P9-CMN-560

*Though Waters Roar*

RARITAN PUBLIC LIBRARY
54 E. SOMERSET STREET
RARITAN, NJ 08869
908-725-0413

11/09

God is our refuge and strength,
an ever-present help in trouble.
Therefore we will not fear, though the earth give way
and the mountains fall into the heart of the sea,
though its waters roar and foam
and the mountains quake with their surging.

Psalm 46:1–3

*Though*
## WATERS ROAR

# LYNN AUSTIN

Minneapolis, Minnesota

*Though Waters Roar*
Copyright © 2009
Lynn Austin

Cover design by Andrea Gjeldum

Unless otherwise identified, Scripture quotations are from the King James Version of
the Bible.

Scripture quotations identified NIV are from the HOLY BIBLE, NEW INTERNATIONAL
VERSION.® Copyright © 1973, 1978, 1984 by International Bible Society. Used by
permission of Zondervan Publishing House. All rights reserved.

All rights reserved. No part of this publication may be reproduced, stored in a retrieval
system, or transmitted in any form or by any means—electronic, mechanical, pho-
tocopying, recording, or otherwise—without the prior written permission of the
publisher. The only exception is brief quotations in printed reviews.

Published by Bethany House Publishers
11400 Hampshire Avenue South
Bloomington, Minnesota 55438

Bethany House Publishers is a division of
Baker Publishing Group, Grand Rapids, Michigan.

Printed in the United States of America

---

**Library of Congress Cataloging-in-Publication Data**

Austin, Lynn N.
    Though waters roar / Lynn Austin.
       p.  cm.
    ISBN 978-0-7642-0728-0 (alk. paper) — ISBN 978-0-7642-0496-8 (pbk.)  1. Women—
Family relationships—Fiction.  2. Social justice—Fiction.  I. Title.
    PS3551.U839T47    2009
    813'.54—dc22

                                                    2009025127

---

*To my husband*
*Ken*
*and my children,*
*Joshua, Vanessa, Benjamin, Maya, and Snir*
*with love*

**1**

It was ironic.

I lay in my jail cell on a squeaky iron bunk, gazing at the stained mattress above me, and I remembered the day I first understood the meaning of the word *ironic*. I couldn't help smiling at . . . well, at the irony of it. The meaning had become clear to me ten years ago on the day my grandmother, Beatrice Monroe Garner, was arrested.

That day had also been a Saturday—just like today. Mother had been distressed because Grandma Bebe, as we called her, would miss church services tomorrow if Father didn't go down to the jailhouse and bail her out.

"She can't spend the Sabbath in prison!" Mother had wailed. "Please, John. We have to get her out of there!"

I was going to miss church services tomorrow, too, come to think of it. Who would teach my Sunday school class of ten-year-old girls? As my father undoubtedly would have pointed out: "Perhaps you should have considered their welfare before getting yourself arrested in the first place, Harriet."

I had been the same age as my Sunday school girls when Grandma Bebe landed in jail that day. My sister, Alice, and I had been eating breakfast with our parents when the telephone rang. The device was brand-spanking-new back then in 1910, and we all stopped eating, listening to see if it would chime our party line exchange of three short rings. When it did, Mother unhooked the earphone and cupped it to her ear, standing on tiptoes to speak into the little cone-shaped mouthpiece. She burst into tears the moment she replaced the receiver.

"That . . . that was . . . the police!" she managed to tell us through her sobs. "They arrested my mother last night and . . . and . . . she's in jail!"

My older sister gasped. She was the feminine, fluttery type of girl who did a great deal of gasping. "Arrested! But why? What did Grandma do?"

"Oh, how could they do such a thing to her?" Mother cried. "She isn't a criminal!"

"Is there any more coffee?" my father asked calmly. "I would like another cup, if you don't mind."

"Oh, John! How can you drink coffee at a time like this? Don't you care?"

"Beatrice Garner cares nothing at all for her family's reputation, so why should I care what happens to her? She knew the consequences when she and that temperance gang of hers started running around smashing whiskey barrels. She made her bed when she decided to become another Carrie Nation, and now she'll have to lie in it."

This brought another cloudburst of weeping from Mother. Alice rose from the table to comfort her. Father sighed and handed me his empty cup. "Fill this for me, would you, Harriet? That's a good girl." Our hired girl had the morning off, so I obediently took his cup to the kitchen to refill it, then sat down and waited for act two of this drama.

"Please, John. I'm begging you, " Mother said. "Please get her out of that terrible place."

"And that's another thing," Father said. "What kind of an example is she setting for our daughters?" He poured cream into the coffee I'd brought him and slowly stirred it as if not expecting a reply.

Aside from begging and weeping, my mother could do nothing to help Grandma Bebe—which was ironic, since Grandma was working hard to give women more power in this world. And Grandma Bebe despised tears. *"Women should never use them as weapons,"* she always insisted, *"especially to prevail upon a man to change his mind."* Yet, ironically, my mother had resorted to tears in order to persuade my father. Grandma Bebe would not have approved.

But Grandma was in jail.

And tears were ultimately what convinced Father to go downtown and bail her out. Alice had joined the deluge of weeping, and Father wasn't strong enough to stop the flood or stand firm against it. No man was. My sister's heart was as soft and gooey as oatmeal. She could turn her tears on and off like a modern-day plumbing faucet and was capable of unleashing buckets of them.

Alice was sixteen and so beautiful that brilliant men became stupid whenever they were around her. The moment her wide, blue eyes welled up, every man in sight would pull out a white handkerchief and offer it to her as if waving in surrender. Grandma Bebe had no patience with her.

"Your sister could do a great deal of good for the cause," she once told me. "Alice is the kind of woman who men go to war over—like Helen of Troy. But she'll squander it all, I'm sorry to say. She'll surrender to the first humbug who dishes her a little sweet-talk. Women like her always do. It's too bad," Grandma said with a sigh. "Your sister believes the lie that women are the weaker sex. Her prodigious use of tears perpetuates that myth. . . . But there's hope for you, Harriet," Grandma Bebe added. Whenever the subject of Alice's amazing beauty arose, Grandma would pat my unruly brown hair and say, "Thank goodness you're such a plain child. You'll have to rely on your wits."

The fact that Alice came to Grandma's rescue with tears is ironic, isn't it? I didn't join the torrent of weeping that morning. I didn't want to let Grandma down.

I loved my grandmother, and I greatly admired her ferocity and passion. Mind you, these weren't qualities that polite society admired in women, but they fascinated me. Even so, I didn't want to be like my fiery grandmother and end up in jail, any more than I wanted to be a dutiful wife like Mother or a virtuous siren like Alice. But how was I supposed to live as a modern woman, born just before the dawn of the twentieth century? What other choices did I have? That's the question I was endeavoring to answer when I ended up in jail.

But I was only ten that fateful day when Grandma got arrested and still young enough to be ignored most of the time unless Father needed more coffee. I was a keen observer, however, absorbing everything that went on around me as I began drawing a map for my life. Grandma Bebe told me that everyone's life led somewhere, and so I needed to have a plan.

*"Grip the rudder and steer, Harriet. Don't just drift gently down the stream. If you don't have a map, you might run aground somewhere or end up crushed against the rocks. Always know where you're headed."*

She had given up on coaching Mother and Alice—her current saviors, ironically—and had begun putting all of her effort into shaping me. She made that decision after she saw me kick Tommy O'Reilly in the shin one day when he tried to bully me into giving him my candy. Tommy was the constable's son, and he bullied all the kids in town. But that day I took a step toward him as if about to give him a cinnamon stick and kicked his bony shin, instead.

"You, my dear, have potential!" Grandma said as Tommy hopped around on one leg, howling. "You'll never float downstream, Harriet. You know how to paddle!"

My map was still just a pencil sketch, to be sure. In later years I would embellish it as each new experience added details to the picture. In time, I would carefully identify all of the dangers to avoid, all of the pitfalls to be wary of. I was trying to heed Grandma's advice, you see, but had she heeded her own? Had she deliberately steered her way into the town jail, or had she let go of the rudder? Or misplaced her map? If she ever got out of jail again, I intended to ask her.

"Please, Father, please!" Alice begged, kneeling at his feet like someone out of the Bible. "Please don't leave Grandma there forever!" Alice had worked herself into such a frenzy that she was about to faint. She was a champion at swooning—another womanly trait Grandma loathed. All Alice had to do was lift her dainty hand to her brow and flutter her eyelashes, and every man in sight would race to catch her before she fell.

Father set down his coffee cup and turned to me. "Get the smelling salts, Harriet. That's a good girl."

Alice was still kneeling, so at least she didn't have too far to fall this time. As I sprinted upstairs to retrieve the vial of ammonia salts, I heard Father say, "Oh, very well. You can stop all the caterwauling. I'll go down and bail Beatrice out of jail."

I didn't blame Father for wanting to flee from the rising floodwaters. I raced back to the kitchen and pulled the cork on the smelling salts, then shoved them under Alice's dainty nose. When order was restored, I followed my father out to the front hallway.

"May I go with you to rescue Grandma?"

"Certainly not! Jail is no place for a delicate young lady."

Back then I didn't believe him, but the truth of his statement was now quite clear to me as I lay in my own jail cell.

Father plucked his duster and driving gloves from the hallstand and stuffed his hat on his balding head, muttering darkly about Grandma Bebe as he headed out the door. I skipped along beside him, nodding in support. Together we started up the Model-T Ford, and I jumped into the passenger seat. The car rattled and coughed all the way to the end of the block before he realized I was still there.

"Wait! Harriet . . . what . . . you can't come along!"

I didn't argue or weep. I simply looked up at him, eye to eye, jutting out my chin a little. That's how I faced Tommy O'Reilly whenever he tried to bully me at school—I would stare silently back at him, arms crossed, my foot aimed at his shin. The stare I gave Father wasn't quite as defiant as the one I used on Tommy, but it had the same effect.

"Oh, bother it all, Harriet! I suppose you're already here . . ." Father turned his attention back to the car as it sputtered and nearly died.

"It needs more throttle," I said, pulling out the lever. "Advance the spark a little."

"But you aren't coming inside, Harriet. I mean it. Jail isn't the sort of place . . . and your grandmother has no business . . ."

I nodded dutifully—and followed him inside the police station just the same. Father went straight in to see the constable, Thomas O'Reilly, Sr. He told us that Grandma Bebe had been arrested after trying to close down a saloon last night. Most of the other members of the Women's Christian Temperance Union had gone home peacefully once the police arrived to break up the protest, but not Grandma. She had refused to give up the fight against the evils of Demon Rum.

"And I'm afraid we had to confiscate her axe," he finished.

Father nodded and paid her fine. In no time at all, Grandma Bebe was liberated from jail. We heard her shouting all the way down the hall as a policeman tried to lead her out of the cell.

"No, wait! Unhand me this instant! I'm not ready to leave! This jail is filled with drunkards—the very people I'm trying to rescue."

Constable O'Reilly rolled his eyes. "It's been a very long night, John. Get her out of here. Please."

"Did you know," Grandma continued as the police handed back her purse and coat, "that there is one saloon for every three hundred people in this country? There are more saloons than there are schools, libraries, hospitals, theaters, or parks—and certainly more saloons than churches."

We drove Grandma home.

Like the brave soldiers who had gone to war forty-five years earlier to battle the evils of slavery, my grandmother was willing to sacrifice her own liberty, if necessary, to set men free from slavery to alcohol. And that was the ultimate irony, I thought, as I lay on the lumpy jail cot pondering my own arrest and imprisonment. You see, Grandma Bebe had recently won the war against Demon Rum. The Eighteenth Amendment to the United States' Constitution had become law a few months ago on January 29, 1920, making the manufacture, sale, and transportation of all alcoholic beverages strictly prohibited.

And I was in jail for defying it.

Yes, I found my situation very ironic. There would be no tears of sympathy for me from Mother or Alice—much less Grandma Bebe. And Father would undoubtedly say, "You made your bed, Harriet, and now you'll have to lie in it."

So how did I end up becoming a criminal? I've been pondering that question all night. Perhaps the best way to search for an answer is to start at the very beginning.

2

My grandmother was young, once, and not altogether sure of herself. I find this unbelievable, knowing the woman she has become, but she has sworn that it's true and my grandmother doesn't lie. "Any assuredness that I now possess, Harriet, has been acquired out of necessity," she insisted. "I was born with no degree of confidence whatsoever. In fact, quite the opposite is true."

She was born in the northeastern corner of Pennsylvania on her parents' farm, nestled in a valley in the Pocono Mountains. Beatrice Aurelia Monroe arrived on the same day, month, and year that the first Women's Rights Convention was held: July 19, 1848. Of course she was too young on the day of her birth to realize what a portentous coincidence this was, but she would later declare her birthday a sign from Providence.

While Elizabeth Cady Stanton, Lucretia Mott, and the rest of that august group of women were signing "The Declaration of Sentiments and Resolutions" in Seneca Falls, New York, and firing the first shot in the battle for women's rights, Great Grandma Hannah Monroe was also doing battle as she labored to give birth to Grandma Bebe—who had the audacity to come out backward. Bebe was destined to do everything in life unconventionally, so arriving feet-first was only the beginning. She also had the audacity to be a girl. Her father, Henry Monroe, had directed his wife to produce a boy—which seems a bit selfish to me, seeing as he already had four sons: James, age nine, William, seven, Joseph, five, and Franklin, who was three.

"What do you mean he's a girl?" an indignant Henry asked the midwife when she told him the news. He stomped into the bedroom in his work boots and peeked into the baby's diaper, convinced that the midwife had missed an important detail. When it was obvious that she hadn't, he handed the howling bundle back to his wife. "This was supposed to be a boy, Hannah. A man can never have too many sons to help him out."

"I know, my dear," she said gently, "but the Good Lord has seen fit to bless us with a girl this time."

Perhaps the Good Lord realized that Hannah also could use some help around the farm, feeding and clothing her strapping husband and four growing sons. That's how Hannah chose to view her little daughter—as God's good gift. She gazed down at the baby and smiled as Henry tromped out of the room. "Don't mind him, my little one. He always gets testy when his dinner is late."

Dinner was late that day on account of Beatrice coming out backward and taking more time to arrive than she should have. But Hannah was a devout Christian woman, and as soon as the midwife spread the news of the baby's arrival throughout the little farming community of New Canaan, Pennsylvania, the other church women quickly drove out to share portions of their own dinners with Hannah's disgruntled husband and four hungry sons. Of course the pantry was filled with the provisions that Hannah had prepared for her time of confinement, but Henry and the boys were incapable of crossing into such feminine territory as the pantry to forage for their own food. They were even less capable of reheating any of it on the stove.

Once Henry's belly was filled, his attitude toward his new daughter did seem to soften, slightly. "I suppose we can learn to make the best of it," he grumbled as he removed his boots at the end of the day and climbed into bed beside his wife. "There's always next time."

Hannah swallowed a rash reply at the mention of "next time," the memory of her harrowing breech labor still fresh in her mind. She whispered a swift, silent prayer to the Almighty, instead. Then she rested her hand on her husband's arm and said, "She's a beautiful, healthy baby—thanks be to God. I would like to christen her Beatrice, if it's all the same to you. Beatrice Aurelia Monroe."

Henry didn't reply to Hannah's request until after she'd finished cooking his breakfast the next morning and had set it on the table in front of him. He crunched into a piece of bacon and said, "That name would be acceptable, I suppose."

Hannah had learned patience during her ten years of marriage. She hadn't expected a reply any sooner than noon. Henry required a sufficient amount of time to pray about such matters and didn't like to be rushed. Three-year-old Franklin, who couldn't pronounce "Beatrice," shortened the baby's name to Bebe. The name stuck, and my sister and I still call her Grandma Bebe seventy-two years later.

The first few years of Grandma's life passed uneventfully, by her account. She grew to be a quiet, nervous child, which was understandable since everyone else on the farm was bigger and louder and stronger than she was. With four older brothers to dodge— along with a team of horses, a pair of oxen, and a herd of milk cows—at times it felt as though there were a conspiracy to trample poor Bebe underfoot. The first useful phrase she comprehended as a toddler was, "Get out of the way, Bebe!"

"I was a skittish child," she told me, "perhaps because I spent a great deal of time skittering out of danger. And so shy! I would cry at the drop of a hat—and there were plenty of hats to drop, not to mention hoes and hay bales, wheels and winches, boots, buckets, and butcher blocks."

I tried to imagine growing up in a home that had butcher blocks dropping from above, and I cringed involuntarily. When I questioned Grandma about it, she laughed and said, "Don't ask, Harriet! The butcher-block incident was my brother William's doing. He was always into some sort of mischief, risking life and limb. That's why it surprised all of us when it was Joseph who lost his life and Franklin who lost a limb. Of course those tragedies happened *years* after the butcher-block episode, but we all remembered it."

Grandma Bebe never did tell a story in a straight line. In order to make any sense of her life, I've had to piece together all of her astounding statements as if working a huge jigsaw puzzle. But I happen to have a lot of spare time as I languish in this jail cell, and her peculiar stories are beginning to make sense to me as I endeavor to figure out how I got here—and what to do about it.

Bebe's brothers were wild, uninhibited boys who took great delight in risking their lives each day in newer and more creative ways. One summer they tied a rope from a branch of the tall oak tree that stood near the river on the edge of their farm. They drilled a hole through an old plank and threaded the fraying rope through the center of it, knotting it beneath the plank to form a seat. Bebe watched from a safe distance as they took turns swinging wildly from it, pumping higher and higher, sometimes falling off and skinning their knees, adding more lumps to their knobby heads. She wondered what it would feel like to fly freely through the air on that swing, the blue sky above her, the wind in her hair. But even though she longed to try it, fear always stopped her.

One day when it was hot enough to roast the chickens right on their roosts, William decided to sail out over the river on the swing and let go of the rope, splashing into the water some twelve feet below, oblivious to the unforgiving rocks. Rain had fallen for weeks that spring and the rushing river looked eager for a victim to drown. But when William bobbed safely to the surface, Bebe's other brothers followed his example, leaping into the water as if eager to meet Jesus. Bebe watched from the side of the path, wary of the snakes that lived in the tall grass near the river. James and Joseph had once caught a thick, glossy black snake three feet long and had scared Bebe half to death with it as they whooped into the barnyard, dangling their prize from the tines of a pitchfork.

After the first five years of Grandma Bebe's jittery life had passed, a momentous change occurred. Harriet Beecher Stowe had published her book *Uncle Tom's Cabin; or Life Among the Lowly* in 1852, and when it made it's way to New Canaan, the ladies from church passed around a well-worn copy of it. Hannah read it by lamplight in the farmhouse parlor and wept. Bebe had never seen her sturdy, devout mother cry before, and she quickly hurried over to comfort her.

"What's wrong, Mama?"

"It's this book I'm reading, Beatrice dear. It describes the daily lives of slaves in our country, and it's simply horrifying. Imagine being *owned* by someone! Just think how horrible it would be to be considered someone's property and thought of as inferior. Imagine having no life of your own, forced to do someone's bidding day and night, body and soul, with no power and no voice."

Hannah talked about the plight of the slaves continually for the next few months as she and Bebe kneaded bread and plucked chickens and scrubbed laundry. She spoke as they weeded the garden and peeled potatoes and mopped the floors and sewed new clothes for the family.

"I believe the Almighty is calling me to do something to help those poor, pitiful people," Hannah decided one fall afternoon while rendering fat to make soap for her household. With her conscience as her guide, she gathered all of the other women who'd read the book and held a meeting in the village church. They decided to form a local chapter of the Anti-Slavery Society. Henry sympathized with the cause after reading the book himself. He even allowed Hannah to hitch the team to the wagon if he wasn't using it and drive into town for the society meetings. Bebe accompanied her mother, watching and listening.

At first the anti-slavery meetings resembled a Sunday church service with lots of praying and hymn singing. But then the women devised a plan, mapping out their battle lines and the course of action they would take. They wrote countless letters and sent innumerable petitions to the government officials in Washington. They raised money to help publish and distribute anti-slavery pamphlets. Hannah contributed to the cause by raising an extra dozen chickens and selling the eggs, along with any spare produce from her vegetable garden.

Every once in a while the Philadelphia chapter of the Anti-Slavery Society would send a special speaker up to New Canaan to give a progress report. One orator told how the society was helping slaves escape, one by one, on an invisible "Underground Railroad." With millions of men, women, and children still enslaved, it seemed to Bebe that it was going to take the society a very long time to reach their goal if the slaves had to escape one at a time.

Then one spring night Bebe awoke to a vicious thunderstorm. Terrified by the howling wind and blinding lightning, she ran downstairs to her parents' bedroom and crawled into bed beside her mother, trembling from head to toe. " 'God is our refuge and strength,' " Hannah whispered to her, reciting her favorite psalm.

" 'Therefore we will not fear . . . though the waters thereof roar and be troubled. . . .' "

Bebe thought the banging noise she heard was caused by the wind until her father said, "I think there's someone at the door."

He rose to answer it. Mama put on a dressing gown to follow him, and when a flash of lightning lit up the room, Bebe scrambled out of bed and ran after both of them, clinging to her mother's leg.

"Come in, come in," she heard her father say as he opened the heavy oak door. "It's a terrible night to be out on the road." Henry was as tall and sturdy as that massive door and not afraid of anything. He invited the dripping stranger into the house without a second thought.

"Thank you, sir. I'm much obliged," the man said. He stood inside the doorway, drenched and shivering.

"What about your horse?" Henry asked, peering out at the drooping animal tethered to the hitching post.

"Well . . . allow me to state my errand quickly, Mr. Monroe. If you're unable to assist me, I'll need to ride on ahead to the next station."

"You know my name—have we met?" Henry asked in surprise. He hadn't bothered to light a lamp, relying on the intermittent flashes of lightning for illumination.

Hannah took a step forward. "I think . . . I think I know you, sir. You're from Philadelphia, aren't you? Didn't you accompany that former slave who spoke at our society meeting last August?"

"That right, Mrs. Monroe. My name is . . . well, maybe it's best if you just call me John Smith." He removed his hat and a puddle of rainwater cascaded from the brim. "I'm glad you recognized me. It makes my request that much easier. You see, I have a . . . a package . . . that I need to deliver to one of the stations in this area. I understand that you are a stockholder in our railroad, Mrs. Monroe?"

Henry stared at Mr. Smith as if he regretted his decision to open the door. But Bebe, who was wide awake now, had attended enough anti-slavery meetings to know exactly what Mr. Smith was talking about. He must be a conductor on the so-called Underground Railroad. The "package" was an escaped slave who needed refuge in a safe house or "station" on the invisible line. Anyone who had contributed money or goods to the effort, as Hannah and her friends had, was known as a stockholder.

"Yes, that's right, Mr. Smith. I am a stockholder," Hannah said with a smile. "Henry, you'd better put our guest's horse in the barn, out of the rain. This might take a while. I'll light a fire and put on some coffee."

Henry grabbed his overcoat and trudged outside with Mr. Smith. Bebe followed her mother into the kitchen and watched as she lit a lamp and gathered kindling and stoked the fire. Hannah didn't seem to notice Bebe until she bumped into her on her way out of the pantry.

"Beatrice, dear, why don't you go back to bed," she said, stroking her hair. "The storm is over for the most part."

Lightning still flashed even though the thunder was only a distant rumble among the hills. Bebe heard the rain hammering on the back porch roof and knew that her father was going to get soaked as he walked from the house to the barn. "I want to help, Mama."

She meant that she wanted to help with the "package," but her mother misunderstood. "Well . . . get out a bowl and some cups, then. Perhaps Mr. Smith would like a little soup to help him warm up."

A fire blazed in the stove by the time the men returned. Hannah hung their coats behind it to dry, filling the kitchen with the sour smell of wet wool. Stripped of his bulky overcoat, Mr. Smith turned out to be a slightly built man, dressed in a city suit and fine leather shoes. He dropped onto a kitchen chair, looking as limp and pale as a plucked pullet. Bebe watched the color slowly return to his pallid skin as he gulped his coffee and ate a bowl of leftover soup. His yellow hair curled into delicate ringlets as it dried.

"What can you tell us about this package?" Hannah asked. "When might it arrive?"

"Well, first I should explain that we don't usually send packages to stations where young children live." He glanced at Bebe. "Ever since the Fugitive Slave Law went into effect, this business has become much too dangerous to risk innocent young lives. If a package is discovered in your possession—"

"The Good Lord can protect my children and me," Hannah interrupted. "We must obey God, not an unjust law. The Bible says we are to feed the hungry and clothe the naked and rescue the perishing."

The stranger smiled slightly. "I'm glad you feel that way, Mrs. Monroe." He wrapped his fingers around his coffee cup to warm them.

"What brings you out our way, Mr. Smith?" she asked. "I didn't think the Underground Railroad passed through New Canaan."

"It doesn't, but we're in a difficult situation. Bounty hunters have discovered our usual rail lines, and our safe houses simply aren't safe anymore. We've been forced to expand the railroad into new territory, and we recalled what a faithful chapter your local society has been in the past. I spoke with your pastor, and he felt that our package would be safer out here on your farm than in town, where the wrong person might accidentally see it. It's so hard to know whom to trust, you see."

"You may trust us completely," Hannah said. "How can we help?"

"All that's required is a temporary place to rest, eat, and hide until the way is clear to the next station. I don't know how long that might be. We're asking you to take an enormous risk, as you probably know. If you get caught you could be fined as much as one thousand dollars and face six months in jail. But if you're willing to help, we would be very grateful. We simply must get our package to Canada. It has traveled so far already."

"I'll need to pray about it," Henry Monroe said. He stood abruptly as if heading to the celestial throne room to consult with the Almighty. "Can you wait for my answer?"

"Certainly. I understand. I'll wait."

But Bebe wondered if the stranger really knew how long it usually took her father to pray about something and make up his mind. Mr. Smith might well be waiting until after the next litter of hogs were born, fattened, butchered, and turned into bacon.

"I'll fix a bed for you, Mr. Smith," Hannah offered. "You should try to get a little sleep. It will still be a few more hours until dawn."

"I don't want to trouble you."

Hannah shook her head. "It's no trouble at all."

"Well, if you're certain. I have been riding all night. . . ."

Hannah evicted William from his warm bed and tucked him in with James and Franklin to make room for the stranger. Bebe crawled back into her own bed, but she had trouble falling asleep. A real live escaped slave might be sent here to hide, in her very own house! She felt scared yet excited.

Bebe had first seen a person with black skin at one of her mother's Anti-Slavery Society meetings. The man's face and arms were the color of dark, rich molasses, and she thought he must have fallen into a vat of blackberries. Her mother told her that the color wouldn't wash off, even if the man scrubbed and scrubbed with lye soap.

"People have made the Negro race into slaves, Beatrice, just because their skin is a different color than ours," she had explained. "But the Bible says that God is no respecter of persons. Man looks at the outward things, but God looks at our hearts."

"Is the man's heart as black as his skin?"

"No, his heart isn't black at all because he knows Jesus. Our sins are what turn our hearts black, but Jesus can wash each heart as white as snow." The conversation left Bebe confused. She wondered why Jesus didn't wash the slave's skin white along with his heart, so he wouldn't have to be a slave anymore. She had never forgotten the beautiful color of that man's skin—and now a slave just like him was coming to her farm.

The next morning when Bebe peeked into her brothers' room to see if Mr. Smith was still asleep, all of the beds were empty. He wasn't downstairs in the kitchen, either. "Did Mr. Smith go—?"

Hannah shushed her. Her father and brothers were tramping indoors after their morning chores, bringing mud, fresh milk, and the scent of cows with them. "We'll talk later," Hannah said. "Sit down and eat your biscuits."

The boys ate breakfast, too, then left for school. While Bebe helped her mother wash and dry the dishes, Hannah explained that Mr. Smith had left at dawn.

"Did Papa decide about the package?"

Hannah nodded. "It will arrive in a few days."

The news astounded Bebe. She had never known her father to make up his mind so quickly. He always emphasized the need to "wait on the Lord" for any answers to prayer, and waiting usually took a very long time. The Lord must have let Henry go straight to the front of the line for an answer this time.

"But listen to me, Beatrice. This is very important." Hannah crouched down so she could look right into Bebe's eyes as she gripped her thin shoulders. "Your papa and I have decided not to tell your brothers about Mr. Smith or the package. The more people who know about it, the more dangerous it will be for that poor soul who is trying to escape. If one of your brothers should happen to have a slip of the tongue and accidentally tell someone at school, we could all be in danger. Do you understand?"

Bebe nodded soberly.

"Promise you won't say a word? To anyone?"

"I promise." No one had ever entrusted her with such an important secret before—and the fact that her brothers didn't know about it made her smile on the inside.

"You aren't frightened, are you, Beatrice?"

"No."

Bebe was terrified.

CHAPTER

3

The package arrived three days later in the middle of the night while Bebe slept. She had no idea it was there. The next morning she watched her mother prepare a second breakfast of bacon and eggs and biscuits after the boys left for school and wondered why. When Bebe asked her about it, Hannah smiled and said, "We have company."

Bebe looked all around, wondering if the package was as invisible as the railroad. Hannah carefully tucked the plates of food inside a basket along with some cups, knives, and forks, then covered everything with a clean towel. She handed Bebe a container filled with fresh milk.

"Will you help me carry this, Beatrice? Be careful not to spill any."

"Are we going down to the root cellar?" She was afraid that her mother had hidden the visitor underground, since that's where the invisible railroad was. Bebe hated the damp, spidery cellar. It smelled like the graveyard on a rainy day, and the crumbling dirt walls always seemed to close in on her.

"No, we're not going down to the root cellar."

Bebe followed her mother upstairs instead, then watched as Hannah retrieved a chair from Bebe's room and moved it into place below the opening to the attic. Hannah climbed up first, pushing the trapdoor aside and carefully lifting the basket up to the attic floor. She reached down to take the container of milk from Bebe and set it on the attic floor, too, then stood on tiptoes and hoisted herself up and out of sight. Bebe scrambled onto the chair to see where her mother had gone, but she was too short to see into the dark hole.

"Mama? Where are you?" she called, her voice quivering. Hannah's face reappeared above her.

"Do you want to come up, Beatrice? Stretch out your arms, and I'll pull you up."

The thought of being hauled up into the unknown void frightened Bebe more than descending into the root cellar had. But she knew her mother was strong and completely trustworthy. Bebe raised her arms above her head and allowed Hannah to grip her wrists and pull her up into the cool, dusty attic.

Dried herbs hung from the rafters along with garlands of cobwebs. Discarded chairs, an old dresser, and a battered steamer trunk lay scattered across the floorboards. Bebe worried about spiders. And mice. And bats. In the middle of the floor lay a heap of bedding, covered with one of Hannah's good winter quilts.

"Good morning," Hannah called into the still, dead air. "I brought you some breakfast."

Bebe's heart raced as the lump beneath the quilt stirred and pushed the blanket aside. When the real live escaped slave sat up, Bebe gaped in surprise. It was a woman! Bebe never imagined that an escaped slave might be a woman. All the slaves she had seen at the society meetings had been men.

The quilt shifted again and a second figure sat up—another

woman, younger than the first. The two "packages" who peered at Bebe with dark, frightened eyes were the most exotically beautiful people she had ever seen. With their dark brown skin and woolly black hair, they seemed like little more than shadows in the dusky attic.

"Don't be afraid," Hannah told the pair. "My daughter, Beatrice, and I brought you some food."

Bebe stayed close beside her mother as she inched across the dusty floor on her hands and knees, dragging the basket. The attic was too cramped for Hannah to stand upright except in the very center beneath the ridge beam, but Bebe could easily stand.

"Beatrice, our new friend's name is Mary," Hannah told her. "And her daughter's name is Katie."

Bebe knew it was rude to stare, but she couldn't help it. The younger slave, Katie, was not much older than Bebe's brother William, who was twelve. Mary looked much too young to be her mother. She smoothed back her sleep-tousled hair as if wanting to make a good impression.

"We appreciate your help," she said softly. She started to crawl forward, but Hannah stopped her.

"No, sit still, Mary. I'll bring it to you. I know you must be exhausted after walking all that way in the middle of the night." Hannah spread the dishtowel on the floor like a little tablecloth, then removed the plates from the basket and placed them on it. She had even packed two napkins.

Tears glistened in young Katie's eyes as she examined the bounty. "All this food for us?"

"Yes, it's all for you," Hannah replied. "We've already eaten our breakfast. And if you're still hungry, let me know and I'll fix more. We have plenty."

Katie scrambled forward to grab her plate. "Ain't you forgetting something?" Mary asked. Katie glanced at her mother, then set down the plate and folded her hands. Both women bowed their heads as Mary prayed. "Lord, we so grateful for these kind people and for all this food they fixing for us. Please bless them, Lord. This a good thing they doing. Amen."

Bebe watched Katie gobble her food, shoveling it down the same way her brothers did after baling hay. If any mice did inhabit the attic, the women weren't leaving them a crumb. When Mary and Katie finished eating, Hannah packed everything back into the basket.

"Please, ma'am . . . I need the privy," Katie whispered.

"Of course," Hannah replied. "Follow me downstairs and I'll show you the way. And I have plenty of hot water if you'd like to wash up."

"You don't need to be waiting on us this-a-way," Mary said. "But we surely do thank the Lord for your kindness."

Hannah lowered herself through the attic opening first, and Bebe had a moment of panic when she realized she would have to drop down into her mother's arms. But she made it safely, followed by Katie and Mary. Bebe offered to show them the way to the privy. Both women followed her cautiously, as if expecting someone to jump out of hiding and pounce on them, the way Bebe's brothers did when playing hide-and-seek. She thought the two women were right behind her as she stepped out the back door, but they had halted before venturing outside, gazing all around, eyes wide and alert.

"Ain't no paddyrollers round here, is there?" Mary asked.

"What's a paddyroller?"

"They the white men on horses who chasing after us. They wanting to take us back to our massa's place, but I sooner die than go back down there." Her words made Bebe shudder, reminding her of the risk they all were taking.

"I haven't seen any," Bebe replied. "Besides, we'd hear them coming up the road a long way off."

The women sat outside on the back steps after they finished washing up, warming their faces in the thin spring sunlight. A grove of fruit trees ruffled with blossoms hid the back of the house from view. A cowbell jangled dully as Henry's cows headed down the path to the pasture.

"It's nice here," Mary said quietly. "But why ain't anybody working all this land?"

"What do you mean?" Hannah asked.

"I ain't never seen a farm that didn't need slaves to keep it going. This late in the morning, we'd already be out there sweating and straining, with the overseer's whip just a cracking on our backs. Sometimes we'd have to start in singing just to keep our spirits up."

"People around here don't farm more land than the family can handle by themselves," Hannah said. "My husband does all of the work with the help of our four sons."

In the peaceful silence of the morning, Bebe heard a crow cawing from the pine tree, a blue jay scolding its mate, a woodpecker hammering into a fence post near the barn.

Mary sighed again. "It's so peaceful here. I wish we could stay."

"I wish you could, too," Hannah said. "I think you're the most courageous women I've ever met."

Mary wrapped one arm around her daughter and pulled her close. "It ain't courage making me do this, it's fear. If I stay down there, I lose my child. Lizzy, up in the big house, say Massa be selling my Katie to another massa—and he planning to use my girl for hisself."

Hannah glanced at Bebe as she patted Mary's shoulder. "There, there . . . I understand." Several years would pass before Bebe understood what Mary had meant—and when Bebe finally did comprehend, she was outraged.

"My Katie is already bought and paid for, so now both our massas is chasing us."

"Well, with the Good Lord's help you'll make it all the way to Canada, where you'll be free," Hannah said.

The women climbed back up to the attic to hide before Bebe's brothers arrived home from school. Hannah repacked the basket with food and water for their supper and sent it up with them, along with a chamber pot. That night Bebe and her brothers slept in their bedrooms beneath the attic as usual, but Mary and Katie were quieter than a pair of mice. They never squeaked a single floorboard. Their lives depended on silence. Bebe listened to her brothers laughing and scuffling as they dressed for school the next morning and smiled to herself. They had no idea that two escaped slaves were hiding right above their heads.

On the third day, as Bebe and her mother packed the breakfast basket, they heard horses trotting up the road to their farm. "Go look out the front window, Beatrice, and see who's coming."

Bebe ran to the front room and peeked through the curtain just as two men on horseback drew to a stop in front of the house. She hurried back to the kitchen. "It's two men, but I don't know them, Mama. Should I let them in?"

"No, stay inside. Your father will talk to them."

"Are they the bad men who are chasing—?"

"They might be."

What had Mary called them? *Paddyrollers*. Bebe ran into the parlor and peered through the window again as Hannah hurried upstairs to deliver the women's breakfast and to warn them to stay hidden. Bebe's father ambled out from the barn with a shovel in his hand and stood talking with the men for a while as if chatting

31

about nothing more important than the weather. When Hannah returned, she took Bebe's hand and led her away to the kitchen.

"Help me wash the eggs, Beatrice. I want to take them into town to sell later this week." Hannah put the basket of eggs they had collected that morning on the table, along with a basin of warm water. Bebe dampened a rag to clean them, careful not to break the delicate shells.

"Mama, I know Papa would never tell a lie. But what if they ask him about—?"

"Your father can honestly say that he hasn't seen any escaped slaves because he hasn't. That's why you and I always bring the food upstairs—and why we can't go outside right now."

"Will we have to hide if Papa invites the men inside?"

"He won't invite them into our home if they're bounty hunters."

Bebe waited in the kitchen with her mother for a very long time. She never knew that her heart could beat so hard and not give out. At last she heard the horses ride away again, but Mary and Katie stayed hidden in the attic all day.

"What did those men want?" Hannah asked when she and Bebe brought Henry's lunch outside to him.

"Claimed they were looking for two escaped slaves. Two women. Showed me a wanted poster and everything. Said there's a reward for finding them."

"I never heard of bounty hunters coming all the way out here. Have you?"

"Greed, Hannah. Men will do anything for selfish greed."

Bebe's brothers arrived home from school that afternoon whooping with excitement and jostling each other as they competed to share their news. "Two strangers on horseback showed up at school today," William said, outshouting the others.

"And guess what they asked us?" Joseph said.

James elbowed him aside. "They wanted to know if we'd seen any Negroes hiding around here."

"My goodness," Hannah murmured. "Imagine that."

"The men said they would give us candy and other treats if we showed them where the Negroes were hiding," Joseph added.

"One of the men had a shiny new silver dollar that he kept flipping up in the air and catching." William tossed an imaginary coin to demonstrate. "He said we could have it if we helped him."

Bebe feared she might burst. Keeping a secret was such a hard thing to do. But her mother crouched beside her and pulled her close, the same way Mary had pulled Katie to her side the other morning. Bebe felt Hannah's courage flowing into her.

"My friend Louis told the strangers that he'd seen Negroes in New Canaan," James continued, "but he was talking about the meetings at church that you and his mama go to sometimes."

"The man gave him a stick of licorice anyway, just for helping," Joseph said. "So then all the other kids started telling stories, too."

"You seen any Negroes around here, Pa?" William asked as their father tromped in from the back porch.

"Who's asking?"

"Two strangers showed up outside the school today and—"

"Oh, them," Henry said with a grunt. "They came out here and asked me the same question. I told them I haven't seen any Negroes. But even if I had, why would I tell some stranger about it?"

"They'll give you a whole dollar, Pa, that's why." Franklin hopped up and down as if he needed the privy. "A whole dollar!"

Their father frowned. "Sure, you would get a dollar. And you know what those poor Negroes would get? Forty lashes with a bullwhip." Franklin took a step backward as if fearing the lash himself. "Then those men would carry the slaves down south again, where they're treated worse than animals. Don't you boys get mixed up with those strangers, you hear?"

"Yes, Pa." Their enthusiasm vanished like a gopher down a hole.

"If you want candy and treats and such, then earn the money the honest way by working for it, not by selling another human being into slavery."

Bebe thought of Mary and Katie, hidden beneath a quilt in her attic, and knew she wouldn't hand them over for all the licorice in the world. She felt like she had grown three years older in the last three days.

On market day, Bebe and her mother drove into town to make their weekly egg delivery and to pick up a few things at the general store. One of their egg customers, the minister's wife, invited them into her parlor for coffee. Reverend Webster himself joined them, which seemed highly unusual to Bebe. He surprised her even more by speaking in a near whisper instead of the booming voice he always used on Sunday mornings. In fact, Bebe had to lean close to hear what he was saying.

"I don't know how to advise you, Mrs. Monroe. It's too dangerous for your visitors to stay and it's even more dangerous for them to leave. Packages usually travel at night, on foot, but the bounty hunters must have tracked them this far because they're hanging around town, waiting for someone to slip up. They take turns patrolling the roads, day and night. They even have dogs on the scent."

"How far is it to the next station?"

"About sixteen miles. It would take the better part of the night to walk that far."

Hannah set down her coffee cup and stared at her hands, folded in her lap. She seemed to be thinking—or maybe praying. "Can you send word to the next station for me, Reverend?" she asked at last. "Tell them I'll deliver the package myself, tomorrow morning. I'll hide our friends in my wagon—"

"In broad daylight?"

"Yes, sir, in broad daylight. Beatrice will come with me, won't you, dear?"

Bebe wanted to say, "No!" but not a sound came from her throat.

4

On Friday morning, before Bebe's brothers left for school, their father ordered them to pitch a load of firewood into the back of the farm wagon. "Who is all this wood for, Pa?" William asked.

"Someone in need. Hurry up now or you'll be late for school."

Henry moved some of the wood aside after the boys were gone and hoisted a small coffin-like box that he'd built onto the wagon bed. Mary and Katie would ride to the next station in this secret hiding place, buried beneath the wood. Before the women climbed into it, Hannah gave them a map she'd drawn.

"It's always best to know exactly where you're headed," she told them. "You can't get anywhere in life without a map. I'll drive you to the next station, but if you find yourself off course after that, you can always look for the landmarks I've drawn."

"I don't know how we can ever thank you," Mary said.

"There's no need." Hannah surprised her with an embrace. "And now I think we should pray and ask the Lord for His protection."

The women joined hands and bowed their heads. Bebe's stomach cramped as if she'd eaten too many green apples as she held on to Katie's and Hannah's hands. She didn't close her eyes. Instead, she watched her mother's face as she prayed.

"Lord, please send your angels to surround us, to guard us and guide us on our way today. Blind our enemies' eyes, Lord, as you did for your servants in times past, so they don't see these precious daughters of yours. We ask you to protect Mary and Katie on their journey and help them reach freedom in Canada. In Jesus' name, amen."

The prayer didn't make the sick feeling in Bebe's stomach go away. Her heart thudded as she watched the women crawl inside the tiny space. Then her father buried the little box beneath the pile of firewood. "Can you breathe in there?" he asked.

"We're fine," came the muffled reply.

Henry helped Hannah climb onto the wagon seat, then handed her the reins. Last of all, he lifted Bebe up beside her. The wagon started with a jolt.

New leaves sprouted from the trees along the way as the countryside burst into life after the long, cold winter. The creaking wheels and plodding horse hooves drowned out the birdsong as the wagon traveled on, but Bebe could hear her mother humming softly as they rode.

"Can God really make our enemies go blind, Mama?" she asked, remembering Hannah's prayer.

"The Bible says that He can. When the prophet Elisha was surrounded by a huge army with soldiers and horses and chariots, he said to the Lord, 'Smite this people, I pray thee, with blindness,' and God did just that. He blinded the enemies' eyes to what they were really seeing, so that Elisha could lead them far away to another place. In the New Testament, Paul and Barnabas were on one of their missionary journeys when an evil sorcerer tried to stop their work. Paul prayed and the sorcerer was temporarily struck blind."

Bebe had heard of Jesus giving sight to blind people, but she'd never known that it worked in reverse. Even so, she hoped they didn't meet any enemies along the way. She would hate for her mother to be responsible for making anyone blind.

A little while later they reached a fork in the road, but instead of turning toward New Canaan as usual, Hannah steered the horses down the other road, toward the distant hills. Bebe had never been this way before. She looked around at the unfamiliar scenery and remembered another part of Hannah's prayer.

"I don't see any angels around us, Mama."

"They're here with us, just the same, dear."

"I wish I could see them." Maybe the sick feeling in her stomach would go away if she could glimpse a halo or two. "Are you scared, Mama?"

"Of course I'm scared. It's only natural. But I've decided to trust God and to follow my conscience. I believe that the Good Lord wants me to help our new friends."

"I heard Mr. Smith say you could go to jail."

"Well, if I have to go to jail for helping Mary and Katie, then so be it. I'm sure God will have a purpose for sending me there, and He'll be with me in jail, too."

Bebe swallowed. "Will I have to go with you?"

"No, you're much too young, dear. But someday when you're all grown up, God is going to give you a task to do in your own time and place. Then you'll have to put your faith in Him as you follow your conscience. That's why I wanted you to come with me today. We grow stronger every time our faith is tested. That's how we learn to trust Him."

Bebe knew that her mother was trustworthy—but her mother

was sitting right beside her. It was much harder to trust a God she couldn't see.

There was very little shade along the road, and the sun grew hot as they traveled. Bebe's hair felt sweaty beneath her bonnet. Buried beneath all that wood, Mary and Katie must feel like two loaves of bread baking in the oven. Bebe turned around to see if she could glimpse them between the logs, and her heart seemed to stop beating when she noticed a dark silhouette in the middle of the road on the horizon behind them. She watched it for a moment, and the shape seemed to grow larger—which meant that it was moving closer, catching up to them.

She tugged at Hannah's sleeve. "Mama, someone's following us."

Hannah glanced over her shoulder. "Yes, I see. Don't worry, dear. Let's recite a psalm together. 'God is our refuge and strength, a very present help in trouble . . .' "

Bebe tried to do what her mother said and not worry, but it was impossible. She kept her gaze straight ahead, watching the horses' rumps until she could no longer stand the suspense. When she turned around again, the shape had split into two figures. They rode horseback and were galloping toward the wagon, quickly closing the gap. Bebe felt like throwing up.

"They're coming closer, Mama. Two of them."

"Can you tell who they are, dear?"

She turned to look behind her again. "I think . . . th-they look like the two men who talked with Papa the other day! Hurry, Mama. Go faster!"

She wanted her mother to lay the lash to the horses and try to outrun the men. Instead, Hannah drew the team to a halt and waited for the riders to catch up. When they finally did, the bounty hunters had rifles strapped to their saddles. Three dogs bounded out of the bushes alongside the road and pranced around the horses, barking at the wagon. Bebe huddled beside her mother in fear.

"Good afternoon. Are you gentlemen lost?" Hannah asked above the clamor.

"Quiet!" one of the men shouted. The barking stopped.

"We're looking for a pair of escaped slaves, ma'am. They're very valuable. We're offering a reward for information."

The dogs circled the wagon while the man talked, sniffing loudly enough for Bebe to hear them. The biggest dog stood on his hind legs with his front feet propped on the tailgate and sniffed the wood. He looked as though he might jump up. Bebe began to cry.

"Would you kindly control your dogs?" Hannah asked. "My little girl is frightened."

The man whistled and all three dogs ran over to him. "Have you seen two Negro women anywhere around here?" he asked again.

"I wouldn't tell you even if I had seen them," Hannah said quietly.

The man stared at her in surprise. He removed his hat and wiped his brow with his forearm. "Well, according to the law, you're required to hand over fugitive slaves."

"I know. But according to the Bible I'm commanded not to. It says in Deuteronomy chapter twenty-three, verse fifteen, 'Thou shalt not deliver unto his master the servant which is escaped from his master unto thee.' So tell me, whose law do you think I should obey, yours or God's?"

"Listen, ma'am—"

"No, you listen. What you're doing is wrong. You're disobeying God's Word."

"We're just trying to make a living."

"Will that be your defense on Judgment Day when you stand before the Almighty to give an accounting of your life?"

The man's face turned red. He looked very angry, but he pressed his lips together and didn't reply.

"If you repent and ask the Lord to forgive you, He surely will," Hannah continued. "I would be happy to pray with you right here and now, if you would like me to."

The men looked at each other, then turned their horses around and trotted back the way they'd come. The dogs followed, noses to the ground, sniffing eagerly. As the dust settled around the wagon again, Bebe buried her face in her mother's lap and sobbed. She had been certain that she and her mother and the two slaves were all going to jail, and the relief she now felt was as real as if the jailer had unlocked the door and set her free.

Hannah flicked the reins to start the horses moving, then wrapped one arm around Bebe to comfort her. "You don't need to be afraid, Beatrice."

"Why did you talk to them, Mama? I was so afraid they would find—"

"Hush now. You learned a valuable lesson today. When you obey the Lord, He will always be with you, no matter what happens. Even if I had gone to jail, the Good Lord would be there, too. As the psalmist wrote, 'The Lord is on my side; I will not fear: what can man do unto me?' "

Bebe thought of several things the men could have done, but she didn't say them out loud. Instead, she wiped her tears with the heels of her hands and decided that she didn't want to be a coward anymore. She would ask God to help her be a woman of faith like Hannah; a woman of courage like the two slaves hiding beneath the firewood. She never wanted to feel afraid again.

A few hours later they arrived at a farm that was much like Bebe's. Hannah helped the elderly farmer push aside the firewood to set Katie and Mary free. The two women were so drenched with sweat they looked as though they had stood outside in a rainstorm.

The farmer's wife—a woman with gray hair and a bent spine—made the slaves hurry inside her house to hide.

"Good-bye," Hannah called to Mary and Katie. "Godspeed!" When she told the farmer about the bounty hunters, they decided that he should keep the firewood in case Hannah encountered the men on the return trip. Bebe helped her mother and the man unload it, tossing down one log at a time until her arms and shoulders ached and splinters pricked her fingers.

Late that afternoon, Bebe and Hannah returned home again. As soon as the wagon stopped, Bebe jumped off and ran down the path that led to the river, feeling as though she could draw a full, deep breath for the first time all day. She halted by her brothers' rope swing. It looked inviting as it swayed gently in the wind. Bebe glanced all around, then lifted her calico skirt to climb onto the swing for the very first time.

She had watched her brothers kick with their feet, then lift up their legs, pumping higher and higher in the air, but her legs were much shorter than theirs were and her feet barely reached the ground. She closed her eyes and let the wind twirl her gently on the breeze. She had been right about riding on the swing—the wind did feel nice on her face. She held tightly to the rope and tilted her head back to look up at the sky, her feet outstretched. She wondered what it would feel like to soar high in the air—not too high, not with abandon the way her brothers did, and certainly not out over the river—but high enough to feel as if she were flying. She imagined that she would feel the same way she had when the paddyrollers had turned around and trotted away. She lifted her face to the sky and tasted freedom.

❧

I had thought of Grandma Bebe's story last night as I set out on my own secret errand. Like Great-Grandma Hannah and the prophet Elisha, I also prayed that the Lord would blind my enemies' eyes so they wouldn't see the cargo I was carrying.

When the patrol car stopped me, I tried to act calm even though my entire body was trembling. Much to my surprise, the officer who stepped up to my car window was Tommy O'Reilly—the constable's son and notorious bully, the boy who had made my school days miserable. Of all the policemen who patrolled our town, why did he have to be on duty last night?

"Would you step out of the car, please?" he asked.

I could barely stand. I had to lean against the fender for support. Tommy looked into the back seat, which was filled with cases of bootleg liquor, and his eyes grew very wide. He stared and stared, blinking in amazement as if he had been struck blind and couldn't quite make out what he was seeing. I thought God surely had answered my prayer. Then Tommy uncorked one of the bottles and sniffed, and I knew I was in trouble. Why hadn't I prayed that his sense of smell would be taken away along with his eyesight?

"I'm going to have to arrest you, Harriet." He seemed truly surprised.

Reasoning with him had been a waste of time last night, just as it had been for as long as I'd known him. I didn't think a kick in the shins would accomplish anything, either. He put me in the back seat of his patrol car and drove me to the police station.

So here I was, in jail. I had remembered to pray before venturing out with my hidden cargo just as Hannah had. I had been convinced that I was doing the right thing for all the right reasons—just like Grandma Bebe.

Now I stared up at the sagging bunk above me and wondered where I had gone wrong. How had I ended up here, so far from where I thought I was headed? And how was I going to find my way back to where I should be?

CHAPTER

5

Grandma Bebe's attic became a refuge for runaway slaves at least
half a dozen times that she could remember. "My mother may have
sheltered a good many more runaways that I never knew about,"
Grandma told me years later. She and I had been talking about
slavery as we sat on her porch swing one sticky summer night when
I was eleven, gently rocking back and forth, sipping lemonade and
swatting mosquitoes. "I think my mother stopped confiding in me
once I started going to school all day," Grandma said with a sigh.

I pushed my foot against the porch floor to keep the swing moving. Grandma was so short her feet barely reached the floor. "Did
your brothers ever find out about the runaway slaves?" I asked.

"No, they did not." Grandma grinned as if she were still a small
girl keeping a very big secret. Her dark eyes gleamed. "My brothers
thought they were so smart—and to this day it tickles me to think
they had no idea what Mama and I were up to."

We were looking through Grandma's box of keepsakes, and
she showed me a photograph of her father and mother. They
sat side-by-side, their shoulders barely touching, Henry's huge

farmer hands splayed on his thighs like a pair of shovels. He wore one of those silly beards that covered his chin and the sides of his face, but without the mustache. Great-Grandpa Henry's wide, generous mouth and full lower lip looked exactly like Grandma Bebe's—although she smiled all the time, and he looked as though he didn't know how to smile. He appeared to be so uncomfortable in his ill-fitting suit and lopsided bow tie that he might have been sitting barelegged in a patch of nettles.

"The suit and tie weren't his," Grandma explained. "The traveling photographer provided a rackful of clothing that you could borrow to get your picture taken."

The photo of Great-Grandmother Hannah intrigued me after hearing so much about her. No one would ever guess from the calm, serene look on her face that she was capable of facing down a pair of armed bounty hunters. Her hands rested on her lap as if they had no bones in them, and there was such an expression of meekness in her pale eyes and faint smile that I thought she probably spoke no louder than a whisper.

I searched her face for any resemblance to my own, hoping I might have inherited some of her fine moral qualities too, but to be honest I didn't see any. I didn't resemble Grandma Bebe either, nor did I look like my beautiful socialite mother, who might have sprung to life and fluttered off one of the pages of the fashion magazines she read so religiously. I not only looked plain and ordinary, but I worried that my life would be ordinary, as well. I wasn't brave and hardworking like Hannah, and I didn't have Grandma Bebe's passion for fighting injustice, and I certainly didn't want to inherit my mother's useless life, even if I did turn out to be as beautiful as she was. I couldn't figure out who I was and how I would ever fit into my illustrious family's story.

"Don't worry dear, I've been a misfit all my life," Grandma said. "I'm sure you'll do just fine. At least you have pluck and spunk.

When I was your age I was as jumpy as a baby rabbit and twice as shy." She showed me a photograph of two dozen children lined up outside her one-room schoolhouse and asked me to guess which one she was. I spotted Grandma Bebe easily. Not only was she the shortest child, but with her shoulders hunched and her head lowered, she looked as though she was trying to disappear.

"Going to school with a bunch of prankster-prone farm boys added to my fears," she said, "making me even more timid than I already was. My goal of becoming a woman of faith like my mother Hannah seemed as distant and unreachable as Canada. . . ."

By the time Bebe turned thirteen in July of 1861, the issue of slavery had become a huge, boiling cauldron that finally grew so hot it overflowed. War broke out between the states. As soon as Bebe's three oldest brothers finished harvesting the fall crops, they marched off to fight. James was twenty-two, William was twenty, and Joseph was eighteen.

"We'll lick those Rebels and be home by Christmastime," William promised as he waved good-bye. All three of Bebe's brothers displayed the same courage and bravado they'd shown as boys, making the Rebels seem like nothing more than a nest of black snakes hiding in the grass.

In a way, Bebe envied her brothers' adventures as they marched off to war. What would it be like to travel beyond the farm and visit new places? But a much wiser part of her thanked God that in His wisdom He had seen fit to make her a girl. She never could have summoned the courage to stand shoulder to shoulder in a line of soldiers and calmly aim her rifle as a horde of angry Rebels charged toward her with bayonets fixed. Bebe had prayed for courage, but so far God hadn't given her any.

With the three oldest boys gone, only sixteen-year-old Franklin remained behind to help Henry with the farm work. And Bebe, of course. The day after her brothers marched away, her father shook her awake before dawn.

"Get up. It's time for you boys to do your chores." He seemed to have forgotten that she was a girl.

"You mean . . . *me*, Papa?"

"Yes, you. Now hurry up. The cows are waiting to be milked." Bebe rolled out of bed and marched out to the barn to do her part, telling herself that the war would be over soon and her brothers would return. Everyone had agreed that the Rebels would be beaten in no time.

Everyone was wrong.

Six months later, when spring came around again, Bebe had all but forgotten that she was a girl, too. Meanwhile, her brothers were on their way to Virginia to conquer the Rebel capital of Richmond.

"Wish I were fighting with them," Franklin said as he and Bebe pitched a load of newly cut hay into the barn loft.

"You don't mean that."

"Sure do."

Bebe paused to lean against her pitchfork. "Aren't you reading their letters, Franklin? All they do is complain about the rain and the mud and the mosquitoes. The food is bad, everyone has a fever, and the Rebels have real bullets in their guns. Why would you want to be a part of that?"

"At least it's something new. I don't want to stay here, pitching hay and milking cows forever. Don't you ever get sick of this place?"

She could only stare at him. Why would he want to go anyplace else?

"Oh, that's right, you're a girl," he said after a moment. "I keep forgetting. Girls can't move around from place to place whenever they feel like it."

Bebe lifted her pitchfork and stabbed it deeper into the hay. "Can to! I just don't feel like it, that's all."

Franklin shook his head. "That's not how it works for women. First you need to find a husband. Then you have to move to wherever he wants to live."

"Who says?"

"Everyone says! That's just the way the world is. Don't you ever pay attention to these things?"

She returned to her work with a fury she didn't understand, stabbing the hay and hurling it aloft. Stubble rained down on her, sticking in her hair and dropping down the neck of her blouse until her body felt as prickly as her mood.

When the last of the hay was loaded off the flatbed wagon, Franklin grabbed Bebe's pitchfork and leaned it against the barn wall beside his. "Come on, let's go jump in the river and cool off."

"But Papa said—"

"He won't know we're finished. Come on! One quick swim before dinner."

Franklin shed his scratchy shirt, shoes, and socks on the way to the tree swing, dumping them in a heap beside the path. With a whoop of pure joy, he swung out over the river and dropped into the water below.

"Come on in, Bebe! It feels great!" he hollered up to her.

Bebe hadn't felt so hot and itchy since she'd had the chicken pox. She caught the dangling rope in her hand and sat down on the board. She was finally tall enough for her feet to touch the ground. But even though she longed for the cooling relief of the water, she simply couldn't bring herself to leap from the swing and drop all that way down into the river. She twirled in halfhearted circles for a few minutes, then got off the swing and picked her way carefully down the path to the river, still wearing her shoes in case of snakes.

"Why don't you jump in?" Franklin called to her. He floated on his back a few feet away, his bare toes sticking out of the water.

"I can't swim." Nor could she take off her clothes as Franklin had done. She was a girl.

Bebe sat down on the riverbank and dribbled water through her fingers, splashing it on her face and neck, aware for the first time of her limitations. She was still hot and prickly, while Franklin floated with the current, cool and refreshed. Bebe was forced to do the same work as a boy, but she couldn't have fun like a boy or travel wherever she wanted. It didn't seem fair. She stood and started hiking up the path away from the river, back toward home.

By the time summer ended, her brothers had marched close enough to Richmond to hear the church bells tolling, but the Union generals made them turn around and march all the way back down the Virginia peninsula to where they'd started. Bebe couldn't believe it. It seemed like the war was going to go on forever. She helped her father and Franklin bring in the harvest and slaughter the hogs. Winter came again.

Bebe rose before dawn on a frigid Sunday morning in 1863 and put on an overcoat that Franklin had outgrown and a pair of his worn-out boots and followed him and her father out to the barn through fresh shin-deep snow. The farmyard looked beautiful in the predawn light, buried beneath a sparkling blanket of pristine snow, unmarred by footprints or wagon tracks. Her breath hung in the air in front of her, as if she could grab it and put it in her pocket.

Warmth from the cows raised the temperature in the barn a few degrees, but by the time Bebe finished her chores and returned to the house, she felt as cold and stiff as a brass weather vane. She had often complained while scrubbing laundry and washing dishes with her mother, but she wished she were helping in the warm, cozy kitchen again. She missed her quiet conversations with Hannah.

"Can you stoke the fire a little hotter, Mama?" she asked as she dumped an extra armload of firewood into the kitchen woodbox. "I'm so frozen I can barely move." Her hair crackled and sparked as she pulled off her woolen hat and shook her long braids free.

Franklin tromped through the door behind her and snatched up his plate, piling on eggs and bacon and biscuits from the warming oven. He was taking more than his fair share, from what Bebe could see. She quickly grabbed her own plate and shoved Franklin aside with her hip.

"Hey, move over. Some of this food is for me, you know."

Franklin laughed and shoved her in return, tussling with her the way her brothers used to wrestle with each other, even though the top of Bebe's head barely reached Franklin's shoulders. At fourteen, she was still as tiny as a ten-year-old, although her back had grown strong during the past two years and her rock-rough hands were callused from wielding pitchforks and shovels and scythes.

"I'm not only frozen, I'm starved!" she said, shoving a warm biscuit into her mouth. Any ladylike manners she once might have possessed had deteriorated significantly since the war began. She didn't care.

"I can't help thinking of James and William and Joseph," Hannah said as she put more wood in the stove. "Imagine eating hardtack and sleeping outside in tents on the cold, hard ground . . . I hope they've found someplace to attend church this morning."

The thought of going outside again made Bebe shiver. "Do we have to go to church?" she asked. "Can't we just stay home and read the Bible here, for once? It's too cold to ride all the way into town—and I could use a rest. Papa thinks we're his slaves."

"You don't know what slavery is," Hannah said gently. "You

should thank God every day that you don't have an evil overseer standing behind you with a whip like those poor slaves down South do. And thank God we have the freedom to attend church."

"Well, I'm going to pray that this war ends soon so the boys can come home and do their own work."

Franklin nudged her with his elbow, frowning. "Don't do that. I don't want the war to end yet. I want my turn to fight."

Bebe stared at her brother. His cheeks were still red from the cold, his sweaty hair mashed flat from his stocking cap. She suddenly realized how much she would miss Franklin if he went off to war, too. The bond between them had grown strong as they'd worked together every day, and Franklin no longer treated her like a pesky little sister the way her other brothers had. She didn't know what she would do if she ever saw his name on the list posted at the general store of all the local boys who had been killed or wounded in battle. But Bebe didn't know how to explain her reasons to Franklin. Instead, she slid the rest of her bacon onto his plate.

"Here . . . I took too much." She lifted one of her biscuits onto his plate, too.

The kitchen door opened and their father came inside, trailing powdery snow from his boots and sending a shiver of cold air down Bebe's neck. "Which one of you boys left my axe lying on the ground?"

"I guess I did," Bebe said meekly. "Sorry . . . I had to use it to chop the ice out of the watering troughs."

"I've told you boys a hundred times to take care of my tools. That axe will be no good to anyone if it rusts."

"Sorry . . . And I'm a girl, Papa, not a boy." Henry didn't acknowledge the correction.

Bebe gulped down the rest of her food and quickly changed into her Sunday clothes, tying a bonnet over her unruly hair. Hannah had warmed bricks in the oven so Bebe could thaw out her frozen feet on the trip to town. She still felt grumpy as she sat down in the church pew between Franklin and her father, fuming about the endless war that might take Franklin away from her, and certain that she smelled as strongly of manure as they did, even though she had washed and changed her clothes and shoes. She barely paid attention to Reverend Webster's sermon until she noticed that an unusual hush had fallen over the congregation. She uncrossed her arms and sat up to listen.

"And so our prayers have been answered," he was saying. "According to the latest news, President Lincoln has signed an Emancipation Proclamation, which means that every slave in every rebellious state is now a free man!"

For a moment, the silence in the church was absolute. Bebe tried to imagine what it would feel like to suddenly be granted her freedom after a lifetime of slavery. Probably even better than if her brothers came home. Then one of the elders began to sing the doxology in a wavering baritone, and one by one the other members of the congregation joined in.

> Praise God from Whom all blessings flow
> Praise Him all creatures here below
> Praise Him above ye Heavenly Host.
> Praise Father, Son and Holy Ghost . . . Amen.

Bebe recalled the feeling of joy and relief she'd felt on that long-ago day when the bounty hunters had turned their horses around and trotted away from the farm wagon, and she felt guilty for complaining about the farm work. She had read the tattered copy of *Uncle Tom's Cabin* with its pages falling out and its back cover missing, and she felt the rightness of the abolition movement with every ounce of her strength.

"God heard the slaves' groaning," Pastor Webster continued, "just as He once heard the cries of the slaves in Egypt. He heard our congregation's prayers, and now He has answered them. But the slaves will still be in bondage until the war is over and liberation comes—which is all the more reason for us to keep praying for our soldiers and leaders, keep praying for the war to end soon. And when peace returns to our land once again, imagine all the other things we can accomplish if we continue to work together as God's people to further His kingdom."

Bebe was quiet for most of the ride home until the wagon reached the fork in the road, reminding her as it always did of the day she and her mother had helped Mary and Katie escape. "Wasn't that wonderful news we heard today about the slaves?" she asked.

"God is so good," Hannah murmured.

Bebe glanced down the other road and remembered the bounty hunters sitting astride their powerful horses. She remembered their hunting dogs jostling and sniffing as they approached the wagon. And she remembered the two brave women huddled beneath the firewood, holding their breath. That's why her brothers were fighting this war. Sometimes it was so hard to take her mind off the daily aches and pains and so easy to lose sight of the bigger goal.

As her farmhouse came into view beyond the turn in the road, Bebe vowed to pray every day for the war to end. And though she knew it was selfish of her, she wanted it to end for her own freedom as much as for the slaves.

CHAPTER

6

Morning comes very early when you're locked in a jail cell. The high, barred windows had no curtains, so I awakened with the sunrise. I sat up, rubbing my eyes with my fists to get out the jail dust, then smoothed my hair off my face. The cell had no mirror, so I could only imagine how disheveled I must look.

Even in the best of times I was never fastidious with my hair and clothing. I had much more important things to attend to than brushing my hair for one hundred strokes or taking hours to pin it up in a fashionable Gibson girl style or applying layers of cosmetics to my cheeks. I wore my hair bobbed, and I purchased clothing that was "serviceable," much to my mother's dismay. I couldn't be bothered with lace that could be torn or silk that would catch and shred easily.

After my wild car ride last evening, and a long uncomfortable night on a lumpy mattress, I figured I must look like Longfellow's *The Wreck of the Hesperus.* I found myself wishing for a hairbrush. And a toothbrush. Never in my life have I slept in my clothes. Mother would be appalled, I'm sure.

There is an old adage that says, "You can't make a silk purse out of a sow's ear," but that didn't stop my mother from trying hard over the years, to transform me into a silk purse. As I lay down on my jailhouse bunk again, trying in vain to go back to sleep, I recalled one of her more memorable attempts. It was during the summer of 1910, when I was a wild and wiry child with scrawny legs and a rat's nest of brown hair . . .

"Harriet, it's time you learned to be more ladylike." My mother made the pronouncement with a firm voice and a determined nod of her stately blond head.

"But I'm not a lady," I argued. "I'm only ten!" I rose from my seat at the breakfast table and began backing slowly from the room, trying to make my escape.

"Halt!" Mother said. "I mean it, Harriet. Your manners are atrocious, and I don't know where to begin to describe your lack of concern for your appearance."

In truth, my appearance was hopeless, so why be concerned? I was mousy and plain, and no amount of wishing would ever transform me into a beauty like my sister, Alice. Or my mother for that matter, who was an older, more elegant version of my sister. God had abundantly blessed both of them with delicate features, golden hair, and alabaster skin. Both had the dainty upturned nose, pointed chin, and mysterious, haughty demeanor of a Gibson girl. Men's heads turned when Mother and Alice sashayed past. Men probably averted their gazes when I did.

"I've let you run wild for much too long," Mother continued. "But starting today that's all going to change."

I gulped. I glanced at Alice and saw her nodding in agreement. I was doomed.

"Mother and I have decided to plan a garden luncheon," Alice said gleefully. "We're going to invite all of our friends—and yours too, Harriet. Won't it be fun?"

"I would sooner be stuck on a spit and roasted over a fire."

"Why must you say such outrageous things?" Mother asked. "Honestly, I never know what's going to come out of your mouth. Perhaps that should be our first task, Alice, teaching the girl to hold her tongue."

I was tempted to stick out said tongue at them, but I knew it would get me into worse trouble. Mother made me sit down at the table again. "And please pay attention to your posture, Harriet. Don't slouch. If you're ever going to learn grace and poise, you'll need to begin with a straight spine."

I listened in horror as they spelled out their plans for me, conspiring to outfit me in a frilly white dress complete with lace and bows. I had no desire to turn all feminine and fluttery. My short, skinny body still resembled a child's, which was fine with me. I wanted no part of womanhood.

But after breakfast Mother and Alice marched me down to Daddy's department store against my will, then stood around my dressing room door *ooh*ing and *ahh*ing and telling me how pretty I looked as I tried on scratchy dresses with lots of ruffles and flounces and frills. "I look like a stray dog trying to fit into a party dress," I told them.

Alice bounced on her toes and clapped her pretty hands. "No you don't, Harriet, you look sweet."

I made a face. The last thing I wanted to be was sweet. "I hope you're not going to buy me a vial of smelling salts and a crochet-edged handkerchief, too," I grumbled.

As soon as we returned home, I bolted away as if my bloomers were on fire and ran straight to Grandma Bebe's house to tell her the terrible news.

"Mercy me, Harriet, who's chasing you?" she asked as I burst through her door, panting like a hound dog. Grandma sat at her dining room table, which was piled high, as usual, with letters and envelopes and copies of the temperance paper, *The Union Signal.* As far as I could recall, I had never actually seen the top of her dining room table—much less eaten a meal on it.

"Grandma?" I asked breathlessly, "I'm not going to start growing all soft and lumpy like Alice, am I?"

"Not within the next few minutes, I shouldn't think. Sit down, dear. Tell me what's wrong."

"Mother is trying to make me wear frilly dresses and go to tea parties, and I don't want to. I don't want to look like Alice, I want to look like you."

"Horrors! Why would you wish for such a thing? I've never grown any bigger than a ten-year-old. Of course, I always blamed my stunted growth on all of the farm work I had to endure while my brothers were away at war, but—"

"Can farm work really stunt your growth?" I was ready to hop on the first hay wagon if it meant avoiding a figure like Alice's and all the attention that came with it.

"I'm not really sure if it can," Grandma replied, "but I always figured that since my father needed another son so badly, my body simply complied. Will you be staying long, Harriet dear? I could use some help with these envelopes."

Grandma was always doing something for "the cause," and I was willing to help her as long as it didn't involve going to jail. After my father bailed her out a few months earlier, I'd heard him say that if she got arrested again she would just have to stay there, no matter how many tears Alice shed.

"How's your tongue, Harriet? Can you lick some envelopes for me?"

"I guess so." Licking envelopes was much better than sipping tea and acting all ladylike. Grandma brought me a glass of water to "wet my whistle."

"I wish I were a boy," I said with a sigh. "Did you hate being a girl, too, Grandma?"

"I didn't know what I wanted to be when I was your age," she replied. "I hated doing my brothers' chores while they were away at war, but I wasn't sure I wanted to be a woman, either. It seemed to me that boys had more interesting opportunities than girls did."

"But isn't that why the suffragettes are marching? So women will have more opportunities?"

"I suppose that's one of the things they're trying to change. But back then I didn't know what I wanted. If you had asked me, I would have told you that I hated doing my brothers' chores, but I didn't necessarily want to do housework, either. That nasty war dragged on and on until I didn't think my life could possibly get any worse—and then it did. . . ."

&

Spring came early in 1863, and as the weather grew warmer, Bebe steeled herself for another season of work. Last spring she'd held on to the hope that the war would end soon. Now she knew better. In March, when she and her father drove into town one morning to pick up supplies from Harrison's General Store, the shopkeeper had more bad news for them.

"How old is your boy now, Henry?" Mr. Harrison asked as he weighed out two pounds of sugar.

Henry gestured to Bebe with his thumb. "You mean this one?"

"I'm a girl, Papa," she said, in case he'd forgotten.

"No, your youngest boy . . . the one who isn't fighting yet."

Bebe's father looked to her for the answer. "Franklin is eighteen," she told them.

Mr. Harrison shook his head. "That's hard luck for you, Henry. Looks like he'll be leaving for the war, too, before long."

"Leaving!" Bebe stared at Mr. Harrison, waiting for him to break into a grin and tell her that it had all been a joke. He was known to be a big kidder. But his expression never changed as he slid the sack of sugar across the counter.

"Yup. Just got word that Congress has passed a new draft law. They're conscripting boys from age eighteen on up—which means my boy will have to go, too." He twirled the ends of his handlebar mustache and shook his head. "Seems the Union army needs more soldiers—which is hardly surprising the way our generals have been sacrificing them left and right. I'm guessing there'll be a lot of folks needing farm help this summer. Don't know how I'll manage the store shorthanded."

Henry scooped up the parcel of sugar and pointed to the shelf behind Mr. Harrison's head. "I'll take some of that lamp oil, too, Herbert."

Bebe stared at her father. How could he remain so calm after hearing the news? She wanted to scream. "What are we going to do if Franklin has to go away?" she asked on the way home.

"One day at a time," her father murmured. "One day at a time."

Franklin's draft notice arrived in the mail a few weeks later. Bebe sat at the dinner table with her family that evening waiting to hear what he and her father planned to do about it. Franklin was the only one who seemed cheerful about the situation. Bebe tried to be patient, waiting until the chicken and potatoes and carrots were all eaten and the rhubarb pie was cut and served, but no one seemed willing to discuss the matter. She cleared her throat, taking it upon herself to start the conversation.

"People in town are saying you can pay three hundred dollars to hire a substitute and get out of fighting in the war," she said.

"That's what Mr. Harrison down at the store might do so his son won't have to go."

Henry frowned. "We don't have three hundred dollars."

"Besides, I want to go," Franklin added.

Bebe could no longer sit quietly. She pushed her chair away from the table and sprang to her feet. "You can't let him leave, Papa! How will we ever manage this farm all by ourselves?"

Hannah laid her hand on Bebe's arm. "Hush, Beatrice. We'll be fine." She would never dream of telling her husband what he could or couldn't do.

"But I'll be the only one left, Mama, and I'm a girl! I can't do all the work that needs to be done around here without Franklin."

"Hush now," Hannah soothed. "With the Lord's help, we can do anything. God is asking the men to do their part to help free the slaves, and we need to do ours."

"Well, I can't do it! I won't!" Bebe ran from the house, past the vegetable garden and through the barnyard, wishing she could run all the way to Canada like the other escaped slaves. That's how she thought of herself—as a slave, forced to labor against her will.

Milkweed and chicory whipped against her legs as she sprinted across the pasture behind the barn. Mud clung to the bottoms of her shoes, but she didn't stop running until she reached her brothers' swing near the river, out of breath and out of tears. She straddled the seat and backed up to push off with her feet. She wished she could make it go as high as her brothers used to go.

It wasn't fair! She wouldn't mind doing something noble and brave, like hiding slaves or fighting a battle, but why was she stuck doing farm work? Endless farm work. She dangled uselessly from the swing, kicking at the dirt and feeling sorry for herself for nearly half an hour before Franklin came looking for her.

"You're not swinging very high, Bebe. Need a push?" He grabbed her from behind and pulled the swing back as far as he could, then let go. Each time Bebe swung back, Franklin gave her another push until she was soaring higher than ever before. The rope creaked as it rubbed against the tree branch and her stomach dropped every time the swing did. Her eyes watered in the wind. She felt like she was flying.

Franklin stopped pushing after a while and sank down on the ground with a sigh. He tore out a wide blade of grass and stretched it between his thumbs to whistle through it—a feat that Bebe had never been able to do. "You have to pump with your legs if you want to keep going," he told her. "Stretch out your legs every time you go forward, then try to scoop air with them on the way back."

Bebe tried it, pouring all of her anger into the task as she reached and stretched, remembering how her brothers used to do it. When she felt the swing respond, she pumped harder, going higher.

"That's it! . . . I think you've got it!" Franklin called.

Bebe pumped as hard as she could, no longer afraid of falling, wishing she never had to stop. "I don't want you to go!" she shouted.

"I know," he said quietly. "But I have to. Somebody needs to lick those Rebels once and for all." She looked down at him, lounging on the grass, and knew that what Franklin faced was much worse than what she did. He could be killed. She stopped pumping and allowed the swing to slow, dragging her feet in the dirt.

"Are you scared, Franklin? Tell me the truth."

"I've decided not to think about it. I'm just going to do what I have to do and take it one day at a time." That was what their father always said—"one day at a time." But those days had already added up to more than two years.

"I'll knit you some socks," Bebe said suddenly.

"Ha!" Franklin laughed. "You hate to knit."

"I know. But you'll need them to keep your feet warm." She

pushed off with her feet and began to pump again, going higher, faster.

"I think you've got the hang of it, Bebe." He gave another piercing whistle, then tossed the piece of grass aside. "We'll be fine, both of us. We'll do what we have to do, and we'll be fine."

When the day finally came for Franklin to leave, Bebe couldn't bear to watch him go. She hugged him tightly, then ran upstairs to her bedroom, stuffing her fingers in her ears so she wouldn't have to hear the wagon driving away. She forced herself not to cry as she wandered into her brothers' room and gazed around at their empty beds. Franklin had left his bureau drawer open, and one leg of his work trousers hung out of it. Bebe started to tuck it inside and close the drawer, then changed her mind. She pulled out the overalls and held them up in front of her. They were miles too long for her, but if she hiked up the straps and rolled up the legs she could make them fit.

"Beatrice, what in the world are you wearing?" Hannah asked when Bebe came downstairs a while later.

"I've decided to borrow Franklin's overalls until he gets back. It'll be easier to do his chores."

"They look quite unbecoming on you. And the Bible says that it's wrong for women to wear men's clothing."

Bebe felt a surge of anger. "The Bible also says not to kill people, and everyone is killing each other, aren't they?"

"Beatrice . . ."

She crossed her arms and lifted her chin. "And what does the Bible say about women doing men's work?"

Hannah displayed relentless patience. "God's Word says that whatever your hands find to do, do it with all your heart as unto the Lord."

"Well then, I don't see why the Lord would care if I did what I have to do in a pair of pants."

Even in trousers, Bebe found it difficult to do her work "as unto the Lord," especially when her father demanded that it be done his way. Before long, the only time Bebe wore a dress was when she went to church on Sunday. That's where she was when she heard the news that General Lee and his Rebel army had defeated the Union forces at Winchester, Virginia, and had now crossed the border into her state, Pennsylvania. The townswomen were all aflutter about it after the service.

"We need to make preparations," Mrs. Harrison told the gathered group of women, "or the Rebels will take all of our food and ravish our daughters."

Bebe wasn't worried about being "ravished"—how would anyone even know she was a girl, dressed in Franklin's clothes and smelling of manure? But she would fight to the death before she'd let those Rebels steal one morsel of the food she had labored so hard to grow.

"We need to buy some extra gunpowder for Papa's shotgun," she told Hannah as they walked back to their wagon. "I'm going to shoot those dirty Rebels if they come near our farm."

Hannah's habitually mild expression grew stern. "Now, listen to me, Beatrice. It's bad enough that my sons are forced to kill—I won't have my daughter killing, as well."

"But what if they try to take our food?"

"Jesus says that if someone asks for your cloak, you should give him your coat also. If the Rebels need our food that badly, we'll let them have it."

"Mama, no! Not after all my hard work! I'm not going to let anyone have it!"

Hannah smoothed back Bebe's hair and caressed her cheek. "Don't borrow trouble by worrying about something that may never happen. 'Sufficient unto the day is the evil thereof.'"

Bebe wondered if she really could kill a Rebel soldier. Two

weeks later on her fifteenth birthday, she thought that perhaps she could. On her family's weekly trip to town, she found all of her neighbors talking about the series of battles that had been fought near the village of Gettysburg, Pennsylvania. Her parents found a telegram waiting for them in Harrison's General Store. Hannah's hands trembled as she tore open the envelope. Bebe watched her face turn pale as she read it.

"What happened?" Bebe asked. "What does it say?"

Hannah choked out the words as if wringing them from her heart. "Your brother Joseph has been killed in battle."

Grief settled over Bebe's household like deep snow, bringing life on the farm to a suffocating standstill and chilling everyone's soul. The neighbors brought food but no one felt like eating it. As Bebe lay awake in her bedroom at night, she heard the floors creaking downstairs as her father paced sleeplessly. She remembered Joseph's wide grin and joyous laughter and wanted to kill a hundred Rebels in retaliation.

"How could God let this happen?" she asked her mother. "We've been praying and asking Him to protect the boys."

"God isn't causing this war, Beatrice, people are."

"Well, why doesn't He stop us?" For once, her mother had no answer.

Bebe never did see her father weep, but he attacked his chores with a ferocity that frightened her. Hannah grieved quietly for her son, allowing her tears to fall silently as she went about her work. But Bebe railed at God, alternating between fits of anger and fits of tears until a day came when she was so hot and weary from the unending work, so feverish with rage, that she dropped her father's hoe in the middle of the vegetable patch and sprinted across the pasture toward the river. When she reached the swing she climbed onto it, remembering the day that Franklin had taught her to pump; remembering Joseph whooping for joy as he'd leaped from the swing into the river.

Bebe started swinging parallel to the river as she always had, then changed her mind. She twisted around on the wooden plank and backed up, preparing to swing out over the river for the first time. The rope creaked against the tree branch as she pumped higher and higher, and she wondered if it might be so rotten after all these years that it would break from the strain. She decided that she didn't care. Even if it snapped off while she was in midair and she tumbled to the ground and broke every bone in her body, she couldn't possibly feel any more pain than she already did.

At first Bebe clenched her eyes tightly shut, afraid to look down at the river as the swing carried her out over it. But the July day was so hot, her smoldering anger so intense, that without thinking she abruptly released the rope and dropped through the air into the river.

Bebe realized her mistake the moment her body plunged beneath the surface. She couldn't swim! Her skin tingled all over from the water's cruel slap, and she felt as if she had awakened for the first time in her life. She opened her eyes beneath the murky river and feared she was about to die—and she didn't want to die.

Somehow, she rose to the surface, coughing and sputtering for air. The shore looked a long way off. Bebe had just enough time to draw a quick breath before the water washed over her head and pulled her under again. The current gripped her as if it were a living thing, and she struggled against it with all her might, flailing and kicking as she tried to fight her way to the top for another gulp of air. Each time her head emerged, she heard birds singing and cattle lowing in the distance. Each time she went under, the growling river muffled the sounds as it tried to hold her down and pin her beneath the surface.

Bebe knew there was no one to save her. If she yielded to the current and allowed it to carry her downstream, she would die. If she wanted to survive, she would have to fight to stay afloat, then fight her way to the riverbank. Bebe made up her mind to fight.

Franklin's heavy work boots felt like rocks tied to her ankles, so she kicked them off, then slipped the straps of his overalls from her shoulders and wiggled out of them. Freed from her cumbersome clothing, she bobbed above the surface again, long enough to drag more air into her lungs, long enough to catch a glimpse of the distant shore. Then she went under.

Bebe fought with all her might until her limbs felt leaden with fatigue. Her stomach ached from swallowing gallons of water. She could feel the current carrying her downstream, but at the same time her efforts were gradually moving her closer to shore. After what seemed like hours, Bebe's feet touched the rocky bottom. She could stand. She struggled upright, sharp stones jabbing her feet, and walked toward the shore as the river tried to drag her under one last time. At last she flopped down on dry land, collapsing with relief. She gazed up at the blue sky and white clouds and realized that in all of her struggles, it had never occurred to her to pray.

Bebe walked through the kitchen door a while later, still dripping wet, wearing only her socks, pantaloons and calico blouse.

"Beatrice, what happened to you?" Hannah said when she saw her. "Where are your clothes?"

"I jumped off the boys' swing into the river."

Hannah stared at her.

"I can't go on much longer, Mama. I hate this ugly war. Why can't things be the way they were three years ago?"

Hannah sighed and drew Bebe into her arms, even though the water from Bebe's clothing soaked through to hers. "Never forget, Beatrice, that the greater goal is to win freedom for the slaves. That's what we've been praying for and working for all this time. That's what Joseph gave his life for. If we ask the Lord to give us love and compassion for those poor souls, then we'll be willing to make any sacrifice."

"But Joseph is gone and . . . and I don't want to lose the other boys, too. When is this war going to end?"

"Do you want to know the secret of contentment, Beatrice?" Hannah released her and stepped back to hold Bebe's water-shriveled hands in her own. A damp spot now darkened the front of Hannah's apron. "We need to live each day as if it was a gift. God gives us that gift every morning when the sun rises, like the tickets they give out when you ride on the train."

"I've never been on a train," Bebe said, sulking.

"That ticket is only good for today. Yesterday is gone and that ticket is used up. We don't have a ticket for tomorrow because life has no guarantees. Each day is a gift. When the sun comes up, we need to ask the Lord, 'What would you like me to do for you today?' That's how you'll find contentment."

"But . . . didn't you always say that we should have a plan so we'd know exactly where we're headed? You said we wouldn't get anywhere in life without a map."

"That's true. But we need to let God draw the map for us, then follow it in faith."

Bebe stared at the floor. She knew that her feeble faith fell far short of her mother's. "I can't do that," she mumbled.

"You're not willing to give your life to Him each day?"

Bebe thought of how she had nearly drowned and how she had saved herself. She shook her head. "If this is what He's going to do with my life . . . then I guess not."

She endured another summer, another harvest—this time without Franklin's help. Another winter arrived, and she learned to split wood and shovel snow. In the spring she watched four new baby calves come into the world and helped her father plant corn and cut hay. And just when it seemed as though the war would never end, it did.

❦

"I wish I could dress up in boys' clothes like you did," I said when Grandma Bebe finished her story. The envelopes were all licked, my water glass was empty, and my tongue felt as raspy as a cat's.

Grandma shook her head. "No, don't wish for that. Those heavy old boots and baggy overalls were nearly the death of me." She tilted her head to one side as she studied me. I loved the way my grandmother looked at me, as if I were a treasure chest filled with glittering gold and precious jewels.

"Harriet, don't give your mother a hard time about the party dress. Let her go ahead and decorate the outside of you. She can't change what's on the inside, you know—and that's the most important part of you. Only God can change you on the inside."

"How does He do that?"

"Sometimes through suffering," she said quietly. Her gaze got all soft and blurry-eyed as she continued to look at me. "I didn't know during those war years that God was preparing me for the future, but He was. He knew that I would need to be strong in order to get through what lay ahead."

"Why, Grandma? What happened?"

I wanted to hear the rest of the story, but Grandma shook her head. "That's a tale for another day." She stood and smoothed the wrinkles from her skirt. "Thanks for your help, dear, but you'd better run along home. And make sure you enjoy that tea party, you hear?"

I made a face. "You can lead a horse to water," I grumbled, "but you can't make him drink."

Grandma's laughter followed me out the door.

CHAPTER

7

My jailhouse breakfast, when it finally arrived, was a terrible disappointment. It consisted of lumpy oatmeal and dry toast. The coffee tasted as though it had been sitting on the back of the stove for the past month, boiling continuously. None of the meal was palatable, so I set the tray on the floor and leaned against the brick wall again to do some more thinking. When you have nothing else to do except think, a lot of strange memories come to mind. One of them featured Grandma Bebe's brother, Franklin.

I had heard stories about him over the years, but I finally met him in person on Decoration Day in 1911, when I was eleven years old. Grandma had purchased her own car by then, much to my mother's dismay. "There's no telling how much trouble she'll get into now that she can drive her own car," my mother said, so she asked me to tag along and keep Grandma out of mischief. Little did Mother know that I was an eager partner in Grandma's mischief, and that I had no intention of keeping her out of it. In fact, Grandma was secretly teaching me how to drive on the dirt roads outside of town now that my legs were long enough to reach the pedals. I couldn't wait for another driving lesson that day.

We left early in the morning and traveled out of town, enjoying the drive through the rolling farmland, admiring the misty forests of the Appalachian Mountains in the distance. Grandma let me slide behind the wheel and practice driving for a few miles as soon as we reached the countryside. She didn't say where we were going, but I hoped she was taking me to one of her temperance rallies and that we'd be pelted with eggs and spoiled tomatoes. Grandma had shown me a story in the newspaper about a saloon owner who had captured several skunks and set them loose on a group of temperance women who were protesting outside his saloon. Since I was all prepared for some excitement, I was a little disappointed when Grandma motored into a village I'd never visited before and parked her car in a cemetery, of all places.

"What are we doing here?" I asked as we removed our driving gloves and dusters and tossed them onto the seat. "Did someone die?"

"Of course, Harriet—*thousands* of people died!" She spread her hands and stared at me in exasperation as if her reply should make perfect sense. "It's Decoration Day!"

"Oh . . ." I still didn't understand, but she linked arms with me and towed me over to a raggedy group of ancient soldiers who were milling around a Civil War monument. They were all holding miniature American flags and waiting for the ceremony to begin. I had seen Grand Army of the Republic veterans before, marching in Fourth of July parades in our hometown, but I had never gotten close enough to see how tattered and moth-eaten their uniforms were after forty-six years. Or how ill-fitting. The passing years were unkind to people's bodies, expanding them in some places, contracting them in others. I gazed around at these somber men, with their aged faces and gray hair, and I tried to imagine them as young men, their uniforms new, their bodies fit and hearty as they bravely marched off to fight a war that would change them forever. I saw a well-deserved pride in their tired expressions, an awareness that they had courageously stepped forward when their country needed them. They had a right to be proud of their accomplishments.

Grandma halted beside a tall, gaunt soldier who looked like the grim reaper in an army uniform. "Harriet, I'd like you to meet my brother, Franklin."

I thought she was joking. The tops of our heads barely reached to his armpits. He didn't resemble Grandma Bebe in the least, and his startling white hair made him look old enough to be her father. But Franklin turned to her with a wide, warm smile that took twenty years off his age.

"Hey, good to see you, Bebe." He wrapped his arm around her neck and pulled her close, kissing the top of her head.

"Franklin, this is Harriet—the granddaughter I've told you so much about."

"Pleased to meet you," I said as we appraised each other. I wondered what she had been saying about me.

"She looks just like you, Bebe, when you were her age."

"Stop it, Franklin. You'll give the girl nightmares." He laughed, and the sound reminded me of a car engine trying to turn over and start.

The ceremony, once it finally began, would have been humorous if it hadn't been so poignant. The pompous officials took turns posing for the news photographer, sucking in their paunches and gripping their lapels, their chins and jowls thrust forward. The mayor sputtered and flapped and tried not to curse after stepping backward into a mud puddle. He stammered his way through a flowery, incomprehensible speech. The next official accidentally dropped the memorial wreath facedown in the same mud puddle that the mayor had stepped in, and half of the flowers fell out of it. When he finally propped up the wreath on the metal stand, it looked as bedraggled and woebegone as the veterans.

The bugler, who looked old enough to have fought in the Revolution, played a barely recognizable rendition of taps. Uncle Franklin closed his eyes while the commander of the local GAR post spoke about sacrifice and duty and freedom, and I wondered if he was dozing or reminiscing. I saw several old veterans wipe their eyes.

After the minister pronounced the benediction, my uncle limped around the cemetery with the other old men, placing flags and GAR stars on various graves. He used an ebony cane with a silver handle, and moved very stiffly, lurching across the lumpy ground as if it pained him to move. The final grave, where he and Grandma lingered the longest, belonged to their brother Joseph.

"What a pity," Grandma murmured.

"Joe deserved better," Franklin sighed. I subtracted the dates on the grave marker while I waited. My great-uncle Joseph had died at the age of twenty—only two years older than my sister Alice was at that time.

Afterward, Grandma and I drove across town to a leafy park, following Uncle Franklin and the other veterans. A Grand Army of the Republic reunion picnic was getting under way, and my great-uncle's spirits brightened considerably as he beckoned to us. "Come on over here, ladies. Sadie and I saved you a place at our table."

Grandma halted, her arms crossed like an Indian chief. "Now, Franklin. There aren't going to be any alcoholic beverages at this shindig, are there?"

"No, ma'am," he said with a grin. "Alcohol is strictly prohibited on village property—thanks to you and the other temperance gals." I didn't tell Grandma, but I saw some of the old soldiers—including

Uncle Franklin—taking furtive sips from silver pocket flasks. The laughter grew louder as the afternoon progressed, the veterans' steps more tentative as if the ground had begun to move like ocean waves.

We sat at wooden picnic tables beneath tall pine trees, and the warm air that blew over us was scented with pine and woodsmoke. The ladies unpacked their picnic baskets and the feast began as everyone shared their bounty with one another. Uncle Franklin's wife, Sadie, brought out pickles and potato salad and cold fried chicken. Someone sliced into a watermelon, and Grandma and I had one of our spitting contests to see who could make the seeds go the farthest. I never have been able to beat her.

"How did you learn to spit so good?" I asked.

"As a matter of fact, Franklin taught me."

He turned around when he heard his name. "What'd you say?"

She held out a slice of watermelon. "Care to give it a try, Franklin? I'll bet I can still beat you."

He laughed and lifted his hands in surrender. "Aw, you're so full of spit and vinegar, Bebe, nobody can beat you."

Late in the afternoon, Uncle Franklin turned to me and pinched my cheek. "Say, there aren't any woodpeckers hiding around here, are there?" he asked.

"Um . . . I don't know . . ."

"Listen, Harriet, I'll pay you two bits if you keep an eye out for them. They might come looking for me, you know."

"Woodpeckers? Are you pulling my leg, Uncle Franklin?"

"No, no!" His laugh sounded more like a cough. "They're not after your leg, they're after mine." He rapped his cane against his calf and it sounded like he had thumped it against the table leg. I thought it was a trick, but he grinned and pulled up his pant leg and thumped it again. "It's made of wood, don't you see?"

I turned to my grandmother for confirmation, and she nodded. "If it weren't for your uncle Franklin, you wouldn't be here, Harriet."

"You mean at the picnic?"

"No, here in this world! I'm talking about the fact that you're alive, dear. It's all thanks to Franklin and his wooden leg."

I had no idea what she meant, and her astounding statement raised a lot of questions in my overactive imagination. But someone announced that the ice cream was ready, and I was swept away in the melee of adults, talking and laughing and enjoying the reunion. Grandma didn't have a chance to explain how Uncle Franklin and his wooden leg were responsible for my existence until the day ended and we were driving home in the car.

"Why did you say that if it weren't for Uncle Franklin, I wouldn't be here?" I asked with a yawn. "And how did his leg get turned into wood?"

"A minie ball shattered it just below the knee, and the army doctors had to cut it off with a hacksaw."

Grandma's grisly description should have repulsed me, but it didn't. I sat up straight, fascinated. "What's a minie ball?"

"It's like a bullet—only bigger." She made a circle the size of a nickel with her thumb and forefinger. "Once a minie ball rips through flesh and bone, there's no saving that limb. It happened on April 2, 1865, during the Union breakthrough into Petersburg. By the time we received word that Franklin had been wounded, the war was over. General Lee had surrendered at Appomattox Courthouse on April ninth, one week after that fateful battle. A few days later, President Lincoln was dead."

"My goodness," I murmured. I never paid much attention during history lessons, but this was my great-uncle we were talking about, a man I'd just met.

Grandma gazed at the road ahead of us as she drove, her chin level with the top of the steering wheel. "For years I wondered why God couldn't manage to keep Franklin safe for seven more days— seven days, Harriet! Especially after everything else my brothers had endured during the war."

"Did God ever give you a reason?" I remembered some of Grandma's other stories, such as the time God had kept her safe while she helped the slaves escape.

"Well, if God did have a reason, He never breathed a word of it to me." She concentrated on her driving for a moment, changing gears as the car chugged uphill. A moment later we flew over the summit and started down again, leaving my stomach on the floorboards. "I've composed a long list of questions to ask God when I arrive in heaven," Grandma continued. "It's nearly as long as a book, by now—and the mystery of Franklin's leg is high on that list."

Before I had a chance to remind her of my original question, she said, "And another thing I would very much like to ask is why I never grew into a properly proportioned woman. Look at me— I'm still built like a ten-year-old boy!"

I rolled my eyes at her oft-said words. "You look fine to me, Grandma."

"No offense, dear, but you're hardly one to judge. You're built like a ten-year-old boy, yourself—in case you haven't noticed."

"Good! I don't ever want to look like a woman! Or be one. Ever since Alice got all 'girly,' she's been impossible to live with. That's why I wanted to come with you today. It's sickening the way her beaux gather around on our front porch every night like flies around a peach pie."

"Well, whether you want to become a woman or not is beside the point. Believe me, it will happen. Although if that war had gone on much longer, I might have completely forgotten that I'd been born a girl. My mother reminded me, just in time when—"

"Wait a minute, Grandma. You still haven't explained how Uncle Franklin was responsible for my existence."

"But that's exactly what I'm about to tell you, Harriet, if you'd just stop interrupting and listen. . . ."

The war ended for Bebe on the day that James and William arrived home. From then on, she never had to do their farm chores again. She had been helping her father smear axle grease on the wagon wheels when she looked up and saw her brothers hiking up the road toward home. She wiped her hands on an empty burlap sack and ran toward them, her oversized boots kicking up little clouds of dust. Her brothers laughed when they saw her.

"I thought we left a little sister behind," William exclaimed. "Where did this scruffy fellow come from?"

"And what happened to little Bebe?" James asked.

Indeed, what had happened? The war had not only changed her, but James and William, as well. The lanky, teasing boys who had marched away four years earlier were grown men now with creased faces and wooly beards. They had arrived unexpectedly, just before lunchtime, and Hannah quickly conscripted Bebe to help out in the kitchen.

"Run upstairs and change into clean clothes, Beatrice. I'm going to prepare a proper feast for my boys, and I'll need your help."

Bebe had never been as close to her older brothers as she was to Franklin, so she eagerly awaited his homecoming, too. The army had sent a letter with the news that he'd been wounded, then another one that said he was convalescing in a hospital in Philadelphia. As the weeks passed with still no sign of him, Bebe began to worry. Franklin wasn't answering anyone's letters. Hannah finally wrote directly to the hospital administrator for news.

*"I'm sorry to say that your son Franklin's condition is showing no improvement,"* one of the nurses wrote in reply. *"He is very depressed about losing his leg and has very little appetite. As a result, he has become quite frail and his wound isn't healing properly. Anything you could do to cheer him would help considerably."*

"I've been praying about Franklin's condition," Hannah told Bebe a few days later, "and I believe God has told me what to do. Franklin needs a loved one to take care of him, and you are the best person to do that. I want you to visit him in Philadelphia and help him get well. Bring him home to us again."

"You want me to travel all that way? All alone? It's more than one hundred miles from here."

"You won't be alone. God will be with you."

Bebe bit her lip to avoid voicing her skepticism about having God for a traveling companion. It would only shock her mother. "What am I supposed to do once I get there?"

"Cheer Franklin up, remind him of home, make him laugh."

"Why can't you go, Mama?"

"Someone has to cook for your father and the boys. Besides, I thought you would enjoy a break from the farm."

"I would, but . . ." Bebe had never gone anywhere alone in her life.

On their next trip to town for market day, Hannah made all of the arrangements. Pastor Webster's wife often visited her sister in Philadelphia, and she agreed to let Bebe travel there with her by train. Bebe would stay with Mrs. Webster's sister and brother-in-law, the Yeagers, while she was there.

When everything was arranged, Hannah took Bebe to Harrison's General Store and picked out lace and yard goods and cotton thread. "We're going to sew new under-sleeves for your Sunday dress," Hannah explained, "and let out the bodice to accommodate your developing bosom."

"Shh! Mother!" Bebe whispered in embarrassment. But it was true. Her womanly figure finally had begun to sprout.

"If we add a new ruffle on the skirt, it will cover up the worn hemline," Hannah continued. "And I do believe you've grown an inch or two since we sewed that dress."

Their final purchase was a new pair of shoes, which were the most uncomfortable things Bebe had ever worn, especially after traipsing around in her brothers' old boots for the past year.

"I don't understand all the fuss and bother with new clothes and shoes," Bebe said that evening. She stood on a milking stool, trying to be patient while Hannah pinned up her hem. The full skirt felt bulky after wearing trousers for the past year, but thank goodness hoops had gone out of style. "What difference does it make what I look like? Franklin won't care. He won't even notice."

Hannah removed the pins from her mouth and stuck them in a pincushion. "Listen, Beatrice. Franklin and the other boys need to see something beautiful again and be reminded of the life that's waiting for them back home. They've witnessed too much horror these past few years."

"But I can't—"

"You did the farm work, now you can do this."

Bebe wasn't convinced.

On the night before Bebe left for Philadelphia, her mother made her take a bath. Bebe tried to back out of the door when she saw Hannah preparing the tub. "You don't need to bother with that, Mama, I can wash off in the river—"

"Oh no, you don't." Hannah snagged Bebe's arm and pulled her back into the room. "You need a proper bath in warm water. And you need to wash your hair. You can't travel to Philadelphia with your hair in braids and smelling like manure and hay. You're a young woman now, and a very pretty one. I'll put some rose water in the tub."

"Rose water!" Bebe wrinkled her nose. "What for?"

"So that you'll smell nice."

Hannah scrubbed so hard Bebe thought all of her skin would come off. Her mother inspected her from head to toe as she helped her dry off. "We have to do something about the dirt beneath your fingernails."

Bebe stared at her hands. They hadn't come clean. "I think the dirt has been there since the Rebels fired on Fort Sumter."

"Well, I have a pair of crocheted gloves you can borrow."

Hannah trimmed off the scraggly ends of Bebe's hair and brushed it until it shone. It was long and dark and thick, with a natural wave in it. Hannah taught her how to part it down the middle and sweep it up on her head, securing it with the new hairpins and fancy tortoiseshell combs they had purchased in town.

Early the next morning, Bebe put on her newly remade dress, fixed her hair, and packed her clothes and toiletries in a carpetbag. Hannah fetched the mirror that Henry and the boys used for shaving and held it up in front of her. "Look at yourself, Beatrice."

She didn't recognize the person she saw in the mirror. She had transformed into a woman—at least on the outside—with a slender waist and a pretty face and thick, luxurious hair. If only she felt like a woman on the inside, too.

"You look beautiful," Hannah murmured.

"I look so . . . different."

"Remember how life changed when the war started and the boys left? And how it changed again when Franklin had to leave? Life is like that, Beatrice—always changing, always flowing forward like a stream. Things never stay the same. And we have to move on and change, too."

Bebe glanced around at her familiar bedroom, then at her image in the mirror again. "What if I don't want things to change?"

"You can't fight against the current. You're no longer a little girl, Beatrice, you're a grown woman. I married your father when I was just a little older than you are. And that's what's next for you—marriage and a home of your own."

She couldn't imagine it. "But I don't want to leave home."

"Nevertheless, you need to trust God and be prepared for wherever the river of life will take you next."

Bebe clutched her carpetbag and a basket of homemade baked goods for Franklin. She felt a mixture of excitement and fear as she began her journey and realized, as she hugged Hannah good-bye, that she had never been separated from her mother before. Panic made it difficult to breathe.

"Mama, I—"

"I'm counting on you to help Franklin get well."

"But I can't…"

"With God, all things are possible."

Bebe nodded and struggled to control her tears. She had longed to do something courageous and meaningful throughout the war, so maybe this was her opportunity. She would be brave for Franklin's sake.

"Don't forget to attend to your appearance, dear. Look in a mirror once in a while and fix your hair. And keep your dress tidy."

Bebe made a face. "It still doesn't feel right to wear a dress all day."

"I know. But you look lovely in one. Don't be surprised if men start looking at you and tipping their hats. They take notice of pretty girls."

Bebe had never ridden on a train before, and when the monstrous thing finally arrived, rumbling into the station with its whistle shrieking, belching smoke and cinders, she walked toward it on trembling legs.

"Ready?" Reverend Webster asked as he prepared to help her

climb aboard. The locomotive hissed at her like an angry barn cat. Bebe nodded. The minister had recently preached on Jesus' command to "fear not," so she was embarrassed to admit her fear.

The train chugged out of the station like an old man wheezing for air, but once it built up speed it traveled so fast Bebe feared it would fly right off the narrow rails. Scenery whipped past her window at a frantic rate. Any minute now, her heart would simply hammer itself to death. Surely there was a less frightening way to travel. She was wondering how long it would take her and Franklin to walk home from Philadelphia, when she remembered his missing leg.

They traveled south to Stroudsburg, then to Allentown, where they changed trains. Late that afternoon the view of Pennsylvania farmland gave way to jumbled buildings and smoking factories as the train neared Philadelphia. The city was a huge, bustling place bursting with people, and more horses and carriages than Bebe had ever imagined. She inched closer to Mrs. Webster, feeling lost and out of place.

Mrs. Yeager met them at the train station and led them to her waiting carriage.

Everywhere Bebe looked she saw soldiers in blue uniforms, and she searched their faces as if expecting one of them to be Franklin. She longed for the peace and quiet of her farm and hoped to convince Franklin to come home with her on the very next train so she wouldn't have to spend a single night in this frightening city.

"Would you like to get settled at home, first?" Mrs. Yeager asked. "Maybe freshen up from your trip?"

Bebe had no idea what "freshen up" meant or how she would go about it. "I'd rather go to the hospital and see my brother, if you don't mind."

"Of course," Mrs. Yeager said. "You must be anxious to see

him. The hospital isn't far." And it wasn't. The carriage halted in front of a large redbrick building before Bebe had time to figure out what to say to Franklin.

"I'll have my driver come back for you in an hour. Will that be enough time?" Mrs. Yeager asked.

"Yes. Thank you." Bebe climbed from the carriage and walked toward the hospital's entrance, where a group of men stood smoking cigarettes. Every one of them had an arm or a hand or a leg that ended abruptly in a bandaged stump. Bebe quickly turned away.

She couldn't do this. The sight of those mangled, wounded men—the sight of her own brother Franklin without his leg—was too awful to contemplate. She had tried not to imagine what his missing limb would look like as she'd planned her trip, and now she couldn't face him. How could she cheer him up when even these strangers' wounds horrified her?

She hurried toward the street, waving her arms and calling to the departing carriage, "Wait! Come back!" But it drove away. Bebe could either stand here on the curb in the hot sun for an hour, or go inside the hospital. She drew a deep breath and turned back toward the entrance. The gathered men had stopped talking. They were watching her. She tried to speak but nothing came out. Then one of them snatched off his hat and gave a little bow.

"Good afternoon, miss." The rest of the men quickly did the same.

"Howdy, miss."

"Ain't you a beautiful sight?"

"Need help with that basket?"

They broke into wide grins as they looked her up and down. Bebe gripped the basket handle. "No, thank you." Her cheeks burned.

One of the men held the door open for her and she scurried inside. A nurse in a white uniform greeted her. "May I help you?"

Bebe's words came out like questions. "I-I'm Beatrice Monroe? I'm here to see my brother? Franklin Monroe?"

"Oh yes. He'll be so glad you've come, Miss Monroe. Follow me, please."

Bebe stared at the floor as she followed the nurse into a long, narrow room. It smelled of iodine and illness. Rows of beds lined the walls on both sides, and Bebe glimpsed white sheets and white faces and a blue uniform or two. She had the uncomfortable feeling that the men in the beds were watching her. Except for the occasional cough, it seemed unnaturally quiet. Halfway down the length of the room, the nurse halted at the foot of a bed.

"You have a visitor, Mr. Monroe."

Bebe never would have recognized her brother if the nurse hadn't led her to him. The sturdy, carefree boy who had marched away a year ago had become a withered old man with a gray face and a shrunken body. The dazed look in his eyes reminded her of the stuffed deer head that hung above the door in Harrison's General Store. Thankfully, a sheet covered Franklin's legs. She smiled as best she could and walked to his side, resting her hand on his arm.

"Hello, Franklin."

He didn't seem to recognize her either, at first. Then his eyes filled with tears. "Bebe? Is it really you?"

She nodded and set the basket down on the floor so she could embrace him. The last time she had hugged her brother was before he'd marched away, and he had nearly crushed her in his arms. Now she was the stronger of the two. She clung to his frail body and asked God to forgive her for complaining about doing farm work.

When they finally pulled apart, Franklin turned his face away to wipe his eyes, embarrassed by his tears. Bebe let hers flow. They were the first tears in four years that she hadn't shed in self-pity or exhaustion. She kissed his whiskered cheek.

"What are you doing here, Bebe? How'd you get here?"

"I came on the train. Mama sent you some food." She lifted the basket and set it on the bed beside him. "She sent me to take care of you until you're well enough to come home."

"I don't think I'll be coming home—unless you mean home to heaven."

His words made her stomach roll over. He looked as though he was knocking on the pearly gates already and St. Peter was about to open them.

"Of course that's not what I mean! You're coming home to the farm, Franklin. I'm tired of doing all your chores."

He shook his head. "I'm worthless now. They should have let me die."

"Don't say that!" Bebe shoved his bony shoulder. "Losing Joseph was bad enough."

"He's better off . . ."

"Stop it, Franklin. Mama grieved something awful for Joseph. Don't you dare let her lose you, too." His self-pity reminded her of her own these past few years. She drew a breath and started again. "James and William came home a few weeks ago. It's wonderful to have them back. Mama is so happy."

"You left her there all alone? Who's helping her in the kitchen?"

"She insisted that I come. She was so glad to have the boys back that she's been cooking enough food for an army. She sent some for you, too."

He shook his head and closed his eyes. "Go away."

Bebe had never felt ill at ease with Franklin before, but she did now. She had no idea what to say to him or how to cheer him up. She was searching for ideas when another patient limped over, leaning on an ebony cane with an engraved silver handle. The bed squeaked when he sat down on the end of it.

"Hey, Franklin. You never told me you had a girlfriend."

Franklin slowly opened his eyes. "She's not my girlfriend; she's my kid sister, Bebe."

"You never told me your sister was beautiful."

"She was just a kid when I left."

"Well, she isn't a kid anymore. A rose would wither in despair if forced to compete with such beauty and grace."

Bebe glanced around, wondering who the man was referring to. When she realized that he meant her, her heart began to pound the same way it had when the enormous locomotive had rumbled into the station. She had no idea why.

"I'm very pleased to make your acquaintance, Miss Monroe," he continued. "It's not every day that I have the good fortune to meet such a lovely young woman. My name is Horatio Garner, by the way."

Mr. Garner had hair the color of mown hay and the palest blue eyes Bebe had ever seen. His mustache and beard were sprinkled with red as if he'd dusted his face with copper shavings instead of talcum powder. Something about the tilt of his chin and the confident, laughing way that he spoke made him seem very self-assured. The simple folk back home would call him a "dandy," with his fancy cane and flowery words, but Bebe was intrigued.

"Your brother and I have had the good fortune to march side by side since the day we reported for duty, isn't that right, Franklin? He used to read your lovely letters out loud to me—so often, in fact, that I feel I already know you. But he never breathed a word about your matchless charms. How old are you, Miss Monroe, if you don't mind my asking? I'm twenty-two, by the way."

Bebe couldn't speak. She wished she had a fan she could unfurl to cool her burning cheeks. The changes Mama had talked about seemed to be coming much too fast, as if the river of life was at flood stage. She'd barely had time to adjust to being a woman, much less learn how to respond to a handsome man's advances.

"Are you always this quiet?" Mr. Garner asked when she didn't reply.

Franklin nudged her. "Answer the man, Bebe. Where's your manners?"

"I-I haven't needed any manners for the last four years. The cows and chickens didn't care about them, and there was no one else on our farm to impress." Mr. Garner laughed as if she'd said something very witty. "But to answer your question, I'm seventeen."

"How lovely. Seventeen. . . As fate would have it, your brother and I were wounded on the same day in the same battle—isn't that right, Franklin? Although I have to admit that the nature of his wounds was much more grievous than mine. The doctors have informed me that my foot has healed, and they have declared me well enough to return home, but I've been hesitant to leave Franklin this way. I'm worried about him, Miss Monroe. I've been trying to cheer him up, but I haven't been very successful. I'm pleased to see that you've arrived to help me. By the way, what did you bring in that basket, if I may be so bold as to ask?"

Bebe folded back the napkin, grateful to have something simple to talk about. "Um . . . there's some of Mama's sourdough bread— she baked it for Franklin this morning. And a jar of that rhubarb jam he always liked . . . and fry cakes. Would you like one?"

The hour passed quickly, with Mr. Garner doing most of the talking. He was a very cheerful fellow and quite interesting to listen to, but Franklin's glum expression never changed. Bebe felt like a failure. She would have to do better tomorrow.

"I need to go," she told Franklin when the hour was up, "but I'll be back in the morning. In the meantime, please eat some of this food so you'll get your strength back. Mama is expecting you to come home with me." She bent and kissed his forehead.

"Well, would you look at that?" Mr. Garner said.

Bebe glanced up. "Look at what, Mr. Garner?"

"I do believe that's the first smile I've seen on Franklin's face in a good long while. Your kiss is like sunshine melting away the frost."

Bebe stared at the floor, embarrassed by his flowery words. "Good-bye for now," she said. "It was nice meeting you, Mr. Garner."

"Wait." He stuck out his cane to block her path. "I won't let you leave until you promise to call me Horatio."

"Very well . . . Horatio. I'll be back tomorrow."

His grin could have lit up a root cellar. "I can hardly wait, fair Beatrice."

CHAPTER

8

Bebe took great care getting dressed and fixing her hair the following morning, hoping she would see Mr. Garner at the hospital
when she visited Franklin. She had loved listening to the smooth,
eloquent flow of Horatio's words—he had called her beautiful.
But when she arrived, she was very disappointed to learn that he
was no longer a patient.

"The doctors discharged him earlier this morning," Franklin
told her. "He didn't lose his leg the way I did."

Bebe heard the bitterness in Franklin's tone and struggled for
a way to cheer him. Nothing came to mind. "Listen," she finally
said. "Mama sent me here to help you get well, and to be honest
with you, I don't know how to do that. I thought about it all last
night, and . . . and I think that the only person who can help you
get well is yourself. You have to want to get better and come home,
but for some reason you've given up."

He flung back the sheet to expose the stump of his leg. "Look
at me, Bebe! Would you want to live with this?"

The sight shocked her, and she averted her gaze. When she

faced him again, the pain she saw in Franklin's eyes made her angry with herself for flinching.

"I can't stand to see people turn away from me like you just did. Or even worse, to look at me with pity."

"Franklin, I'm sorry—"

"Why? It's not your fault that you couldn't stand the sight of me. I'm not a whole person anymore, Bebe. There's part of me missing . . . and I don't want to live this way." He pulled the sheet over his leg to hide it, but Bebe yanked off the cover again.

"Part of you is missing, yes. But back home, *all* of you is missing. We feel that loss the same way you feel this one. Joseph is gone, and it's horrible to see his empty chair at the table and his empty bed upstairs. Losing you would be even worse for me. You're not just my brother, you're my friend." She saw his jaw quiver as he struggled with his emotions. "I missed you so much after you left home, Franklin, and not just because I had to do all of your work. If you died I would miss you forever. Yes, they cut off your leg— but it will heal if you let it. Don't cut yourself out of my life. That wound will never heal."

"Don't you get it, Bebe? I'm useless this way. How can I work on the farm?"

"We'll figure something out. Remember how useless I was with the chores at first? But we made adjustments for the fact that I was smaller and weaker, and eventually things got done. You can adjust, too, Franklin—if not to farm work, then you'll find something else to do. Your family doesn't love you for the work you do, but because you're our brother. You mean so much to us. I don't know how else to say it, but I love you and I want you to come home!"

She bent to embrace him and felt his weaker hug in return. At last she pulled away. They both wiped away tears.

"Listen, I'm going to get you well enough to come home if it's the last thing I do." She set the basket of food on his bed and began rummaging through it. "Mama made you some apple turnovers, and I want you to eat one right now!"

"Better do what the pretty little lady says, Franklin. I think she means business."

Bebe looked up, surprised to see Horatio Garner limping toward them, leaning on his cane. "What are you doing here? I thought you went home, Mr. Garner." She saw the wry, admonishing smile on his face and quickly corrected herself. "I-I mean Horatio."

He grinned. "Ah, how sweet my name sounds when it flows from such sweet lips. But to answer your question, Miss Monroe, I've decided not to go home until Franklin does. We started out in this war together, we were wounded together, and it's only fitting that we leave here together. And so I pledge to partner with you, fair lady, for as long as it takes. I place myself at your service." He ended with a bow and a little flourish that made Bebe laugh.

She had never met anyone like Horatio, and she wanted to know all about him. He obliged by freely talking about himself, filling the long hours at Franklin's bedside by telling stories. Horatio described the modestly sized town of Roseton where he'd grown up, not far from the state capital of Harrisburg. He talked about the home he'd shared with his parents and his staff of servants, and the leather factory his family owned. He told tales of the two years he'd attended Dickinson College in Carlisle, Pennsylvania—and how a draft notice had ended his education.

"Why didn't your father pay the three hundred dollars to hire a substitute?" Bebe asked.

He stared at his feet as if suddenly bashful. "It was his wish to do so—but it wasn't mine. I felt it was my duty to serve my country."

By the end of the week, Bebe was smitten with Horatio Garner. She hurried through breakfast every day, impatient to get to the hospital to see him. Mrs. Webster stopped her with an invitation one morning as Bebe was about to leave the house.

"Beatrice, it must be tiresome to spend all day at the hospital. My sister and I are planning to attend a very interesting anti-slavery meeting this afternoon, and we would love to have you join us. We could pick you up at the hospital on our way."

"Um . . . Thank you very much, but I think I should stay with Franklin. I do believe he is making some progress."

"He wouldn't mind if you were to come with us, would he? Just for one hour? I believe the lecture would be of great interest to a young woman like you."

Bebe thought that nothing in the world could be more interesting than listening to Horatio Garner, but she didn't say so out loud. "Thank you, Mrs. Webster, but my mother is counting on me to attend to my brother."

Bebe arrived at the hospital before Horatio did and couldn't help glancing at the door while she waited, watching for him. As she cajoled Franklin into eating everything on his breakfast tray, she felt light-headed and a little breathless. She used to get this same shaky, stomach-reeling sensation when she was starved for food after working in the fields all day, only now she was starved for Horatio.

"Ah, good morning, my dear friends!" he finally called out in greeting. His warm smile made Bebe smile in return. "Franklin, you're looking hale and hearty today. I do believe your charming sister is better for your health than a hundred nurses."

Bebe loved the way Horatio's eyes would soften each time he looked at her—even though she knew it could be nothing more than sisterly affection. The differences between them were much too great for it to be anything else. She was the timid daughter of a simple farmer, he the gregarious son of a well-to-do factory owner.

But the biggest obstacle as far as Bebe was concerned was the fact that the woman Horatio had met was a fraud. He saw a cleaned up, dressed up, sweet-smelling version of her, while the real Bebe had only recently changed out of men's overalls and work boots and put away her manure shovel. The real Bebe still had dirt beneath her fingernails, hidden under a pair of scratchy crocheted gloves that she wished she could yank off and toss into the trash. Her own father kept mistaking her for a boy, yet Horatio thought she was the epitome of womanhood.

"I have never met a more selfless, caring woman," he told her. "Imagine, traveling all this way to help your brother with his convalescence. What a brave, devoted woman you are."

"Um . . . but you see, Mr. Garner, the truth is—"

"Say no more. I see that blush of modesty, and I am moved by your humility."

Indeed, she was a fraud.

It hadn't been her idea to come to Philadelphia to take care of Franklin. She hadn't been the least bit brave about it. And now that she was there, she had no idea how to nurture him or anyone else back to good health. The Beatrice that Horatio Garner saw was a creation of his own flowery imagination and her mother's frugal grooming. She would have told him the truth if he had asked—or if he had let her get a word in edgewise—but Horatio never stopped talking. And, oh, how she loved to hear him talk. His words sounded just like poetry.

Little by little, Bebe's feelings for Horatio Garner began to grow and bud and blossom until she was certain she resembled one of her father's apple trees in full, glorious bloom. And little by little, the food she'd brought from home, and the laughter she shared with Horatio and Franklin, coaxed life and health back into her brother. By the end of the second week, Franklin was eating like a farmer again, and the color had returned to his cheeks. Bebe and Horatio managed to convince him to take a few hobbling steps on a pair of crutches. When he could limp as far as the front door, Horatio boosted him into a hired carriage and the three of them toured Philadelphia. The carriage rides soon became daily ventures. Sitting close to Horatio gave Bebe the same dizzy, giddy feeling she'd had when soaring through the air on the swing. She tried to forget that they soon would have to go their separate ways, certain it would feel much like the shock of plunging into the river when she had let go of the rope.

All the while, Bebe's hostess continued to invite her to attend the anti-slavery meetings. "They have such wonderful speakers— you really should hear them, Beatrice." Bebe made excuses, but truthfully she didn't want to give up a single moment of time with her new friend.

It took a month for Franklin to regain his health, but at last he was strong enough to go home. Bebe knew it had very little to do with her influence and everything to do with Horatio Garner's. The day of Franklin's discharge was a bittersweet one. Bebe was elated for her brother, who had learned to maneuver quite well on his crutches, but devastated to have to say good-bye to Horatio. He drove them to the train station, making sure Franklin's bags were loaded on board and that the porters were well compensated. And just before saying farewell, he presented his ebony and silver cane to Franklin, holding it out to him like a medieval king bestowing a great honor on his knight.

"This is for you, my friend. I want you to keep it as a token to remember me by."

Franklin scowled. "I can't use that. I need two crutches to get around."

"Only for now, my good man, only for now. I've heard there is a doctor here in Philadelphia who can outfit you with a fine wooden leg when you're ready. By this time next year you'll be running relay races."

Franklin mumbled his thanks and gave the cane to Bebe to carry. Horatio turned to her next. "Before we part, may I ask a very special favor, Beatrice?"

"Of course."

"On the day you arrived, you graced your brother with a kiss, and it was like watching the sunshine melt the frost. Would you favor me with one farewell kiss before we part? It would mean so much to me . . . I don't know when I might meet another woman as beautiful and kind as you are."

"You must have a sweetheart back home. . . ."

"No, I have no one." He leaned toward her and pointed to his cheek. "Please?"

Bebe had never kissed anyone who wasn't a family member. Tears filled her eyes as she stood on tiptoes and briefly pressed her lips to Horatio's cheek. His ruddy beard felt soft, not scratchy as she had supposed. His warm, rich scent smelled like something she would eat for dessert.

"Thank you," he said softly. He took her hand in both of his and pressed it to his heart, then raised it to his lips. "Before you came to Philadelphia I had forgotten how sweet and good a woman smells, how soft her skin feels. Tenderness . . . gentleness . . . beauty . . . I've missed those things these long, dark months when I've been surrounded by death. But a woman is made for life. How beautiful that reminder is to me." He gave her captive hand a gentle squeeze and released it.

"Good-bye," she murmured. "I'll never forget you."

Horatio helped her and Franklin climb aboard, then waved to them from the platform. Bebe waved back, her heart aching. Horatio had filled her life with laughter and delight these past few weeks, and now she would never see him again. Their parting had been inevitable. She wasn't the vision of loveliness and gentility that he imagined her to be. The rose water that had provided her with the sweet fragrance he'd admired belonged to Bebe's mother. From now on, Bebe was much more likely to smell like the bacon that she fried for breakfast every morning rather than rose water. She leaned out the window, watching until the train station—and Horatio—disappeared from sight.

"Why are you crying?" Franklin asked when he saw her tears.

She quickly dabbed her eyes with her handkerchief and forced a smile. "I'm so happy that you're finally coming home, Franklin." It wasn't a lie.

Philadelphia had seemed like a strange, foreign place when Bebe had first arrived, but after being away from home for a month, the village of New Canaan now seemed like a foreign place to her, shabby and colorless after the glittery bustle of the city. Each day on the farm moved as sluggishly as mud as she settled back into her daily routine. For Bebe, the river of life had dwindled down to a trickle, and the most she could hope for was to cool her toes in its shallows. She wondered if her brothers felt as restless and bored as she did. After all, she'd spent only a month in Philadelphia and they had marched all over the country for the past few years, seeing new things and meeting new people. She remembered complaining to her mother about not liking change, but now she longed for it.

Then one Sunday morning Mrs. Webster stopped to speak with Bebe and her mother after church. "I have good news, ladies. Our local chapter of the Anti-Slavery Society has decided to hold meetings again. We have a speaker coming from Philadelphia on Wednesday evening, and I just know you'll be fascinated when you hear what she has to say. You remember one of our society's most outstanding proponents, Mrs. Lucretia Mott, don't you? Well, she's coming to speak to our organization, Hannah. Do you think you and Beatrice might attend?"

"We'll see," Hannah replied.

Bebe hated it when her mother said, "We'll see." It usually meant "no." Bebe remembered attending meetings before the war, and although they hadn't been very exciting, hiding the occasional slave in the attic had been. She couldn't imagine what work the society would do now that all the slaves were free, but she was curious—and more than a little bored. She decided that she would go, with or without her mother.

"I would like very much to go into town for a meeting on Wednesday evening," she told her father on the drive home. "May I please borrow the wagon?"

"Is it a prayer meeting?"

"No . . . it's for the Anti-Slavery Society."

The horses traveled a full quarter of a mile before Henry said, "Seems to me the abolition people got what they wanted, didn't they? Didn't Mr. Lincoln free the slaves?"

"Yes . . ."

"Then why are the abolitionists still meeting?"

"I don't know, Papa. I guess there must be other things they would like to accomplish. May I please go and find out?"

Her father began shaking his head, his expression already warning her that he was about to say no. Surprisingly, Hannah intervened.

"Let her go, Henry . . . please."

He drove all the way home in silence. He remained silent on the subject throughout the afternoon and into the evening hours. Bebe didn't know how her mother could be so patient with such a taciturn man. She thought of Horatio Garner—as she had every day since leaving Philadelphia—and wished he were there to fill the silences in her life with his ever-flowing words.

As Henry rose from his customary chair in the parlor at bedtime, he turned to Bebe and said, "You may go, but you'll have to take care of the horse and wagon yourself." She would have hugged him, but her father never had cared much for affectionate displays.

Bebe rushed through her chores on Wednesday evening, then hitched one of the horses to the wagon for the long, dusty drive into town. Only a handful of women had gathered at the church for the meeting, and Bebe was the youngest. Several of them took out their knitting as they sat in a circle, waiting to hear what Mrs. Webster and her guest had to say.

"Like all of you, I thought our work for the society was finished," Mrs. Webster began. "I'm sure you recall the many meetings we held before the war, and all the prayers we offered up to heaven in order to end slavery here in America. The Scriptures say, 'The effectual fervent prayer of a righteous man availeth much.' And I do believe that the same can be said about the fervent prayers of women. We all thank God that He heard our prayers and freed the slaves. But while visiting with my sister in Philadelphia recently, I became aware that there is still more work to be done. Ladies, I would like to introduce our special guest this evening, Mrs. Lucretia Mott, who is going to explain what our next task must be."

Mrs. Mott looked like a peacock among hens in her fashionable city clothes. She wore her hair coiled in an elaborate knot that Bebe wished she could copy. Her alert, observant expression told Bebe she was very intelligent, yet she seemed to have the same kind, gentle nature that Bebe always admired in her mother, Hannah. Mrs. Mott waved away the spattering of applause and remained seated as she began to speak.

"It's clear that women like us, united for a heavenly cause, can accomplish great things. Let the men shoot it out on the battlefield or argue politics; women fight best on their knees.

"Our United States Constitution has now been amended to grant Negro slaves their freedom, which is what we've been praying for. Soon another amendment will grant civil rights to those former slaves, but only to the men. That means that half of the population of America—its women—are still denied the basic rights of our Constitution. Ladies, this simply isn't fair. Shouldn't the women who worked so hard on behalf of the slaves be accorded the same civil rights that they now will enjoy?"

Bebe glanced around at the others as Mrs. Mott paused and noticed that the ladies had stopped knitting. Everyone gazed intently at her, waiting to hear more.

"We were the force who, through our prayers and hard work, won freedom for them. We are all educated, literate women, while the vast majority of Negroes are illiterate. Yet those uneducated men will now be allowed to vote while we will be denied. Is it fair, I ask, that those of us who've worked so hard to see the Negroes raised to a position of equality—and Negro men have been so raised—is it fair that the very women who've helped raise them are still considered inferior?"

Bebe could barely sit still. She wanted to leap up and shout, "No! It isn't fair!" Mrs. Mott's cheeks flushed with passion as she continued.

"If I were to go around this circle and ask each of you to describe the sacrifices you've made for the cause of abolition and for the recent war, I believe I would hear tales of great courage and devotion. Many of you risked your own freedom to help slaves escape on the Underground Railroad. Others supported the cause with your time and donations. And you continued your volunteer work during the war, sending packages to our soldiers, and supplying the army hospitals with nurses and food and bandages. You took over your families' farms and businesses when the men marched off to fight, and sat at the bedsides of wounded loved ones when they needed you. Some of you paid the ultimate price, losing a loved one on the battlefield for the cause of freedom.

"In light of all these sacrifices and accomplishments, don't we deserve to be counted as full citizens? After everything that we have done during the war, haven't we proven our equality?"

Once again Bebe longed to shout, *"Yes!"* She had worked just as hard as her brothers had, so why should she be treated differently? Lucretia Mott's speech made sense to her, and she wanted to send up a cheer. The other townswomen sat so quietly that it was impossible to tell what they were thinking. Mrs. Webster, the minister's wife, glanced around at the ladies, and seemed surprised that no one had responded. She turned to Mrs. Harrison, who was seated alongside her.

"Tell me, Grace. Don't you work just as hard in the store as your husband does? I've seen you waiting on customers and making change and ordering goods—then you have to go home and cook dinner and clean house. And all you other women, didn't you take over a great deal of the work when your sons and husbands were away?"

"I did," Bebe said—but she didn't say it nearly as loudly or forcefully as she would have liked to. Mrs. Webster smiled at her.

"Yes, Beatrice. You took over for all four of your brothers and helped raise the food that fed the armies."

Mrs. Morgan, the doctor's wife, lifted her hand for a chance to speak. "But if the government does grant us equality with men, might we also be required to take up arms and fight in the event of another war? I, for one, am grateful that I didn't have to fight in the recent conflict. I wouldn't care at all for equality if that were to be the case."

Bebe pictured the rows and rows of wounded men she'd seen in the hospital and had to agree with Mrs. Morgan on this point. She turned back to Mrs. Mott in confusion.

"It's true that women currently aren't required to fight," Mrs. Mott quickly replied. "Thank goodness for that. Our gentler, more tender natures don't equip us for the rigors of battle. Our soldiers displayed outstanding courage during the recent war—but who was responsible for shaping those young men's characters so that they developed the necessary courage to fight? Their mothers, of course—women like all of us. Is the task of molding and nurturing the next generation of leaders any lesser of a role, deserving lesser rights? Of course not. If we are the ones who help mold our future leaders, why shouldn't we be granted the right to help choose those leaders?"

When no one else challenged her, Mrs. Mott continued. "We need a plan, ladies. Winning civil rights for women is the next logical step. In the past, we used prayer, petitions, and pamphlets for the cause of abolition—now we will use those same methods to accomplish this new goal. Those of you who disagree"—she smiled pleasantly at Mrs. Morgan—"are of course free to engage in other work. But if you believe, as I do, that 'there is neither bond nor free, there is neither male nor female,' as the Scriptures say, 'for ye are all one in Christ Jesus,' then let's get to work tonight."

Bebe needed no further convincing. She already had proven her equality with her brothers. She would join the cause. She would give it her all.

As I said before, Grandma Bebe never did tell a story in a straight line like the chapters in a book. Following the thread of her sagas was like chasing a startled rabbit through the woods—you never knew when it was going to turn and head in a new direction. I hated to interrupt her, but we were more than halfway home from the picnic that Decoration Day, and if she veered off the path of Horatio's story, I was afraid she would never find her way back to it. Grandma had wandered in a new direction with Lucretia Mott, and while I'm sure her story would be very interesting, I was losing patience with this new rabbit trail.

"Um . . . Grandma Bebe?" I said when she paused for a moment. "Could you go back to the story of—?"

I never finished my sentence. We heard a *bang!* that was as loud and explosive as a gunshot, and it scared the thoughts right out of my head.

Grandma hit the brakes and gripped the steering wheel with both hands to control the car's sudden swerving. "Hang on tight, Harriet! We've had a blowout!"

I've watched my father struggle to wrestle his car into submission after a blown tire, and I was pretty amazed that my tiny grandmother could manage to control her behemoth of a car. I was also glad that I hadn't been driving at the time. The sound the ruined tire made as it slapped against the roadbed was like a dozen maidservants beating carpets on a clothesline. The car came to a halt at last on the side of the road, enveloped in a great cloud of dust.

"Well!" Grandma said with a sigh. "Don't you hate when that happens?"

We climbed out of the car and walked around it to look at the rear tire. There must have been a pond nearby, because I could hear frogs *thrump-thrump*ing in the distance. I looked around for a farmhouse, but the only light I saw came from the moon high above us. We seemed to be on a desolate stretch of road, surrounded by forested hills. I hoped there weren't any hungry bears in those woods.

"Now what?" I asked. "I suppose we'll have to wait for another car to come by and rescue us?" I shivered and folded my arms tightly against my chest. The air in that mountain hollow felt as damp as the inside of a cave.

"Nonsense!" Grandma replied. "Only women in fairy tales wait to be rescued." She twisted the handle on the trunk, and it opened with a squeak. She had to raise her voice to be heard above the clamor that she made as she rooted through the shadowy bin. "No, Harriet, I made up my mind when I bought this car that if I was responsible for driving it, then I should be responsible for fixing it when something went wrong. Here, hold these . . ." She handed me a car jack and a tire pump, then disappeared into the trunk again. She emerged a moment later, waving a rubber inner tube in the air like a deflated black snake. "Always carry a spare, dear."

I watched in awe as Grandma crouched down and wedged the jack under the car frame as expertly as my father did. Her driving gloves were getting greasy and the front of her duster was smudged with dirt, but she didn't care one whit. I wanted to be just like her.

"Let me do that, Grandma," I said as I knelt beside her. "I want to learn how." She taught me to change an automobile tire that day, step by step, and I wished the boys from school could have been there to watch me work. They thought all girls were helpless and empty-headed like my sister, Alice. I would have loved to show them how wrong they were. Grandma was right—why wait to be rescued when I was perfectly capable of rescuing myself? Her example inspired me—and it was one of the reasons why I had refused to call anyone on the telephone to come and rescue me from jail. I had thought of Grandma's words as my cell door slammed shut: *"Only women in fairy tales wait to be rescued."*

After Grandma Bebe and I fixed the tire that damp May evening and started down the road toward home again, I was eager for her to continue the story of my great-uncle Franklin and grandpa Horatio.

"So how did you end up marrying Horatio Garner, Grandma? If you went home to the farm and he went back to Roseton again, how—?"

"Patience, Harriet, patience. I'm getting to that part . . ."

Bebe couldn't wait to tell her mother all about the Anti-Slavery meeting as they prepared breakfast the next morning. "You should have come last night, Mama. Lucretia Mott came all the way from Philadelphia, and she told us that—"

"Not now, Beatrice . . . please . . . and mind what you're doing— you're letting the bacon burn."

Bebe slid the cast iron skillet to a cooler place on the stovetop, then turned the crisping pieces with a fork. The fat sizzled, stinging her bare arms like wasps. She knew better than to raise the subject of equality for women after her father and brothers trooped in from the barn, but when the men had eaten their fill and she and Hannah were alone, Bebe brought up the subject again as they washed the breakfast dishes.

"It was such an interesting meeting last night, Mama. Mrs. Mott said that we proved our equality with all the work we did during the war. She said we're entitled to the same rights as men, seeing as we were created equal."

Hannah put away the stack of plates she had dried and closed the cupboard door. "But I don't agree that men and women are equal, Beatrice. God created us to be different, with different skills and qualities that complement one another. Women don't have the muscular strength to be blacksmiths and men don't have the tenderness required to nurture a baby. To say that we are equal is foolishness."

Bebe looked up from her scrubbing, genuinely surprised that her mother disagreed. "But didn't we work just as hard as men while they were away?"

"Those were special circumstances. I don't think you'd want to do men's work for the rest of your life, would you?"

"No . . . but Mrs. Mott said that women are considered inferior to men, and we're not inferior, Mama. So it isn't fair that—"

"It's not a question of who is superior; it's a question of who is the head of the household. Someone has to assume leadership in the home, and God decreed that it should be the husband. This isn't something for you or me or Lucretia Mott to decide. We can't change what's written in the Bible. "

Bebe felt confused. Everything had seemed so clear to her at the meeting last night, but she didn't know how to explain it to her mother the way Mrs. Mott had. Bebe finished scrubbing the last pot and handed it to Hannah to dry. "I don't think you understand what I'm saying."

"Listen, Beatrice. The roles God has given us as wives and mothers are of the utmost importance. The standard He set for us is found in the thirty-first chapter of Proverbs. We are to be a help-meet to our husband so that he can accomplish his God-given work. And we are to raise obedient, moral, God-fearing children."

"Yes, that's exactly what Mrs. Mott said last night. And she said our work is just as important as what men do—maybe even more important."

Hannah smiled and spread her palms. "Then what more could you possibly want?"

Again, Bebe felt confused. "Well . . . Mrs. Mott said that women deserve the same civil rights as men, including the right to vote."

"Why would you want to vote, Beatrice?"

"I-I don't know . . . That's why I need to go to the next meeting, so I can learn more about it. She said that women like us helped win freedom for the slaves, and that equality for everyone should be our next goal. That's what I want to do, Mama. I want to help accomplish something important."

"The most important thing that any of us can do is to serve God and build Christ's kingdom. My religious convictions were what led me to help all those slaves escape. I was simply doing the work that God gave me to do."

Bebe huffed in frustration. She wished she could explain it better. Her mother just didn't understand. "Well . . . well, maybe this is the work God is giving me to do. That's why I want to go to another meeting."

Hannah hung the dish towel near the stove to dry and rested her hands on Bebe's shoulders. "If you would determine in your heart to put that same amount of time and effort into Bible study and prayer, you would find the purpose and contentment that you're seeking."

"Yes, but . . . can I still go to the meeting?"

"That's up to your father, Beatrice."

When Bebe's father learned what the meetings were about, he forbade her to attend any more of them. She voiced her frustration to Hannah, who responded by reciting Bible verses such as "godliness with contentment is great gain." Bebe resigned herself to living a boring life on a boring farm outside a boring town—but she was not very happy about it, let alone content.

She found it especially hard to be content whenever she shopped in the general store and heard the other women discussing the meetings. Mrs. Harrison never failed to invite Bebe to come back. She invited her once again after Bebe drove into town on a beautiful Indian summer day to buy vinegar and salt and the other supplies that she and Hannah needed to make pickles and sauerkraut.

"Thank you, Mrs. Harrison. I would love to come again. Maybe when the harvest is over."

She hurried out of the store to avoid further conversation and noticed an unfamiliar horse and buggy drawing to a halt across the street. No one she knew could afford such a fine rig. Three other women from town had stopped to stare at it, too.

"Who in the world could that be?" one of them asked.

"Someone who is lost, no doubt."

But to Bebe's amazement, the man who stepped down from the high leather seat to tie the horse to the hitching post was none other than Horatio Garner. He looked as rich as the king of England in his waistcoat and bowler hat and shiny black shoes. He would have been right in style on the streets of Philadelphia, but he looked quite overdressed among the simple, hardworking people of New Canaan. The other women stared at him, as slack-mouthed as a string of dead trout.

Horatio turned when he'd finished securing the reins, and headed across the street toward the women. When he spotted Bebe his grin outshone the moon. He swept off his hat and bowed, his fair hair and reddish beard glinting like gold in the sunlight.

"Good afternoon, Miss Monroe. How fortunate that we should meet this way. You're the very person I came to see."

"Me?" she squeaked.

"Yes, you!" His laughter filled the quiet street. "Why are you so surprised?"

She didn't know what to say. Happiness and dismay began a tug of war inside her heart. She was thrilled to see Horatio again, but he had stumbled upon the real Bebe Monroe, dressed in a patched skirt and a faded shirtwaist, not the idealized version of her that he had met in Philadelphia. Now he would see that her life in the village was as dull as a log of wood, that she lived in a simple frame farmhouse, and that she worked as hard as his servants did.

"Will you excuse us, please?" he asked the gaping women. He grasped Bebe's elbow and gently led her away. "Is there a café where we could find a bite to eat?"

Now it was Bebe's turn to laugh. "This isn't Philadelphia, Mr. Garner. There's no café. In fact, you'll have to drive all the way back to the last town you passed just to find a place to sleep tonight."

"Is your home nearby? Perhaps I could trouble you for a glass of lemonade on the porch?"

"I live two miles down that road," she said, pointing. "But I'm quite sure there are no lemons in the pantry . . . and I wouldn't know how to make lemonade, even if we could afford such luxuries."

"How is Franklin doing?"

"Good . . . good . . . a little better every day."

"I'm very pleased to hear it. And although he is my very good friend, the truth is that it was you I came to see."

Bebe's heart thrummed inside her chest like hummingbirds' wings. She tried to speak but nothing came out.

"I've missed you, Beatrice," he said softly. "Ever since you left Philadelphia, I haven't been able to get you out of my mind."

She had to find her voice, had to say something. "I-I missed you, too. But I'm afraid that you have the wrong impression of me. As you can see, my hometown is—"

"I brought you something. I'm dying to see how you like it." He rooted through his coat pockets while he talked. "I happened to pass a jewelry store one afternoon on the way to my attorney's office, and I saw this in the store window. It was so dainty and beautiful—it reminded me of you."

He pulled out a velvet-lined jeweler's box and opened it to show Bebe a small gold locket inside. She couldn't breathe. How was it possible that a handsome, wealthy man like Horatio had come looking for her, bringing her a present?

"I would be so honored if you would accept it as a gift from me. May I see how it looks on you?" He removed it from the box and reached over her shoulders to fasten it around her neck. They stood inches apart. She smelled the clean, spicy scent of his hands.

"But I . . . this old dress . . ."

"Nothing you wore could ever diminish your loveliness."

"Thank you, I-I . . ." Bebe felt completely overwhelmed. She wanted to let go of all caution and allow herself to be swept away by Horatio, but she was terrified that he would leave when he discovered the truth about her, and she would drown in disappointment.

"I forgot to show you, but look—the locket opens." He took another step closer as he pried it open for her. "See? There's a place inside to put a picture of your beloved or a lock of his hair."

"Oh . . . it's beautiful," she whispered. "Thank you, Horatio. No one has ever given me . . . I mean, I've never . . . I don't know what to say. . . ."

Bebe's heart lost the battle. The grip he had on her was too powerful to escape, even if she had wanted to. Seeing Horatio again thrilled her, and she was so amazed by the gift he'd given her that she wanted to whirl and dance in the street. She could have floated home on a cloud of happiness. She drew a shaky breath and said, "Come home with me, Horatio."

"Thank you. I would be honored."

She untied her own horse and wagon and led the way to her farm. Her mother stopped removing laundry from the line to watch as Horatio's buggy pulled into the yard behind the farm wagon. Bebe took his arm and led him over to meet her mother. Hannah silently eyed the locket.

"Look who I met in town, Mama. This is Franklin's friend, Horatio Garner—"

"I hope that I am your friend, as well, Beatrice."

"Yes, of course. But Franklin knew him first, Mama, from the war. And then they were in the hospital together in Philadelphia . . . and that's where I met him."

Horatio swept off his hat and bowed. "How do you do, Mrs. Monroe?"

Hannah smiled in return. "I'm very pleased to meet you, Mr. Garner. I'm sure Franklin will be glad to see you, too. He's working out in the barn at the moment. If you just walk through that open door across the way, I'm sure you'll find him."

"Thank you." But Horatio gazed at Bebe, not in the direction where Hannah had pointed. Bebe didn't want to let him out of her sight and would have escorted him to the barn, but Hannah gently pulled her away from Horatio, linking arms with her.

"Come, Beatrice. You can help me finish folding the laundry, and then we'll get started in the kitchen. You'll stay for dinner, won't you, Mr. Garner?"

"Thank you. It's very kind and gracious of you to offer."

Bebe couldn't take her eyes off Horatio as he crossed the barnyard, mindful of where he stepped in his shiny black shoes. She continued to stare at the empty barn doorway after he'd disappeared through it. Hannah finished taking the clothes off the line, then led Bebe into the kitchen.

"I see he brought you a present."

"Yes. Isn't it beautiful?" Bebe fingered the necklace, amazed that he would give her something so lovely.

"It looks very costly."

"I-I guess so . . . Horatio's family is wealthy. His father owns a tannery. They have servants." None of those statements had anything to do with the joy and wonder Bebe felt at that moment.

Mama stopped working and turned to look at her. "Oh, Beatrice," she said with a sigh. "Anyone with a pair of eyes can see that you have feelings for each other."

"Really, Mama? Do you really think he has feelings for me?"

"I don't know where this is going to lead, but before you get swept away, you need to remember that the strongest marriages are between couples who share the same faith and the same values. If money is the most important thing to him—"

"It isn't, Mama! I mean . . . at least it doesn't seem to be important. He has always been very kind and generous to Franklin. They're friends."

"And what about Mr. Garner's faith? Does he trust in God or in his wealth and position?"

Bebe didn't know the answer. She turned away so her expression wouldn't betray her doubts. Horatio had never spoken of his faith.

"It's a wonderful thing to fall in love, Beatrice. But make sure that both you and the man you marry love the Lord even more than each other."

She nodded but her mother's words were sliding off like rain on glass. She felt as though she'd been caught up in a whirlwind as she tried to comprehend the fact that Horatio Garner was here—on her farm. He had come to see *her*. And he had brought her a present.

Horatio looked even more out of place at dinnertime, seated

at the table beside her burly father and brothers. But if Horatio felt uncomfortable, he never showed it. He gazed across the table at Bebe as if she were the only person in the room while he filled the normally quiet dinner hour with a never-ending stream of words. Now that he'd entered her world, Bebe would never be content without him. The emptiness he would leave behind would be just like the ache she felt every time she saw her brother Joseph's vacant chair or his unused bed. Was this what falling in love was like?

"What are your plans, Mr. Garner?" Bebe's father asked when dinner ended and Horatio had praised Mama's cooking for several minutes.

"Well, as I explained to Franklin earlier, one of the reasons I've come is to pass along the name of a doctor I've heard about. He has the knowledge and expertise to fix up Franklin with a brand-new leg. And to show my appreciation for the friendship we shared, I also came to offer him a job in my family's business. We're in need of a new clerk, someone to handle the customers' orders and keep the books."

"That's very generous of you, Mr. Garner. I'm sure Franklin is grateful."

"I am," Franklin said. "But I don't think I'd make a very good clerk. I never cared much for schoolwork—and I don't think I'd like to sit at a desk inside a building all day. I'm not exactly sure what I'll do for a job, but thanks for the offer."

"Of course, of course. But be sure to let me know if you change your mind."

"You're welcome to spend the night if you'd like more time to visit," Bebe's mother said. "It's too late to travel anywhere else to spend the night."

"Thank you. It's most kind of you to extend such wonderful hospitality to me. I shan't burden you for very long, I promise. I noticed this afternoon how hard everyone works, and I would hate to get in your way, especially at harvesttime." Horatio glanced at Bebe and smiled before turning back to her father. "But there is one other matter of great importance that I would like to discuss with you, Mr. Monroe. Might I have a moment to speak with you in private?"

Henry nodded in agreement. Horatio started to rise, then quickly sat down again when Henry reached for his Bible to read the evening's Scripture passage. Bebe didn't hear a word of it. Her heart galloped in anticipation of what Horatio was about to ask her father, hoping and praying that he was going to ask for her hand in marriage. She thought her father would never finish reading the passage. His closing prayer seemed endless. At last he said "Amen" and scraped back his chair. As Henry led Horatio into the parlor, Bebe abandoned her mother and the supper dishes and ran upstairs to eavesdrop through the vent in the bedroom floor.

She arrived in time to hear Horatio say, "I want you to know, Mr. Monroe, that I developed very tender feelings for your daughter, Beatrice, during her month-long stay in Philadelphia. I had the opportunity to get to know her as she cared for Franklin, and I discovered what a remarkable woman she is. Those feelings didn't diminish after we parted. In fact, I found myself unable to get her out of my mind. And so what I am trying to say is that I would be very grateful if you would grant me the honor of marrying your daughter—if she will have me."

Tears of joy filled Bebe's eyes. She longed to cover her face and weep at the wonder of Horatio's proposal, but then she wouldn't be able to hear her father's response. She pressed her fist against her mouth. The pressure of holding back her happiness felt like a dam about to burst.

"I want you to know that I am able to provide well for her," Horatio continued. "My family owns a very profitable leather tannery, which I will inherit one day. I'm in a position to build Beatrice the finest house in town and staff it with servants and—"

Henry interrupted with a grunt, as if unimpressed with Horatio's wealth. Bebe held her breath, waiting to hear his reply. "Are you a believer, Mr. Garner?" To Henry, that would be the most important question.

"Oh yes, sir. Most assuredly so. I've been baptized and confirmed in the Christian church, and our family worships together regularly. Your son Franklin can attest to my character, having shared a tent with me while we served together in the army."

Another lengthy silence followed. Bebe peeked through the grate and saw Horatio perched on the edge of his chair as if anticipating an answer at any moment.

"I'll pray about it," Henry finally said. Bebe closed her eyes in despair, well aware of how long that might take. Why couldn't her father be like other people, who made prayer seem as simple as tossing a ball up in the air and catching it again when it came down?

"Yes . . . of course," Horatio replied. But when her father stood to return to his evening chores, Bebe saw Horatio's shoulders slump. She composed herself and hurried downstairs to rescue him from her father's silence.

"Would you care to go for a walk with me, Horatio?"

"That would be lovely, if . . ." He glanced at Hannah, who was clearing the table, then back at Bebe. "If . . . if you would excuse us, please, Mrs. Monroe."

Bebe led Horatio past the barn and through the pasture and stopped beside the swing overlooking the river. "What a charming swing," Horatio said. "And in such in a charming setting. I can picture you as a rosy-cheeked girl playing here on a summer afternoon."

Bebe nodded, certain that he pictured her in a lacy white dress with her dark hair in ringlets and ribbons. What would he think if he saw her swinging in Franklin's baggy overalls and work boots? "Horatio, I need to tell you about my childhood—"

"I'm certain it was more idyllic than mine. A bout of rheumatic fever as a child left me too weak for outdoor activities. I confess that afterward my mother coddled me in many ways. How I would have loved the rugged outdoor life that Franklin and your other brothers led. But as the only son, I was expected to inherit our family's business."

"That's just the thing . . . you see, while my brothers were away at war . . ."

He turned to Bebe and took her hand. "I've asked your father for your hand in marriage."

"Yes, I know. I was eavesdropping."

"Did I do something wrong that your father didn't answer my question?"

"No, he always takes a long time to pray. That's just Papa's way."

"Then if he agrees, will you marry me? Please say yes, sweet Beatrice."

"Are . . . are you sure you want *me*? Your family is so wealthy and . . . and I don't know anything about your way of life—"

"My life will be empty and pointless without you. Please say yes . . . please!" He dropped to his knee like a prince in a fairy tale, leaving Bebe breathless.

Could she really live the life of a wealthy, genteel woman? She owned only one good dress. The rest were work clothes that were stained and tattered. She needed to confess her ignorance and tell him who she really was. But as Bebe gazed into Horatio's eager, expectant face, she realized that if she could transform herself into a boy during the war and learn to do a man's work, why not transform herself into the woman he thought she was? Anything was better than saying good-bye to him and never seeing him again and living her life without him. If the river of life was going to carry her into marriage and motherhood next, why not choose her own vessel and chart her own course?

"I don't care what my father's answer is, Horatio. My answer is yes! Yes, I will marry you!"

"Oh, Beatrice . . ."

Happiness filled his eyes as he gazed at her. He was speechless for the first time since she'd met him. Then he scrambled to his feet and pulled her into his arms to hold her tightly.

⁓

By the time Grandma Bebe and I arrived home from the reunion of the Grand Army of the Republic that Decoration Day, I had a better understanding of what she'd meant when she said that I was here because of my uncle Franklin. But at the same time, I was left with the unsettling feeling that life resembled a game of chance more than a river, and that we were all at the mercy of a heavenly game master. I existed because of the random firing of a minie ball that just happened to strike Great-Uncle Franklin's leg at the same moment that another one struck Grandfather Horatio in the foot.

The minie balls might explain why I was here on earth, but why was I *here*, in this jail cell, some fifty years later?

I rose from the rusty cot to stretch and yawn. My night's sleep had been anything but restful. I paced from one end of the cell to the other for a few minutes, then lay down again. I couldn't help worrying about Grandma Bebe. I loved her so much—and her heart was going to break in two when she found out what I had done.

CHAPTER

10

I heard footsteps in the hallway outside my cell. It was lunchtime, so I figured someone must be bringing me a meal. I sat up, then groaned aloud when I saw Tommy O'Reilly stop outside my cell door. He balanced a tray on one of his brawny hands and fumbled with a ring of keys with the other hand as he tried to unlock the door.

"You can take back the food," I told Tommy. "I'm not hungry." It wasn't true. I was starved. But I thought I should maintain an aggrieved attitude for a while longer.

"Nonsense," Tommy said. That's what he'd said last night, too, when I'd tried to explain what I was doing driving a carful of bootleg hooch.

Tommy finally managed to unlock the cell door. He took a step inside, glancing around for a place to set down the tray before deciding on the floor. It was the only place he could put it other than the bed, and since I was sitting with my legs crossed and my arms folded in a posture of defiance, I didn't blame him for not venturing any closer. Lunch consisted of a cup of coffee, a slice of buttered bread, a bowl of soup—it smelled like vegetable beef—and a dish of pudding. Tapioca. My favorite. It was going to be hard to resist.

"Don't you want to call someone to come down and bail you out, Harriet?"

I heaved a bored sigh. "As I explained to you last night, Tommy, there is no one I can call. Besides, the liquor wasn't mine. I don't understand why you don't believe me."

He looked down, and I had the wild thought that he was staring at his shins, which had received their fair share of kicks from me over the years. The kicks had all been well deserved, I might add, but they had done nothing to endear me to Tommy O'Reilly. He probably thought it would serve me right if I spent the rest of my life in jail.

"Well," he finally replied, "the evidence against you says otherwise, Harriet." His voice was soft and a little sorrowful, I thought. "As an officer of the law, I'm obliged to make assumptions based on the evidence, which in your case was a load of bootleg liquor. It'll be up to a judge to determine your guilt or innocence."

"Oh, I'm quite sure the judge will find me innocent, once the facts are known."

"Maybe so, but why sit here starving in the meantime? In fact, why sit here at all?" he asked with a shrug. "You're entitled to a phone call, you know."

I looked at him in amazement. From all outward appearances, Tommy looked . . . well . . . sympathetic! It must be a trick. He probably thought he could wheedle a confession out of me if he smiled his wide Irish grin and pretended to be nice. Tommy had grown into a fine-looking man, filling out every inch of his policeman's uniform. He'd been blessed with classic Irish good looks: dark, straight hair that fell into his brilliant blue eyes, and shoulders that were broad and strong enough to rescue innumerable damsels in distress. Any other woman might have swooned when he grinned at her the way he was grinning at me, but Tommy O'Reilly and I had a long, checkered history. My heart fluttered only a little.

"I'm sure there must be someone who's getting worried about you by now," he continued. "Someone who's wondering why you didn't come home last night."

I shrugged. My personal life was none of Tommy's business.

"I really hate to see you like this, Harriet."

I sighed again and lay down on the bunk, crossing my ankles and folding my hands behind my head. "Don't you have work to do, Tommy? Aren't there laws in this town that need to be upheld?"

He stared at me for a long moment before walking away, locking the cell door behind him.

My thoughts drifted back to my grandmother. She was going to be so disappointed in me after all her work for the Women's Christian Temperance Union, wielding hatchets and closing down saloons. She had been gloriously triumphant when the Prohibition Amendment had passed a few months ago and might have celebrated with a glass of champagne if she hadn't taken The Pledge years earlier.

I knew full well why she had become involved in the Temperance Union. I groaned and pulled the pillow over my head, wishing I could hide in jail forever.

℘

On her wedding night, Grandma Bebe nearly died of fright. One moment she was sleeping peacefully beside Horatio Garner, nestled in the warm, safe curve of his body, and the next moment a piercing cry startled the life right out of her. She leaped out of bed, terrified, ready to run, and saw that the anguished cries were coming from her new husband. She grabbed his shoulders and shook him.

"Horatio! Horatio, wake up!" His eyes shot open. He stared at her as if at a stranger. "Horatio, it's me . . . your . . . your wife . . ." When Bebe's heart slowed again and she was able to catch her breath, she sat down beside him on the bed and gathered him into her arms.

"Oh, Horatio . . . what is it? What's wrong?"

"I'm so sorry. I should have warned you . . . but sometimes . . . sometimes I have nightmares. They are always about the war. I dream about all the things I've seen . . . I thought they might go away in time, but . . . but they haven't."

Bebe rocked him in her arms and felt a tremor course through his body, shaking the bed. She wondered if it would help to light a lamp in the unfamiliar hotel room, but he was clinging to her like a drowning man in a flood.

"When my brothers and I used to have bad dreams," she told him, "my mother always made us talk about them. It seemed like the nightmares lost their power once we spoke them out loud. Maybe if you told me—"

"No, Beatrice," he said with a shudder. "You don't want me to describe the things I dream about."

"Yes I do. I think it will help. Please?" He didn't reply. She squirmed out of his embrace and stood to light a lamp, then coaxed Horatio to sit propped against the pillows. She sat cross-legged on the bed facing him, waiting.

"It isn't really a dream," he finally said, "because I'm remembering things that really happened. It's like . . . like I'm reliving the war all over again. Tonight I was back in Virginia, fighting outside of Richmond." He shivered, hugging himself as if to ward off a chill. Bebe longed to take him in her arms again but was afraid he would stop talking if she did.

"We had fought a hard battle two days earlier . . . and lost nearly two thousand men. Now the Rebels were entrenched behind earthworks at the top of a rise. We all knew there was going to be another slaughter when we tried to take that hill, so the night before the battle, some of the men sewed tags in their clothes with their names and addresses printed on them. That way people would know whose body was whose after the Rebs shot us all to pieces.

"And that's just what happened the next morning. It was a slaughter. The generals kept sending our men up that stupid hill . . . charging forward in nice, neat rows . . . and the Rebels kept mowing us down like a field of wheat. As fast as one row of men would fall, we'd send up the next batch. Our commanding officers were asking us to commit suicide!"

His Adam's apple bobbed as he swallowed a knot of emotion. His voice didn't sound like his own, and Bebe realized that it was the first time she'd ever heard him speak plainly, without all of his flowery words and inflections.

"I was so scared as I waited for my turn," he continued, "that I could hardly stand up for shaking. It seemed like a terrible waste to me, and I didn't want to go. But people were determined to shoot me either way. If I sat down and refused to obey orders or ran off like a coward, the Yanks would put me up before a firing squad. And if I charged up that hill like they were telling me to do, I would face Johnny Reb's firing squad. No matter which course I chose, I was a dead man. So you know what I did? I got out a nickel and flipped it in the air. Heads, I would die by a Yankee bullet, tails by a Rebel one."

"It must have come up tails," Bebe said quietly.

"It did. So I started reciting the Lord's Prayer. Everyone was reciting it. A lot of us were vomiting our guts out, too. I was all set to die, like I'd been ordered to do. But just before my turn came, they stopped the slaughter. Someone finally saw the senselessness of it, I guess. I heard later on that when General Grant ordered another attack, his officers refused. I don't know if that's true.

"But even though the shooting stopped, our wounded men were lying out on that hill, pinned down. You could hear them begging for help, moaning and weeping and dying—all day and all that night. I tell you I cried like a baby for those men. Some of them were my friends. Except for the grace of God, it might have been me."

He swallowed again and drew a ragged breath. "They say that seven thousand men died that day in less than an hour. *Seven thousand*, Bebe! And I watched it all happen. It's something I'll never forget. And now . . . well, my body may have survived, but my nerves were shot all to pieces that day. Sometimes . . . sometimes I think I would have been better off if I had—"

"Don't say it, Horatio! Please!" Bebe scrambled forward to hold him in her arms again, gripping him tightly as if trying to squeeze her own strength into him. "Don't you ever dare to say such a terrible thing." The tremor that ran through his body was like the rumbling Bebe felt when riding the train.

"You know how much longer we had to keep on killing each other after that battle near Cold Harbor? Ten more months! I felt like a condemned man on death row all that time, following those generals around Virginia as they sacrificed us like so many sheep just to win some little piece of worthless land or a burned-down town. I was one of the walking dead, waiting for my turn to go down into the grave."

Bebe looked into his eyes and brushed his damp hair from his forehead. "But you didn't die, and it wasn't a useless sacrifice. You kept our country united and you won freedom for millions of slaves."

"Well, why couldn't they have settled those issues like gentlemen? Isn't that what governments are for? War is a horrible way to decide an argument, Bebe. You saw the aftermath of it when you visited the army hospital." He released her and fought free of the covers to climb out of bed.

"Where are you going, Horatio? Can I get you something?"

"Stay in bed, dear one. I'll get it myself." He crossed the room to retrieve his small traveling case and set it on top of the dresser to open it. Strapped inside were four glass decanters of golden liquid and two sturdy glasses.

"What is that?" she asked.

"A little something to calm my nerves." His hand shook as he poured a generous amount into one of the glasses and carried it over to her, sitting beside her on the bed. The smell of it made Bebe's eyes water. "Would you like some?" he asked.

"Is it liquor?"

"It's the only thing that helps chase away the ghosts."

She pushed the glass away. "No, thank you. My parents never allowed alcohol in our home. Reverend Webster always preached against strong drink."

Horatio drained half of the liquid in one gulp. "Well . . . I would hate to wake you up again with another nightmare, beloved Beatrice. This was not at all how I envisioned our first night together, and I am so very sorry for frightening you the way I did. You must know that I would never do anything to hurt you." He drained the second half and pulled her into his arms. "Do you think you can ever forgive me for the way this night has turned out?"

"Of course. There's nothing to forgive. You can't help having nightmares."

He stroked her hair. "You're the best thing that has ever happened to me, do you know that? Who would have thought that fighting the war and getting wounded would lead to meeting you?" He kissed her, and she didn't like the taste of the liquor on his lips. When he pulled away again, he looked at her for a long moment, then rose and crossed the room to the dresser. She thought he was going to put the glass away, but instead he poured another drink. It seemed like a lot.

"Why don't you come back to bed, Horatio?"

"I will in a moment, dearest. I want to make certain that I stay asleep this time." He raised the glass in the air in a toast: "To no more bad dreams." And after he'd refilled his glass a third time and drank it down, there weren't any. In fact, Horatio slept like a dead man. Bebe had to shake him awake in the morning so they wouldn't miss their train to Niagara Falls.

They spent their honeymoon in a lavish hotel near the falls, and the first time Bebe saw the thundering cascade, she clung to Horatio's arm, unable to speak. They stood so close to the rushing water that she could feel the spray on her face when the wind blew their way, and she had to fight against the sensation that she would be swept over the edge.

"Can you feel the river's power, Beatrice?" he asked, raising his voice to be heard above the roar.

"Yes! It's . . . it's overwhelming!"

"That's how I felt when I met you—overwhelmed. Swept away."

Bebe clung to him a little tighter, not caring if it was improper to show affection in public. "The falls are so terrifying . . . and yet so beautiful. I never dreamed I would see anything this magnificent." She drew her gaze away to look up at her husband. "Or that I would ever love anyone as much as I love you."

Bebe would remember those two weeks as the most wonderful days of her life. Horatio didn't have a single nightmare after the first one, and they both believed it was because of the healing power of their love.

Then they returned to Horatio's hometown of Roseton in a mountain valley in central Pennsylvania and Bebe's nightmares began. Her new mother-in-law met them at the front door with crossed arms and an angry glare. "How could you do this to us, Horatio? How could you run off with some . . . some *farm* girl with no thought or consideration at all for our feelings? After everything we've done for you?"

Bebe drew back from the force of her words. Her instinct was to turn and run, but Horatio remained calm, his smile never wavering.

"I'm sorry you feel that way, Mother, but this is my new bride, Beatrice Aurelia Garner, and—"

"She's a child! Is your marriage even legal?"

"She's not a child; she's merely dainty and petite."

"I-I'm seventeen," Bebe said just above a whisper.

Mrs. Garner ignored her. "It may not be too late to have the marriage annulled, Horatio. Your father can talk to a judge and—"

"He'll do no such thing." Horatio draped his arm around Bebe's shoulders and pulled her close. "I love her, Mother. And if you can't accept my choice, then perhaps Beatrice and I will have to move to her hometown and live with her parents, instead."

Bebe looked up at him, wondering if he'd lost his mind. Then she remembered her manners and turned back to her mother-in-law, offering her hand. "I'm very pleased to meet you—"

Mrs. Garner whirled away with a rustle of taffeta, leaving Bebe on the doorstep with her hand still outstretched. Horatio squeezed her shoulder and led her into the house. "That went better than I expected," he said with a grin.

"Are you joking, Horatio? She hates me!"

"She'll get over it. She's angry because we had a simple marriage ceremony in your church and she didn't have the opportunity to plan a huge, lavish wedding. And also because I chose my own bride instead of marrying someone from her social circle. But don't worry, by this time next week she'll be planning an extravagant ball to introduce you to all her friends."

Bebe didn't know which frightened her more, the idea of meeting more women like Mrs. Garner, or the knowledge that it would be at a fancy ball. She didn't even know how to dance. "Oh, Horatio . . . a ball? I-I—"

"Mother will have so much fun shopping with you, buying your trousseau, outfitting you in a new wardrobe—"

"Outfitting me?"

"Of course." He took her face in his hands. "You're beautiful, Beatrice. You're like a tiny porcelain doll. I can't wait to dress you up and show you off myself."

*Show me off?* For a second time, Bebe fought the urge to turn and run. She gazed around the mansion's soaring foyer and sweeping staircase—and noticed, for the first time, the row of uniformed servants standing like stiff, unsmiling soldiers. The man whom she guessed to be the butler gave a little bow.

"Welcome home, Master Garner," he said. The row of maids all curtsied.

"Thank you, Robert," Horatio replied. "I trust that you and the rest of the staff will help make my bride feel welcome in every way. You're all dismissed for now." The butler went to see about their luggage. The maids curtsied again and scattered. Horatio smiled as if they'd been greeted with hugs and kisses and a fattened calf instead of harsh words and unfriendly faces. "Would you like a tour of the house, my dear?"

"I-I feel a little dizzy, Horatio." She had made a wrong turn and had wandered onto the pages of a tragic fairy tale. If only she could read the ending and find out what would happen. A week ago she'd been certain that she and Horatio would live happily ever after. Now she wasn't so sure.

"You must be exhausted, my dear," Horatio said as he led Bebe into an enormous parlor. It overflowed with so much overstuffed furniture, gewgaws, and bric-a-brac that she could barely see the walls. He made her sit down on a stiff horsehair sofa. "Shall I have the servants bring you something?"

"I don't want to bother anyone. . . ."

Horatio's laughter filled the high-ceilinged room. "My dear, it's their job to wait on you!" He crossed to a tall cabinet in the corner and took out a glass decanter. It was like the one in his traveling case, only larger. The crystal tumbler that he poured the liquor into was larger, too. Bebe watched him take a long drink. "Would you like some, Beatrice?"

"No thanks. I think . . . I think I need to lie down." Her nerves felt so fragile that she feared she might throw up or burst into tears—perhaps both—and she wanted to be someplace private when she did. Horatio laughed again and set down the glass. Before Bebe could protest, he scooped her up in his arms and carried her into the foyer and up the stairs. She was in tears before he reached the first landing. "This . . . this is all too much, Horatio!"

He kissed her forehead. "You'll get used to it, my dear Beatrice. I promise you."

But for the first time since she'd met her husband, Bebe had cause to doubt him.

## 11

Three days after arriving home with Horatio, Bebe crept down the wide staircase all alone in search of breakfast, leaving her husband asleep in bed. The first two mornings he had convinced her to stay in bed with him and sleep until much later in the day as they rested from their journey. "The maids will serve us our breakfast here," he'd told her.

"You mean we'll eat while lying in bed? Not at a table? I couldn't do that."

"Why not?" He had grinned, as if her efforts to adapt to his lifestyle were very amusing.

"Well . . . I'm just not used to staying in bed past dawn unless I'm sick—and I'm hardly ever sick."

She had yielded to Horatio's wishes and remained in bed for the first two days, but by the third day Bebe couldn't sleep a moment longer. When the hall clock struck seven, she put on her clothes and tiptoed downstairs. She heard laughter and the rattle of dishes coming from the kitchen and would have been content to go through the forbidden doorway and eat with the servants.

But Horatio had scolded her for socializing with the help after he'd overheard her chatting with the chambermaid.

"Servants often become lazy and presumptuous if their masters are overly friendly," he told her. In truth, Bebe had much more in common with those simple, hardworking people than with Horatio's family.

Except for the voices in the kitchen, the house was cold and silent. Bebe missed the sound of the rooster crowing in the morning and the cows lowing to be milked, and all of the other clanking, bustling noises of the farm. She crept into the dining room and saw steam rising from a row of silver chafing dishes on the sideboard. She lifted one of the lids and found enough bacon for a dozen people. Should she wait for Horatio's parents? And how in the world would she converse with them without Horatio alongside her?

In the three days that Bebe had lived in the Garner home, her mother-in-law had not once spoken to her or addressed her by name. Mr. Garner had barely spoken to her, either. Horatio had carried the conversation throughout their meals, describing Niagara Falls and the other sights they had seen in such beautiful, poetic language that Bebe could have listened to him for hours.

She replaced the lid on the chafing dish and was about to go back upstairs when Horatio's father strode into the room. He stopped short when he saw her.

"You're up early."

"Yes, I can't seem to sleep past—"

"Where's Horatio?"

"In bed—"

"What did you say? Speak up!"

"I-I said that he is still in bed." She saw no need to mention that the three tumblers of liquor he drank last night had knocked him out cold.

"Well, he needs to get up. I need him at the tannery this morning."

"I'll go wake him." Bebe turned to leave.

"Not you. Sit down. The servants can do it." He sank into his place at the head of the table and rang a little silver bell. Servants poured through the door from the kitchen as if he had opened a spigot. Bebe jumped out of their way.

"Kindly awaken my son," Mr. Garner commanded them. "I would like my coffee and my newspaper right away. Then fix me a plate—but I don't want any of that disgusting orange marmalade on my toast. I'd sooner eat earwax."

The maids scrambled to do Mr. Garner's bidding as if he were King Solomon and they were his many wives. Once he began to read his newspaper, he didn't speak another word to anyone. Someone filled his coffee cup. Another maid prepared a plate for him at the buffet and set it before him. Bebe watched her father-in-law silently turn the pages of his newspaper and tried not to form a harsh opinion of him. Her own father had never been a talkative man, but he wouldn't have ignored another person at the table this way. Nor would he have begun to eat, as Horatio's father had just done, without first offering thanks to God for his food.

Mr. Garner rang the bell once again when he wanted more coffee, pointing mutely to the empty cup. Then, when he'd finished his breakfast, he folded his newspaper, laid it aside, and rang for his carriage.

"I don't have time to wait for Horatio," he told Bebe. "Tell him I left without him." The front door thumped shut behind him.

"Can I get you something, ma'am?" the serving girl asked as she cleared away Mr. Garner's breakfast dishes.

"No, thank you . . . I'm waiting for Horatio."

"If you please, ma'am . . . he told us not to disturb him again for another hour. And then he would like his breakfast upstairs, as usual."

Bebe stood to serve herself from the chafing dishes, swallowing a knot of tears as she remembered standing at the stove with her brother Franklin, tussling over the scrambled eggs and biscuits.

It didn't take long to eat breakfast alone. She longed to carry her plate into the kitchen, where she would feel more comfortable and where there were other people to talk to, but she didn't dare. She was trying to decide where she should go in this enormous house, and what she should do until Horatio awoke, when Mrs. Garner swished into the room in her ruffled dressing gown, carrying a stack of books.

"Do you know how to read?" she asked.

"Yes, of course, Mrs. Garner. I—"

"Then you'll need to study these." She dropped the pile onto the table in front of Bebe. "They'll teach you proper etiquette and other important social conventions. I don't have time to teach you all of the things you failed to learn on your rustic little farm. And your first social engagement is in a few weeks."

"My first—?"

"When you're finished reading these, I have several back issues of *Godey's Lady's Book* for you to peruse. Have you heard of it?"

"Yes, it's a magazine for women that—"

"You'll need to begin reading it regularly. Otherwise, heaven only knows what you'll find to talk about in polite company. My dressmaker will be coming to measure you at nine o'clock this morning. Kindly be prepared for her."

Bebe wondered what in the world she had to do to prepare to be measured, but before she could ask, her mother-in-law said, "Once you are properly educated and outfitted, you'll be included in the regular round of social duties."

"Social duties?"

Mrs. Garner rolled her eyes toward the ceiling as if beseeching the Almighty for patience. "Your ignorance is astonishing." She turned and swished away, her chin in the air.

Bebe swallowed another knot of tears as she looked at the pile of books in front of her, scanning the titles: *Good Morals and Gentle Manners; The Manners That Win; Our Deportment; The Complete Book of Etiquette*. She opened one of them at random and began to read: *Never loll, fidget, yawn, bite the nails or be guilty of any other like gaucherie in the presence of others*. She had no idea what *gaucherie* meant, but she suspected she would find out after studying all four books. She opened to another place and read, *The proper form of introduction is to present the gentleman to the lady, the younger to the older, the inferior to the superior.*

*The inferior to the superior?* She thought of the Scripture verse that Lucretia Mott had quoted at the anti-slavery meeting back home: *"There is neither bond nor free, there is neither male nor female: for ye are all one in Christ Jesus."*

Bebe thumped the book shut. Trying to memorize all these trivial things seemed daunting and useless. She recalled, with great regret, the advice her mother had offered: *"If you would determine in your heart to put that same amount of time and effort into Bible study and prayer, you would find the purpose and contentment that you're seeking."*

Bebe was still sitting alone at the table a while later when a maid came in and began preparing a breakfast tray from the food in the chafing dishes. "Is that for my husband? Horatio Garner?"

"Yes, ma'am."

"I'll bring it up to him."

"Oh, no, ma'am. Mrs. Garner would never allow such a thing."

Instead, Bebe waited until the tray was ready, then followed the maid upstairs, lugging the stack of books. Horatio was awake but still in bed. "Why are you dressed already, Beatrice? What time is it, anyway?"

She walked over to his dresser to look at his pocket watch. No one had ever cared about the time of day on the farm, following the rhythm of the animals and the sun and the seasons. But Horatio and his family scheduled everything according to the clock. There were several of them scattered throughout the house, including the tall case clock in the foyer that chimed four times every hour. It made Bebe uneasy to hear regular reminders of the passing of time, especially since so far she had not accomplished anything useful.

"It's ten minutes past eight," she told him. Horatio groaned and closed his eyes. Bebe waited, wondering what to do. "Your father said he needed you at work this morning."

"Too bad. Let him wait. I have a pounding headache, and the last thing I need is all that racket at the tannery. . . . What are all those books for?"

"Your mother loaned them to me. She says I need to read them so I can learn proper etiquette and prepare for my social duties. And a seamstress is coming before long to measure me."

Horatio smiled and stretched out his hand to her. "Come here, my love. Why so glum?" The tears that Bebe had held back all morning spilled over as Horatio pulled her close. "Are you sorry you married me, Beatrice?"

"No! Never! But I wish . . . I wish it could just be the two of us, and that we lived all by ourselves so that I could cook for you and take care of you myself and—"

"It will be that way soon. Didn't I promise to build you your very own house?" He tried to kiss her, but she freed herself from his embrace. "What's wrong, dear one?"

"Your breakfast is getting cold, and your father needs you at work, and I need to get ready for the seamstress. She's coming shortly."

The woman arrived promptly at nine and made Bebe strip

to her chemise and drawers while Mrs. Garner and one of the chambermaids stood right there in the room with her, watching. Then the seamstress measured every inch of Bebe from head to toe, shaking her head and muttering as she bemoaned the fact that Bebe was so small.

"I may have to use children's patterns," she told Mrs. Garner, "and even then they may not fit her properly."

"I'm not a child," Bebe tried to explain. "I'm seventeen."

Mrs. Garner and the seamstress exchanged looks. While Bebe put her clothes back on, the two older women paged through pattern books and examined fabric samples and discussed lace and trim. Neither of them bothered to consult Bebe or ask for her opinions as they planned an entire wardrobe for her. If she had tiptoed out the door, she doubted anyone would have noticed.

"The girl doesn't have a single decent thing to wear," Mrs. Garner told the seamstress. "I'll need to take her shopping for shoes and hats and gloves—and undergarments, too, from the look of hers."

Bebe pressed her lips together and tried not to cry.

Their shopping trip a few days later was an exhausting affair. Back home in New Canaan, Bebe could have purchased everything she needed at Harrison's General Store, but Roseton had so many stores to choose from that she and Mrs. Garner spent two long days traipsing from one to the next. Mrs. Garner made all of the decisions. When Bebe first arrived in Roseton, all of her belongings had fit inside two modest-sized carpetbags. But by the time she finished shopping and her new dresses had arrived, she needed a bureau, an armoire, and a vanity table to hold everything. It seemed like a sin to own so much.

"Tomorrow you will receive callers for the first time," Mrs. Garner told her when she and Horatio had lived there for a month.

"Be dressed and ready to greet our guests by two o'clock sharp. Wear the blue taffeta gown. My maid will arrange your hair."

"You'll do fine, my darling," Horatio assured her as he kissed her good-bye in the morning. "There's no reason in the world to be ill at ease. You will win over the other women with your charms in no time, just as you captivated me."

Horatio's confidence seemed unfounded to Bebe. But as she gazed at her husband's handsome face, she decided that she would walk through fire and flood for him. Surely a simple tea party wouldn't be so difficult.

That afternoon as Bebe sat in front of her looking glass watching the servant arrange her dark hair in an elaborate knot, all of her confidence suddenly evaporated. What had ever made her think she could transform herself from a simple farm girl into a society woman? Laboring like a man alongside her father had been easy compared to facing a roomful of women like Mrs. Garner. What would she say to them? And how would she ever manage to pour tea with shaking hands?

"All finished, ma'am." The maid had secured the last hairpin in place. "You have lovely hair, ma'am. So full and thick."

Bebe stared at her reflection and saw a stranger. *"Life is always changing,"* her mother had said, *"always flowing forward like a stream."* It was time for Bebe to wade into the current and change, as well. She rose from her seat at the dressing table, gracefully lifting her skirts, and went downstairs to the parlor to face her guests.

Mrs. Garner wore a tense smile as she introduced Bebe to the chattering ladies. Bebe hated being on display, scrutinized by a roomful of strangers. Some of the guests boldly questioned her about her age, others commented rudely on how short and girl-like she was. Bebe wished she could retaliate by pointing out how stout and wrinkled they were or by asking their age in return. But according to the etiquette books, she was supposed to answer their questions politely, no matter how inconsiderate they were, and above all to smile.

As the afternoon wore on, Bebe thought she was doing well until one of the younger women approached and asked her a question she hadn't expected. "Which clubs will you belong to, Beatrice?"

"I-I'm not sure what you mean."

"Which women's organizations do you plan to participate in? Which causes have you supported?"

Bebe stuttered to form a reply. "W-well . . . back home, my mother and I worked with the Anti-Slavery Society."

The woman frowned and waved her hand in dismissal. "That's all in the past. The war is over. The slaves are free."

"Yes, but there is still so much work to do. One of our guest speakers, Lucretia Mott, pointed out that since women proved their equality during the war by running their husbands' farms and businesses, we should be allowed the same civil rights as men, and—"

"Excuse me? You're not talking about woman suffrage, are you?" The room grew unusually still. Bebe felt everyone's attention shift to her. She had no idea what the correct response was, so she told the truth.

"Well . . . Mrs. Mott explained that it was compassionate, educated women like ourselves who have worked hard to abolish slavery. And now all of the former male slaves are being granted civil rights, even though many are illiterate, while literate women are still being denied those rights."

For a long moment, no one seemed to breathe. The room felt as hot as the hayloft on an August afternoon. Bebe had been certain that this gathering of women would agree with Lucretia Mott's conclusions. Instead, they appeared shocked.

Finally, the woman who had asked Bebe the question mumbled,

"I see. Would you excuse me, please?" She scurried away as if Bebe had head lice. Within minutes, everyone seemed to be saying good-bye and leaving. Bebe had no way of knowing if it was because of what she'd said or if afternoon teas always ended this abruptly. She soon found out.

"How could you!" Mrs. Garner roared the moment they were alone. "Didn't you read the books I gave you?"

"Y-yes. All four of them."

"Then why did you decide to ignore all of the warnings about never discussing politics?"

"I . . . I . . . she asked me about the clubs I belonged to, and—"

"And you told her you supported woman suffrage? Of all the outrageous things!"

"I didn't mean . . . I only went to one anti-slavery meeting back home and—"

"You've not only embarrassed me in my own home, you've also ruined your chances of being invited to any of their homes! No one wants to entertain a woman with such radical views."

"But don't women deserve the same rights as—?"

"Certainly not! The public sphere of labor and politics is a man's domain. Ours is the more exalted sphere of home and family. Motherhood is a woman's highest goal. Our success can be seen in the character of our children and in the respite we provide for our husbands at home."

"But—"

"Don't you *ever* mention woman suffrage in my house or in my presence again! Do you understand?"

Bebe wanted to run down the hill and jump into the wide, cold river that flowed through Roseton. She was still in her room, crying, when Horatio returned home from work. He went to her immediately and folded her in his arms. "Oh, my poor Beatrice. Is it safe to assume that the afternoon didn't go very well?"

"It was awful," she whimpered. "I'm so sorry, Horatio. I know how important this event was to your mother, and I embarrassed her, and . . . and I let you down."

"Beatrice, I love you. Nothing will ever change that. I don't care what you said or what happened today. It isn't important to me."

"But your mother—"

"You don't have to be part of Mother's social circle if you don't want to be," he said gently.

"That's good. Because after today, I doubt if she'll ever allow me to be seen with her in public again."

"I'll smooth things over with her. Now, please don't cry anymore. It breaks my heart to see you so upset."

She drew a breath and tried to pull herself together, but her tears wouldn't stop falling. "But what will I do all day, Horatio? The house is cleaned for us, all of our meals are prepared, our clothes are all sewn and laundered and pressed. The chores that I used to do back home are all done for me, and I have nothing to do. Your mother doesn't like me and never talks to me. You told me I mustn't talk to the servants, and I don't have any friends . . ."

He smoothed her hair off her face. "You'll make new friends soon. The first day of any new venture is always the most difficult one. I'm certain that when you try again, you'll find someone in Mother's crowd or among their daughters who will be a friend to you."

Bebe wanted to believe him but couldn't. She longed to be honest with him, to tell him that she really wasn't graceful and refined, to confess that she had been playacting ever since the day they'd met. But the only certainty in her life right now was that she loved him—more and more each day, if that was possible. And she would do anything in the world for him. She dried her eyes with her new linen handkerchief and smiled up at him.

"Forgive me for complaining, Horatio. I'm so sorry. I'll do better the next time. I promise."

When Tommy O'Reilly arrested me last night, he'd had the audacity to ask if I was married. I stuck out my chin, looked him square in the eye, and said, "No, I am not, Tommy—are you?"

He took a step backward, holding up his hands as if I might take a swing at him. It wouldn't have been the first time. "I meant no offense, Harriet. I just thought that if you were, I could call your husband to—"

"To do what? Come and rescue me? Talk some sense into me? Take control of me?"

"Sorry I asked," he said, shaking his head. He was careful to keep his hands in a defensive position. "And the answer is no, I'm not."

"Not what?" I was too angry to keep track of the conversation.

"Not married. I'm single. Like you." He smiled, and if I hadn't known him as well as I did, I would have thought he was being flirtatious. But I was immune to men's advances in general—and to Tommy's in particular.

Grandma Bebe may not realize it, but she had played a huge

part in forming my opinions of men and marriage. To be honest, I couldn't see why I needed either one. She no longer had a husband and she fared just fine without one. She went wherever she pleased and did whatever she pleased, and I planned to do the same. I knew how to start an automobile, how to drive it down the road, and how to take care of it when it rattled to a halt. What did I need a husband for?

My parents' marriage had also contributed to my opinions—but not in a positive way. Mind you, I never heard them arguing, and our house was, for the most part, a peaceful, happy place. But that was largely because my mother treated my father like a maharajah in his palace: *"Yes, dear. No, dear. Whatever you say, dear."* On the odd occasion when my father became unreasonable she resorted to tears, which nearly always worked in her favor. I was much too proud to weep, so how could I have a marriage like theirs? I planned to navigate my own path through life, and I had no intention of handing the rudder over to anyone else.

My low regard for marriage had solidified into rock-solid aversion when my sister Alice became engaged. Where should I begin to describe that turn of events? After breaking hundreds of hearts, Alice finally made up her mind and settled on one beau. If her decision surprised me, imagine the astonishment of her innumerable spurned suitors. The fact that she'd made up her mind at all was shocking. My empty-headed sister had trouble deciding which hat to wear for a stroll down the block, let alone choosing something as momentous as a mate. Alice insisted on seeing the good in everyone, so she had been forced to rely on Mother's skills at dissecting people and analyzing their pedigrees. It was the only way Alice ever could have narrowed her choice down to one.

I was thirteen that spring of 1912 when Alice got engaged. She was twenty. The lucky winner of Alice's heart was a banker's son named Gordon Shaw, grandson of one of Roseton's founding fathers. I had absolutely no idea what Alice saw in him. Gordon was a bore. His favorite topics of conversations were himself and his bank full of money.

But before the marriage could occur I had to endure . . . *The Wedding*. When General Pershing and his troops set off for France in 1917, they didn't go through nearly as much rigmarole as Mother and Alice did as they prepared for *The Wedding*. Digging the Panama Canal was simple in comparison. One afternoon, when they were trying to narrow down the guest list to slightly less than circus-like proportions, the hullabaloo became so unbearable that I fled to Grandma Bebe's house for refuge. I found her seated at her desk, writing a speech for a temperance rally.

"May I move in with you until the wedding is over?" I begged. "Please?"

Grandma smiled and blotted the ink on the last line she'd penned. "Well, as much as I would love your company dear, your mother would never allow it. . . . But as long as you're here, Harriet, maybe you can listen to my speech and tell me what you think of it. I'll make us some tea, first."

I would've rather had a bottle of sarsaparilla, but Grandma didn't have any in her icebox. I sat down at her kitchen table while she put the kettle on to boil, savoring the peace and calm. I liked eating in Grandma's kitchen. Our kitchen was the domain of Bess, our Negro cook, and Maggie our hired girl, and they didn't like anyone venturing into their territory. Grandma didn't have any servants and preferred sitting in her kitchen more than any other room.

"I'm never getting married," I said with an elephant-sized sigh.

"Never is a very long time, Harriet. And marriage is what gives you a purpose in life—not to mention a family. Just think: If I hadn't married Horatio, your mother never would have been born. And if your mother hadn't married your father, you never would have been born." She scooped tea from the canister into the pot while she talked, then set cups and saucers in front of us.

"If having babies is the only reason to get married," I said, "then count me out for sure! The last thing I need is a drooling, squalling baby. And if Alice decides to have one, I'm moving in with you for good."

"Most people get married for love, Harriet. . . . No, don't make a face. I know you don't understand it now, but someday some lucky man will come along, and when you fall in love with him it will be like plunging over Niagara Falls. You won't know how you ever lived without him. That's how I felt about Horatio."

"I don't think Alice 'fell over the falls' with Gordon Shaw. I think Mother steered her straight into him, like beaching a ship on a sandbar. I can't figure out what Alice sees in him. Or what he sees in Alice, for that matter."

"I hope that both of them are looking for the right qualities in each other. And I hope, for Alice's sake, that there is more to Mr. Shaw than a handsome face and a wealthy father."

"Well, there's nothing more to Alice, I know that for sure. Aside from a pretty face and fluffy blond hair, she's completely hopeless. She has trouble remembering how to uncork her smelling salts, and she needs them at least three times a day—that's how often she swoons."

"Now you're exaggerating," Grandma said with a smile.

"What do men see in women like Alice—and my mother? No offense, I know she's your daughter, but Mother doesn't do much of anything except look pretty and fuss over Father and go to club meetings."

"I know. Poor Lucy," Grandma said, shaking her head. The kettle reached a boil and she rose to pour the water over the tea leaves. "Lucy was overly influenced by Horatio's mother, I'm sorry

LYNN AUSTIN

to say. I wasn't home much of the time when she was little, so my mother-in-law made her into the woman she is today. Lucy acquired a taste for expensive things because Mrs. Garner kept buying her extravagant toys—imported dolls, a rocking horse, an enormous dollhouse. She even bought a miniature porcelain tea set so Lucy could learn the tea ritual from a very young age. And the last thing Grandma Garner did before she died was to make sure Lucy married well."

"You mean to my father? He was a prize? I don't believe it. He owns a department store, for goodness' sake. He has a moon face and spectacles. His forehead gets higher and higher every year. What in the world did Mother see in him?"

"He was a very nice looking, up-and-coming gentleman back in the early nineties, when they married. Not as handsome as my Horatio, but not every woman can be as fortunate as I was."

I didn't say so, but I had seen pictures of Horatio and I didn't think he was handsome at all. He looked scrawny and pasty-faced to me.

"Horatio and I went to Niagara Falls on our honeymoon, and it's a perfect metaphor of what love is like: powerful, beautiful, terrifying, overwhelming—and there's no turning back once you fall over the edge."

"But you've told me stories about how hard your marriage was, especially living with Horatio's parents and trying to learn all those society rules. You made it sound horrible."

"Did I? I didn't mean to. Marriage can be difficult at times, I'll grant you that. But being married to Horatio gave me a great deal of joy, as well." She smiled, and even with silver streaks in her dark hair, I could see remnants of the lovely woman Grandma Bebe must have been. She poured tea into my cup and pushed the sugar bowl across the table to me. "Here. I know you like it sweet."

"But you were pretty, Grandma. Mother and Alice are, too.

You and my mirror have told me countless times that I'm plain. I look like Father's side of the family. Even if I was interested in marriage, who would want to marry me?"

"Outward beauty can be a distraction for many men. Count it a blessing that you're plain, Harriet. That way, you'll know that a suitor is attracted to the real you, not the fancy wrappings. Believe it or not, I was very plain when Horatio met me. I was dressed in a simple calico gown with my braids coiled up on my head. I was a shy, small-town farm girl with no social graces at all. What he saw in me, I'll never know."

Grandma was getting more nostalgic about marriage by the moment. I needed to bring her back to the present. "I'm going to go to college when I finish school—and not some sissy female seminary, either. I want to go someplace substantial like Cornell or Oberlin. I want to be like you, Grandma, and do something important with my life. Didn't you say that your work for the Temperance Union gave your life meaning?"

"Yes, but you can be married and still serve a cause. I did. Besides, I probably never would have joined the Union if I had remained single."

"I don't believe it." Her insistence on the joy of marriage was starting to frustrate me. I blew into my cup to cool the tea and my temper, then said, "You need to explain yourself, Grandma."

"It's a long, sad story . . . are you sure you want to hear it?"

"We have plenty of time. I'm not going home until the wedding is over. And if Alice has a baby, I'm never going home."

"Every marriage has its good times and bad, Harriet. Change is the only constant in life. . . ."

⁓

By the time Bebe and Horatio had been married for three years, she had perfected her ability to perform in society. She could pay visits to the wealthiest homes in town and make meaningless conversation for hours on end without committing a faux pas or a gaucherie. But even with flawless social skills, Bebe never achieved full acceptance by Mrs. Garner and her friends. That came by birth, not by marriage. She would always be poor little Bebe Monroe, a dairy farmer's daughter. Many of the young women who were Bebe's age held a grudge against her for capturing Roseton's most desirable bachelor. The older women never forgave her for denying them a huge society wedding—a major social event among the well-to-do. They would consider her a gold digger, an upstart, a newcomer in town, even if she resided there for fifty years.

Bebe may not have been allowed to mention woman suffrage, but she did find something more meaningful to do than attend tea parties and social events. Since the Garner men owned one of Roseton's largest industries and employed hundreds of workers, it was the duty of the Garner women to be charitable to the poor workers' families. Once every month, Bebe and Mrs. Garner would travel by carriage to The Flats, as the sorry side of town was called, accompanied by the driver and the family butler for protection, of course.

Before Bebe visited The Flats for the first time, she had never imagined that such poverty existed. Her family had always worked hard on their farm, and life had been primitive in many ways, but at least they'd always had plenty of food to eat. In The Flats, the ramshackle tenements and bungalows were bounded by the river on one side and the railroad tracks on the other. Sewage oozed down open gutters alongside the streets, and freight trains rumbled past day and night, rattling windows and foundations. There was no grass or trees, and the yards behind the buildings were so tiny and barren that the workers couldn't even grow food or raise animals. It seemed like a miserable way to live. Yet in the eight-block area of The Flats, Bebe counted six saloons.

"Those saloons are the reason you must never venture into this part of town alone or at night," Mrs. Garner warned.

On Bebe's first trip to The Flats, they visited a tannery worker's wife, who had recently given birth. "Her sixth or seventh child, I believe," Mrs. Garner said with a sniff. Bebe wondered where everyone slept at night in that tiny, crowded apartment. The new mother barely spoke English, but she did know how to say "Thank you," which she repeated over and over as she expressed gratitude for the meal they'd delivered—as if Bebe and Mrs. Garner had cooked it themselves. Bebe felt like a fraud.

Two of the woman's ragged, barefooted children had coughs and runny noses. The three oldest, who looked as though they should be in school, sat at a table doing piecework with their mother, sewing on buttons. "Can't we do something more for that family?" Bebe asked after they returned to their carriage that first day.

"Of course not. It's important to be charitable, but we mustn't allow the poor to become dependent on us."

"Shouldn't the city officials be doing something about the sewage and all the garbage that's piling up?"

"That's entirely up to our civic government. It isn't our duty to meddle in men's affairs."

Three years after Bebe's first visit to The Flats, the neighborhood looked exactly the same. The garbage and sewage, the fleas and the flies remained unchanged. The only thing that had changed, as far as Bebe could tell, was the population, which had grown considerably larger.

"I don't know how these families can afford to live with so many mouths to feed," Bebe said after delivering yet another meal to yet another new mother. She felt guilty for parading into these families' lives, well dressed and well fed, reminding them of what they lacked. To Bebe, her attempts at charity seemed like a tiny drop of goodwill in an ocean of need. "I counted five children in that apartment, and none of them looked well nourished," she continued. "Surely there must be something more we can do than simply deliver one meal."

"At least these women are willing to have their husbands' babies."

Bebe knew that Mrs. Garner had directed the jibe at her. She had turned twenty in July, she and Horatio had been married for three years, and she had yet to become pregnant. Bebe's insides burned like hot coals as she forced herself to ignore her mother-in-law's barb—just as she ignored countless other barbs every day. As if it were Bebe's fault for being childless! Mrs. Garner herself had produced only one son. Bebe longed to speak her thoughts out loud but didn't dare, and the coals of her anger burned hotter each day.

Her mother-in-law seemed convinced that Bebe was somehow to blame for her childlessness, when the fault rested entirely with Horatio. A man needed to be at home with his wife at night in order to produce babies, and Horatio rarely was. He arrived home with his father at six every evening, swearing that he'd missed Bebe and professing his undying love. He would eat dinner with her and his parents and then go out again.

"I have business to attend to," he would say if she questioned him. She was often asleep when he returned late at night, the smell of alcohol strong on his breath. "So my nightmares won't bother you, my dear one," he explained. The more Horatio drank, the less he resembled the carefree, talkative man she had fallen in love with. The distance between them seemed to be growing wider and wider.

Bebe arose and got dressed long before he did in the morning, steeling herself to endure another long, lonely day with only his mother and her socialite friends for companionship. During the war years, when her life had been a daily struggle of hard labor, she had feared that the work would never end. Now that she didn't have the usual women's chores to do, her empty, work-free life also seemed as though it would never end. She hated her life. Then one night Horatio stopped coming home for dinner altogether.

"Where's Horatio?" Mrs. Garner demanded when Mr. Garner arrived home alone.

"How should I know?" he replied.

Bebe had been waiting for Horatio in the parlor and didn't intend to eavesdrop on his parents' conversation in the foyer, but there was no other way out of the room without being seen. She shrank away from the parlor door as the Garners began shouting at each other by the front staircase.

"Well, he was with you all day at work. Why didn't he come home with you?"

"If you must know, your son hasn't been with me all day at work for a very long time. He fails to show up at all, half the time, nor does he do a full day of work when he does show up. He comes in late every morning and leaves whenever he feels like it."

"Where does he go?"

"How should I know? I have more important things to do than follow him around all day. But I'll tell you this much, I'm not going to put up with it any longer. I hired a new general manager last month to replace him. I warned Horatio that I was going to do it, and now I have. As soon as the fellow learns his way around, Horatio can look for work elsewhere, as far as I'm concerned. I'm taking him off my payroll."

"You can't do that! He's your son."

"No, he's *your* son—you spoiled him shamelessly when he was a boy and—"

"Only because Horatio was so ill."

"—and you're still spoiling him to this day. It's your fault that he never grew up."

"How dare you blame me when the fault is yours? I told you not to force him to go to war. I begged you to hire a substitute for him when his draft notice came. He's our only son! Horatio wept and pleaded with you, too, and you turned a deaf ear."

A chill shivered through Bebe at their words. Horatio had told her the opposite story—that his father had offered to hire a substitute, but he had insisted on fighting. She wanted to believe Horatio's version, except his nightmares told her otherwise. She felt stunned. Duped. He wasn't the man she'd thought he was. And what did he do all day if he wasn't working?

"I thought that going away to war would do him some good," Mr. Garner said. "Make a man out of him."

"Well, you forced him to go and look what happened. He not only came back wounded, he brought home that ridiculous wife of his."

"Well, you can't blame me if he doesn't come home now. He's obviously not very happy with his ridiculous wife or he would be here, wouldn't he?"

Mr. Garner's words hit Bebe with the same shock she'd felt when she'd plunged into the river. Could it be true? Had Horatio stopped loving her? If so, she wanted to sink into the cold, dark water and drown.

Silence settled over the foyer as the Garners stalked off in opposite directions. As soon as the way was clear, Bebe ran upstairs to her room. She refused to come down for dinner and refused the servants' offer of a tray. How could she eat? Horatio didn't love her anymore.

On other nights when Horatio stayed out late, Bebe usually went to sleep before he came home. But tonight she sat up in a chair beside the bed waiting for him, growing angrier and angrier with each passing hour. Horatio was not the man she'd thought she had married. He was an irresponsible liar who seldom went to work, leaving her trapped at home with his hateful mother. He never was going to build a home for her—small or grand. How could he afford one if he never went to work to earn a living?

Anger kept Bebe awake until Horatio stumbled home at two o'clock in the morning. She knew the time by the hall clock, which had chimed every hour, half hour, and quarter hour before he arrived. Horatio blinked when he opened the bedroom door and saw all of the bedroom lamps burning. He shaded his eyes against the brightness. His clothes and hair looked disheveled.

"What are you doing up, my sweet Beatrice? It's very late, you know."

"I know. I've been waiting for you to come home. I need to ask you something."

"What's that, my dear?"

"Do you still love me, Horatio?"

"Of course! Oh, my dearest, how could you even think that I don't love you?" He moved toward her with wavering steps. Drunk.

"You never spend time with me. You didn't even come home for dinner tonight."

"I'm sorry. Something unforeseen came up. But you must believe that I love you, my darling. I adore you."

"I don't know whether to believe you or not, especially when you're like this."

"Like what?"

"You've been drinking. Excessively, it seems." She wanted to confront him with all of the other lies he had told her: how he hadn't really volunteered for the war; how he wasn't going to work every day; how he'd promised to move out of his parents' house and build a house for her. Instead, she continued in a calm voice.

"I don't know what to believe. Where do you go all day and all night, Horatio? You're never home. Your father says you haven't been working at the tannery with him."

His smile faded into a troubled frown. "I hate working there. It's too noisy, for one thing. And Father and I don't get along. He never listens to any of my ideas." Horatio began to undress, kicking off his shoes and dropping his suit coat onto a chair. "He should have given me the foreman's job. It belongs to me. But instead he hired Neal MacLeod, an outsider. So I left."

Horatio turned toward the cupboard where he kept the bottle for his nightly drink, then seemed to change his mind. He wobbled toward Bebe, stopping in front of her chair to face her.

"I wanted to surprise you, Beatrice, but I suppose I'll have to tell you now. I haven't been going to work because I've been looking into another job possibility. I'm tired of being dependent on my father, and I've decided to start a business of my own choosing."

His words offered her a tiny seed of hope, but she was afraid to plant it, afraid that it, too, would shrivel and die. "A job? Doing what?"

"I don't want to say, just yet. I'd rather surprise you. But I'm working on something big."

"Will we be able to move out of your parents' house? They hate me, Horatio, and I'm sick of this boring, shallow life. I want to do something meaningful."

"Yes, my love. We'll move out just as soon as we possibly can." He leaned forward and reached for her hands, gripping them in his. "It will be wonderful with just the two of us. You can do whatever you wish with your time. It will all happen soon, I promise you, my dearest."

"And will you stop drinking, too?"

He released her hands and tugged off his tie, collar, and cuffs, tossing them on the bureau top. He dropped his suspenders and shirt on the floor. "I've tried to stop drinking, Beatrice, you know I have. But the nightmares always begin again."

"But do you have to drink so much? Do you really need to get drunk every night?"

"I don't get drunk—you're exaggerating. Listen, can we talk about this tomorrow? I've had a very long day, and I have a very important appointment tomorrow. Our future is at stake, Beatrice. I need my rest."

She wanted to remind him that he could get all the rest he needed if he hadn't stayed out until two o'clock in the morning, but she held her tongue. He dropped his trousers onto the floor and left them there in a heap, then climbed beneath the covers.

"I've made up my mind, dear Beatrice. I believe I'll accept that business proposition tomorrow. And as soon as the deal is signed, I'll begin looking for a new house for us. Now, please, come to bed, my darling."

Bebe wanted so badly to believe him. She rose from the chair, her muscles stiff with tension, and went around the room picking up his clothes and turning off all the gas lamps. By the time she took off her dressing gown and climbed into bed beside him, he had already passed out.

Horatio slept late the next morning, finally rising at noon. Bebe wondered if he remembered what they had talked about last night—and if he would keep all of his promises. He awoke in such a foul mood that she was afraid to confront him.

"I'll go see about that job now," he said when he'd dressed and had his coffee. He kissed her good-bye and rode off in the family carriage.

Bebe spent the next hour in an agony of waiting. As she paced in their bedroom she tried to think of Horatio's good qualities and the reasons she had married him—but all she could remember were the lies. Maybe he was lying about the important appointment, too, and about the new business venture, and about their new home. When the carriage returned awhile later, she went downstairs to speak with the driver.

"Could you please tell me where you drove my husband?"

His eyes shifted all around. He seemed reluctant to answer. Bebe refused to back down, mustering all of her courage and standing in the man's path as she waited for his reply.

"Same place I take him every day, ma'am—to his gentleman's club on Foster Street."

"I would like you to drive me there. Right now."

Again, the driver hesitated, glancing around as if he wanted to run and hide in the bushes. "Begging your pardon, ma'am . . . but the club is no place for a lady."

"I see. Can you please tell me what Horatio does at this club?"

"It's . . . it's a place where gentlemen go to drink . . . smoke cigars . . . maybe play cards . . ."

"You mean gambling?"

He gave an uneasy shrug. "I can't really say for sure. They don't let me inside, ma'am. And I doubt if they would let you inside, either, even if I did take you there."

"I see."

And she did. There was no important appointment, no new job. There would be no home of their own. Their future was not foremost in Horatio's mind—liquor was. The man she had married was a liar and a fraud. She leaned against the carriage to keep from falling as her world collapsed on its foundations.

"Are you all right, ma'am?"

"Yes. I'll be fine. Wait right here for me, please. I'll be back shortly."

Bebe hurried upstairs to her room, her decision already made. She removed the locket from around her neck for the first time since Horatio had given it to her and laid it on her dressing table.

Then she rifled through Horatio's pants pockets and bureau drawers, collecting all of his loose change and dollar bills. After stuffing a few belongings inside two carpetbags, she hurried downstairs to the waiting carriage. The driver tossed aside his cigarette when he saw her and crushed it beneath his shoe.

"Where to, ma'am?"

"Please take me to the train station."

CHAPTER

13

Bebe didn't realize how much she had missed home until the crowded city was far behind her and acre after acre of rolling farmland and forests came into view. She had spent the night in the train station since there wasn't a train home until morning, praying that Horatio wouldn't come looking for her. Thankfully, he hadn't.

The train reached the station in New Canaan by early afternoon. Bebe breathed a sigh of relief that it wasn't market day, when all of the townsfolk would be milling around. Hopefully, no one would recognize her beneath her veiled hat and city clothes, and she would be able to sneak out of the station and walk home unnoticed. She pulled the hat down low over her face, just to be sure, before stepping off the train. But there on the platform, hurrying to put a small stool in place for the convenience of the passengers, was her brother Franklin. She stared at him in astonishment. His crutches were gone and he was standing on two legs, using Horatio's ebony cane for support. Bebe had to remind herself that her brother was only twenty-three. His trials during the war made him look years older.

"Franklin!"

He looked up at her in surprise. "Bebe? What are you doing here?"

"I could ask you the same question. And why are you wearing that uniform?"

He gave a bashful grin as he helped her down from the train. "I'm the assistant stationmaster now. But . . . why didn't you tell us you were coming? Are you home for a visit?"

Bebe hated to lie, but there were other people on the platform, unloading mail and freight, replenishing the train's supplies of coal and water. If she confessed that she had left her husband and was returning home for good, the news would spread all over New Canaan before she walked through her mother's kitchen door.

"I haven't been home for a visit in three years," she said instead. It was the truth.

"Well, why didn't you tell us you were coming? There's no one here to meet you."

"I wanted to surprise everyone."

"They'll be surprised, all right. I can hardly believe my eyes . . . Say, where's Horatio? Didn't he come?"

Bebe shook her head. She was going to cry, and she didn't want to. She pulled Franklin into her arms, hugging him tightly, avoiding his question. When she held him at arm's length again, she said, "You look wonderful, Franklin. I'm so happy to see you doing so well."

"I get around pretty good these days on my new leg." He glanced around at the flurry of activity on the platform and said, "Listen, I'm supposed to be working. I don't finish until six but I can drive you home then. Can you wait a few hours?"

She shook her head. "I'm eager to see Mama. I don't mind walking home. I've done it before, you know."

Bebe left her two carpetbags with Franklin and walked all the way home from town. Her fancy city shoes pinched her feet so badly that she took them off and carried them the last mile. Hannah was in the garden, hoeing weeds, but as soon as she spotted Bebe, she put aside the hoe and hurried up the road to meet her. Bebe's tears started the moment she felt Hannah's embrace.

"My goodness, Beatrice. Why didn't you write and tell us you were coming for a visit? I would have driven to the station to meet you. Did you see Franklin?"

"Yes, I saw him. And I'm not visiting, Mama, I'm home to stay. I've left Horatio."

"Oh my." Hannah hugged her again, then said, "Let's go inside. I think there's still some coffee in the pot. And I picked rhubarb yesterday and made pies." Neither of them spoke again until Hannah had poured the coffee and had set a slice of pie and a fork on the table in front of Bebe. "Now, tell me why you left your husband, Beatrice. Does he abuse you?"

"No. Horatio has always been gentle and kind. He would never hurt me."

"Does he fail to provide for you?"

"No. Money isn't a problem . . . even though he skips work most of the time. I suppose it will become a problem if he doesn't start working soon. We live with his parents, and they provide everything for us."

"Is there another woman in his life?"

"I don't think so."

Hannah sighed. "Listen, all married couples have disagreements from time to time, but he is still the head of your household and—"

"This isn't a silly disagreement."

"Then why did you leave him?"

"I don't want to be his wife anymore. He's not the man I thought he was when we married. All this time I thought I was the fraud, and I've been trying so hard to become the woman he thought

I was. But now I found out that he's the fraud, Mama. He's been lying to me about everything."

"What aren't you telling me, Beatrice?"

She hesitated. It was a terrible thing to admit that her husband had a weak moral character. And why did she still want to protect him, now that she had left him? She took a breath and finally blurted out the truth. "Horatio is a drunkard. The bottle is his entire life. I thought I could help him. I thought that he would get better—but he's getting worse. And he has been lying to me to cover it up. He has broken every promise he ever made to me. So I left him." She pushed the plate of pie away, uneaten. Her stomach felt as bitter as unsweetened rhubarb.

Mama rose and turned to the stove, poking the coals, checking the stew that was simmering on the back of the stove. Bebe wondered what she was thinking. Mama had tried to warn her before she married Horatio, asking about his faith and questioning her about their shared values. *"Make sure that both you and the man you marry love the Lord even more than each other,"* she had said. Bebe should have listened to her. Horatio had sworn that he was a regular church member, but it had been another lie. He'd only attended services with her half a dozen times in the past three years, sleeping late on Sundays, instead.

When Hannah returned to the table and sat down again, she took Bebe's hands in hers. Her words were unexpected. "You must go back to him, Beatrice."

"Go back! Why? . . . I told you, he's not the man I thought he was."

"Nevertheless, you made a vow before God that you would cleave to him 'for better or for worse, in sickness or in health.' "

"I know, but—"

" 'As long as you both shall live.' "

"But he's a drunkard, Mama. You want me to live with a drunkard?"

"You made those solemn vows to each other before God. If Horatio isn't abusing you, and if he is providing for all of your needs, then you must keep your vows—for better or for worse. I understand that this is one of those 'worse' times, but you made a solemn promise. You have to go home to him."

"Mama, no! Please don't make me go back there."

"It isn't up to me, Beatrice. You promised God. In His eyes, you and Horatio are no longer two separate people. You've become one. And Scripture says, 'What God therefore hath joined together, let not man put asunder.' I would be disobeying Him if I allowed you to stay here."

"But I'm so miserable in Roseton. There's nothing for me to do all day, and his parents hate me, and Horatio doesn't care about me anymore, and I'm so angry with him for lying and for drinking—I don't want to go back to him!"

"You can stay for a visit and take some time to calm down. But you are a married woman now, and the Bible says you must leave your father and mother and cleave to your spouse."

Bebe folded her arms on the table and lowered her head on them. "I can't live that way for the rest of my life!" she wept. "It's like a prison."

"No one says it has to remain that way for the rest of your life. That choice is up to you. You can always pray for your husband. Ask God to help him overcome his weakness. Fight for him. God is stronger than the enemy who has captured Horatio. Do you believe that?"

"I don't want to fight for him. I don't care what happens to him! I'm tired of holding all my feelings inside, tired of trying to be polite to his hateful mother and trying not to nag my husband. I can't stand living there another day!"

Hannah stroked Bebe's hair. "I hear a lot of anger and bitterness,

Beatrice. Even if your circumstances created those feelings, you've been wrong to harbor them and nurture them. Horatio and his family might have helped to sow the seeds, but you're the one who has allowed them to grow in your heart, untended. Bitterness is like a weed. Remember how hard it always was to pull out thistles once they take root? Remember how deep those roots grow, and how if you just snapped off the end of it, the plant would grow right back? You have to dig down deep inside. Let God search your heart. Let Him show you what's there and help you root out all that bitterness. Then you can pray for forgiveness."

"Why should I ask for forgiveness? This is all Horatio's fault."

Mama rose from the table and tied an apron over her dress. She would have to get dinner on the table soon. "You may stay for a few days, Beatrice, and we'll talk some more. I'll pray with you, if you want me to. Once you've asked God to search your heart, you'll be able to go home with a renewed love for your husband. You'll be able to help him. And you'll also be able to show God's grace to his parents."

"They've never liked me, Mama. They're probably glad that I'm gone."

"Nevertheless, it sounds as though they've been showing grace to you if they've been feeding you and clothing you and providing a roof over your head."

Bebe didn't want to hear any more of her mother's advice. And she certainly wasn't going to heed it. The fault in her marriage was Horatio's, not hers. Mama was wrong. And Bebe was never going back to him.

"I'm going for a walk." Bebe knew her mother could use help, but she didn't want to talk about Horatio anymore. She put on her tight-fitting city shoes and went outside. Hannah didn't stop her.

The farm was so beautiful and lush during these early summer months. Bebe had missed the view from the barnyard of rolling hills and fences, the verdant green pastures and trees, the sedate

black-and-white cows grazing in the distance. She could see a wide
swath of azure sky above the Pocono Mountains, and smell fresh
earth-scented air—so different from the city. If Mama wouldn't let
her stay, maybe she could find a job in New Canaan like Franklin
had, or work as a hired girl for one of the town's more prosperous
families. Maybe she could be a schoolteacher. No matter what, she
would never go back to Horatio.

Bebe followed the familiar path beside the pasture that led to
the river and the rope swing. The riverbank had become overgrown
with brush and weeds since she'd left three years ago, and the river
had dried up into a stream half its size. She looked around for the
swing but it was gone. All that remained was a ragged, rotted end
of rope dangling from a branch high above. Bebe felt the loss as
if the swing had been an old friend. She sank down in a heap on
the dusty ground.

*"Let God search your heart,"* Mama had said. Deep down, Bebe
knew that she still loved Horatio—the old Horatio from their days
at the hospital in Philadelphia and when they'd visited Niagara
Falls. She wanted him back.

*Fight for him.*

Bebe remembered how she'd nearly drowned after leaping
from the swing into the river. That's how she felt now—like she was
drowning. She had wanted to die when Mr. Garner said Horatio
must be unhappy with his marriage. But should she let despair
overwhelm her this way? She had fought to survive her plunge
into the river, battling her way back to shore. And if she wanted
to save her marriage, she would have to do battle again. Where
would she ever find the strength?

A long time later, Bebe returned to the farmhouse, still unsure
what to do. Franklin had arrived home for supper and her father
had come in from the barn. "Hello, Papa," she said as she gave
him a brief hug. "It's so good to see you again."

"Where's your husband?"

Bebe glanced at her mother before replying. "Horatio didn't come with me." She hoped her face didn't reveal her emotions as the four of them sat down at the table to eat, along with the hired hand who now worked for her father. Bebe strained for something to say to change the subject. "Mama never mentioned in her letters that you've been working in town," she told Franklin.

"That's because they just hired me about two weeks ago. I can get along pretty good on my new wooden leg, but Pa and I figured out that farming is just too hard for me. Too much mud and manure to slip around on."

"Do you like your new job?" She thought of Horatio and how he hated working at the tannery.

Franklin shrugged. "I'm getting used to it, little by little. Mr. Freeman wants to retire as stationmaster, so if all goes well, I'll be replacing him in a few years."

"Did Franklin tell you that he has a girlfriend in town?" Mama asked. She wore a pleased smile on her face.

"That's wonderful, Franklin. Who is she?"

Franklin's cheeks colored, and Bebe remembered how ghostly pale he had been in the hospital. "Remember Sadie Wilson?" he asked. "Her pa has a farm west of town. I haven't asked her to marry me or anything. She's only my girlfriend." He paused and his blush deepened. "But I think I might like to marry her, if she'll have me. I'm going to save my money to build a house for us in town, near the station."

Bebe had to hold back her tears when she remembered all of Horatio's promises to build a house for her. She hoped Franklin mistook them for tears of happiness. "I wish you and Sadie a lifetime of happiness," she said.

They finished their meal and the rest of the rhubarb pie, then the men went out to do the evening chores while Bebe and her mother washed and dried the dishes. Late in the evening, after her parents had gone to bed, Bebe decided to confide in her brother. "Can I ask you something, Franklin? . . . Do you ever dream about the war?"

He shrugged. "Not really. Why?"

"Horatio has terrible nightmares about the war. He wakes up screaming and trembling. . . . He says that the only way to make the dreams stop is to drink whiskey."

Franklin sighed and sank onto his chair again, massaging his knee. "We both saw some pretty terrible things, Bebe. Men blown to pieces . . . and some of them were our friends." He shook his head as if to erase the image. "Horatio seemed more bothered by sights like that than the rest of us. I always figured it was because he was a city boy and wasn't used to seeing animals slaughtered—all the blood and guts. . . . Yeah, he had a pretty hard time with it. I was surprised he enlisted in the first place, him being wealthy and all. I always gave him a lot of credit for not buying his way out like a lot of other rich fellows did. But it seems like he got sick more often than anyone else and couldn't always make roll call."

"That's because Horatio was weak and ill as a boy," Bebe said. "His mother told me that they nearly lost him several times from pneumonia, pleurisy, influenza . . ." Bebe didn't know why she had come to his defense. Why make excuses for him if she was furious with him?

Franklin nodded. "I remember one doctor who seemed to have it in for Horatio. He kept sending him back to fight, even if he was coughing or feverish. Accused him of faking. Horatio tried to report in sick on that last day when we were both wounded. Said he had the flux real bad, but the doctor sent him right back to fight with the rest of us. Bad luck that he got shot that day."

Bebe wasn't sure she wanted to know the answer to her next question but she asked it anyway. "How did it happen? Did you see him get wounded?"

"You never see the bullets coming, Bebe. We were fighting side by side. Horatio always stuck pretty close to me. Said I was his good luck charm." Franklin smiled crookedly. "Some charm! Anyway, the Rebels were throwing all the ammunition they had at us. I suddenly felt this jolt in my leg like I'd been kicked by a mule. Then unbelievable pain. Blood everywhere. Horatio put down his rifle and helped me tie a tourniquet around my leg like they showed us how to do. Probably saved my life. He was supposed to keep charging forward with all the others, but he didn't. When I finally got up the nerve to look down again and saw what was left of my leg, I passed out. Horatio dragged me back to an aid station. Next time I woke up, he was still there beside me. He'd been wounded in the foot."

"Was it a minie ball?"

"No, a bullet. Doctor said it was from a revolver—like the one Horatio always carried."

"What are you saying? . . . You think Horatio shot himself?" Along with everything else Bebe was discovering about her husband, she was beginning to fear that she had married a coward.

Franklin held up his hands. "I'm not saying anything. He's a good fellow at heart. And quite a talker. He kept us entertained on those long marches and on the nights before a big battle when we were all too keyed up to sleep."

"I wish you would have told me that he drank a lot. I wouldn't have married him if I had known."

Franklin stared at her in surprise. "I didn't know that he drank, Bebe, I swear. I never saw him drinking—least not any more than the rest of us. If he was drinking on the sly, I think I would have known. Why? Is there a problem?"

She shook her head. Horatio's problem was no longer hers. She had left him for good.

Franklin climbed wearily to his feet, hanging on to the arms of the chair for support. "Well, I'm bushed. We should call it a night. Can we talk another time?"

"Sure. And I'm sorry for making you think about the war."

"It doesn't bother me."

She watched him hobble toward the downstairs bedroom that used to belong to their parents. It was his now that he had difficulty climbing stairs. "Franklin?" she called. He stopped and turned to her. "Make sure you keep your promise and get that house built for Sadie, even if it's just a cottage. She won't care how fancy it is if she loves you."

"Hey, don't cry," he said when he saw her tears. Franklin was as awkward with his emotions as their father was, but he limped back over to her. "Are you all right? Can I do anything? You helped me out when I was low, Bebe."

And helping Franklin was how she had met Horatio. She quickly wiped the tears away. "I'll be fine. Good night, Franklin."

The rooster awakened Bebe the next morning at dawn. She joined her mother in the kitchen. Bebe hadn't cooked in three years, but she mixed the dough and rolled out the biscuits as if she'd made them only yesterday. She had missed the sticky warmth of the dough beneath her fingers, the velvety softness of the flour. By trying so hard to be the woman Horatio envisioned her to be, she had lost part of herself. Worse, she didn't like the person she had become, a woman who did nothing productive day after day, living a life of gossip and frivolity. But Bebe also realized as the day progressed that she didn't belong here at home, either. She was no longer a child.

After lunch, she joined Hannah in the vegetable garden. The early summer sunshine warmed her back as she attacked a crop of weeds with the hoe. Hannah knelt in the dirt, thinning a row of young carrot plants. "I'm sorry that your life hasn't been what you'd hoped it would be, Beatrice," she said. "I understand how you feel, because the early years of my marriage were very difficult and lonely for me, too."

"At least Papa was never a drunkard."

"True. But like most women, I also came into my marriage with expectations. I imagined that my home here on the farm would be a little paradise, where Henry and I would work together side by side, sharing our lives and our dreams. But you know what a solitary man your father is. He's a good man, and he lives right before God, but he doesn't have any idea how a woman needs to be loved. His first love is for his land. He knows his farm and his animals inside and out, but he doesn't know me at all."

Bebe stopped and leaned on the hoe, looking down at her mother in surprise. She had never imagined that Hannah was discontented.

"The first years after I married your father I was very lonely and unhappy. Henry never knew how to talk to me. Then the boys came along, one right after the other—and they didn't talk to me very much, either," she said with a little laugh. "I don't think I ever told you how grateful I was for your companionship, Beatrice. But by the time you came along I'd learned to turn to God. We can't expect other people to meet all of our needs, all of the time. Only Christ can do that perfectly. That's why I know that if you turn to Him, you'll find contentment."

Bebe didn't reply. She watched as Hannah moved to the next row of carrot sprouts and began to tend them. "I put in many hours of prayer during those years," she continued. "I figured as long as I was going to be down here on my knees anyway, I may as well pray."

"But trusting God comes easy for you, Mama. You've always been devout."

Hannah shook her head. "A life of faith and prayer doesn't come naturally to me or to anyone else. It grows from tiny seeds that we have to plant and nurture ourselves. What I'm trying to tell you is that my marriage hasn't always been easy, either. I felt, at times, like I was Henry's property, not his partner. That instead of appreciating all the work I did for him, he felt that it was his right and my duty. When we don't get our own way, and when our life doesn't turn out the way we think it should, we face a choice. We can let bitterness grow or let the love of God grow. So instead of becoming bitter toward Henry, I asked God to help me change and to use me for His purposes, not my own."

Bebe laid down the hoe and knelt beside her mother to help finish the row. Hannah's words had moved her, and she felt selfish for thinking only of her own unhappiness. "I never knew you were unhappy, Mama. I don't understand why God would allow anyone to struggle. I thought He loved us."

"He does love us. But as the saying goes, 'Smooth seas don't produce skillful sailors.' It's the rough waters that train us to be His disciples. He uses the turbulent times in our lives to prepare us for His purposes—if we'll let Him. God taught me to see the plight of slaves and have compassion for them because I had once felt so unappreciated and used. That's why I became involved with abolition. The rough seas in my life prepared me to reach out to others."

"You were so courageous, Mama, hiding the slaves the way you did and helping them escape."

"I didn't have any courage, Beatrice. I had God. Over the years, as I drew closer to Him and saw His faithfulness in my life over and over again, I learned to trust Him. But I learned it the hard way—by being tested. That's why I urge you to turn to God. Ask Him to show you how He wants to use your marriage for His glory."

"But I'm miserable there. How can I possibly do any good?"

"There are still many evils in the world, even though slavery has been abolished. And if Horatio can't stop drinking, it sounds like he's as much of a slave as those poor Negroes were. God wants us to fight evil and take part in His redemption. You always said you wanted to do something important with your life, remember? Maybe this is what God is asking you to do."

Bebe wasn't so sure. She was still angry with Horatio, and she still couldn't face the idea of going back to Roseton and living with him and his parents after overhearing their conversation. Yet she couldn't deny what Mama was saying, either. She had long admired Hannah's faith and her willingness to risk going to prison for what she believed.

"How did you know what God wanted you to do, Mama?"

"Have you been reading His Word, Beatrice? It's the best way to get to know God and discover His will. And prayer, of course. I spent a lot of time praying. I did it all day long, while I worked. I still do. And see these weeds we've been attacking?" Hannah yanked out a dandelion and held it up. "They'll take over this garden and choke out all of the good vegetables if we don't get rid of them—every day. We can't see His will clearly until we get rid of our anger and bitterness and all those other weeds that choke out His life. Give up your right to them."

"But Horatio broke my heart. How can I go back to him? I'm not even sure I love him anymore."

"Ask God to heal your broken heart. He can put the pieces back together the right way so you'll be able to love your husband the way God does—forgiving him seventy times seven and wanting only the best for him. Ask God to give you Christ's love for Horatio, not your own imperfect love."

Hannah stood and surveyed the row they had just tended. She offered Bebe a hand and pulled her to her feet. "I won't lie and tell you it will be easy, Beatrice. If you want a fruitful life, it requires a lot of hard work, and daily attention—just like this garden does. But love is the most powerful force there is—Christ's love and our love for one another. It has the power to change us and to save the whole world. It can surely save your husband."

Five days after Bebe arrived at the farm, Horatio drove into the barnyard in a new runabout. Bebe saw him through the kitchen window as she was cleaning strawberries to make jam. For a moment she couldn't breathe. When he drew to a halt, her first impulse was to run upstairs and hide.

"Mama, please! I'm not ready to talk to him yet. Send him away . . . or . . . or tell him I'm not here—"

"He's your husband, Beatrice. You belong with him."

"But I don't want to hear what he has to say. I won't believe a word of his lies anyway."

"You don't have to believe him. But you do have to listen to him with an open heart and with God's love."

"I'm not ready to forgive him. And his parents said such hateful things about me. How can I go back there and live with them? How can I forgive them?"

"Do you deserve forgiveness? None of us do. But we need to forgive each other because God forgave us."

Horatio had walked around to the front of the house. He knocked on the door.

"Go answer it, Beatrice."

"This is too hard! I can't do it!"

"That's what you said during the war when you had to take over your brothers' chores, remember? And do you remember what I told you then? We can do all things through Christ who strengthens us."

Horatio knocked again, louder.

"Go on, Beatrice. I'll be praying for you."

Bebe walked through the house, whispering a prayer for help. She drew a deep breath, then opened the door and looked up at her husband's pale face. He still looked handsome to her with his hair the color of mown hay, and his copper-flecked mustache and beard. His eyes filled with tears.

"I don't blame you for leaving me, Beatrice. I know I lied to you. But I'm telling the truth when I say that I love you. Please forgive me. Please give me another chance."

Bebe couldn't speak through the knot of tears in her throat. Horatio dropped to his knees.

"Please . . . I can't live without you. I don't want to try. I'll change, Beatrice, I can change, I know I can. Can't we please start all over again?"

Bebe longed to believe him. She prayed for the strength to believe him. Then she dropped to her knees, too, and took him in her arms, knowing that she needed forgiveness as much as he did.

Grandma Bebe and I finished the pot of tea at the same time that she finished her story. "So you see, Harriet, I loved Horatio dearly, but liquor had a very tight grip on him at times. We had some wonderful years together when he was sober. But it drove me to my knees—and to the railroad stations to smash whiskey barrels—when he wasn't. Living with him was like soaring on a swing—high in the air one day, feet dragging on the ground the next. But the Lord used the circumstances of my marriage to bring about something good for many, many people."

I stared at Grandma in disbelief. "Was that story supposed to make me eager to get married? I'm sorry, but I still say *no thanks!*"

Grandma Bebe laughed. "You'll have to fall in love in order to understand, Harriet. When you do, I promise you that everything I just told you will make perfect sense."

I was about to ask another question when the telephone rang.

Grandma got up from the table and climbed onto a little stool to answer it. I had always admired Grandma for being among the first people in Roseton to purchase a telephone and to have electricity wired into her home. But the man who'd installed the telephone had hung it too high on the wall for Grandma to reach, insisting that all telephones needed to be hung at the standard height.

"Poppycock!" Grandma had told him. He had ignored her protests and mounted it at the standard height, just the same.

"Hello?" she said into the mouthpiece. "Yes, Lucy. Yes, Harriet is here. . . . Yes, I see . . . I'll tell her, dear. . . . Good-bye." She replaced the receiver and smiled at me as she stepped down from the stool. "Your mother is looking for you. You're needed at home."

"Did she say why she wants me? She's not going to make me go shopping with her, is she? Grandpa Horatio may have had nightmares about the war, but my recurring nightmare is of the time that Mother and Alice made me shop for that horrible dress with all the flounces and frills and furbelows. I don't ever want to—" I stopped short, struck by a newer version of my nightmare. "Mother isn't going to make me dress up in something horrible for The Wedding, is she?"

"Well, you can't go looking like that."

"Why not?" The century was only a few years old, but I'd already discarded my voluminous petticoats in favor of the modern, streamlined look and shorter hemlines. Mother thought I looked scandalous—even though my high-button shoes covered my ankles. "If Mother thinks I'm going to get all done up like a Gibson girl, she's going to be sorely disappointed. I refuse to wear one of those enormous hats with all those ridiculous feathers. And I steadfastly refuse to wear a corset. Ever! Even if I do get a figure someday."

Grandma Bebe rested her hand on my arm. "Calm down, dear. Your mother didn't say anything about shopping for hats or corsets. She would like you to come home and help Alice address her wedding invitations. She said you have lovely penmanship."

I moaned. "Do I have to? You were going to practice your temperance speech on me, remember?"

"Next time, dear."

"And you didn't finish telling your story. What about the right to vote? When did you join the suffragettes?"

"That story can wait for another day."

"Can't I *please* join the suffragettes with you?"

Grandma shook her head. "Your parents said no, and I have to respect their wishes."

I huffed in frustration. "Please don't make me go back to that crazy house."

"Stop being melodramatic, Harriet, and get going." Grandma made sweeping motions as if trying to shoo me out the door with a broom.

I dragged myself to my feet, sighing and making faces, hoping Grandma would feel sorry for me. Instead, she smiled and wiggled her fingers to wave good-bye. I got as far as the back door and turned around.

"Are you sure I can't stay a little longer? You never told me what happened to Horatio. Did he give up the bottle for good that time? You tell all of your stories in bits and pieces, Grandma, and you never finish any of them."

"Another day, Harriet," she called as she walked from the kitchen to her dining room. "Go home."

I realized as I slouched down the street toward home that even though I was thirteen years old, I didn't know what had become of my grandfather. I had never met him, nor had I ever visited his grave.

In fact, I had no idea if Grandfather Horatio was dead or alive.

CHAPTER

14

In the frantic weeks before Alice's wedding, my mother's greatest fear was that Grandma Bebe would get herself arrested again and cause a family scandal. Grandma did have a reputation in town, make no mistake about that. In fact, one of my more memorable fights with the school bully, Tommy O'Reilly, occurred when he started teasing me about her on the way home from school one day.

"Harriet's grandma is a jailbird!" he announced in a singsong voice, loud enough for all of the other kids to hear. His father was the town constable, so he had firsthand knowledge of every arrest in Roseton. I should have ignored him but I didn't.

"I dare you to cross the street and say that to my face!" I yelled in a very unladylike manner. Tommy shouted even louder.

"Jailbird! Jailbird! Harriet's grandma is a jailbird!"

I sprinted across the street and tried to kick him in the shins, but he knew me well enough by then to sidestep my foot. He laughed and said, "You're going to be a criminal just like her!"

I took a swing at him and my fist smacked into his chin. He

howled like a baby. "Ow! Ow! You broke my jaw! I'm telling my father to arrest you!"

"Hit her back," one of his friends advised.

"Naw, let's get out of here. Her whole family is crazy! You'll be sorry someday, Harriet Sherwood!"

I was sorry immediately. My hand hurt so badly I was certain I had broken a few bones. At least my parents never found out about the fight because it hadn't taken place on school property, but my hand was sore for a week.

I hated the fact that Tommy O'Reilly had been right: I did grow up to be a jailbird just like Grandma Bebe. This was only my first offense, but Grandma had been arrested several times, following in the footsteps of her heroine, Carrie Nation, who had a reputation for smashing up saloons with a hatchet. Carrie had an alcoholic husband, as well, but other than that she and my tiny grandmother were as different as night and day. Carrie stood nearly six feet tall and weighed at least one hundred eighty pounds, according to the policemen who were required to arrest her. I read one newspaper account where she described herself as "a bulldog, running along at the feet of Jesus, barking at what He doesn't like." She inspired Grandma's temperance group to adopt some of her hatchet wielding tactics—giving my mother good cause to be worried.

"Why not let me live at Grandma Bebe's house until after the wedding is over?" I asked my mother. "She'll stay out of trouble if I'm with her."

"What about school?"

"I can walk to school from her house. It isn't that much farther." My plan had a dual purpose: It would keep me away from the wedding mania that had taken control of my house, and it would provide me with a new route to school that didn't include crossing paths with Tommy O'Reilly—who might be seeking revenge for his aching jaw and injured dignity.

My mother eventually agreed, and I packed a satchel. Deep inside I hoped that I would get to see my grandmother and her axe in action. That's why I was thrilled when she got a phone call from one of her temperance friends on a Saturday night, and the two of them arranged a meeting. I was even more thrilled when Grandma let me come along with her.

The saloon they had chosen was down by the river near the brickyard. Out of the dozen women who showed up, I was the youngest protester by about fifty years and the only one without gray hair. I craned my neck, trying to get a peek inside the "den of iniquity" while Grandma shouted to the saloon owner through the open door, asking for permission to come inside and pray. She didn't seem surprised when he refused.

"Never mind, ladies. Let's all stand out here near the curb," Grandma said. "Remember, we have strict orders from the police not to block the sidewalk or the doorway."

The women arranged themselves in a long row, and after some preliminary throat clearing we began singing hymns. Horses and wagons drove past us on the street, and laborers hurried by on the sidewalk, but nearly every man raised his hat in respect as he passed. After we'd sung two or three hymns and a small crowd had gathered, one of the ladies told the tearful story of how her son had fallen into the clutches of Demon Rum in a saloon just like this one. When she finished her sad tale, the prayer meeting began—and it lasted so long that I began wishing I had a whiskey barrel to sit on. Finally the prayers tapered off, and we ended the meeting with another hymn. I hoped that the hatchets would come out now and I would witness a little excitement, but the ladies simply wished each other a good night and went home. My first temperance meeting was a great disappointment.

"I don't see how praying and singing hymns is going to accomplish anything," I told Grandma when we returned to her house. "I didn't see any drunks suddenly turning sober."

"Progress doesn't happen overnight, Harriet. But if we close down the saloons one by one, the men will finally get out of that terrible atmosphere. A change of scene always worked very well for Horatio—especially when he took a vacation from the city altogether. I noticed the beneficial effects of good country air for the very first time when he came to fetch me from my father's farm after I ran away. We ended up staying there with my parents for a week. . . ."

*e*

"This week has flown by," Horatio said as he and Bebe walked along the path from the barn to the river. "It's so peaceful compared to the city. I feel different here."

He looked different to Bebe, too. The sun had bronzed his face during their long walks and burnished his hair. His hands no longer shook the way they had at first. "Why don't we move here, Horatio? Maybe Franklin could help you find work in town."

"That's tempting," he said with a sigh. "Especially when I see how happy Franklin is. But I owe a debt of loyalty to my parents. My father worked hard to build up our family's business, and I'm his only son."

"But you hate working at the tannery."

"I know. But I need to try again, for his sake. We need to go home, Beatrice. I think it will be better for both of us this time. And I'm going to keep my promise to build you a house of your own."

Bebe wanted to trust him, but she was still afraid. They walked until they reached the spot where the swing used to be, and as she looked up at the frayed rope she tried not to think of Horatio's other broken promises. She listened in the afternoon stillness to the sound of the wind in the leaves and the murmur of the river.

"Let's build a small house," she told him. "Just big enough for the two of us. I want to cook for you, and—"

"You shouldn't have to cook. I'll hire servants."

"But I like to cook. I've missed being in the kitchen. Besides, my biscuits are much better than the ones your cook makes." She had hoped to make him smile, but he stood looking into the distance, his face somber. Bebe wondered what he was thinking. "Horatio?"

He turned back to her, and his gaze was tender as he studied her face. He loved her. She had no doubt. "Let me hire just one servant then, my sweet Beatrice. I insist. So you won't become overly tired."

She smiled up at him. "Very well. Just one."

"Things will be different this time," he said as he drew her into his arms. "I promise."

They returned home to a reception that was as frigid as the first one had been. It reminded Bebe of the first winter morning every season when she would awaken to a coating of frost on the hardened ground and tree branches that were barren and brittle. She knew from her mother-in-law's expression that Mrs. Garner hadn't hoped for reconciliation. She didn't speak a word to Bebe for three days.

The first thing Bebe did was to throw out the whiskey bottle that Horatio kept in their bedroom. He handed over his key to the liquor cabinet in the drawing room and Bebe made sure it always remained locked.

"I've cancelled my membership in the club downtown," he told her. "I promise I'll stay away from there."

Horatio rose early every morning and went to work with his father, even when his nightmares kept him awake much of the night. Father and son arrived home for dinner together in the evening, and Bebe could see their relationship begin to change. Their conversations flowed more easily and the men seemed much more relaxed at the table. Mrs. Garner remained cool and distant, but Bebe consoled herself with the thought that she and Horatio would be moving out soon. Whenever the family carriage wasn't in use, Bebe borrowed it to search for a home of her own to purchase, unwilling to wait for a new one to be built.

On a warm autumn afternoon three months after she and Horatio reconciled, Bebe found the perfect house. She met Horatio in the foyer the moment he returned from work that evening and told him about the house before he even had time to remove his hat.

"I know it's going to seem small compared to this mansion," she said, "but it will be just right for us. It's in a lovely neighborhood on a quiet street, not too far from the tannery or the center of town. Come with me after dinner and look at it with me. Please, Horatio?"

"If you wish." His voice sounded flat and toneless. She saw none of her own excitement mirrored in his expression. But in spite of his lack interest in the venture, he went to see it with her after dinner. His face fell when he saw it.

"That little cottage? It's much too small, Beatrice. I want something better for you. Why won't you let me build you a proper house? We can hire the same architect that Father used."

"Because it will take too long. I want our own place now. Please? I like this little house."

He was quiet for such a long time that she thought he would refuse. She saw lines around his eyes that she hadn't noticed before, and his face looked strained as he stared at the house. She reached to take his hand, but he held it tightly clenched into a fist. "Is something wrong?" she asked.

He shook his head. "Everything's fine. If you're certain you want this place, I'll go to my lawyer's office tomorrow and ask him to buy it for you." His lack of enthusiasm worried her.

"If . . . if you'd rather not, Horatio—"

"I said I would buy it!" He raised his voice with her for the first time. Tears sprang to her eyes, but he didn't seem to notice. They rode home in silence.

At breakfast the next morning, Horatio still seemed preoccupied. He hadn't said another word to Bebe about the house, and she was afraid to raise the subject again. She watched him poking at his eggs while his father silently read the newspaper and decided not to remind him of his promise. Maybe he would be in a better mood that evening.

Mr. Garner folded the newspaper and rang for his carriage. "You ready?" he asked Horatio. He nodded and pushed away his untouched plate.

Bebe gave his arm a gentle squeeze as he rose to his feet. "I'll see you tonight," she whispered. She remained at the table to finish her tea as the men headed toward the front door. A moment later she heard a loud thud, as if someone had dropped a sack of grain.

"Father!" Horatio shouted. "Help! Somebody, help!"

Bebe ran out to the foyer and saw that Mr. Garner had collapsed to the floor. His face was the color of ashes, his arms and legs splayed lifelessly. Horatio dropped to his knees beside him and lifted his head. "Father? . . . Father!"

Bebe flung open the front door and called to the waiting carriage driver. "Fetch the doctor! Hurry! It's an emergency!"

But moments after he'd collapsed, Mr. Garner died in Horatio's arms.

Bebe stayed close to Horatio's side for the next three days, throughout the wake and the funeral. His spirits had plummeted into a depression that was as deep and dark as the grave they had dug for his father. Horatio barely spoke. He closed his eyes as the men lowered the casket into the ground. Bebe gripped her husband's hand, trying to will her own strength into him. They rode home in the carriage together after the graveside service, but he wouldn't come into the house.

"I need to go to the tannery," he said. "Father left some unfinished business that I need to take care of."

"Let me go with you, Horatio. I'm sure it will be hard for you to go into your father's office all by yourself and—"

"I would prefer to do it alone. I'll be home shortly." She released his hand reluctantly and climbed down from the carriage. When she looked back to where he still sat, he seemed to have shriveled in size, like bread dough that had been punched down, releasing all the air.

He arrived home after midnight. Drunk.

Bebe's anger kindled when he staggered into their bedroom, bumping into a chest of drawers, knocking over a chair. "How could you, Horatio! You promised me you wouldn't start drinking again and—"

"He was my father!" he shouted. "And he's *gone!*"

The anguish in his voice tingled through her. Bebe laid aside her own anger to offer Horatio comfort instead of condemnation. "Thank goodness you made your peace with him, Horatio. Your father was so glad to have you working with him these past few months, wasn't he? At least you had that time together."

Horatio stood with his fists clenched, just as he had when they'd looked at the little cottage together three days ago. His eyes looked dull and lifeless. "My father fell down dead right beside me . . . I couldn't do anything for him."

"It wasn't your fault that he died. There was nothing you could have done." But Horatio stared straight ahead, not at Bebe, and she saw the gleam of tears in his eyes. He looked as fragile as glass, as though he might shatter if tipped the wrong way, if she said the wrong words. "Horatio, talk to me," she begged.

"Did I ever tell you about my friends? Jacob Miller and Peter Griffin? We met during the war. . . . One day we were all charging forward with our bayonets fixed, one fellow on either side of me. . . ." Horatio held up an imaginary rifle and stumbled forward a few steps to demonstrate. "Then they both fell down dead, just like that . . . and I was left standing. I don't know why God would do that, do you, Beatrice?"

"That's something only He can know."

"So do you know what I did that day? I wasn't wounded, but I dropped down on the ground, same as them. . . ." Horatio sagged to the floor. "And I covered my head, and I . . ." He fell facedown, weeping, his arms folded over his head. Bebe leaped from the bed and sank down beside him to comfort him.

"It's all in the past, Horatio. It happened a long time ago. There was nothing you could have done—"

"Yes there was!" He raised his head to glare at her. "I could have stood up and fought like a man. But I was a coward, Bebe . . . and my father knew it, too. I didn't want to go to war, but he made me go. He refused to pay the money and forced me to go!"

"Shh . . . shh . . ." She pulled him close and sat with his head on her chest, stroking his hair.

"Your brother Franklin wasn't a coward. He wasn't afraid of anything. But when Franklin fell . . . when the Rebels shot him in the leg, I—"

"Hush now!" Bebe put her hand over his mouth to cut off his words, afraid of what else he might confess. He pushed her hand away.

"First thing tomorrow, I'm going to go down and enlist. I'll go out West and fight the Indians and prove to my father that I'm not a coward."

"No, Horatio. Tomorrow you're going to go down and run the tannery in your father's place. You can prove yourself to him that way."

He shook his head. "I don't think I can. Running that place is . . . is too much for me . . . and I . . . I feel like I'm drowning."

Bebe could see how overwhelmed he was. No wonder he had started drinking again. Horatio had never liked working at the tannery in the first place, and now he was in charge of it. She hugged him tightly, rocking him. "You can do it, darling. I believe in you."

He clung to her like a child. "I'm so sorry, Beatrice, but having a drink was the only way that I could cope. You understand, don't you? Just one drink . . . ?"

"We'll start all over again tomorrow." She held him until he relaxed and his breathing eased, then helped him to his feet to undress.

"I never bought that little house you wanted. I promised I would, and now—"

"That doesn't matter right now. Let's get you into bed."

"But don't you see? Now I can't keep my promise. My father is dead, and I own this house."

Bebe froze. "Doesn't it belong to your mother?"

He shook his head. "It's mine . . . yours and mine."

"But what about your mother? Where will she live?"

"She'll live here, too. We have to take care of her from now on."

Bebe fought the urge to moan. She wanted her own house, far away from Mrs. Garner. She wanted Horatio all to herself. She hated this monstrous house and the three years of bad memories that it held. She had hoped to move out soon so she wouldn't have to see her mother-in-law anymore. For the past three days, Mrs. Garner had been insufferable as the grieving widow—more so because Bebe had never seen any sign of affection between the Garners, much less love.

As Bebe's anger and bitterness sprouted and bloomed, she tried to recall the advice her mother had given her. Mama would say that she needed to change her attitude toward her mother-in-law and learn to love her. She would tell Bebe to let go of her plans and make the best of her situation. Again.

Wasn't that what she had been doing all her life?

Horatio passed out quickly once she helped him into bed. But Bebe lay awake for a long time, unable to sleep.

Bebe wasn't surprised when Horatio was too ill the next morning to get up and go to work. He didn't seem to recall last night's conversation or that he had confessed to being a coward. She left him in bed and went downstairs to eat breakfast alone. The dining room looked the way it always had, with the chafing dishes on the buffet, but now Bebe was the only one at the table. The room was so quiet that she could hear the case clock ticking out in the hallway and the low rumble of the servants' voices in the kitchen. She looked at Mr. Garner's empty chair and marveled at how quickly life could change. Why did he have to die now, just when she and Horatio were going to move out of this place and away from his mother?

Bebe folded her arms on the table and lowered her head onto them. She didn't want her love for Horatio to slowly erode again, but if he continued to drink she feared that it might. The only thing she could think of to do was to pray.

Her prayers, it seemed, went unanswered. Horatio's one night of drinking turned into two, then three. Mrs. Garner was no help to him or anyone else. She remained in her bedroom, consoled by the laudanum pills that the family doctor had prescribed. Bebe felt utterly alone. When she could no longer stand the silence in the cold, echoing house, she decided to follow the maid upstairs when she took Mrs. Garner her breakfast, determined to offer comfort.

Bebe's mother-in-law looked years older, lying in the rumpled bed with her hair loose and disheveled. "Leave the tray on the table," she mumbled to the maid. The girl obeyed, then quickly left the room. Bebe cleared her throat.

"Mrs. Garner? Is there anything I can do for you? I'd like to help."

Mrs. Garner rolled over to face her, frowning. She looked Bebe up and down for a moment, as if wondering who she was and where she'd come from, then pointed to the pile of condolence cards heaped on her nightstand. "You can write thank-you notes on the family's behalf . . . and you can leave me alone." Bebe scooped up the cards and backed from the room.

One week after her father-in-law's death, Bebe was writing notes at the desk in the parlor when someone arrived at the door. "My name is Neal MacLeod," she heard him say to the butler. "I'm the foreman down at the tannery. Might I speak with Horatio Garner, please?"

Horatio was still in bed, of course, passed out cold at eleven o'clock in the morning. Bebe hurried out to the hall, and when she saw a ruddy young man about the same age as Horatio standing in the doorway, she could only stare in surprise.

"Excuse me . . . did I understand correctly that you're the foreman down at the tannery?"

"Yes, ma'am. Neal MacLeod." He swept off his hat and bowed slightly.

No wonder Horatio had viewed MacLeod as a rival. No wonder

he had been angry with his father for hiring him. He looked no older or more experienced than Horatio was.

"I'm Beatrice Garner, Horatio's wife." She offered her hand, and it seemed to disappear inside his large, freckled one. "I saw you at the funeral, but we weren't properly introduced."

Neal MacLeod reminded Bebe of one of her father's yearling calves—sturdy and square and large-boned, with all of the latent power of a bull but none of the brashness. His round boyish face and gentle nature made her feel as comfortable with him as with her own brothers.

"My husband isn't feeling well, Mr. MacLeod. May I relay a message to him?"

"I wouldn't want to trouble you, ma'am. I understand that your household is still in mourning. I'll come back another time." He ducked his head shyly and began backing away.

"Wait. Please. It's no trouble at all, Mr. MacLeod, I assure you. Especially if it's important. Won't you please come into the parlor and have a seat?"

He seemed to step carefully as he followed her into the over-stuffed parlor, as if picking his way across a stream on uneven stones. He gazed around uncomfortably at the abundant bric-a-brac just as Bebe had the first time, then sat down on the very edge of the sofa, gripping his hat in his hands. Why would her father-in-law, known to be a ruthless businessman, hire such a gentle, unassuming man to run his tannery? Could it be that MacLeod's lumbering physique discouraged arguments among the workers or threats of labor unrest? Judging by his deferential manner and threadbare suit, he probably had grown up in The Flats alongside the other workers.

"Tell me what brings you here, Mr. MacLeod?"

"First of all, please extend my sympathy to your family once again for their loss. Mr. Garner was a very fine man and—" His voice faltered as he choked back his grief. Bebe had no doubt that it was genuine, and it surprised her.

"You were fond of him, weren't you?" She saw his eyes glisten as he nodded.

"He was like a father to me, ma'am. I will miss him. . . . Excuse me . . ." He cleared his throat.

Bebe waited, liking Neal MacLeod more and more every minute.

"I understand that your husband, Horatio Garner, will take over for his father according to the terms of his will. And I know that in the past he didn't always agree with his father's decisions and even argued against some of them. I've been running the tannery the same as usual for the past week, but I've begun to worry that I've been too presumptuous. I came here to ask your husband if I should continue with the plans that his father set in motion before he died, or if he—young Mr. Garner, that is—has different plans."

Bebe's stomach turned over in dread. Horatio wasn't capable of running the business in his present condition—and perhaps not even when he was sober. His father hadn't seemed to trust him and had hired MacLeod precisely for that reason. Nor had Mr. Garner promoted Horatio to the foreman's position even after three months of sobriety. The fact that Horatio hadn't always agreed with his father's more experienced decisions made Bebe feel ill. Might his decisions sink the company, now that he was at the helm?

"I see," Bebe murmured. "I'll certainly convey your message to my husband, Mr. MacLeod. But in the meantime, I don't see how it would be presumptuous of you in the least if you continued to operate the tannery the way you did when Mr. Garner was alive. I'm certain that Horatio would trust your judgment completely until he's feeling better."

And then what would happen? Would Horatio fire Neal MacLeod when he did return to work? Bebe feared that he would. The young foreman's plain, honest face revealed that he had arrived here fearing the same thing. And she had done nothing to relieve those fears.

MacLeod rose to his feet, squaring his broad shoulders. "Thank you, ma'am. I will continue the daily operations as usual, for now. Please tell your husband that I hope he feels better soon. I know that there will be documents that will require his signature, and while I have the authorization to sign in some instances, I don't in all of them."

Bebe remained seated as another wave of fear washed over her. Horatio's oversight would be required soon. If he didn't pull himself together, the business could suffer serious consequences.

"You are welcome to bring the papers here for Horatio's signature whenever necessary, Mr. MacLeod. I'm not certain how long it will be until he's well." Her future rested in his drunken, shaking hands. If only Horatio could go back to her family's farm to dry out again, as he had the last time. If only the farm wasn't so far away. As she finally stood to walk the foreman to the door, Bebe struggled to think of a way to convince Horatio to make the trip.

"We may be leaving the city for a few days so that my husband can rest and recuperate in the countryside. It's so much better for him, you see."

MacLeod nodded. "I know that your father-in-law always enjoyed visiting his fishing cabin up on Iroquois Lake. I can see how spending some time up there might bring consolation. It shocked all of us when he died so suddenly."

Bebe hadn't known about the existence of such a cabin, but she nodded as if she had. "Thank you for coming, Mr. MacLeod. I'm certain that Horatio will be back to work very soon."

As soon as MacLeod left, Bebe hurried upstairs and began

packing two satchels with clothing and toiletries for Horatio and herself. The foreman's visit had fueled her rising fears for the future, but he'd also given her hope for a way to help Horatio. He heard her rustling through the bureau drawers and rolled over in bed to face her, squinting in the light.

"What are you doing, Beatrice? Must you make so much noise? What time is it?"

*Time for things to change,* she wanted to tell him. But she didn't, aware that she needed to console him and coax him, not confront him. "Have you ever been to your father's fishing cabin on Iroquois Lake?" she asked.

"Yes, of course. Why?"

"I think we should go there for a few days."

"What are you talking about?"

"The factory foreman was just here. You're needed at work. He says there are questions for you to answer and papers for you to sign, and you can't do your work when you've been drinking this way."

"I don't think I can—"

"Nothing can bring your father back, Horatio. But if you loved him—and if you love me—then you need to take charge of the business that he worked his entire life to build. You need to stop drinking. And you need to keep all of your promises to me—" Fear and grief choked Bebe's voice. She couldn't finish.

Horatio closed his eyes. "You don't know how hard this is for me. I want to stop . . . and I don't mean to drink so much, but I . . ." He sank back against the pillows and covered his face.

Bebe quickly wiped her own tears. "I know it's hard. But maybe if we went to the lake for a few days, just the two of us . . . Remember how peaceful and rested you felt when you visited our farm?"

"I don't think I can—"

"You have to!" she shouted. She hadn't meant to, but fear drove her to it. "I can't live this way and neither can you!" He stared at her as if she had slapped him. Bebe swallowed, forcing herself to speak calmly. "Please, Horatio."

When he finally agreed, Bebe immediately ordered the driver to prepare the carriage before Horatio could change his mind. "Please pack a hamper of food for us," she told the cook. "Enough for three or four days." All the while, Bebe kept a close eye on Horatio to make sure he didn't bring along any alcohol.

"Do you know the way to Mr. Garner's fishing cabin?" she asked the driver as he loaded their belongings into the carriage.

"Yes, ma'am. It's about an hour's drive outside of town, up the mountain."

Horatio was silent and sullen throughout the trip, slumping forward on the seat with his head in his hands, elbows on his thighs. He seemed oblivious to the beauty all around him, and the flaming colors of the changing leaves. Bebe sat back and enjoyed the view of the countryside, trying to let it soothe her, praying that this cure would work. The road followed the same river that flowed through Roseton, climbing steadily uphill until it reached Iroquois Lake at the top of the mountain. The mirror-like lake was peaceful and serene, surrounded by a forest that was so quiet Bebe could hear her own heartbeat. She wished they had brought enough food for a month.

"It's beautiful up here, isn't it Horatio?"

"I suppose so. The lake is man-made, you know. They dammed up the river about ten years ago to form a reservoir for the city."

The carriage halted in front of a rustic cabin with log walls and a stone fireplace for heat. The driver had to kick the swollen door a few times before it would open. Bebe followed him inside. Judging by the cobwebs on the rafters and the mice nests in the corners, the cabin had been vacant for quite some time. Puffs of dust trailed behind Bebe as she crossed the room to open a window. The curtains crumbled in her fingers when she touched them.

Horatio stood in the doorway, watching her. "This is much too crude for you, my darling. We should let the servants come up here first and clean it before we try to stay here. It's uninhabit-able. Let's go back."

"I don't mind doing a little cleaning," she replied. "I can have this place tidy in no time, you'll see. I love it up here." She brushed the dust off her hands as the driver brought in the last of their things. "Please come back for us in four days' time," she told him. She feared it wasn't long enough, but that was as long as Horatio would agree to stay. He stood outside and watched as the carriage drove away as if watching the last ship set sail, leaving them stranded on a deserted island. During the drive up to the cabin the sky had been steadily lowering on them like a gray wool blanket, but the moment the carriage disappeared from sight among the trees, the blanket split open and rain began to pour down. It rained for the entire four days they were there.

Horatio's recovery was much rougher than the last time. His moods rose and plummeted from high to low, from anger to despair, as if he were on a swing and couldn't jump off. Bebe read books to him, prayed for him, talked to him. They took walks together in the dripping woods whenever the rain let up—which wasn't often. Some evenings they stood on the fishing pier in front of the Garners' cabin in the cold drizzle and watched the waves wash over the planks. Little by little Bebe encouraged Horatio to talk about his father.

"I could never please him, Beatrice," he said one stormy afternoon as they sat in front of the fire. "I never heard him say that he was proud of me. Not once. Not even during these past few months when I've been working so hard for him."

Bebe leaned into Horatio's shoulder as she listened, grieving for her husband and not for the man who had hurt him so deeply.

"You know what his lawyer told me after he died? My father put a condition in his will that I have to keep Neal MacLeod on as foreman for at least five years after my father's death. Otherwise, I won't inherit anything. What an outrage! He didn't trust me—his own son! He gave my job to a stranger!"

Bebe squeezed his hand a little tighter and tried to form her reply. She knew she should be as outraged as her husband was, but instead she felt relieved to know that Mr. MacLeod would manage the tannery for a while longer. It would give Horatio more time to learn the business—and more time to remain sober. If only Horatio would see him as a friend instead of a rival.

"Don't be so hard on yourself, Horatio. I'm sure your father trusted you. It's just that Mr. MacLeod has had a little more experience than you've had, hasn't he? Your father loved you. He provided well for you, didn't he?"

"I suppose so." He stared into the flames for a long moment before saying, "I never could figure out the connection between my father and Neal MacLeod or why he hired him in the first place. He isn't even from our social class. He grew up in The Flats. He barely has an education."

"I only met him once," she said, "and it was obvious to me that he came from the working class. But please don't hold that against him, Horatio. I grew up poor, too, you know. Would it be fair for your mother and her friends to judge me by where I grew up rather than by the person I am now?"

"That's different."

Bebe wanted to ask how it was different, but she held her tongue. "Can't you try to see Mr. MacLeod as someone who can share the burden and the responsibilities with you?"

"There was always something between him and my father. I can't explain it. . . ."

"Did you ever ask him about it?"

Horatio didn't seem to hear her. He was sunk too deeply in his own misery. "Father used to brag that MacLeod had earned the Medal of Honor for bravery during the war. He worked with some big general or other. Why does everything always come back to that blasted war?"

Bebe had to change the subject before memories of the war pulled Horatio any lower. "Hey, I think the rain has stopped. Let's go fishing. We can use your father's fishing poles." She jumped up. "Do you think they'll still work?"

"My father taught me how to fish when I was a boy. We had some good times up here—when Mother would allow me to come, that is. I told you how sickly I was when I was young, didn't I?"

"You did. Thank goodness you're strong and healthy now." She dragged over a chair to stand on and managed to lift down one of the poles resting on wooden pegs on the wall, sneezing from the dust. "Look, these rods still have strings and hooks on them. We can dig up a few earthworms and we'll be all set."

Horatio hadn't moved. He wore a frown on his face as he watched her. "How do you know so much about fishing?"

"Franklin used to take me with him once in a while. I was pretty good at it, too. Sundown is supposed to be a great time to catch fish. Come on." She held out her hand to him.

Horatio rose from the sagging sofa like a man twice his age, and they bundled up against the autumn chill. Bebe easily found a few earthworms squirming on the rain-soaked ground, then she and Horatio walked out to the end of the pier together. The wind had stopped blowing, and the lake resembled a wide sheet of smooth gray metal. She watched Horatio untangle one of the poles, attach the bait, and cast his line into the water. The ripple from the hook made an ever-widening circle on the glassy water.

"Look at that," she whispered.

"Look at what?"

"You disturbed the water in only one tiny place, yet the circle is growing wider and wider until it will reach all the way to the shore." She watched as he cast his line, over and over again, and she never grew tired of watching the ripples widen and spread. When a gentle, misting rain began to fall, thousands of tiny raindrops transformed the smooth lake into a mosaic of intersecting ripples. "How could something as tiny as a raindrop create such beauty?" she asked.

Horatio turned to her and caressed her cheek. "I've learned that true beauty sometimes comes in very small packages." He smiled, and for the first time in a very long time, it seemed genuine.

Horatio caught three fish for their dinner. Bebe cleaned them and cooked them in the fireplace in a cast-iron frying pan. "These are the best fish I've ever tasted," he told her.

Later, as Bebe lay in Horatio's arms, listening to the patter of raindrops on the cabin roof, it seemed as though the rain had finally washed away his grief and nourished his withered spirit. He began to talk to her the way he had in the hospital in Philadelphia, and as he spun stories like silk, hour after hour, the beauty of his words made Bebe remember why she had fallen in love with him.

CHAPTER

15

The rain was still falling steadily when the carriage arrived to take Bebe and Horatio home from the cabin. The driver looked drenched and shivery. "Come inside and warm up by the fire," Bebe told him. "I'll fix you a cup of coffee. Your name is Peter, isn't it?"

"Yes, ma'am."

Horatio looked irritated with her. He probably would scold her later for being too friendly with the help, but she didn't care. She didn't view class differences the way Horatio and his mother did, and besides, the driver's hands were raw from the cold. He wrapped them around the coffee cup she gave him and sat down in front of the fire. Horatio stared out of the window at the horses, huddled beneath the woodshed's sloping roof. Silence settled over the three of them.

"Did you have any trouble making it up the mountain in all this rain?" Bebe asked the driver. "I imagine the roads are very muddy by now."

"Yes, ma'am. I ran into some muddy patches along the way, and a few slippery spots with the wet leaves and all. But I don't think we'll get stuck going home. The horses are plenty strong."

Bebe nodded. Rain drummed against the roof and plinked into the tin pan she'd placed below a leak. "We've certainly had a great deal of rain these past few days, haven't we?" she asked. "Has it rained this much back home?"

"Oh yes, ma'am. Some of the folks down in The Flats are having a really rough time of it."

"What do you mean?"

"The river overflowed its banks down there. You almost need a boat to get around in some places. The floodwaters forced a lot of people out of their homes with no place to go."

"What will happen to them? Where will they live?"

Horatio spun around abruptly to face them. "Fortunately, my father had the foresight to build our home on the ridge, overlooking the river. We'll be high and dry, my dear."

"Yes, I know, but—"

"I think we should get going." He scooped up their satchels himself and carried them outside while the driver gulped the rest of his coffee. Bebe quickly doused the fire. She had the unsettled feeling that Horatio was already thinking about his first drink.

Cold rain and low gray skies greeted them when they arrived in town. The road had disappeared completely beneath the floodwaters in several places, forcing the horses to wade or make a wide detour.

"Do you think the tannery will be flooded?" she asked Horatio. "It's closer to the river, isn't it? Maybe we should go there first."

"Nonsense. I want to get you home, where it's warm and dry. I'll head over there and see for myself after I speak with Mother."

Bebe's loneliness returned the moment she walked through the door into the quiet house. "Where's Mother?" Horatio asked the servant who opened the door for them.

"Mrs. Garner is in bed, sir—where she's been for the past four days."

"Is she ill?" Bebe asked.

The butler shook his head. "It's grief, ma'am."

"I'll go up and talk with her," Horatio said.

Bebe didn't volunteer to go with him. Her conscience whispered that she should, but she had no desire at all to see her mother-in-law. Nor would Mrs. Garner be eager to see her. Horatio returned five minutes later.

"She's fine," he assured her. "But I'll ask Dr. Hammond to come by and see her today, just the same."

"Why don't you take your coat off and warm up, Horatio. You're all wet."

He shook his head. "I'm going down to the tannery. I'll be home by dinnertime, my dear."

A shiver of mistrust slithered through Bebe as Horatio kissed her good-bye and left the house. Maybe she should go with him. Maybe she should warn the driver not to take him to any saloons. She should have checked with Mr. MacLeod to see if Horatio kept any alcohol hidden at work. As her suspicions rose as steadily as the river, threatening to overwhelm her, Bebe searched for a distraction. She picked up Mr. Garner's newspaper from the table in the foyer, and carried it into the parlor to read. The unused room felt damp and cold, and she knelt by the hearth to light the logs that the servants had laid in the fireplace. The chill she felt didn't come from the cold, rainy weather but from her fear for Horatio.

She pulled a chair close to the fire and opened the newspaper. Bad news covered every page, drawing her in as she began reading about problems larger than her own. The mayor called the flooding the worst the town had seen in fifty years. Workers filled empty sacks with sand to try to protect the downtown area from the swollen river. Store owners scrambled to move their merchandise to the second floor whenever possible. But worst of all, an outbreak of cholera had already taken two lives down in The Flats.

Bebe closed the paper and stared into the flames. After she'd reconciled with Horatio and returned from her parents' farm three months ago, she had vowed to do something purposeful with her life rather than simply attending social events and delivering food that the servants had prepared. Instead, she had wasted the past few months searching for a house to buy—a house she never would live in. The needs she had just read about seemed enormous, and she longed to keep her promise and do something useful to help. But what could she do?

By the time Bebe finished reading four days' worth of newspapers, the family doctor had arrived to see Mrs. Garner. Bebe poked the fire and added more wood as one of the servants led him upstairs. She felt a tremor of fear when she thought about how helpless and self-pitying Mrs. Garner was—and how weak Horatio was, too. Might she end up just like the two of them someday? Bebe brushed sawdust off her hands and went into the foyer to wait for the doctor.

"Do you have a moment, Dr. Hammond?" she asked when he came downstairs from Mrs. Garner's room. "I would like to ask your advice on what I might do to be of help."

"Don't worry, your mother-in-law should be back to normal soon. Grief affects people in different ways—and the gloomy weather and all this rain haven't helped, either. I suggest you spend some time with her, talk with her, read uplifting books to her to help raise her spirits." He reached to remove his coat from the hall tree.

Bebe looked away so he wouldn't see her irritation. "That wasn't quite what I meant. I was talking about the much greater needs here in Roseton because of all the flooding. I've been reading the newspaper reports and wondered what you can tell me about the cholera outbreak down in The Flats."

"You have nothing at all to worry about. It won't spread up here to this part of town."

She nearly stomped her foot in exasperation. "I'm not concerned for myself. Our tannery workers and their families live down in that area."

The doctor stopped buttoning his coat and studied her for a moment. Bebe grew impatient. "I'm not my mother-in-law, Dr. Hammond. I may appear young and delicate to you, but I am determined to help those poor people if at all possible. I need to know what to do."

He exhaled, and she saw the lines in his face soften. "The cholera is being spread through the sewage. Someone must have brought the disease to town unknowingly—perhaps one of the newer immigrants. With all of this heavy rain we've had, the sewage spilled over into the drinking water. People don't know they're drinking contaminated water and the disease keeps spreading."

"I've visited The Flats on occasion to do charity work. I've seen the open gutters and raw waste. I've also noticed that the sewage is taken care of in this part of town. Why haven't the city officials done something about The Flats long before now? On our farm back home, we kept our barn cleaner than those streets are kept."

"You'll have to ask the mayor and our city councilmen, ma'am."

"Perhaps I will. In the meantime, what can be done for those poor people?"

"The disease could be stopped if they were taught to boil all their drinking water. And once someone becomes ill, people need to avoid contact with contaminated bedding and clothing."

"Is it really that simple?"

"Yes. The problem is, once a mother contracts the disease, her children quickly get sick, as well, because there is no one to care for them or boil their water. The diarrhea can become so severe that if the patient isn't rehydrated, death can occur within several days for an adult, within hours for a child."

"If I gathered together some volunteers, what would we need to do to help?"

"Teach people to boil all of their water. The city is supposed to post signs with the warning—but many of the people in The Flats can't read. Patients that are already ill need to be kept well hydrated with clean drinking water. Get rid of any soiled clothing and bedding—boil it or burn it if you have to—and make sure no one comes in contact with it."

"Would volunteers be in any danger?"

"Not if they're careful. If they scrub their hands in hot soapy water and don't drink any untreated water, they should be fine."

As soon as Dr. Hammond left, Horatio's mother descended the stairs wearing her nightclothes and dressing gown. Her hair hung loose and limp, reaching past her shoulders. She halted on the landing, staring down at Bebe like a hawk watching a mouse.

"Are you feeling better—?"

"I heard what you and Dr. Hammond were discussing just now. I forbid you to get involved, Beatrice."

"But I'm concerned that the cholera outbreak might spread to our workers and their families. Dr. Hammond said it could be stopped with a little effort. Might we ask some of the women we know to help?"

"Absolutely not! I forbid it! You will not embarrass me by making such a request. Women of refinement and delicate sensibilities must be sheltered from such unpleasantness. How can you even think of asking such a thing?"

Bebe felt anger building inside her chest. Mrs. Garner responded to tragedy by taking a dose of laudanum and going to bed. Worse, she had coddled and sheltered Horatio until he was unable to endure the miseries of life without a glass of scotch. But Bebe carefully suppressed her anger before speaking.

"Helping those poor people is the Christian thing to do, Mrs. Garner. And it needs to be done quickly, before more people die."

Her mother-in-law descended the remaining stairs, standing so close that Bebe could see her jaw trembling with rage. "If you step one foot in that neighborhood in the middle of this epidemic, don't you dare come back to my house!"

Bebe took a deep breath. "This is Horatio's house now, and I'm his wife. I know that I need to ask his permission before I go down there, but I'm certain he won't forbid me to help people who are suffering and dying. Now if you'll excuse me, please, I need to change into my work clothes."

She brushed past her mother-in-law and hurried up the stairs, aware that she probably had sacrificed all hope for a peaceful relationship with her. Bebe slammed her bedroom door a little louder than necessary and tore two buttons off her blouse in her haste to change out of her clothes. Mrs. Garner had purchased these clothes for her, and they were as suffocating and pretentious as she was. The woman was heartless. So were all the other women in her social circle. Mrs. Garner probably had been right about one thing: Those snobs would never lower themselves to help someone else, even if it meant saving a life.

Bebe thought of her own mother as she slipped into the dress that Hannah had sewn for her, the one she had worn when she arrived there three years ago. If only she could be more like Hannah, whose gentle, loving spirit never seemed to waver. But Bebe despaired of ever becoming like her mother.

She sighed and dropped to her hands and knees to search for her sturdy work shoes from the farm, digging through the back of the wardrobe. Horatio had nearly convinced her to throw them away since they were too small for any of the servants to wear, but Bebe's frugality hadn't allowed her to toss out perfectly good shoes.

She tried to think of someone else who might volunteer to help her, and thought of the tannery foreman, Neal MacLeod. If his wife had grown up in The Flats as he had, she might know some of the families in that neighborhood. Since Bebe intended to go to the tannery anyway to ask Horatio for his permission, she could easily ask Mr. MacLeod about his wife at the same time.

Bebe hurried down the servants' staircase and out the rear door to avoid running into her mother-in-law again. In her heart she knew that asking for Horatio's permission was simply an excuse to go to the tannery and check up on him. Was he really at work or had he already left for the saloon?

Bebe had never been inside the tannery before and had viewed it only from a distance—a messy, sprawling collection of buildings situated near the railroad tracks and the river. She asked the driver to take her to Horatio's office, and he halted the carriage in front of a long, low building with a small overhanging roof. The aroma of freshly cut wood scented the air as Bebe climbed down, along with the smell of smoke rising from the tall smokestack. But nearly drowning out all the other scents was an animal-like stench she couldn't quite place.

As soon as she walked through the main entrance, Bebe understood what Horatio meant about the terrible noise. The deep rumble of machinery roared in her ears like a dozen locomotives, and she had the urge to put her hands over her ears to drown out the deafening sound. Much worse than the noise was the terrible smell that caught in her throat and made her want to gag. She had grown up on a farm and was used to the odor of animals and manure, but this was something altogether new and horrid—a combination of strong chemicals and putrid flesh.

Her eyes adjusted to the dim light, and she saw that the noise came from several huge machines a few yards away. Two workmen stood in front of each one, feeding hides into the machine's mouth while the monster spit piles of discarded animal fat, flesh and hair at their feet. Another row of workers bent over wooden stands, scraping flesh and hair from animal hides with two-handled blades. Farther back in the shadowy building she glimpsed huge wooden vats and bales of hides stacked in tall bundles.

Poor Horatio, forced to spend his days in such a dreary, airless place. No wonder this job had killed his spirit. No wonder he preferred to remain in bed every morning than to come here. The stench of death was everywhere—and Horatio had experienced his fill of that stench on the battlefield.

As she stood looking all around, trying to decide where to go, she saw Neal MacLeod striding toward her. She had forgotten how tall and solidly built the foreman was—like a walking oak tree.

"If you're looking for your husband, Mrs. Garner, he's upstairs in his office. Would you like me to take you there?"

The relief Bebe felt was like shedding a heavy, wet coat. Horatio was at work, just as he said he would be. "Yes, you may take me to him in a moment. But may I have a word with you first?"

"Certainly, Mrs. Garner."

"I've been reading about the cholera outbreak down in The Flats, and I'm worried about our workers and their families. I just spoke with our family doctor, and he believes the epidemic could be stopped if we gathered some volunteers together and educated the people about the need to boil their drinking water. I'm willing to do that, but I'll need help. I wondered if your wife might be willing to assist me."

He looked away, already shaking his head. "I'm sorry, Mrs. Garner, but—"

"We will be perfectly safe," she said angrily, "as long as we take the precautions that the doctor outlined."

He stared at the floor, rubbing his square chin as if she had landed a punch to his jaw. "You've misunderstood me, Mrs. Garner," he said softly. "I was about to say I'm sorry—but I'm not married."

"Oh." Her anger drained away, replaced by embarrassment.

"But my sister Mary may be willing to help you," he continued. "I share a home with her and my mother. I can give you our address, if you'd like. I think that what you're doing is very courageous."

"My fair Beatrice is undoubtedly courageous," Horatio said as he approached Bebe from behind. She hadn't heard him coming because of the factory noise and his voice startled her. He rested his hands on her shoulders as if staking his claim. "How is it that you've discovered my wife's courage?" he asked his foreman.

Bebe saw MacLeod glance from Horatio to her and back again, as if unsure if he should reply or allow her to explain. She quickly told Horatio about the cholera epidemic and what Dr. Hammond had advised her to do. "You're not going to forbid me to help, are you, Horatio?"

"No, darling. Of course I'm not going to forbid it." But Horatio's cheeks colored as he glanced at MacLeod, and Bebe sensed from the way that he shifted his feet that he might have refused her request if they had been alone. "I'm proud of you for being so brave. You are certain that it is safe, though?"

"Yes, of course. Ask Dr. Hammond."

"Well, then." Horatio smiled. "You had better be on your way while we get back to work."

The carriage driver followed Neal MacLeod's directions, halting in front of a small, plain bungalow on a quiet street. Bebe was surprised to discover that the foreman lived only one block west of the house that she had wanted to buy. She wondered if Horatio had known where MacLeod lived, and if that was the reason he had seemed so tense the day she had taken him to see the house. Bebe suddenly had second thoughts about initiating this friendship. What if it enflamed Horatio's jealousy? She nearly turned away from the door, but Mary MacLeod must have spotted Bebe's carriage through the window because she opened the door before Bebe had a chance to change her mind.

"Please, come inside out of the rain," she said, beckoning to her. Her smile was warm and welcoming. Bebe liked the woman the moment she saw her. Mary was sturdy and large-boned like her brother, with the same ruddy complexion and plain, honest face. Bebe glanced around at the inside of her cottage and wished that she and Horatio lived here instead of in their cold, echoing mansion.

"Thank you so much, Miss MacLeod. I'm Beatrice Garner, Horatio Garner's wife."

"Yes, I know. I saw you at the funeral."

Bebe stared for a moment, too surprised to speak. She could understand why Neal MacLeod would attend Mr. Garner's funeral, but why would his sister? She decided not to pursue it and quickly explained why she had come. "Dr. Hammond assured me that we'll be perfectly safe," she said when she finished, "as long as we're careful to take precautions."

"Of course I'll help you," Mary said without hesitation. She untied her apron, wrapped a warm shawl around her shoulders, and climbed into Bebe's carriage without a second thought. "I'll talk to my minister tonight," Mary promised. "Perhaps we can gather a few more volunteers from my church to help out tomorrow."

"That would be wonderful. I don't think the women from my church would ever volunteer. They're mostly high-society women, and . . . well . . ."

"You don't need to explain," Mary said. "I've lived in Roseton all my life. I understand."

"Back home in New Canaan, the women from my church would gladly help out. Some of them risked their lives to help slaves escape before the war." Bebe listened to the horses' hooves splashing through the rain-drenched streets, then added, "I wish I could attend a different church, but Horatio's family has belonged to this one for several generations."

"And it isn't our business to judge them, is it? The choices people make are between them and God. And may I say that I admire you very much for going against their opinion and doing this, Mrs. Garner."

"Please, call me Bebe."

By the time they arrived in The Flats, Bebe was certain she had found a new friend. In the few minutes that they had conversed, it seemed as though they had always known each other. But they both fell silent when they reached their destination and saw the devastation. Water flooded the streets in every direction as far as Bebe could see. It surrounded all of the houses and tenement buildings until they appeared to be floating in a vast lake.

"This is as far as I can go," the driver told her. "The water is too deep."

"That's fine. We can walk from here." Bebe's concern for the residents increased as she and Mary climbed out of the carriage and waded into the knee-deep water. Bebe headed for the nearest tenement, snatching down one of the signs the city had posted to warn of the cholera epidemic and carrying it with her.

"How many of these people can even read?" she asked.

"Not many," Mary replied. "Most children are forced to drop out of school so they can work and help support their families."

Bebe pointed to the nearest building and said, "Let's start right here."

Shin-deep water filled all of the main floor apartments. The tenants had salvaged whatever items they could from their meager possessions and carried them to the upper floors. Bebe was astonished to see that many of the families were now living in the hallways or on the landings. She saw small children asleep on the floor beside mounds of soggy bedding, cooking pots, and rickety wooden chairs. Some upstairs tenants had taken pity on their neighbors, jamming dozens more people into the apartments on the upper floors.

For the next few hours Bebe went door to door with Mary throughout that first tenement, then to every other home and apartment building on the block, showing residents the sign and explaining what it meant. "Don't drink that water," she warned, pointing to the public faucets. "It isn't safe. It's making people very sick. Drink only boiled water. You must boil all of the water you use from now on."

In house after house they found the main floors flooded and the tenants doing their best to live in despicable conditions. "Doesn't the city realize that these people have no place to live?" Bebe asked her new friend. "I wish we could do something."

"I'll ask our minister if we can open a shelter for some of them at our church—if these people will come to it, that is. They don't always like to accept charity."

Bebe nodded. She thought of all the extra rooms in Horatio's spacious home. They could house entire families there. But she knew better than to extend the offer without Horatio's permission. And she knew that his mother would never allow him to grant it.

Bebe and Mary talked to as many people as they could that afternoon, then promised to come back tomorrow with more help. When she returned home, Bebe put her own cook and all of the maids to work preparing extra food to distribute. They filled crocks and pails with clean drinking water for Bebe to take with her tomorrow. She loaded everything into the carriage early the next morning and stopped to pick up her new friend on the way. Mary had recruited six other women from her church. "And a dozen more ladies are working to turn the church into a temporary shelter," Mary told her. "Others are collecting donations of food and blankets and clothing."

"That's wonderful news, Mary." Bebe knew it was what her own mother would have done—and what all Christians should do—and she made up her mind to live her life differently from then on.

In one of the first tenements Bebe entered, a little girl met her at the door, begging for help. "Please come. My mama is sick. She needs help."

Bebe found the mother and three of her children lying on soiled bedding, sick with cholera. The apartment stank so badly of illness and mildew that Bebe feared she might become sick herself, but she knelt beside the mother's bed with a cup of clean drinking water. "Here, you need to drink this. Your children need water, too."

The woman's lips were parched. She gulped thirstily. She looked both young and old at the same time. "What's your name?" Bebe asked her.

"Millie," she whispered. "Millie White. Please help my babies."

"Don't worry, Mary is taking good care of your children. Let me help you wash and change your clothes and bedding."

"Wait, let me do that job," Mary said, stopping her. "It's not fitting for a woman like you to do it. You shouldn't have to."

"No task is beneath me, Mary. I'll change this bed while you look after the children."

"The baby looks very ill to me," Mary whispered a few minutes later. "He's so weak he can't even swallow."

"I'll run downstairs and have my driver fetch Dr. Hammond."

All day long the women cared for the sick and moved flood

victims to the shelter at the church. Bebe and Mary returned the next day and the next. "You are angels, sent from above," an elderly woman told them.

But even with additional volunteers, their efforts weren't always successful. Four days after Bebe first helped Millie White, she watched helplessly as Millie's baby boy died in his mother's arms. Bebe was so furious that she climbed into her carriage and drove straight to the mayor's office.

"Is the mayor expecting you?" his clerk asked.

"I'm Mrs. Horatio Garner," she said with as much dignity as she could, mindful that she was wearing muddy shoes and dripping work clothes. "The mayor's wife and I belong to the same social circle. I need to have a word with him." When the surprised clerk didn't respond, Bebe stormed past him and through the open door into the mayor's office. He appeared surprised and disgruntled, as if she had awakened him from a nap.

"My name is Mrs. Horatio Garner," she began, calmly enough. "My husband owns the tannery, as you well know. I have been helping out down in The Flats for the past several days, and I thought you should know that people are dying. Needlessly! Every single one of the cholera deaths this past week—including Millie White's infant son who died a few minutes ago—could have been prevented if this city had provided proper sanitation down there."

His obstinate expression never changed. With his long narrow face and overly large ears, he reminded Bebe of one her father's mules. "I don't understand how this concerns you, Mrs. Garner. Your family isn't affected in the least."

His attitude fueled her rage. "It concerns me because these are our workers and their families. We owe them a decent place to live. Furthermore, it concerns me as a citizen of this town, because our public works are supposed to be for the good of all, not just for the wealthy. And finally, it concerns me—as it should you—because the Bible commands us to help the poor."

The mayor looked her up and down. "My wife has mentioned making your acquaintance. She told me that you were . . . unusual." He had the audacity to smile as if she were an entertaining child. "You're not originally from Roseton, are you?"

"What does that have to do with anything?"

"You have no idea how we do things here, so allow me to give you some advice. If you value your husband's reputation in this community, I suggest that you run along home now and leave this business to others."

Bebe wanted to leap across the desk and punch him. "You think this is a joke? How would you like it if I dumped contaminated water into your well or your cistern? How would you like to watch your children die of cholera?"

"Does your husband know you're meddling this way?"

"My husband cares about his workers just as much as I do. And since most of our workers are eligible to vote, perhaps you should care about them, as well. I intend to hold meetings at the tannery and inform our workers of their rights—and of your lack of concern for them during this crisis. The population of The Flats is quite large, you know. We're talking about a sizable group of voters. They may be interested to know how their informed vote can bring about change for their neighborhood. And who knows, perhaps someone from that community might decide to run for councilman—or even mayor."

He pushed papers around on his desk as if Bebe were an annoying fly and he were searching for the swatter. "Are you finished, Mrs. Garner?" he asked without looking up. "I believe I have another appointment."

"I'll see you at the next city council meeting," she said with controlled fury, "along with some citizens from The Flats. We'll see what you have to say then!"

"Women aren't allowed in our council meetings. Only registered voters may attend. Good day."

Bebe had never felt such helpless rage in her life. She stalked out to her waiting carriage, sank down on the seat, and wept with anger and frustration. The driver surely could hear her, but she didn't care. She thought of Millie's heartrending tears as she'd held her lifeless child, and Bebe sobbed harder.

"Shall I take you home, Mrs. Garner?" the driver asked when her tears finally subsided.

"No. Take me back to The Flats, please. I have more work to do."

Horatio stared at Bebe in amazement that evening when she told him about her conversation with the mayor. "You really said all of those things to him, my darling?"

"I would have said a lot more if he had taken me seriously. But he was laughing at me, Horatio!"

"To your face?"

"No . . . but he was laughing inside, I could tell. Lucretia Mott is right, you know. She came to one of our anti-slavery meetings back home and told us that women must win the right to vote. Coldhearted men like the mayor will never have the same compassion for children and poor people that women have. It's going to be up to us to make every neighborhood safe from disease."

By the time the epidemic and the flooding subsided, Bebe and Mary MacLeod had become good friends. "Won't you come inside and share a cup of tea with me?" Mary asked when they finished their last workday together. "Our home isn't fancy, but—"

"I would love a cup of tea," Bebe replied. They sat by a cozy fire in the cottage kitchen, eating Mary's homemade scones.

"I wanted to show you this," Mary said, handing Bebe a

photograph. "He's my fiancé, James Lang. He died at the Battle of Shiloh."

He looked like a boy to Bebe. But hadn't they all been mere boys? "He has a very kind face," she said. "I'm so sorry for your loss."

"I loved him," she said simply. "I still love him. No other man can ever take his place."

"I fell in love with Horatio when I visited my brother Franklin in the army hospital in Philadelphia." Bebe remembered how different Horatio had been back then compared to the Horatio who had to get up and work at the tannery all day.

"Do you hear what everyone in The Flats is saying about you?" Mary asked as she poured more tea. "You have won undying gratitude from the workers and their families."

"I'm not finished down there. The cholera epidemic may be over, but the city still needs to do something about the sewage. Are you willing to fight that battle with me, too, Mary?"

"Of course. Tell me what I can do."

Bebe looked up at her new friend and smiled. Mary might have been large-boned and plain, but her kind, gentle nature made her seem pretty. Mrs. Garner's society friends worked so hard at dressing up the outsides of themselves but they could never compete with Mary's inner loveliness and strength.

"I don't know exactly how I'm going to fight that battle, yet," Bebe said. "We need to figure out a way to storm the city council meeting and get someone's attention. We'll talk about it some more tomorrow."

But the next morning when Bebe tried to get out of bed, the room spun so wildly that she had to close her eyes to make it stop. When she opened them again, her stomach seemed to turn inside out and she was struck by such a violent wave of nausea that she barely made it to the chamber pot before vomiting. Nor could she stop vomiting. Horatio leaped out of bed in a panic, ordering the servants to send for Dr. Hammond, immediately.

"Oh, my darling," he moaned. "I was so afraid you would catch that vile disease."

"It's not cholera," she told him. "Vomiting isn't a symptom."

"Please don't die on me! Please! I can't live without you, Beatrice." He looked so pale and shaken that she wondered if he was ill, too.

"I'll be fine," she assured him. But she wasn't fine. She felt so wretched that she had to lie down again.

Dr. Hammond arrived an hour later. By the time he'd finished examining her, he was smiling as he called Horatio into the bedroom. "I expect your wife to make a full recovery in approximately eight months," he said. "That's when your baby will be born. Congratulations, Mr. Garner."

"M-my baby?" Horatio stammered. "She's having a baby? . . . Oh, my darling, how wonderful!" He broke into a wide grin, then hugged Bebe so tightly she feared her ribs might break. When Horatio finished walking Dr. Hammond to the door, he returned to the bedroom. His handsome face was somber as he took Bebe into his arms again.

"Now listen to me, my dearest. No more excitement of any kind for you. No more trips to The Flats, no arguments with the mayor."

She gently freed herself from his arms and started to get out of bed, feeling much better now that the nausea had passed. "But there's more work to be done down there and—"

"No, Beatrice. I withdraw my permission for you to go down to that place ever again. From now on you need to stay at home. In bed. For the baby's sake."

She tried to laugh away his concern. "Don't be silly, Horatio. Women have babies all the time, and they don't stay in bed."

"I don't care what other women do. You're my wife, and I want you to stay home and not exert yourself. I want to make certain our child is delivered safely into this world."

"But I can still do some sort of charity work even though—"

"No. I would never forgive myself if something happened to you down in that terrible place. I want you to follow Mother's example and be a respectable wife from now on. Women from our social station are supposed to have a proper period of confinement when they're in your condition. I'm sure Mother will explain it to you."

"Your mother hates me, Horatio."

"That isn't true. Please give her a chance, Beatrice. My fondest wish is that you and Mother would become friends."

Bebe could only nod. Her own mother had advised her to make peace with Mrs. Garner, too. "I promise to try, Horatio. Now may I please get out of bed? Mary MacLeod is expecting me to call on her this morning."

"We need to talk about her." Horatio looked like a stern schoolmaster about to scold his pupils. "Now that the flooding has subsided, I don't want you to see her anymore."

"But why not?"

"Why not? I hardly know where to start. The MacLeods are not our kind of people, Beatrice. It's bad enough that Father has saddled me with her brother for the next five years, but I don't need you socializing with the rest of his family, as well. Please respect my wishes, darling."

Bebe felt another wave of dizziness, as if the bedroom walls were floating toward her. "But Mary is my friend. Can't I just visit her now and then?"

Horatio looked wounded. "I've given you a life and a home that many women would envy. Isn't that enough for you? Aren't I enough?"

"Of course you are." Bebe pulled him into her arms so he wouldn't see her tears. If she had to choose between losing her new friend and losing Horatio there was no contest. He was working hard and staying sober, and those were the most important things right now, especially with a baby on the way. But she couldn't help feeling the loss of her friend along with her hopes of living a more meaningful life. She would have to lay aside her own wishes once again, and she didn't want to. She felt the seeds of bitterness and resentment begin to sprout in her heart and recalled Hannah's warning about weeding them out before they grew. If only she knew how to do that.

"I'll do whatever you want," she told Horatio.

*For now*, she said in her heart.

On a warm morning in May of 1869, Bebe went into labor. The delivery proved to be very difficult and painful, lasting nearly two days. Horatio worried and paced and fretted the entire time.

"Your wife is having a hard time," the doctor told him, "because she is so tiny and her baby is so big."

Bebe thought her pain worthwhile, though, when she finally held her daughter in her arms. She was a beautiful baby, ruddy and fair-haired like Horatio. "Are you all right, my darling?" he asked when the doctor finally allowed him into the room.

"I'm fine now. Just very tired." Bebe remembered how disgruntled her own father had been after she'd been born and asked, "Are you disappointed that we didn't have a son, Horatio?"

"Not at all! How could anyone be disappointed in this wonderful child? She is the most beautiful baby in the world!"

"Do you like the name Lucretia? We could call her Lucy." She didn't tell him that she had chosen the name in honor of Lucretia Mott.

"Could we give her my mother's name for her middle name?" he asked.

"Yes, of course."

Horatio lifted Lucretia Frances Garner from Bebe's arms and waltzed slowly around the room with her, talking to her nonstop and telling her what a strong, brave mother she had.

"I'm so tired, Horatio. Can you talk to her later? Lucy and I both need to rest."

"Yes, of course." He gave the baby to the nurse he'd hired and kissed Bebe's forehead. "Go to sleep now, my darling. You deserve a very long nap. The nurse will take good care of both of you."

Bebe sighed and closed her eyes. Moments later, she was asleep.

While she slept, Horatio went downtown to his former club with a fistful of cigars to celebrate his daughter's birth.

He came home roaring drunk.

## 16

My sister Alice's wedding was two weeks away, and I was still safely tucked away at Grandma's house, enjoying the peace and quiet. Then Grandma heard about a big temperance rally that was going to be held in the state capital of Harrisburg. "Should we go, Harriet?" she asked. "It would take us about two hours to drive there."

I felt torn. On the one hand, I had promised my mother that I would keep Grandma Bebe out of trouble so there wouldn't be any family scandals before the wedding. But on the other hand, maybe I finally would get to see some axe-wielding at a gathering this big. "What do people do at these rallies?" I asked her.

"Oh, the speeches are very inspirational. Some of our national leaders will be there, and there is usually a call to sign The Pledge and abstain from alcohol. I heard Frances Willard speak at one rally, but she has since passed away, I'm sorry to say."

"Will Carrie Nation be there?"

"She passed away last year."

"Oh. That's too bad." I was beginning to get the feeling that I had missed the boat when it came to the more exciting exploits of the temperance movement. "I would still like to go, Grandma. Can we? Please?"

Grandma agreed. But when we awoke to a downpour on Saturday she began to have misgivings. "I've driven to Harrisburg in the springtime before," she told me. "The dirt roads can be quite muddy this time of year."

"But we *have* to go! Please, Grandma? Please?" She didn't know it, but I planned to surprise her by signing The Pledge, swearing to forsake all alcoholic beverages for the rest of my life. After hearing about my grandfather, I never wanted to take a single sip. Grandma was going to be so pleased.

We left Roseton early in the morning and made it over the first range of hills without any trouble. We saw some pretty huge puddles in the road, and the mud looked deep and squishy in places, but Grandma steered smoothly around all the obstacles. Twenty minutes into our trip, though, we came to a quagmire that had completely swallowed the road. Grandma stepped on the gas to plow straight through it, but the car never made it to the other side. We ground to a halt, stuck in the mud—sunk clear up to our axles, judging by the spinning sound that the wheels made. A shower of muck sprayed out from the rear wheels and splattered down on the rear window. We were going nowhere. Grandma lifted her foot off the accelerator and let the car engine die.

"Oh, dear," she said with a sigh. "I was afraid this would happen."

I started to open the passenger door, certain that if Grandma knew how to fix a tire, she would surely know how to get us out of this mess, too. But she stopped me before I could climb out.

"Where are you going, Harriet? Stay in the car. It's much too wet and muddy out there. You'll ruin your shoes."

"But we're stuck. Shouldn't we do something? Jack up the car, maybe? Or start pushing?"

"No, we'll just wait. Another car is bound to come along soon and help us out."

I stared at her in disbelief. "But . . . but you said that only women in fairy tales wait to be rescued."

"Harriet dear, neither one of us is capable of getting this car out of the mud by ourselves."

"But you said—"

"I know, I know. But there are exceptions to every rule, and this is one of them."

My disappointment was as deep as the mud. How was I supposed to learn anything about life if Grandma was going to contradict herself? I heaved a loud sigh to let her know how frustrated I was. "First you say, 'Don't wait to be rescued.' Now you say, 'Wait for help.' How am I supposed to know what to do when?"

"Well, I suppose time and experience will teach you the difference."

I sighed again and sat back with my arms folded, waiting for an explanation. Grandma stared at the fog-shrouded mountains in the distance for a long moment. Rain pattered softly against the roof and slid down our windshield like thin, glassy fingers.

"Sometimes you can look at circumstances," she finally said, "and you can clearly see what needs to be done. Take my mother's situation, for instance. She didn't wait for someone else to help the runaway slaves; she did what she could to rescue them herself. And in my own situation, I knew that I had to do whatever I could to rescue Horatio so that he wouldn't drink us all into ruin."

I waved my hand impatiently. "I understand that part. Like you said, 'Only women in fairy tales wait to be rescued.' "

"Yes. But there were other times in my life when I took matters into my own hands, and . . . well, things didn't turn out the way I'd hoped. . . ."

$\backsim$

Bebe sat in the parlor with her four-year-old daughter on her lap and held up two books for her to choose between. "Which story shall we read today, Lucy?"

"Both! I want to hear both of them!"

"No, we have time for only one of them before your nap."

"But I want both!" Lucy pouted.

Reading stories before Lucy's afternoon nap was one of Bebe's favorite rituals, and one of the few times she had Lucy all to herself. Lucy resembled a little angel, with her halo of curly blond hair and her sweet rosy face—but her temperament didn't always match her appearance. Bebe glanced at Lucy's nanny hovering nearby. The woman always gave in to Lucy in order to avoid a temper tantrum, but Bebe was determined not to spoil her only child. She laid one of the books aside.

"If you can't make up your mind, we'll read this one."

"No! I want two books!"

Bebe ignored her daughter's stubbornness and opened the book, hoping Lucy would settle down once they started reading. Several pages into the story, the front doorbell chimed. Bebe paused, waiting for the servants to answer it, listening to hear who it was. Lucy listened, too, and when it became obvious that a deliveryman had arrived at the front door with a package, she slid off Bebe's lap, squealing with delight and clapping her hands. "For me? Is it for me?"

Bebe laid aside the book and followed her to the front hallway.

"Yes, Miss Lucy. It's for you," the butler said. Lucy snatched the package from his hands without a word of thanks and began tearing off the brown paper wrapping, scattering it all over the floor. Mrs. Garner descended the stairs to watch the destruction, wearing a pleased smile on her face.

"I was wondering when my surprise might arrive for you, Lucy.

Open it carefully, dear. You wouldn't want to break it before you've had a chance to play with it, would you?"

Bebe stifled a groan. "Not another toy, Mother Garner. The playroom is overflowing with toys as it is. No child needs that many playthings."

They were expensive toys, too. Last week Mrs. Garner had purchased a wooden rocking horse for Lucy, with a mane and tail made of real horsehair. The week before, she had brought home a stuffed bear with glassy eyes and velvety fur and paws that really moved.

Lucy tore open the box and quickly dug through the straw packing material to retrieve her prize. "Look, Mama! A dolly!"

Bebe crouched beside her daughter. She had to admit that the doll was beautiful—even more so than the five other dolls Lucy already owned. Its hair felt like real human hair and the eyes in its dainty porcelain head opened and closed when Lucy moved her. She even had tiny eyelashes. According to the label, the doll had been imported all the way from Germany.

"She's lovely, Lucy. You must give her a very lovely name to match."

"And you must be careful with her," Mrs. Garner added. "You don't want to get her hair mussed or her clothes wrinkled."

"Aren't toys meant to be played with, Mother Garner?"

The older woman ignored Bebe's question and reached for Lucy's hand. "Come, Lucy dear. Let's go find a place for her in your playroom."

"But it's time for her nap, and—"

"Lucy wants to play with her new doll, don't you, darling?" They walked upstairs together, followed by the nanny.

"Lucy?" Bebe called up the stairs after her. "Did you thank Grandmother Garner for the present?" She didn't reply.

Bebe looked down at the torn paper and straw that Lucy had strewn all over the floor for the servants to clear away. She sighed in frustration and bent to pick up the mess herself. Her daughter was growing into a spoiled, demanding child, who didn't know how to do anything for herself, but whenever Bebe complained to Horatio, he took his mother's side.

"She'll only be a child for a few more years, Beatrice. You want her to grow up happy, don't you?"

"Of course I do." Bebe wanted everyone to be happy—most importantly, Horatio.

His drinking binge following Lucy's birth had lasted nearly a month. Bebe had begged him to stop, appealing to his love for his new daughter and for her. When he finally agreed, she took him up to the fishing cabin for a week. Once again, Horatio sobered up, apologizing and promising that it would never happen again. He had kept his promise for four years now. In return, Bebe had done her best to settle into the Garners' social world at his request, planning dinner parties and open houses and teas, attending social gatherings and balls and fetes. In fact, she was supposed to attend the ribbon cutting ceremony at Roseton's new women's club this afternoon. She wished she didn't have to go.

"I own the tannery now," Horatio had told her. "I have certain duties to perform in this community, and so do you and Mother." Like it or not, those duties included pointless ribbon-cutting ceremonies. Bebe trudged up the stairs to get ready, ignoring the commotion in Lucy's playroom as the nanny tried in vain to coax her into taking a nap.

"Let her stay up and play with her new doll," Bebe heard Mrs. Garner say. "I insist."

Bebe's maid was waiting in her room to help her dress. "Mrs. Garner chose this gown for you to wear today," she said. Bebe nodded, tight-lipped. It seemed as though Horatio's mother made every decision in her life. While the maid tightened her corset laces and slipped the chosen gown over her head, Bebe struggled to stay afloat in a sea of resentment. She hated the control that Mrs. Garner had over her—and now over Lucy. She felt as though she were navigating through rocky waters without a map: praying Horatio would remain sober, trying to please Mother Garner, hoping to maintain a façade of normalcy for her daughter's sake.

As she sat at the dressing table, watching in the mirror as the maid arranged her hair, Bebe thought her life resembled a lavishly written novel without a plot. What good was all of the pageantry and posturing without a purpose? And what good did it do her to look beautiful on the outside when she seethed with frustration and resentment on the inside? She wished she would get pregnant again so she would have something useful to do—and so Lucy wouldn't become so spoiled—but that hadn't happened, either.

Bebe and Mrs. Garner arrived side by side at the ceremony, smiling and greeting the other women as if they were as close as mother and daughter. On lonely afternoons like this one, Bebe longed for a true friend. Her relationships with the other society women were superficial, and none of the women had become what she would call a friend, much less a confidante. She missed Mary MacLeod, even though their friendship had lasted barely a month. After Lucy's birth, she had begged Horatio again and again to allow her to visit Mary, but he always refused.

"Why do you need her?" he had asked. "She's not like us, Beatrice. Please stay away from her."

Three hours after the ribbon-cutting ceremony began, Bebe returned home, her face stiff from holding a phony smile in place all afternoon. She trudged upstairs feeling exhausted, even though she'd done nothing more strenuous than eat *petit fours* and listen to boring speeches. After changing out of her dress, she sat down in her dressing room to read the newspaper. Mr. Garner's subscription had never lapsed, and Bebe had developed the habit of reading the news every day. Occasionally, she would find an article about the Woman Suffrage movement—the paper always described their activities in negative terms, of course—and sometimes an article would mention Lucretia Mott.

But what interested Bebe even more were the descriptions of a temperance crusade that had swept across upstate New York, Ohio, and Michigan this year, quickly gaining momentum. Like the abolition crusades, it had begun when groups of Christian women joined together in prayer meetings, seeking the abolition of all alcoholic beverages. As the movement spread, the women began holding their prayer vigils on the streets outside of saloons until the embarrassed customers went home and the saloon owners caved in to the pressure and closed their doors. So far, the women had driven dozens of saloons out of business.

Bebe cut out all the articles she could find with news of either movement and kept them in a cigar box in her dresser drawer. If Horatio wouldn't allow her to become involved, she could at least enjoy reading about what other women were doing.

Bebe was disappointed to find nothing about either the Temperance or Suffrage movement in today's paper. Instead, every headline and article described the shocking news that yesterday, September 18, 1873, the nation's best-known banking house, Jay Cooke and Company, had collapsed. Business affairs usually were of little interest to Bebe, but she could tell that this news was momentous. She read every word. Experts predicted that more bank failures would quickly follow; that businesses and industries would be forced to close their doors once they could no longer borrow money; that workers would be laid off, leading to labor unrest, riots, and starvation. The newspaper painted such a grim picture that Bebe whispered a prayer that the experts would prove to be wrong.

Late that night, Horatio startled her awake, moaning and thrashing in bed.

"Horatio! Horatio, wake up!" she said, shaking him. His eyes finally flew open and he sat up, looking frantically around the room as if he didn't know where he was. "You were having a nightmare, Horatio. Everything is fine, it was only a bad dream."

She could feel his body trembling, shaking the bed. Sweat drenched his silk pajamas. He groaned and ran his hands through his hair and then climbed out of bed. Bebe got out of bed, too, and started to light a lamp, but he stopped her.

"Don't! I don't want a light on." She tried to draw Horatio into her arms to soothe him, but he refused her consolation, pushing her away. He began to pace as if trapped in a cage with no way out.

"Tell me about your dream, Horatio. Was it the war again?" He shook his head. She could see that he longed for a drink, and she was glad that she had thrown out every drop of alcohol after his father died. She sat on the edge of the bed, still feeling shaky after being startled awake.

"Please tell me what's wrong." He didn't reply. "Talk to me, Horatio. Are you worried about something? I read in the newspaper about the huge bank that went broke—are you afraid it will affect the tannery?"

He finally turned to her, and she could hear the controlled anger in his voice, even though she couldn't see him clearly in the dark. "This house is my refuge, Beatrice. I don't want to talk about work when I'm at home. Besides, you don't need to concern yourself with financial matters. You shouldn't even be reading the newspaper in the first place. Why can't you read *Godey's Lady's Book,* like other women do?"

His words stung and she knew he had meant them to. She lashed back without thinking. "I don't care about the latest fashions. I care about real life! You think I'm too stupid to understand the news, don't you?"

"I didn't say that. But why concern yourself with the world

outside our home? I work hard so that you can be free from worry, like Mother is."

Comparing her to his mother infuriated Bebe. She sprang to her feet. "Well, I'm not stupid! I know that Cooke's was one of our country's largest banks and that business loans are going to be hard to come by in the next few months. I know that if factories like yours can't borrow money to purchase supplies, and if stores can't borrow money to buy stock, then the store shelves are going to be empty by Christmastime and workers are going to be laid off and—"

"Stop it! I never said you were stupid. I said I didn't want to talk about it at home!"

Bebe realized her mistake and softened her tone. "But why can't you share your life with me? We could help each other." She tried to take him into her arms again, but he fended her off.

"You're not the man of the family—I am!" He snatched up his dressing gown and opened the bedroom door. "Go back to sleep. I'm sorry I awakened you." He slammed the bedroom door on his way out.

Bebe sank onto a chair and lowered her face to her lap. She didn't know what to do. She could hear Horatio wandering around downstairs, unable to sleep, but at least he wouldn't find any alcohol. She sat in the chair for the rest of the night, waiting for him to return to bed, but he never did. In the morning, she saw dark circles beneath his eyes as he dressed for work.

"Horatio, I'm sorry for making you angry." She wanted to hold him, but she was afraid to approach him after he'd pushed her away twice last night.

"I'm sorry, too," he said. "About everything." He reached out to her, and the sorrow she saw in his eyes nearly stopped her short. His grief seemed much deeper than regret over a marital spat. And what had he meant by "everything"? She went into his arms and held him tightly, afraid to risk another argument by questioning him.

"I won't be home for supper tonight," he told her. "We are very busy at work right now, and I'm needed there to handle things."

He still held her tightly in his arms, so she couldn't look into his eyes to see if he was lying to her. "Shall I have the servants save dinner for you?" she asked.

"No. I'll be very late." And he was. But Bebe didn't detect the smell of alcohol on his breath when he did return home, and he didn't appear to be drunk.

The following afternoon, Bebe was sitting in the parlor reading in the newspaper about the growing financial crisis when someone arrived at the front door. Lucy, who was supposed to be napping, barreled down the stairs, shouting, "For me? Is it another present for me?"

Bebe laid down the paper and hurried to the door. When she saw that it was the foreman from the tannery asking for Horatio, her stomach clenched in a knot. "Go back upstairs, Lucy. Right now."

"But I want another present!"

Bebe stood aside and waited while the nanny scooped up the struggling child and carried her upstairs. The dread Bebe felt overwhelmed any embarrassment over her daughter's tantrum.

"Won't you come in, Mr. MacLeod?"

He shook his head, choosing to remain on the front step. "I'm very sorry to bother you, Mrs. Garner, but your husband is needed at work. I'm afraid it can't wait until tomorrow."

The knot of pain in her stomach tightened. "Horatio's not here. . . . Isn't he at the tannery?"

MacLeod's face reddened with embarrassment. "Um . . . well . . . no, ma'am. He isn't." He began backing away, preparing to leave. "I'm sorry I bothered you with this."

"Wait . . ." The foreman halted, but he wouldn't meet Bebe's gaze. "How long ago did Horatio leave?" She was trying to convince herself that he had simply gone for a haircut or a shoeshine.

"About three hours ago. . . . I'm sorry. I never would have disturbed you, but he told me he had another headache, and I thought he said he was going home. I must have misunderstood him. I'm sorry." Once again, he began backing away. Once again, she stopped him as dread and suspicion billowed inside her like smoke.

"Wait! Does he complain of headaches often? Has he left work this early before?" MacLeod hesitated as if he didn't want to reply. "I need to know the truth, Mr. MacLeod. I want to do what's best for the tannery, and I want to help my husband. But I can't do either one if I don't know the truth."

"He has been complaining of headaches for some time now," he said, rubbing his jaw. "Lately, it has become a habit for him to leave work early. Usually around noon. I'm sorry."

"Does he return to work, or is he gone for the remainder of the day?" She dreaded hearing his reply.

"He doesn't return, ma'am. Listen, I'm sorry for disturbing you. I wouldn't have bothered you if I had known . . . I'm sorry . . ."

"Stop apologizing and tell me how long he has been doing this."

He cleared his throat. "For about two weeks."

*Two weeks.* What had Horatio been doing all that time? Where had he been going? The pain in Bebe's stomach grew so fierce she wanted to double over. Instead, she held her head high.

"Horatio hasn't been coming home with these headaches. And he didn't come home last night until well after dinner. He told me he was working late."

"I'm sor—" He caught himself and stopped. "I worked late last night and . . . and he wasn't there. Listen, I guess this can wait one more day, Mrs. Garner. I'll talk to him about it tomorrow morning. I'm sorry for bothering you."

"No, wait!" He halted again, and this time Bebe paused until he finally looked up at her. "You need to know the truth, Mr. MacLeod. The reason that Horatio isn't here and the reason he's been lying to you about his headaches is probably because he is down in a men's club or a saloon somewhere, getting drunk."

MacLeod didn't reply. Nor did he appear surprised. His emotions were easy to read on his plain, honest face, and Bebe guessed from his expression that many of Horatio's other actions had begun to make sense to him.

"You aren't surprised, are you, Mr. MacLeod?"

"It does explain some things that have happened lately."

"Like what?"

"I would rather not say." He lowered his gaze again to stare at the ground.

Should she go looking for Horatio? Bebe felt so angry and betrayed that she wanted to storm into his club and confront him. She knew that she should wait until she could let go of her anger and could confront him in love, but she felt no love at all for him at the moment. She had given up everything for him, had agreed to all of his wishes—and he had deceived her.

"You mentioned that you came here on important business, Mr. MacLeod. I would like you to come with me now and help me find my husband. That way, Horatio will know that he can't lie to us anymore."

"I'm sor—" He stopped and cleared his throat again. "Listen, nearly five years have passed since your father-in-law died. Your husband has already made it very clear that I will be fired as soon as the time is up. He was forced to keep me on as foreman according to the terms of Mr. Garner's will, and . . ." He looked very uneasy. "And when he fires me, I'll need a recommendation from him if I hope to find another job. I don't want to do anything to make him angry."

"Horatio can't run the business by himself," Bebe said. "I think you already know that. Especially if he has begun drinking again. And I believe you know what might happen to the tannery during this economic crisis if you're not at the helm."

He didn't reply. His unease grew as he continued to rub his jaw and shuffle his feet, his gaze directed at his shoes. Bebe admired his unwillingness to speak ill of Horatio, even if his motivation was fear of unemployment. But she could no longer disguise her fear from him.

"I know about the banking crisis in this country," she told him. "If Horatio doesn't sober up, we stand to lose everything, don't we? The tannery, all of our income, our savings?"

"Please don't ask me to confront your husband, ma'am. I'm very sorry for disturbing you, but I need to get back to work."

This time he turned around and kept walking without looking back. Bebe closed the front door. It required a great effort on her part to remain calm and not burst into tears of rage and fear and disappointment. Instead, she went out to the carriage house to find the driver. Bebe made up her mind that if Horatio was using the carriage, she would walk downtown alone, searching every men's club in town until she found him and dragged him home. But the driver and all of the horses and vehicles were in the carriage house.

"I need to find my husband," she told him. "He isn't at the tannery. I need you to drive me around to some of the other places he frequents."

The driver didn't reply, but his pained expression told her what she needed to know. He didn't want to be in the middle of this confrontation any more than Mr. MacLeod did.

"I know that you must feel a great deal more loyalty to Horatio than to me," Bebe continued, "but I need your help. If Horatio is drinking during the daytime instead of working, and if we lose the tannery because of it, you could be out of a job."

He lifted a set of reins from a hook on the wall and slowly opened one of the horse stalls to lead the animal out, his reluctance displayed in his every movement. He silently harnessed the horse to the vehicle, then helped Bebe into the carriage. He paused before climbing aboard himself. "I'll take you to a place where he sometimes goes, ma'am."

Bebe closed her eyes. "Thank you," she said softly.

They drove to one of the poorer parts of town and halted in front of a two-story brick building with a striped awning in front. The sign read *Logan's Tavern*. Horatio was frequenting a common saloon. In the middle of the afternoon.

The driver hopped down to help Bebe, but she couldn't seem to move. Lively piano music drifted out of the open door, but the saloon's interior looked very dark, as if the people inside were trying to hide. A deliveryman had propped the door open as he hurried in and out, carrying blocks of ice.

Bebe finally climbed down and went up to the door for a closer look, pausing before entering, waiting for her eyes to adjust to the darkness so she could recognize her husband. Through a haze of cigar smoke, she saw a bartender standing behind a long, wooden counter, wiping glasses. Dozens of liquor bottles filled the shelves behind him, and Bebe fought the urge to pick up the brick that held the door open and hurl it at the shelves, smashing every bottle in the place. She drew a breath to calm herself, inhaling smoke and the yeasty aroma of beer. The row of men who leaned against the counter wore filthy work clothes, their faces smudged with soot and grease, as if they had just finished a day of work and had stopped off for a drink on their way home. Horatio wasn't among them.

Her eyes adjusted a little more and she watched the iceman shove the dripping blocks inside a wooden icebox beside the bar. A rotund man sat on a little round stool, playing an upright piano that sounded as though it needed to be tuned. In between the tinny notes she heard the clink of glasses, the rumble of voices and laughter. The saloon had smoke-stained walls and a wooden floor and a tin ceiling.

In the rear of the long, narrow room, groups of men sat hunched around tables while a woman served drinks to them. One of the men was Horatio. He had a glass in one hand and a fistful of playing cards in the other. He had slung his suit coat over the back of the chair and rolled up his shirtsleeves. He looked happier than Bebe had seen him in months, laughing and tilting his chair back on two legs.

The iceman brushed past her and shoved aside the brick he'd used to prop open the door. Bebe caught the door as it slowly closed, but before she could step inside, the bartender rushed over from behind the counter.

"Whoa, whoa! You can't come in here, lady. Women aren't allowed." He held up his hands to block her path.

"Then kindly send my husband out. His name is Horatio Garner, and he is needed at home."

The man stroked his bushy mustache and shook his head. "I never disturb my customers in the middle of their euchre games. Go home, little lady."

"I said he is needed at home! This is an emergency!" She had raised her voice, hoping Horatio would hear it above the chatter and the music. She hadn't lied about the emergency; Horatio was putting his family's future at risk by neglecting his work at the tannery.

"Sorry, but you'll have to send your driver in to get him. No women allowed." He pushed the door closed in her face.

Bebe returned to the carriage, where the driver stood waiting for her. "I'm sorry," she told him. "I hate to make you take my side over Horatio's, but as I said, you could lose your job if the tannery goes bankrupt. Kindly fetch Mr. Garner for me."

"Yes, ma'am." He shuffled through the door and disappeared inside. Bebe climbed into the carriage to wait. Several minutes passed before he returned with Horatio, and while she waited, Bebe thought of her cigar box full of newspaper articles describing the new women's temperance movement. She felt much too angry to ever kneel in front of this saloon and quietly pray the way those women did. Instead, she envisioned herself throwing bricks through the windows and smashing all the tables and chairs to pieces in anger.

Horatio finally emerged with the driver, wearing a silly grin on his face, as if he wasn't the least bit concerned. "What's the emergency, Bebe?"

"Your foreman came to the house. He needs you at the tannery. You have to come home and sober up so you can go back to work."

He stood staring at her as if he hadn't understood a word she'd said.

"Please get in, Horatio. We need to go home."

The driver had to take his arm and help him climb in. Bebe's tears began to fall as the carriage jolted up the hill toward home. Horatio had brought along an unfinished bottle of vodka, but when Bebe tried to take it from him, he became as stubborn and petulant as Lucy did during one of her tantrums.

"No! You can't have it, Bebe. This is mine. I need it."

She glared at him in disgust and his silly smile vanished.

"Don't look at me like that, Bebe."

"How should I look at you? You're drunk, Horatio. You broke your promise to me."

His eyes filled with tears. "Remember the first time we met in the army hospital? You looked at me as though I had just hung the moon in the sky. I saw it on your face . . . in your eyes. . . . You never look at me that way anymore."

*That's because you're a drunkard,* she wanted to shout. *I gave up all of my own wishes and dreams for you!* But she bit her lip and remained silent.

Horatio finished the vodka at home that evening after locking himself in his father's study. He didn't come upstairs to their bedroom until after midnight. The next morning, when Bebe tried to awaken him for work, he refused to get up.

"Go away and leave me alone," he mumbled.

"Horatio, you have to go to work. Please, for my sake . . . for Lucy's sake . . . for your mother's sake . . ."

He clapped his hands over his ears. "Shut up and leave me alone!"

Bebe got out two satchels and packed clothing for both of them, then shook him awake again. "Everything is ready, Horatio. We can leave for the fishing cabin right away. We'll take Lucy with us this time. She'll like it up there."

"No she won't. She'll hate it."

Bebe knew it was true. Even at four years of age, Lucy was as accustomed to luxury as her grandmother was. Bebe pulled back the covers and tugged on his arm. "Come on, Horatio. You need to go down to the tannery and—"

"I'm never stepping foot in that cursed place ever again!"

She remembered yesterday's visit from the foreman and felt the pain in her stomach return. "Neal MacLeod was here yesterday, and he said there was something important to take care of at work this morning."

Horatio sat up in bed to face her. "Don't ever mention that man's name to me again, do you hear me? And stop telling me what to do, Beatrice. I'm in charge of my life, not you!"

The rage she saw on his face frightened her. She backed up a step. "I know you are in charge, but—"

"All my life, everyone has been telling me what to do. First my mother, then my father, then the army officers . . . Don't you dare start telling me what I have to do, too! This is my life, and I'm never going back to that tannery again! Ever!"

She turned her back on him and walked from the room and then downstairs to the foyer. She needed to get away from him before she said something she would regret. She grabbed her hat and shawl from the hall tree, sick with fear and worry, and hurried outside to the carriage that stood waiting to take Horatio to work. Something was terribly wrong at work, and if Horatio wouldn't go, then she would have to go in his place. She would find out what the crisis was, then return home and beg him to take charge of it. Surely he hadn't meant it when he said he would never go back there again.

She strode through the tannery's main entrance, and the smell of death immediately assaulted her. As she pulled out a handkerchief to cover her nose, she spotted Neal MacLeod examining one of the huge scraping machines as if trying to determine why it had stopped. A workman alerted him to her presence, and he spun around with a look of surprise.

"Mrs. Garner, I hope nothing is wrong."

"May I speak with you for a moment?" She led him further away from the workers so they wouldn't overhear. "Horatio won't get out of bed. He has started on another drinking binge. I know you said yesterday that something important needed his attention, but since it isn't possible for him to attend to it this morning . . ." She paused to swallow her tears. "I-I wondered if you could advise me on the best course of action to take. What exactly is the problem?"

MacLeod hesitated, and she saw his back stiffen. He reminded Bebe of one of her father's mules refusing to follow her order to plow. "Please tell me the truth," she begged. "Is the tannery in financial trouble?"

"Let's go up to the office."

She followed him up a short flight of stairs to a cramped, cluttered office that was not much bigger than her dressing room. Horatio's name was painted in gold lettering on the glass window of the door beneath his father's name. A window on one side of the desk looked down on the tannery floor, offering a view of the workmen and blunting some of the terrible odors and noise. A window on the opposite wall looked out on the tannery yard behind the main building. But that view was far from scenic, marred by untidy storage sheds and a row of railroad cars, a smokestack and water tanks, and piles and piles of tree bark. The river in the distance resembled a sluggish brown smear. Bebe couldn't picture Horatio working in this stifling room all day, nor working down on the factory floor or out in the filthy yard. Yet Neal MacLeod had looked confident and comfortable striding among the men and machines. His work had become part of him. She wondered if Horatio had noticed it, too.

MacLeod closed the door behind them and motioned for Bebe to sit down behind the desk. He pulled up a chair on the other side of it. "Our financial situation is not good, Mrs. Garner. We are nearly out of money. If we can't convince the bank to extend our loan, the tannery will have to close."

Pain gripped Bebe's stomach and twisted it. "Does Horatio know the truth?"

"Yes. I've been begging him to sign these loan forms so we can stay in business, but to be honest, he doesn't seem to care. It's almost as if he wants the tannery to close."

MacLeod paused, and Bebe was surprised to see him struggling to control his emotions. He seemed to care about the tannery's future as much as she did. She wanted to lean on him, and put her trust in his quiet strength and competence. "In that case, you need to take control, Mr. MacLeod. You need to sign the loan forms in his place."

He shook his head. "I can't. I won't be working here much longer. Two weeks ago, your husband went to see his father's attorney to find out exactly when my contract here was finished so he could be rid of me. I don't know what the lawyer told him . . . but that's when he stopped caring about what happened here. That's when he started leaving work early with headaches. I don't have the authority to save this place, even if I wanted to."

Bebe felt her life spinning out of control as if as she were battling a swift current. She remembered the day she had nearly drowned in the river, and once again she was struck by the overwhelming knowledge that no one was going to save her. If she yielded to the current and allowed it to carry her downstream, she would go under. But if she wanted to survive—and if she wanted her family to survive—she would have to fight to stay afloat, fight her way toward the riverbank. She would have to save herself. She gripped the arms of Horatio's chair.

"Then I'll do it. I'll take over for him until he's sober. Give me the loan forms."

The foreman stared at her. "I don't think that's legal—"

"Do you like your job here, Mr. MacLeod?"

"Yes, but—"

"Then we need to make certain that you keep it. Who's going to know that it isn't Horatio's signature, besides you and me?"

He didn't reply. Their staring contest lasted several long moments.

"Are you still unmarried?" she asked him.

"Yes, ma'am."

His answer surprised her. Why would a young, nice-looking

man with a good job be unable to find a wife? "Why is that?" she asked him.

"I support my mother and sister."

"What about your father?"

His face colored slightly, but Bebe couldn't tell what had caused it. "He died," MacLeod said. "Why is my personal life so important to you?"

"I'm sorry if it sounds like I'm prying, Mr. MacLeod, but I need to see where things stand. I read the newspaper every day, so I'm well aware of the bank collapse and the financial crisis. I don't want this tannery to shut down. Too many families are depending on us, including yours and mine. Agreed?"

He nodded slightly. "Agreed."

"Good. Then this is the way it is: Horatio has started on another drinking binge. You and I are the only ones in this place who know the truth. Neither of us knows how long it will last this time. Like it or not, you and I will have to run things until he decides to get sober again." She folded her hands on top of the desk, trying to appear calm. "So. Kindly give me the loan papers to sign."

She watched as MacLeod searched through the stacks of documents on Horatio's desk. Bebe didn't want to run her husband's business any more than she had wanted to do her brothers' chores during the war. *This is temporary,* she told herself—just as she had told herself back then. *It's only until this crisis ends—until Horatio pulls himself together.*

The foreman finally produced the documents and spread them in front of Bebe, pointing to the lines that required a signature. She took Horatio's pen out of the holder and dipped it into the inkwell. When she finished signing them, she stacked them in a neat pile and handed them to MacLeod.

"Kindly take these papers to the bank right away. And let's pray that it isn't too late."

**17**

Bebe tried in vain to get Horatio out of bed and off to work the next morning. When he wouldn't budge, she knew she would have to get dressed and go in his place. "Please tell the driver to prepare the carriage for me right away," she told the serving girl.

"You mean after breakfast, ma'am?"

"No, immediately. I don't want any breakfast." The food would only seethe and boil in her stomach, along with her anger and fear.

"I'll fetch your shawl and bonnet, ma'am."

Bebe had hoped to leave quickly, before encountering her mother-in-law, but Mrs. Garner swished down the stairs in her dressing gown just as Bebe's carriage arrived. "Where do you think you're going?" she asked.

Bebe hesitated, forming her reply. Horatio needed to stop drinking and take responsibility, but that would never happen if she lied for him and pretended nothing was wrong. She needed to tell her mother-in-law the truth.

"I'm not going to cover up for Horatio anymore. He is on a drinking binge, and he is unable to run the tannery."

"That's a lie!" She rushed toward Bebe as if she wanted to strike her. "Horatio has always had health problems, but to accuse him of drinking—"

"This isn't a health problem, it's a drinking problem. He drank so much last night that he can't get out of bed and go to work this morning. So I'm going to work for him."

"That's absurd! It's unseemly! What will people say?"

"The better question is, what will people say if the business fails and we go bankrupt? How will we continue to live in this house or pay the servants or put food on our table if the tannery closes?"

Mrs. Garner glanced around in horror as if one of the servants might have overheard them talking. She lowered her voice to a harsh whisper. "I don't believe any of this. You're exaggerating. What do you know about such things? You're just an ignorant farm girl."

Bebe held her temper at an enormous cost. The pain in her stomach burned like fire. She knew that arguing wouldn't help any of them, and she refused to stoop to Mrs. Garner's level and hurl insults. "If you don't believe me, then go upstairs and speak with your son. And if you want to be helpful, talk some sense into him. Convince him of the need to sober up so his 'ignorant' wife won't have to run the tannery in his place."

"How dare you speak to me this way!"

Bebe clasped her hands together in frustration. "I don't know how else to convince you that I'm telling the truth. This country is in the middle of an economic crisis. If things go the way the experts are predicting, we'll have to cut back on our household expenses and let some of the help go. At the very least, you'll need to stop buying new clothes for yourself and expensive toys for Lucy every week. And if the tannery closes, not only will your fancy dinner parties have to stop, we may not be able to feed our own family. The morning newspaper is in on the breakfast table. You can read about it for yourself."

"You don't know what you're talking about. If my husband were alive—"

"If he were alive, he would tell you the same thing. It's not just our business that's having trouble, but businesses everywhere. I'm sure that finances are getting tight for your friends, too. They're just not admitting it." She paused and took a calming breath. The maid had returned with Bebe's shawl and hat, holding them out to her. "Thank you. I need to leave now. Kindly explain to Lucy that I've gone out."

Helpless dread overwhelmed Bebe as she rode the carriage to work. What would happen to all of them if the business did go bankrupt? Where would they live, how would they survive? Horatio couldn't get another job in his condition even if he did manage to find one somewhere.

How had she ended up living this useless, lonely existence in the first place? She would like nothing more than to go down to the station and board the next train out of town, leaving everyone and everything behind. She was furious with her husband, sick of her mother-in-law. But where would she go? Her life had deteriorated into a huge mess, and she didn't know what to do about it. What could she do?

Bebe dried her tears as the carriage slowed to a halt at the tannery. She lifted her chin and strode inside, passing the foreman's desk and hurrying upstairs to Horatio's office. She hung her hat and shawl on his coat-tree and sat down behind his desk. A moment later, the foreman knocked on her door. "Come in, Mr. MacLeod."

He stood in the doorway, his head inches from the lintel, his broad shoulders filling the frame. "My husband won't be coming to work today," she told him. "I can't convince him to stop drink-ing, so I've decided to take his place."

"I see." He rubbed his chin. He seemed incapable of hiding any of his emotions, and she could tell he was not happy with her decision.

"Together, we're going to figure out a way to keep the tannery going, Mr. MacLeod, and to keep our workers employed and pay back the loan I signed for yesterday. I need you to tell me exactly what's going on so I can decide what else I need to do."

He hesitated for a long moment, and she wondered if he was going to become mulish again and refuse to plow under her orders. But he finally pulled a chair over in front of her desk and sat down across from her, accepting the fact that he needed to work with her.

"Business is slowing down in many industries, not just ours," he began. "More and more of our orders are being cancelled. Customers are reluctant to spend money in this economy. The loan you signed for yesterday will tide us over for a while, but if business doesn't improve, we won't be able to make any payments on it. We may have to lay off some of our workers."

"But they'll need money for food and for a roof over their heads. What will those poor people do?"

"I don't know."

Bebe pressed her fist against her stomach to ease the pain. "The newspapers speak about labor unrest and even riots in other cities because of unemployment. I don't want that to happen here."

"Neither do I." He paused for a moment, then said, "I believe we might be able to ward off some of the labor unrest if you and I spoke honestly with our workers. They respect you, Mrs. Garner, because of the way you helped them during the cholera outbreak. And they know that my family was once just as poor as theirs."

"That's a good idea. And maybe I could speak with some of

the local charities and churches and women's clubs. If I could convince all these groups to coordinate their efforts during the financial crisis, they would be able to provide for more families. Do you think your sister Mary might help me?"

He looked away. "I can't speak for my sister."

"Listen, I know I treated her very badly. I tried to explain everything to her in my letters—I hope she read them. Horatio didn't approve of our friendship, but he promised he would stay sober if I became more involved with his mother's social circle. . . . As you can see, he hasn't kept his promise."

"I'll talk to Mary."

They spent the morning outlining what they would tell their workers and labor leaders, then gathered them together for a meeting shortly before the whistle blew at the end of the day.

They had agreed that MacLeod would speak first. "We will do our best not to cut jobs or hours," he explained. "But we can't increase wages or pay any overtime until this crisis is over. Please work with us. We're trying to keep the factory doors open and keep all of you employed."

"We'll also try to provide the practical help that your families need," Bebe told them when it was her turn. "Please feel free to come to me whenever you need help. Every one of you should have a decent place to live, and none of you should ever have to go hungry."

Bebe spent the next few days meeting with church leaders and women's clubs in an effort to get them to work together. Mary MacLeod went with her, volunteering to serve as coordinator for the combined charities. The work distracted Bebe from her problems with Horatio and with their finances, but by the end of the week, Bebe was able to leave everything in Mary's hands and return to the tannery. The responsibility frightened her. She felt much more capable running a charity than running a business, and she sat behind Horatio's desk wondering where to begin. She was paging through the ledger books and trying to make sense of them when the foreman knocked on the office door.

"Come in, Mr. MacLeod."

"You're back," he said. She could tell by his somber expression that he was not happy about it.

"Listen, I can see that you're uncomfortable with the idea of having a woman in charge of the tannery, and I want you to know that I'm not happy about this arrangement, either. Horatio should be here, not me. But he isn't, and so we'll simply have to make the best of it. Now, kindly sit down and explain these ledger books to me."

MacLeod picked up a chair and dragged it behind the desk beside hers, drawing out the action as if to display his reluctance. But he spent the rest of the morning going over the books with her and answering her questions. When Bebe finally thought she grasped the bigger picture, she sat back with a sigh.

"If I understand what you're saying, there really is nothing we can do about the orders that have been cancelled. But I believe we would be wise to start searching for new markets. There are more uses for leather than simply for shoes. Couldn't we offer to create new leather products along with sole leather in order to win new customers? And if we shaved off our profits and sold our leather for a cheaper price, wouldn't that win more business for us, too?"

"I suggested that we do all of those things, but your husband disagreed with me."

"Well, I agree with you, Mr. MacLeod. I would like you to explain some of the ideas you have for finding these new markets."

He sat back in his chair and studied her. "May I ask how you know all of this, Mrs. Garner?"

Bebe's temper flared. "What do you mean by that?"

"I'm sorry. I meant it as a compliment, and it came out wrong.

It's just that you seem to know how to run a business, and I wondered how you learned."

She shrugged. "It seems like common sense to me . . . and I read the newspaper. Listen, I don't think we need to be so formal. I would like to call you Neal—and please call me Beatrice."

"If you wish."

They worked together all the following week, outlining ideas, forming a plan, delegating duties. When Friday came and the payroll was due, Neal came into her office again. "I hate to mention this, but the five-year anniversary of Mr. Garner's death is next week. I will be working without a contract after that. I know your husband planned to fire me, and—"

"And you know that I can't run this place without you." The thought of losing Neal brought the burning pain to Bebe's stomach again. "I'll speak with Mr. Garner's attorney and have him extend your contract for you."

"Without your husband knowing about it? It won't be valid. The attorney will know very well that Mr. Garner didn't sign it."

"Let me worry about that. Kindly tell me the name of Mr. Garner's attorney."

"William Harris. His office is on Central Avenue."

Bebe went to see him that afternoon and felt even more out of her element than she had when sitting behind Horatio's desk. Legal affairs were a man's domain, not a woman's, and Mr. Harris greeted her with suspicion after his clerk ushered her into his office. He was old enough to be Horatio's father, with a full head of yellowing white hair and a stern expression on his wrinkled face.

"What can I do for you, Mrs. Garner?"

She lifted her chin, reminding herself that the attorney worked for her. She had seen his name in the ledger books for doing legal work for the tannery. "I understand that the contract for Mr.

MacLeod's services as foreman is about to expire. I would like you to draw up a new one for him."

His white eyebrows met in the middle as he pierced Bebe with hawkish eyes. "I don't know why you're attending to this business in place of your husband, Mrs. Garner, but I'm quite certain that Horatio did not wish to extend Neal MacLeod's contract."

"He changed his mind."

"And he sent you here? I'm sorry, Mrs. Garner, but I don't believe you. Can you prove to me that you're authorized to act for Horatio?"

Bebe drew a deep breath. She had proven years ago that she could do men's work, and she knew that she could do Horatio's work, too. She kept her head high and her voice level, trying not to be intimidated by Mr. Harris's gaze or his office full of leather-bound books and framed diplomas. She wondered if her mother had felt this way when she faced the gun-wielding bounty hunters on that long-ago day.

"No, sir. I can't prove that I'm authorized. But I'm going to be honest with you in the hope that it will convince you to help me." She paused until the pain in her stomach eased a bit. "The truth is that my husband has been drinking very heavily for the past few weeks. He is in no condition to run the tannery or make wise decisions. If Mr. MacLeod doesn't continue to work as our foreman, we'll lose everything. But in order for him to work, he needs another contract. Once Horatio sobers up, he can hire or fire whomever he chooses, but in the meantime I have a daughter to support and I don't want to lose our home or our livelihood because of my husband's moral failures. Is that clear enough?"

The attorney looked away while Bebe wiped her tears. When he turned to her again, his eyes had lost their hawkish gleam. "I'm very sorry about your situation, Mrs. Garner. I know that you never would have divulged such personal information unless it was absolutely necessary."

She drew a deep breath. "Will you help me?"

Mr. Harris hesitated, propping his elbows on the desk and lacing his fingers. His lips pursed as if he was carefully considering his response. "What I'm about to tell you," he finally said, "is very confidential. Please understand that I will deny I ever told it to you. Is that clear?"

"Yes."

Mr. Harris paused again, staring at the littered desktop as if trying to decide where to begin. Bebe couldn't imagine what he was about to reveal.

"I was your father-in-law's legal counsel before he died. He told me all about Horatio's weaknesses, so what you've just told me isn't news to me. Mr. Garner asked me to put a provision in his will to keep Neal MacLeod on as manager for five years after his death in order to make certain that Horatio had time to remain sober and learn the business. But there was another reason why he made MacLeod his foreman." He paused, looking her in the eye. "Neal MacLeod is Mr. Garner's illegitimate son. Mary MacLeod is his illegitimate daughter."

Bebe heard the words, but it took a moment for her to comprehend them. The lawyer waited, aware that he had shocked her. She suddenly recalled that Mary MacLeod had attended Mr. Garner's funeral with her brother, and it finally made sense to her.

"Mr. Garner supported the MacLeods while he was alive," Mr. Harris continued, "and he wanted to ensure that they were taken care of after his death. However, he didn't want his wife and son to know the truth. If he had made provision for the MacLeods in his will, the truth would have become obvious."

"His wife doesn't know?"

Mr. Harris shook his head. "As far as I know, she does not."

"Does Horatio know?"

"Not until recently," he said with a sigh. "He came to see me for the same reason that you've come—because five years have elapsed since his father's death, and Horatio was determined to be rid of MacLeod. I asked him about the financial situation at the tannery, and he admitted that the business was in trouble. Before he died, Mr. Garner instructed me to tell Horatio the truth if his mismanagement ever threatened the business—or if he continued to drink. I felt I had no choice but to tell Horatio. The news shocked him, to say the least."

Bebe couldn't speak. She couldn't move. Added to the tannery's financial woes, the shock of this revelation would have given Horatio more than enough reasons to start drinking again.

"I'm sorry if I've shocked you," the lawyer said.

"It-it's not your fault . . . Thank you for telling me."

Poor Horatio. What a terrible blow he must have suffered. He had harbored jealousy toward Neal MacLeod for a long time, but to discover the truth about his father's indiscretions, along with the reason for his favoritism toward his "other" son—it must have been more than Horatio could bear. How could Bebe let him know she sympathized without telling him how she had learned the truth?

But deciding what to say to Horatio would have to wait until later. Bebe quickly turned her thoughts back to Neal's contract. "In light of what you've told me, Mr. Harris, you certainly must agree that Neal MacLeod should continue as foreman."

He gave a reluctant nod. "Yes, I know it would be what Mr. Garner would want. I'll draw up a contract that will remain in force until your husband is able to take charge again."

When Bebe returned to the tannery, it seemed like a different place to her. She had never felt much affection for her father-in-law, but now that she knew his secret sins and the mess they had created, she felt only hatred toward him. She saw Neal working at his desk on the tannery floor and wondered why she had never noticed before that his hair was the same color as Horatio's—and their father's. He looked up as Bebe approached.

"Is something wrong?"

"Please come upstairs to my office, Neal."

She heard him following her up the steps and closing the door behind them. She hung her hat and wrap on the coat-tree, then drew a deep breath as she turned to him.

"How long have you known the truth?"

It took a moment before Neal seemed to realize what she was asking. He sank down in the chair in front of her desk, and Bebe sat down, as well.

"All my life," he said quietly. "Mr. Garner . . . my father . . . met my mother when she worked here at the tannery. She said that Mr. Garner's wife didn't . . . I-I mean . . . he said he didn't love his wife. He had married her because it was the socially acceptable thing to do. I was born six months after your husband was. My sister arrived a year and a half later."

He paused, staring down at one of the ledger books as if he were the one who needed to be ashamed. "I would like to believe that our father loved us in his own way. He visited us once in a while. He took me to his fishing cabin a few times. When I was old enough to work, he gave me a job at the tannery. When the war started I enlisted right away. Afterward, we often talked about my experiences. My father never said much, but I knew he was proud of me."

Bebe's heart ached for Horatio. He had never felt that assurance from his father. "And did you love him?" she asked.

"Not always. There were times when I resented him. I couldn't understand why he didn't leave his wife and marry my mother, or at least acknowledge her and her children. But he did provide for us. He bought the house where we live and deeded it to me before he died. And he made me his foreman."

"You're his son, Neal," she said softly, still trying to comprehend it. "That's all the more reason why you must continue working here. The tannery can't run without you. The attorney agreed with me and is drawing up a temporary contract."

She saw him smile for the first time.

## 18

Grandma Bebe was right in the middle of her story when a farm wagon with a team of horses approached us from the opposite direction. On board were a farmer and his two burly sons. The wagon bed held a dozen crates of wet, squawking chickens.

"Need help, ladies?" the farmer called to us from the other side of the mud bog.

Grandma lowered her window. "Yes! We would be very grateful for your help. Thank you."

The men climbed down and unhitched the horses, then harnessed them to our rear bumper. With the horses pulling from behind and the farmer's two sons pushing from the front, they managed to heave our car backward out of the mud.

"Where are you headed?" the farmer asked after Grandma thanked him profusely.

"We're on our way from Roseton to Harrisburg."

"Well, ma'am, I suggest you turn right around again and go home," he said, shaking his head. "We've just come from that direction and the road gets much worse a little farther along. We were going to deliver these chickens, but we've had to turn around ourselves."

I knew how brave Grandma Bebe was. She would never retreat. "Thanks for the advice," she said with a smile. "As soon as I get this car turned around, I believe we will heed it."

"No, please . . ." I begged. "Don't listen to him." But Grandma started up the engine, and after executing a perfect three-point turn, we headed home to Roseton.

"We could have made it to Harrisburg," I grumbled, slouching in my seat. "What do they know?"

"There is no shame in changing direction, Harriet. In fact, once you've seen the warning signs, it's always wise to turn around."

"You could easily get us there, I know you could. You ran a tannery all by yourself. A little mud is nothing."

Grandma glanced at me in alarm. "I don't know where you ever got the idea that I'm invincible, Harriet. And as for managing the tannery . . . well, things didn't turn out very well for me, in the end. . . ."

$\backsim$

Bebe realized on her way to work one morning that a year had passed since she first went to work at the tannery in her husband's place. She had been reminded of the fact after hearing Mrs. Garner making plans to place flowers on her husband's grave to mark the sixth anniversary of his death. How could so much time have passed so swiftly? And how could Horatio have remained a drunkard for an entire year? Bebe had stopped pleading with him long ago, becoming accustomed to rising early every morning and going to work in his place. She wondered if Neal MacLeod realized how long it had been.

"Come up to my office," she told him as she passed his desk. "There's something I want to tell you."

250

"I'll be right there."

Bebe enjoyed working with Neal. He had a gentle smile and a quiet strength that enabled him to remain calm in any crisis. Working alongside him reminded her of the war years when she and her brother Franklin had labored together, sharing the chores, becoming friends. Over the past several months, she and Neal had found new customers and gradually improved their sales. None of their workers had been laid off. The fiery pain in her stomach was gone.

Bebe removed her hat and shawl and hung them on the coat-tree, remembering how angry and resentful she had felt a year ago on her first day there. She stood by the window in her office, looking down on the tannery yard and outbuildings, and realized that she knew exactly what each one was for: the drying shed and bark shed, the buildings for the soaking vats and the steam generator, the warehouse to store all the hides that arrived by rail from the slaughterhouses. And as she looked out at the rainy September afternoon, Bebe realized that her anger was gone, too. She no longer cared if Horatio drank all day. Her life had a purpose, just as it had when she'd helped with the cholera outbreak.

She heard someone tap on the door and turned to see Neal filling the doorframe. He was holding a ledger book. "You wanted to see me?"

She smiled up at him. "Do you realize that I've been working here with you for a full year?"

"Has it been that long?"

"Yes. I started in September, five years after Mr. Garner—your father—died. And it will be six years this week."

"The year sure went fast." He rubbed his jaw, smiling slightly. "I hope you take this in the way that it's meant, but when you first came in here and told me that you were going to run the tannery for your husband, I thought we were ruined for certain."

Bebe laughed out loud.

"I was certainly wrong about you," he continued. "You're just a little bit of a thing—no offense—but you have the courage and common sense of someone three times your size. And a real mind for business, too."

"Thank you. No offense taken," she said with a smile. "And I have to say that you surprised me, too. You reminded me of one of my father's mules that first day, and I thought for sure you were going to dig in your heels and refuse to plow for a woman."

"You know, in many ways you're much better at this job than your husband was."

Bebe's smile faded. "I can honestly say that I'm sorry to hear that. I wish Horatio enjoyed working here, but I know that he never did. I don't think he is very well suited to being a businessman. I wish he could find something that he truly enjoyed—besides drinking, that is. I thought he would sober up and return to work here within a few days, and that I would be able to return home to raise my daughter. But that's not what happened."

"I'm sorry about the circumstances, Beatrice, but I'm very glad to have worked with you."

"Please don't say anything more, Neal." She was going to cry, and she didn't want to. She wished she'd had the good sense to marry a man like Neal instead of Horatio.

"Let's change the subject," Neal said. He opened the ledger book he was holding and traced his finger down the page, pointing to the bottom line. "Here, I wanted to show you these figures. Thanks to our new customers, we've made a very nice profit for the third month in a row. That means it might be a trend, not an accident. And if the trend continues, we may be able to pay off our loan ahead of time and save money on the interest. I think the worst is finally over, Beatrice. We're going to stay solvent."

"Oh, Neal, that's wonderful!"

Bebe threw her arms around him and hugged him tightly. She acted spontaneously, responding the same way she would have if she and her brother Franklin had shared good news. But the gesture quickly changed into something more when neither one of them tried to pull away.

Bebe felt the warmth of his body spread through her own as he held her close. She rested her head against his chest and closed her eyes, inhaling his scent. She could feel his heart racing as rapidly as her own. She never wanted to let go of Neal MacLeod.

For months, she had relied on his strength as they'd weathered the financial crisis; now she felt the full force of his physical strength as his arms surrounded her. Horatio hadn't held her this way for a very long time. She wouldn't allow him to if he had been drinking—which was all of the time. Bebe had even moved into a separate bedroom, hoping to bribe him into sobriety. It hadn't worked.

Now the embrace that she and Neal shared lingered much longer than it should have, but she didn't want it to end. He knew the real Bebe, not the false image of her that Horatio had fabricated when they'd met. And she had come to know Neal, as well—his quiet resourcefulness, his integrity and courage.

Neal finally drew back to look into her eyes but their arms still encircled each other. Bebe saw the truth written on his face—he never had been able to disguise his feelings. He was in love with her. She saw it so clearly. And she loved him.

"Neal . . ." she whispered. She lifted her face toward his, longing to kiss him.

Suddenly Neal's expression transformed into one of horror. He released his hold on her and pulled her arms from around his waist.

"What are we doing, Beatrice? We never should have . . . I-I'm sorry . . ." He turned and fled from the office as if the room were on fire.

"Neal, wait!"

He kept going, lumbering down the stairs to the main floor.

Bebe couldn't breathe. Her entire body trembled. She wanted Neal's arms around her again. She wanted him to hold her. Neal MacLeod had become the rock she had clung to in the middle of the rapids, and she didn't know how she would survive without him.

"Please don't leave me . . ." she whispered. But it was much too late for pleas.

She grabbed her hat from the coat-tree and settled it haphazardly on her head. Somehow she kept moving, stumbling out of Horatio's office like a blind woman and hurrying down the stairs. The noise from the tannery floor throbbed in her ears along with her pounding heartbeat, but she kept walking, moving toward the main entrance, then through it. She ran out of the building and onto the street, into the rain.

Bebe had no idea where she was going as she walked and walked. The rain fell steadily, soaking her back and shoulders and thighs, wicking up from the hem of her skirt as it trailed through the puddles. The rain drenched her hat until the ruined straw wilted and dripped. She didn't care. Her tears fell as steadily as the rain, pouring down her face, blurring everything around her.

At last she halted, realizing through her haze of grief that the gray stretch of nothingness ahead of her was the river. She pulled a handkerchief from her sleeve and wiped her tears to look around. She was standing on a deserted stretch of waterfront between the railroad tracks and the wide, rippling water. On her left, fifty yards away, the tall fence that surrounded the sprawling brick factory blocked her path. On her right, beyond piles of gravel and trash, stood the shantytown that bordered the area called The Flats.

Walking alone in that direction would be too dangerous. She had no business being in this place—just as she had no business falling in love with Neal MacLeod.

She turned to leave and realized that the deep rumbling sound she heard was a locomotive moving closer and closer. She started running toward the tracks to re-cross them before the train blocked her path, but she was too late. The long line of freight cars created a slow-moving fence, barring her escape. She was trapped by her own mistakes.

What was she doing there? What had become of her life? If only she could figure out how she had ended up at this dead end, maybe she could find her way back. She looked up at the heavens as the rain flowed down her face, but God seemed a long way off.

Bebe knew she had married Horatio for all the wrong reasons— his handsome face and fancy clothes and the way he had wooed her with romantic words like the hero in a novel. But most of all, she had liked the image of herself that she'd seen reflected in his eyes, the beauty and goodness he'd imagined seeing in her—things she knew weren't really there. She had known nothing of his true character, nor had she cared to look beneath the surface. That mistake was hers, not God's. But what should she do about it?

She heard the squeal of steel against steel as the train halted on the tracks, trapping her. She turned around and walked toward the river again, watching the raindrops dimple the surface. The rapidly spreading rings collided and created more rings, roiling the surface. Bebe remembered the day she had stood at the lake with Horatio, watching the spreading ripples, realizing that one rain-drop—one person—could make a difference. Multiple raindrops and multiple people, all interacting and colliding and stirring up the placid surface could create a tidal wave of change. Mr. Garner's infidelity had created a son out of wedlock, who had collided with Horatio, leading to his misery, his drunkenness—and because of his drunkenness she had fallen in love with Neal MacLeod. It hadn't happened overnight, but little by little, working with him day after day—the same way tiny raindrops could create a flood.

Freight cars banged and slammed behind Bebe as the locomotive added more cars to the train and released others, coupling and uncoupling. The engine rumbled, hissing steam. She bent to pick up a stick from the ground and snapped it in half.

She had made a terrible mistake. The love she had once felt for Horatio had slowly eroded while her feelings for Neal MacLeod had grown steadily stronger. Had her father-in-law fallen in love with Neal's mother the same gradual way? Had he overlooked the warning signs, too, until he'd fallen into temptation?

Horatio's drunkenness had happened with one sip of alcohol at a time. He had made the wrong choice day after day until those choices accumulated into something more, just as Bebe's wrong choices had. She knew that she no longer left home every morning to work in the tannery out of necessity. She went every day because she wanted to be with Neal. She loved talking with him, loved the nearness of him when they worked side by side, loved everything about him.

She tossed half of the broken stick into the river and watched the current sweep it away. That's what had happened to her. She had allowed the current to carry her away to a place she had no business going.

*God forgive me. God forgive us all.*

Bebe glanced behind her. The train hadn't moved. In front of her, the river flowed through town and out of sight. The rain continued to fall. She was soaked to the skin, her dress plastered to her back and arms and thighs. She turned in a circle like a trapped animal with no way out.

Should she go home to the farm? No, that was another dead end. Her mother would never allow her to stay. Hannah would say,

"*What God hath joined together, let not man put asunder.*" She would tell Bebe that she had to forgive Horatio "seventy times seven." But how could she go back to Horatio when she loved Neal?

Maybe she should go back to the tannery and beg Neal to run away with her.

Bebe's tears flowed faster when she realized that he would never do it. Neal had too much integrity. He had turned away from their embrace before she had, just now, as if fleeing the scene of a crime. And that's exactly what it had been. Bebe was a married woman. And Neal knew firsthand the devastation that adultery always caused.

What was she going to do? She hated living in the mansion on the ridge, hated all the turbulence in her marriage and in her life. Her mother-in-law despised her. Horatio loved liquor more than he loved her. And for the past year, she had spent so much time at work that her daughter barely knew her anymore.

Bebe watched a small ship navigate upriver against the current and remembered her mother's words: "*Smooth seas don't produce skillful sailors.*" Mama said that the rough waters in life made people strong, ready for God to use. But what could possibly be God's purpose in all of this mess? She couldn't even remember the last time she had prayed.

Bebe threw the other half of the stick into the water as hard as she could. She longed to shout aloud to the heavens, "*What do you want from me, God?*" Maybe she should leap in after the stick, let the shock of the icy water steal her breath away, let the water fill her lungs and carry her away to the sea.

All of her mistakes were of her own making. She couldn't blame God. Whether she had married Horatio for the right reasons or not, she had vowed to be his wife until death parted them. She knew that her life was never going to get any better than it was right now unless she asked God to change her, first. She had walked into this dead end on her own. Bebe lifted her face to the sky again. *Help me, God. Please show me what to do.*

She heard another crash as more freight cars collided. She turned toward the tracks and saw that the train had begun to move again. She watched it slowly lumber away, and when the track was clear she started walking back the way she had come.

Bebe already knew what God wanted her to do. It wasn't a mystery. She needed to help Horatio get sober so he could return to his job. She needed to pray and ask God to forgive her and restore her love for Horatio. She recalled Horatio's words on the day she had fetched him from the saloon: *"You used to look at me as though I had just hung the moon in the sky. . . . Why don't you look at me that way anymore?"*

Hannah had been right; love was the most powerful force in the world. But Bebe had allowed its strong grip to pull her in the wrong direction, pulling her toward Neal MacLeod and away from Horatio. Now she had to redirect that force. She had to look at Horatio with love again, to do the loving thing for him whether she felt like it or not. She had to work for his good, encourage him, pray for him.

And if he continued to drink?

Bebe choked back a sob. Regardless of the outcome, she had to turn away from Neal MacLeod and go home to her husband and daughter.

She trudged up the street the way she had come and found herself back at the tannery a few minutes later. Two figures, a woman and a young boy, stood outside the door, huddled beneath the overhanging roof. They looked nearly as drenched as Bebe was. As she drew closer, she saw that the woman held an infant bundled in her arms. Then a third child, a little girl Lucy's age, peeked from behind the woman's skirts.

"Mrs. Garner!" the woman called.

Bebe halted, startled to hear her name.

"You're Mrs. Garner, aren't you?" the woman asked.

"Yes. . . . How do you know my name?"

"I'm Millie White. You helped me once before when I was sick with cholera. Please, Mrs. Garner, I need your help again."

Bebe stared. She was in no position to help Millie or anyone else after making such a mess of her own life. "What . . . what do you want me to do?" she finally asked.

"My husband works at your tannery and today is payday. Please, I'm begging you to give the money to me this week, not him. He'll only drink it away in the saloon. My children need to eat. I need to pay the rent. Can't you please give the money to me?"

Bebe looked at Millie White and saw herself. She easily could have ended up in Millie's situation. Her husband was also a drunkard, and if Bebe hadn't come to the tannery a year ago and taken over for him, she might have lost everything. Her own daughter would be the child who was hungry.

Bebe rested her hand on Millie's shoulder. "I don't know the answer to your question, Millie, but if you'll come inside with me, I'll find out." She would have to talk to Neal MacLeod. She would have to face him again, even if it broke her heart. She opened the door and motioned for Millie and her family to follow her inside.

The children cringed at the noise and huddled around their mother. Bebe led the way to Neal's desk on the main floor. He had all of his drawers open and a wooden crate at his feet, and she realized that he was emptying his desk, packing his things. He glanced up long enough to see her approaching, then looked away. His eyes were red, as if he had been weeping.

Bebe cleared the knot from her throat and quickly explained Millie White's request. "Can we do that, Neal?" she asked. "Can we give Mrs. White her husband's pay?"

He shook his head. "I'm sorry. I would like to help her out, but her husband earned his pay. By law, we have to give it to him."

"Let me work, then," Millie begged. "Give me a job here instead of him."

"But who will take care of your children?" Bebe asked.

Millie pushed her son forward. "Hire my son, then. He can run errands for you or sweep the floor. He's a good boy; he does what he's told."

The boy couldn't have been more than seven or eight years old. Bebe hated the idea of a child laboring in her tannery. It was bad enough that most children did piecework in their tenements at night. But Neal looked at the boy and nodded. "I think I can find something for him."

Bebe imagined her own daughter being forced to work and shuddered. Horatio might be a drunkard, but he owned the tannery and had the means to support his family. Women like Millie had nothing.

Bebe glanced at Neal again and longed to feel his arms around her—just one more time. Tears stung her eyes as she remembered the starchy scent of his shirt and the sound of his heartbeat. She looked down at the little boy instead, and suddenly knew that this family was an answer to her prayer. She swallowed her tears and said, "Listen, Millie. If the only way we can keep our husbands out of the saloons is to close them down, then that's what we'll have to do."

"How can we do that?"

"Can you gather together a group of women who are in the same situation that you're in?"

"Yeah, sure," she said bitterly. "That won't be hard at all."

"Do you know which saloon your husband usually goes to on payday?"

"Ozzie's Tavern down on Sixth Street."

"I want you and the other women to meet me there tonight at six o'clock."

"Meet you . . . ?" She started shaking her head. "You shouldn't go down there, Mrs. Garner, believe me. The tavern is down in The Flats, and—"

"I'm not afraid. I've been to The Flats before. We have to stop the men from getting drunk on their way home, right after they get paid. Will you meet me there?"

Millie nodded and caressed her daughter's damp hair. "Yeah. I'll be there, Mrs. Garner. And I'll gather the other women, too. Thank you."

Bebe waited until Millie left before turning to Neal again. She couldn't meet his gaze. She drew a painful breath as she looked out over the floor of the tannery that had become so familiar to her this past year. "I think my work here is finished, Neal. The tannery is yours to run, alone, until Horatio returns. I don't know when that will be, but I've been reading in the newspaper about a new temperance organization, and I think I'll start a chapter here in town. I'm not going to quit until every saloon is forced to close its doors and my husband—" She paused as her voice broke. She covered her mouth with her hand until she could finish. ". . . and my husband is sober again. Until then, our family would appreciate it if you would kindly manage the business for him."

"Yes . . . of course . . . but listen, Beatrice. I-I'm sorry—"

"So am I, Neal. So am I."

She turned and hurried away from him. She felt as though her heart had been slashed in two. She strode out of the building and back out into the rain, walking all the way home to her mansion on the hill. She went inside through the servants' entrance in the rear of the house and climbed the back stairs to her room, too ashamed to go through the front door, too ashamed to face her mother-in-law. One of the servants met Bebe on the stairs.

"Goodness' sakes, you're soaking wet, Mrs. Garner. Let me draw you a hot bath and take care of your wet clothes."

"That would be wonderful, thank you. Your name is Herta, isn't it?"

"Yes, ma'am."

It shamed Bebe to realize that she had kept all of the servants at a distance, just as Horatio and her mother-in-law did, as if she were better than these simple, hardworking people. That was going to change. From now on Bebe was going to stop trying to fit in with the Garners' socialite friends and be herself—a simple farm girl.

"And, Herta, kindly tell the driver—his name is Peter, isn't it?" The girl nodded. "Please ask Peter to have the carriage ready for me at six o'clock tonight."

Millie White and two dozen other women stood waiting for Bebe outside Ozzie's Tavern when Bebe arrived. They looked desperate but determined, and she felt an instant kinship with them. She should have done this a year ago.

"My husband is a drunkard, too," she told them as they gathered in front of the saloon door. "We're going to pray and ask God to help us close down this place. And we're going to come back here every night if we have to, until it does close."

"It won't help," one of the women said. "Our men will just find another saloon."

"Then we'll do the same thing until that one closes. I've been reading in the newspaper how women in other cities have done this very thing—and it works. Dozens of saloons have been forced to close their doors. The organization is called the Women's Christian Temperance Union. I'll write to them and ask for advice. We'll start a chapter here in town. We'll have more power and influence if we join together with other women."

"What do we have to do?" someone asked.

"Well, besides praying, one of the Union's methods is to write down the names of all the men who are patronizing the saloon and list them in the newspaper. The men should be ashamed of what they're doing, spending your rent money on alcohol and taking food out of your children's mouths. We'll bring their actions out into the open and make people aware of how drunkenness affects families like yours."

"I say let's try it," Millie said. "It can't hurt none."

"Good. Shall we bow our heads?" Bebe closed her eyes as she prepared to pray aloud. She had never done anything like this before, always praying silently in church or in the privacy of her room. "Heavenly Father . . ." she began. Her throat closed with emotion.

Desperation had forced her to turn to God, and she suddenly felt closer to Him than she ever had before. He was here, right beside her. This was the task that He wanted her to accomplish. And although nothing in her life was as it should be, God was still with her and she was going to be fine. She drew a deep breath and started again, pouring all of her passion and sorrow, all of her guilt and grief into her prayer. She didn't stop until the saloon door opened a few minutes later and the owner began to shout.

"Hey! What do you think you're doing out here? You're blocking my door! Get away from here!" He waved his arms as if shooing a flock of chickens.

"This is a public walkway," Bebe told him. "We have every right to stand here."

"You're going to interfere with my business. Go home where you belong!" He looked down the street past the women and scowled. Bebe turned in that direction and saw a group of workmen approaching from the brick factory where their shift must have just ended.

"Let's pray, ladies." Bebe closed her eyes again, ignoring the owner's angry shouts as she beseeched the Almighty to turn the workers' steps away from the saloon and toward their homes. The women joined in with cries of "Yes, Lord!" and "Hear us!"

When Bebe opened her eyes to peek again, the workers had halted at the corner as if afraid to wade through the mob of women. "Come on, come on, gentlemen," the owner called out. "We're open for business. Don't let these crazy women get in your way."

Bebe raised her voice to outshout him. "Ladies! Do you know the hymn 'Give to the Winds Thy Fears'? Come on, sing it with me: 'Give to the winds thy fears, hope and be undismayed; God hears thy sighs, and counts thy tears, God shall lift up thy head.' " Bebe sang with all her might even though only a few of the women joined her and none of them seemed to know all the words. " 'Through waves and clouds and storms, He gently clears the way. Wait thou His time, so shall the night soon end in joyous day.' "

The workmen held a huddled conference on the street corner, then slouched away. The women cheered, drowning out the bar owner's angry rant.

⁓

Three months later, Ozzie's Tavern closed its doors for good. Bebe, Millie, and the other women now began gathering in front of Logan's Saloon—Horatio's favorite place—to pray and sing. Bebe had made the rounds to all of the local churches, giving speeches to their ladies' groups about temperance and asking them to join her crusade. Hundreds of women had signed The Pledge, vowing to abstain from alcohol. Her local chapter of the Women's Christian Temperance Union had grown to nearly three hundred members.

On a Friday night well into their crusade, Bebe's women forced Logan's Saloon to close its doors for lack of patronage. Horatio was the last man to stagger out that final night, gripping a half-empty bottle. The bartender cursed at the women as he hung up a *Closed* sign and locked the door. Bebe had the carriage waiting for her husband at the curb, and Peter, the driver, helped him climb in beside her.

"Let's go home, Horatio," she said.

"Are you happy now?" he asked as they rode up the hill in the quiet night.

"Yes. I am." She nestled close beside him and took his hand in hers, lifting it to her lips and kissing it. She didn't feel love for him yet, but God willing it would soon begin to grow.

"Horatio?" She waited until he met her gaze. "I love you."

He looked away as tears filled his eyes. He still gripped the half-empty bottle and she took hold of it, as well. "May I have this, please?" She waited until she felt his grip loosen, then pulled it gently from his hand and dropped it over the side of the carriage. She heard glass shattering on the cobblestone street behind them.

Bebe wondered what Horatio would have done if liquor hadn't been readily available. Might he have found a better way to cope and saved all of them a great deal of grief? She knew in that moment that she wouldn't stop her temperance crusade until every last saloon had closed its doors and alcohol was banned everywhere. With God on her side, how could she lose?

She helped Horatio up the stairs to their bedroom when they reached home, then helped him undress. His clothing stank of cigar smoke.

"You'll be happy to know that the country's financial crisis is much improved, Horatio. The tannery is earning a profit again. You got overwhelmed, I know, but when you go back to work, you'll see the improvement."

He sat on the bed and kicked off one of his shoes. It fell to the floor with a thud. "Thanks to Neal MacLeod, I suppose?"

Bebe wasn't sure what would anger him more: knowing that

Neal had saved the business or that she had helped him. She decided to tell him the truth. "Mr. MacLeod and I worked together until things turned around."

"You worked with *him*?" He kicked his other shoe across the room. "I suppose he found great satisfaction in that. He has stolen everything else from me—my father, my job . . . What's left to steal except my wife?"

Bebe cringed, aware of how close to the truth Horatio's words were. "It isn't like that at all," she told him. "You're my husband, not Mr. MacLeod. You're the man I vowed to spend my life with. And I've kept my vows. But you also made vows to me, Horatio. You vowed to honor and protect and cherish me. You can't do those things when you're drunk."

"I've tried to stop and I can't!"

She helped Horatio put on his pajama top and buttoned it for him. "No one can get through life's trials alone. We all need God's help."

"God wants nothing to do with me, and I want nothing to do with Him!"

His words shocked Bebe, but she tried not to show it. She had to keep coaxing him to talk, to unload all of the reasons he had started drinking in the first place. Maybe then he would be able to stop.

"What makes you think that God doesn't care about you, Horatio?"

"Because God never answers my prayers. He never answers anyone's prayers. Why doesn't He right all the wrongs here on earth? Put a stop to war and killing? All my friends . . . all my friends . . ." He paused, passing his hand over his face. "I prayed for courage, and He didn't give me any. I was scared all the time during that war."

"But Franklin and your other friends will tell you that they were terrified, too. There's no shame in being afraid."

"Neal MacLeod won a Medal of Honor, did you know that? My father made sure that I knew all about it—and he called me a coward. God is supposed to be our Father, isn't He? Well, if He's anything like my father, then I want nothing to do with Him!"

"Oh, Horatio . . . listen—"

"My father turned away from his family, did you know that?"

"Yes, I know, but—"

"He didn't love my mother and me anymore, so he left us and started another family. Then he sent me out to die on a battlefield to be rid of me. How could a loving father do that? How could he force his son go to war? He wanted me to die!"

The anguish in Horatio's voice made Bebe ache for him. She wrapped her arms around him and held him tightly. "I don't know, Horatio . . . but I know that God isn't like your father at all. God loves you."

"Then why does He stand aside and watch us hurt and betray each other?"

"I don't know the answers to your questions, Horatio. But I promise that we'll try to find them together. . . ."

❧

Grandma and I arrived back in Roseton that rainy afternoon just as she finished telling her story. "So you see, Harriet, there is a time to fix your own flat tires, and a time to recognize that all of your efforts to help yourself are only making matters worse. You'll only end up soaked and muddy and trapped in an even deeper rut. That's when you need to know enough to turn around. That's when you need to call on the Lord for help. Do you understand what I'm saying?"

"I suppose so."

"Listen, I'm sorry that we didn't get to the meeting. I know you're disappointed, but—"

"I was going to take The Pledge today. I made up my mind, and I was going to surprise you."

She looked at me in dismay, not pride. "You're just a child, Harriet. You're much too young to understand what you're promising."

"I'm not too young, I'm twelve! And I know that I'll be promising never to touch a single drop of alcohol all my life and to do my best to stop other people from drinking it, too. I want to get my own pledge book to carry, so I can get other people to sign it, like you do."

"You also would have to promise to banish alcohol from your sideboard and your kitchen, and that's not something you can promise yet. And you would be pledging not to court a man who drinks or to marry one—"

"That's easy. I'm never getting married."

"You see, Harriet? You're much too young to be making such rash decisions. Let's wait a few years to see if you change your mind about drinking alcohol—and about getting married, too."

She parked the car in the garage and went into the house, leaving me sitting there, mystified. Grandma was working so hard to get other people to take The Pledge. Why wouldn't she let me sign it? I didn't understand my grandmother at all. She was turning out to be a woman of great contradictions.

19

In June of 1912, my sister Alice married banker Gordon P. Shaw. It was the society event of the year in Roseton, and people considered it a social triumph to be invited. I considered it a triumph when I successfully avoided wearing a hat, a corset, and any article of clothing with frills or ruffles. I watched all the other women's heads wobbling beneath the weight of their voluminous hair and enormous hats, and I ran my fingers through my short, bobbed hair and gloated.

The weeks and weeks of fluttering preparations for Alice's wedding, along with several last-minute emergencies, had exhausted everyone in our family. The worst crisis had been the heated argument that had erupted over whether or not liquor would be served. Grandma opposed it, of course, and wanted all types of alcohol completely banned from the event. Mother worried that a "dry" reception might offend the groom and his well-to-do family.

"Poppycock!" Grandma said. "Are they such lushes that they can't celebrate a happy occasion without a drink? If so, perhaps

Alice should think twice before marrying into that family. We already know there are lushes on our side."

"Shh! Don't say such things!" My mother always became horrified whenever Grandma implied that drunkenness ran in our family. "Think of the girls! Do you want to tarnish their reputations?" she whispered.

"Our family's 'secret' isn't exactly a secret, Lucy. Everyone in town knows that I'm the president of the local Women's Christian Temperance Union—and most people know why. Besides, how will it look if my granddaughter's wedding reception turns into a drunken brawl, especially after all my hard work preaching temperance?"

"Really, Mother. My friends are respectable people. The reception is hardly going to turn into a brawl. You always exaggerate."

I listened to weeks of such arguments. The truth was, Daddy's relatives also would have been offended if the liquor didn't flow freely. They figured Daddy owed them a lavish party in exchange for the gifts they were giving Alice. My father finally announced his decision, attempting to meet both sides in the middle and avoid a rift between Grandma and Mother.

"Liquor will be served in small amounts," he decreed as he stroked his clean-shaven chin. He looked as wise and decisive as King Solomon had when he'd ordered the baby to be chopped in half. "We will serve enough liquor for a decent toast and a festive celebration, but not enough to encourage drunkenness."

In other words, neither side would be happy.

As I sat at the wedding reception watching the festivities, my father wore the dazed look of a man whose hard-earned money had been stolen by pirates and carted away in fat treasure chests. My mother looked flat-out exhausted. The bright rouge on her cheeks couldn't distract from the dark circles beneath her eyes. Presiding over this lavish wedding had been the pinnacle of all her achievements, the fulfillment of all her dreams. This extravagant party for Roseton's most important citizens had kept seamstresses busy for months, while the local jewelers had made hefty profits polishing everyone's heirloom diamonds. The drama and pageantry of the occasion represented everything Mother loved most in life. In one glorious evening she would exercise all of the etiquette skills she had learned from Grandmother Garner—who would have reveled in the event, too, had she been alive. Best of all, the wedding united Mother to the groom's impeccable family. What would she do for an encore?

I asked to sit beside Grandma Bebe at the wedding reception because I enjoyed her company more than anyone else's in my family. Neither one of us fit in with this crowd. We were two social misfits who didn't care one whit about what people thought of us. By the time I had eaten all of the food I wanted to eat, and Alice and her groom had cut the wedding cake, I was ready to go home. The dancing had begun, and I didn't see a single gentleman in this sorry assembly of social climbers who I cared to dance with—even if I had known how to dance.

Grandma gazed at the waltzing couples in their glittering finery and sighed. "It's on joyous occasions such as this that I miss my Horatio the most." She smiled and yet at the same time she looked sad.

"Whatever happened to him?" I asked, hoping I wasn't opening a Pandora's box of bad memories. "Why doesn't he live with you?"

"Don't be obtuse. You've heard the story a hundred times, I'm sure you have."

"No, I haven't. Mother never talks about him. That's why I'm asking."

"Well," Grandma said with a sigh, "it's really quite a long story."

"Good. The longer the better. This party is boring."

e⁓

Horatio looked wretched as he sat on the edge of the bed. "Very well, Beatrice, I give up. I'll go up to the fishing cabin with you."

Bebe closed her eyes in joy, wondering if she were dreaming. She had formed the local chapter of the Temperance Union more than a year and a half ago, and had fervently prayed ever since that one day she would hear Horatio say those words. She went to him, hugging him tightly. His embrace felt limp in return. His once ruddy skin had turned dull and gray, his sunken eyes looked lifeless. But Bebe believed that the man she once loved still lived inside this sad, tired body. He would be his old self again once he quit drinking.

"Thank you, Horatio. It will be wonderful to get away from here for a while, you'll see." She got out their satchels and began to pack. "I'll tell Peter to get the carriage ready and—"

"No, don't. I want to drive up there myself. Tell him we'll take the runabout."

Bebe hesitated, wondering if she should try to talk him out of it. It would be easier for Horatio to change his mind and return home if he didn't have to wait for Peter to come back for them. On the other hand, he might decide not to go to the cabin at all if she argued with him. She decided to say nothing and let him drive the runabout. She had waited much too long for Horatio to get sober.

After Bebe and her temperance women had closed down Horatio's favorite saloon, he had found another—and another. Then he'd begun drinking at home. Neal MacLeod continued to operate the tannery for them in Horatio's absence, but Bebe was careful never to mention his name.

Forgetting Neal proved much harder than she ever imagined.

She kept busy with her temperance activities: holding prayer vigils in front of saloons, attending rallies and conventions, writing articles and speeches that told about the high cost of alcoholism. Now, as she prepared to climb into the runabout with Horatio to drive to Iroquois Lake, she was almost afraid to hope that her prayers were finally being answered.

Rain began to patter against the roof of the runabout before they even left the city limits. Thunder grumbled in the distance. Bebe nestled closer to Horatio. "Good thing we bundled up in our warmest clothes."

"It always rains when we go up to the cabin. Did you ever notice that?"

"No, I can't say that I have. But it's nearly April, after all—and you know what they say about April showers. Besides, I don't care if it does rain. We can just sit by the fire together in the cabin."

Fifteen minutes later, the sky opened up and rain poured down on them. The canopy could barely keep them dry. "Maybe we should turn back," Horatio said. "We're getting wet, and besides, I've never seen the river this far over its banks before."

Neither had Bebe. The rain-swollen river they had been following up the mountain had seeped into the woods, leaving trees stranded and the forest flooded with several feet of water. It surged across their path in some places as if trying to swallow the road. She urged him on. "The weather won't matter once we're up there. And I'm sure everything will be dried out by the time we go home."

The higher they climbed, the more rapidly the river seemed to flow. Once again, Horatio talked about turning back. "I don't like the look of that current, Beatrice. I've never seen it flowing so swiftly."

"We're almost there now, aren't we?"

Thankfully, he kept going. But as they neared the lake, Bebe heard a roaring noise in the distance like the rumble of a locomotive. "What's that sound, Horatio? Stop the carriage for a minute." He pulled to a halt and listened with her. It wasn't the wind. And it sounded much louder than the rush of rapids in the nearby river.

"I don't know what that is," Horatio said. "A train, maybe?"

"It sounds like a waterfall, doesn't it? Remember our wedding trip to Niagara Falls? Remember how loud the water was?"

"I remember." He flicked the reins and the horse started moving again. "I'll be glad when we're inside, out of this rain."

The roaring sound grew louder the farther up the mountain they climbed, and when they neared the dam that had created Iroquois Lake, the mystery was finally solved. "Look, Horatio. It *is* a waterfall! I don't remember seeing it before—or hearing it, either. Do you?"

"That's because it isn't supposed to be here. There isn't supposed to be that much water going over the dam. It was just a trickle the other times we came up here, remember?"

Horatio drove the wagon a little farther up the road and stopped when they reached a clearing. "Look at that!" he breathed. Bebe gaped in awe at the power of the water thundering over the earthen dam. Behind it, the lake looked twice as vast as she remembered. It seemed to strain against the flimsy barrier that held it back.

"I've never seen the lake so high . . . or the water flowing over the dam so fast," Horatio said. "They must have had a lot of snow higher up in the mountains last winter, and now it's all melting."

Bebe rested her hand on his knee, worried that he would decide to turn back. "The waterfall brings back memories, doesn't it? It's hard to believe we've been married for more than ten years already, isn't it?"

"Mmm . . ." He didn't seem to be listening. He stared at the falls and shook his head before moving forward again. "I don't like the look of that dam, Beatrice. It was built right after the war, you know. It was never designed to hold back so much water."

They barely recognized the cabin when they finally reached it, either. The beach along the lakefront was under water, the fishing pier submerged. The lake engulfed all the trees that had once stood near the shoreline, and Bebe had to remove her shoes and lift her skirts to wade from the road to the doorstep.

"The flooding up here seems even worse than the last time," she said. "That was when we had the cholera epidemic in town, remember?"

"Maybe we should go back."

Bebe shook her head, aware of the temptations he faced in town. "We'll be fine. I'm just remembering."

Two days later it was still raining. Horatio couldn't stop worrying about the earthen dam. He walked outside so often to check on it that Bebe wondered if he had a flask of alcohol hidden somewhere. She watched him from the cabin window as he waded down the beach for the third time that day and disappeared among the trees.

"The dam doesn't look sound to me," he told her when he returned. "The structure has aged over the years, and it has developed a nasty bulge on one side. I wonder if anyone from town has bothered to inspect it lately."

"Who is in charge of the dam?"

Horatio shrugged. "This land is all privately owned up here. I suppose all of the landowners are."

Each day the lake continued to swell before their eyes. Horatio worried and paced, walking out in the rain every few hours to check on the dam. By the end of the week the waves lapped at their doorstep. "I think we should go home," he said. "I want to send someone up here to inspect the dam and see if it's sound."

Bebe resisted his pleas, convinced that Horatio wanted an

excuse to go home and get drunk. His latest binge had lasted more than two and a half years—much longer than any of his others had—and she knew it would probably take more than a week for him to dry out. She had been afraid this would happen when he had decided to drive up here himself. Having transportation handy made it too easy for him to leave before he was ready.

That afternoon, when he returned from his walk, he begged Bebe to come outside with him. "Please, I want you to look at it for yourself, Beatrice. You'll see why I'm so concerned."

She pulled on a pair of his trousers and waded out to the dam with him, slogging through water up to her thighs in places. She heard the roar of the falls long before she saw them. Horatio stopped in a clearing overlooking the dam, and what Bebe saw frightened her so badly that she clung to his side. Water rushed over the dam with unstoppable power. The river below the falls had become a raging rapids.

"Can you see how the dam is bulging over there?" Horatio shouted above the noise. "It's only made of earth. I'm afraid it's going to burst."

"What will happen if it does?"

"If that dam gives way, all of the water in Iroquois Lake will go surging down the river at once. The houses in The Flats would be demolished by the tidal wave. Remember the flood eight years ago when we had the cholera epidemic? If this dam lets go, that entire neighborhood could be washed right off its foundations."

Bebe knew he wasn't exaggerating. Even as they stood watching, a small, boulder-sized section crumbled away before their eyes. Horatio gripped her arm. "Look, Beatrice. It's starting to go! We have to go home and warn people!"

He grabbed her hand as they hurried back to the cabin, struggling as if in a dream to move through the deep water. Bebe packed as quickly as she could while Horatio harnessed the horse to the runabout. For the first time she was grateful that they had driven up to the lake and wouldn't have to wait for the driver to return for them. But when the vehicle was ready, Horatio stopped her from climbing on board.

"I want you to stay here, Beatrice. The road follows the river most of the way and if the dam bursts while we're on our way home . . ." He drew a breath as if his chest ached. "If it bursts, we'll never make it. We'll be washed downstream with the surge, carriage and all."

Bebe's heart hurt from pounding so hard. "Well, if it's too dangerous for me, then it's too dangerous for you, too."

"I can drive faster if I'm alone. I'll come back for you when it's safe. I want you to stay here on higher ground."

"Never! I'm going with you, and don't you dare try to stop me!" She clutched his jacket in her fists as if she never intended to let go. "I love you, Horatio Garner, and if you get washed away, then I want to be right beside you."

"What about Lucy? She needs a mother—"

"And she needs a father, too. Now, come on. You're wasting time. Let's go."

He lifted her onto the wagon and they took off down the mountain as fast as they dared on the flooded road. "I hope you're praying," Horatio murmured.

"Yes—with all my might." Bebe pleaded with God to help them make it back to town before the dam burst. He had protected her and her mother from the bounty hunters years ago, and she prayed that He would send His angels to protect her and Horatio now. *"When you obey the Lord,"* Hannah had said, *"He will always be with you, no matter what happens."* Bebe prayed that her mother was right.

Horatio sat on the edge of the seat, concentrating on the path ahead as they traveled down the steep, muddy road as fast as the horse would go. Bebe helped point out some of the deeper ruts and holes, while glancing anxiously at the swollen river on their left. The current had uprooted trees, carrying them along in the brown, swirling water. The river rushed madly alongside them as if they were in a race against it. Perhaps they were.

*Please help us, God,* she silently pleaded. *Please spare the town and our home. Please help us make it in time to warn people. . . .*

She suddenly remembered how much Lucy and Mrs. Garner loved to go shopping downtown. She tugged on Horatio's sleeve in panic. "What about the downtown area? Do you think the tidal wave will hit there, too?" She tried not to picture her daughter and mother-in-law strolling innocently down Central Avenue when the flood hit.

"I don't know," he mumbled. "I don't know. . . . The stores aren't far from the river."

Horatio had to stop three times and climb down from the runabout to lead the horse through the deep water that flooded the road. The sound of the rushing river spooked the animal, and Bebe saw its eyes rolling in fear. Horatio was getting soaked but he spoke calmly as he coaxed the horse along. He looked strong and determined. She had never loved him more.

Whenever she thought about the crumbling dam and the water that was powerful enough to sweep them away, Bebe could barely breathe. *Please, God . . . please . . .* she prayed. And when the town finally came into sight below them, she wept with relief. "We made it! Thank God!"

"Yes, we're almost there," Horatio breathed. "Hang on, darling."

The lathered horse was panting with exertion when Horatio stopped at the tannery. They came to it first along their way, and he rushed inside, shouting, "Shut the place down, MacLeod! Send everyone home! The dam on Iroquois Lake is going to burst. Everyone who lives near the river needs to evacuate. Now!"

They stopped next at the mayor's office, where Horatio delivered the same warning. "Sound all the town's fire alarms! Get the police and firemen to spread the word! Everyone needs to get up to higher ground!"

Bebe chewed her fingernails while she waited for him. Fear gnawed her insides. Finally, Horatio turned the exhausted horse up the hill toward home. Bebe didn't even wait for the vehicle to halt out front before she leaped off and ran up the steps into the house.

"Lucy!" she cried. "Lucy, where are you?" If her daughter were downtown, how would Bebe ever find her in time? She would have to go from store to store, searching for her. "Lucy!"

It felt like an eternity before the playroom door opened at the top of the steps and Lucy's golden head appeared. "I'm up here, Mama."

"Thank God! Thank God!" Bebe bounded up the stairs toward her daughter, tripping over the last step, struggling to her feet again, hugging Lucy tightly. "Thank God, you're safe!"

"Ow . . . not so hard, Mama. You're wrinkling my dress!"

Mrs. Garner emerged from her bedroom down the hall. "What's going on? Why all this shouting?"

"The dam up on Iroquois Lake is going to burst," Bebe said breathlessly. "All that water is going to flood the town. People have to get out. Horatio says the tidal wave could wipe out The Flats."

Horatio had followed Bebe inside after tethering the horse. He stood downstairs in the foyer, calling up to them. "Are all of the servants at home, Mother?"

"Yes, I believe so."

Horatio ran into the parlor, dripping muddy water on the floor, and rang the service bell to summon them. One after another, they hurried to the front hallway in response. Bebe saw him counting heads to see if they were all there.

"Make sure everyone stays inside," Horatio told the butler. "Don't let anyone go downtown. It's not safe. The dam up on Iroquois Lake is about to give way and all of that water . . ."

"Don't stand there with the door open," Mrs. Garner told him as she descended the stairs. "Come upstairs, Horatio, and let the servants fix you a hot bath. You need to change out of those wet clothes before you catch your death of pneumonia."

He shook his head. "I'm going back out to finish sounding the warning."

"I'll go with you." Bebe released her hold on Lucy and started down the stairs.

"Oh no, you won't," Horatio said. "You're staying right here with Mother and Lucy."

"And you're staying, as well," Mrs. Garner said. "There's no reason in the world why you should risk your life. You can very well send someone else."

Horatio took another step toward the open door. "People are going to need a place to go for shelter. I'm going to bring as many people as I can up here to the ridge where it's safe." He turned to the servants, who were whispering fearfully among themselves. "Get some coffee and food ready for them. I'll be back shortly."

"No, Horatio. I forbid it!" Mrs. Garner said. Lucy began to wail as if the panic had become contagious.

"Daddy, Daddy!" She started down the steps toward her father, stretching out her arms to him. Bebe caught her and tried to comfort her, but she squirmed in protest, trying to reach Horatio. He was almost through the door when Peter, the family's carriage driver, stepped forward.

"I'll go with you, Mr. Garner. We can rescue more people if we take two vehicles."

"Very good. Thank you, Peter." They left hurriedly, making plans.

"Daddy! I want Daddy," Lucy cried. Bebe finally released her after the door closed behind Horatio, and Lucy fled into her grandmother's arms.

Mrs. Garner glared at Bebe as if the commotion were all her fault, then turned her attention to Lucy. "There, there. Come with me, dear. The cook will fix us some tea and cookies." She led her away by the hand.

For the next hour, Bebe tried to distract herself from her fears by helping the servants turn the house into a shelter for the refugees. Church bells clanged incessantly all over Roseton and fire bells sounded a warning in the distance. When Bebe went into the parlor to build a fire to warm the room, she found Lucy and Mrs. Garner sitting side by side on the horsehair sofa, sipping tea. Bebe wasn't sure if she should be irritated with Mrs. Garner for not helping or grateful that she was distracting Lucy.

"What are you doing?" Mrs. Garner asked as Bebe knelt to pile the wood in the fireplace. "Let the servants do that."

"I don't mind. I'd rather work than pace the floor and worry. And I'm sure everyone will be wet and cold when they arrive, so I thought I would warm the room for them."

Mrs. Garner surveyed the overstuffed room with a worried look. "You're not going to allow strangers to come into my parlor, are you? What about all of my things?"

"That's all they are, Mother Garner—things. People's lives are at stake."

But Mrs. Garner rose from her chair like a queen rising from her throne and strode from the room with Lucy close behind her. Bebe crumpled up a piece of newspaper and lit a match to it. By the time she got the fire kindled, her mother-in-law had returned with two chambermaids.

"I don't care what you were doing," Mrs. Garner told them, "I want you to help me protect my things." She paraded around the room, pointing to all her bric-a-brac and silver pieces. "Take this . . . and this . . . and this . . . upstairs to my bedroom suite for safekeeping." Lucy followed her grandmother around, whining for attention as Mrs. Garner pointed to each item. The maids ran up and down the stairs, hauling everything away.

Two hours after he left, Horatio returned. Bebe felt weak with relief as she hugged him, not caring if she got wet. He led a bedraggled group of people into the house, half of them small children. "I'm so proud of you," Bebe whispered as she brushed his wet hair off his forehead. A moment later, Lucy raced into the foyer to see her father.

"Daddy! Lift me up, Daddy," she said, reaching up to him. "Carry me."

He patted her head. "Not now, sweetheart. I'm all wet. Your nice dress will get all wet."

Bebe looked at the frightened, shivering children that Horatio had herded into the foyer and saw them gaping at the enormous rooms and sweeping staircase. She remembered how overwhelmed she had felt the first time she'd entered Horatio's home—and these poor souls were fleeing for their lives.

"Come, Lucy. Let's take these children upstairs and show them where your playroom is. They must be terribly frightened."

Mrs. Garner moved to bar their way. "You can't be serious! These people can't be trusted. They'll break all her nice things."

Bebe winced at her mother-in-law's insulting words, spoken loudly enough for the children and their mothers to hear. "We can always buy more, Mother Garner," she whispered. "Please, I don't want Lucy to grow up to be selfish." She motioned to the refugees again. "Come, children. This way. Mothers, too, if you wish. Lucy, you go first and show them where your playroom is."

Mrs. Garner glared at Bebe, then turned to Horatio. "Aren't you going to stop her?"

He shook his head. "They need a place to stay. It isn't safe downtown. The warning is going out, and we're evacuating all the people—"

"Good. Then you can change out of those wet clothes right now, and warm up. You look drenched, Horatio."

"We're not finished, Mother. It's a big town, you know. I won't rest until I've made sure everyone has heard the warning."

Bebe halted halfway up the steps when she heard Horatio's words. The refugees continued on as she hurried back downstairs to him. "You can't go out there again! What if something happens? The dam could break any minute. You said yourself how danger-ous it was."

He glanced around at the flurry of activity all around them and reached for Bebe's hand. "Will you excuse us please, Mother?" He led Bebe into the dining room, where no one could hear them, then took her other hand as he faced her. "I have to do this, Beatrice. I'm tired of being a coward. Why should you be the only brave one in the family?"

"No! I won't let you go!" Bebe clung to him, weeping, not caring how wet he was. "Please don't go back out there, Horatio! Please! It's too dangerous. Stay here with me. I need you! You're not a coward, I know you aren't."

He pried her arms from around his waist and looked down at her, holding her hands in his again. Tears filled his eyes. "I know the truth, and I'm tired of running scared. I want you and Lucy to be proud of me for once. Most of all, I want to be able to face myself in the mirror every morning. I have to do this, Bebe." He kissed her forehead and turned toward the foyer.

"No!" Bebe clung to his clothing, desperate to hold him back.

"Don't, my darling," he said quietly. "Let me go. Let me do this."

Bebe saw his courage and determination and released her hold.

"I love you, Horatio." For the first time in months, she meant it. He nodded and hurried through the door, closing it behind him. Bebe sank down on the bottom step, covering her face.

"I hope you're happy now!" Mrs. Garner said before swishing past her up the stairs.

Several minutes passed as Bebe sat on the stairs. She knew she had to pull herself together, but fear for Horatio threatened to overwhelm her. She felt a hand on her shoulder and looked up. It was one of the refugees.

"My husband is helping, too," she said.

Bebe wiped her eyes and let the woman pull her to her feet.

Peter returned to the house three more times that afternoon, bringing more refugees to safety. Nearly one hundred people crowded into the downstairs hallways and rooms, and Bebe did her best to help them get dried off and settled and fed. During a lull in the activity, she went up to her own bedroom and fell on her knees to pray. Suddenly, above the rumble of voices in the rooms below her, she heard a loud roar outside in the distance.

The dam had burst.

She fell on her face, pleading with God for Horatio.

Bebe had no idea how long she had prayed when she heard hoofbeats and the sound of a carriage rolling to a stop outside. She raced downstairs and threw open the front door, expecting Horatio. Instead, Peter sat on the driver's seat, badly shaken. His carriage full of refugees appeared dazed; many were weeping. Bebe wanted to weep with them, but she opened the carriage door and offered her hand to help them down.

"Please, come inside where it's warm. We have coffee and food waiting." When the last one climbed out, she looked up at the driver. He hadn't moved. "Where's Horatio?"

Peter stared into the distance as if he hadn't heard her. "I've never seen anything like it," he mumbled. "The dam burst. The water was like a wall—"

"Is Horatio with you?"

He slowly shook his head. "The water carried trees and debris, and everything crashed into the railroad bridge north of town . . . a-a huge pile! It got hung up on the railroad trestle, but then that gave way and the bridge collapsed and all the debris thundered into town. I-I saw freight cars carried away like toys!" He paused when his voice broke. Tears overflowed and ran down his face. "The water crushed every building in The Flats into matchsticks. Houses were lifted right off their foundations by the force of the water and carried away downriver. I saw . . . I saw people hanging from their windows, screaming for help. . . . There was nothing we could do. . . ."

Bebe climbed up to his seat and grabbed the front of his jacket, shaking him. "Peter! Where's Horatio!"

"I-I don't know. We split up hours ago. He was driving the other carriage."

"Driving it where? Did you see where he went?"

"No, ma'am. We went in different directions. I'm sorry. . . ."

Bebe knew better than to direct her anger and fear at Peter. She released her grip on his jacket. It was drenched. She dried her hands on her skirt. "Come inside and get dried off and warmed up," she told him. "We'll fix you some food and hot coffee. It was very courageous of you to help Horatio this way. I'm glad you're safe."

She kept busy for the rest of the evening, soothing people, making them comfortable, feeding them. Herta, one of the maids, tried to offer Bebe a plate. "Here, Mrs. Garner, sit down and have something to eat. You must be hungry, too."

"No, thank you. I can't eat."

At last she went upstairs to the playroom searching for Lucy, longing to hold her and fill her empty arms. A dozen children were playing quietly with Lucy's toys, carefully watched by their mothers. "Have you seen my daughter, Lucy?" she asked.

"Her grandmother came for her a few hours ago," one of the mothers said.

Bebe went down the hall to Mrs. Garner's bedroom suite and knocked on the door. "Come in," Mrs. Garner said. Lucy lay asleep on her grandmother's lap.

"Have you eaten anything, Mother Garner?" Bebe asked. "Would you like me to bring you something?"

"Where's Horatio? It's getting dark outside."

"He's still out there, helping people."

"The fool!"

"He's not a fool. He's a very courageous man." She lifted Lucy from her mother-in-law's arms, holding her closely for several minutes before laying her on the bed. "I'll be downstairs if you need anything." Bebe left, closing the door behind her.

Later that night, the servants brought out every blanket and pillow in the house for the refugees to use, and they bedded down wherever they could find space, sleeping on the parlor floor and in the dining room and even in the front hallway. Everywhere Bebe looked she saw bedraggled people, some sleeping, some talking quietly, others holding children in their arms, soothing them to sleep.

She finally went upstairs to her bedroom—Horatio's bedroom—but she didn't undress. She would never be able to sleep. She found her Bible and opened it to her mother's favorite psalm: *"God is our refuge and strength, a very present help in trouble. Therefore we will not fear, though the earth be removed, and though the mountains be carried into the midst of the sea; though the waters thereof roar and be troubled . . ."*

At dawn Bebe went downstairs. Peter was gathering all of the able-bodied men to go downtown to help. "I want to go with you and look for Horatio," she told him. "Show me where you last saw him, please."

He shook his head. "You'll only be in the way, ma'am. There's work to do, and they'll need the carriage and horses."

"I can help—"

"No, ma'am. People are buried under all that mud and debris. It's not something a woman should see. Mr. Garner would never forgive me if I let you go down there."

Three days passed before it was safe enough for the women and children to leave Bebe's house. When the ordeal ended and the last refugee had moved out of the mansion, Bebe finally walked down the hill alone. Some areas of town were still under water. Others had mud and wreckage piled as high as the windowsills. Most of the downtown area had flooded, and many buildings had sustained damage. Debris floated everywhere in the hip-deep water, pieces of people's lives and possessions—a chair, pots and pans, an oil lantern. Bebe saw the bloated bodies of rats and dogs and horses. Trees that had avalanched down the mountain in the flood lay piled everywhere, along with ragged planks of wood from houses, shards of window glass, bricks, and shingles.

There was nothing left of The Flats. Not a single house remained standing along either side of the river. Bebe never could have imagined that the once-placid river could cause so much destruction. It had destroyed her town, her life.

Fifty-six people perished in the flood along with her husband. According to the newspapers, the death toll would have been much, much worse if not for the heroism of Horatio T. Garner.

## 20

Bebe barely coped with her sorrow. Horatio's funeral was one of many, many others in town, yet she felt utterly alone in her grief. She walked through the motions of laying her husband to rest as if walking in her sleep. The nanny took little Lucy home after she threw a tantrum during the church service, and Bebe longed to throw herself on the floor, too, and weep like a child. If she could just get through the burial, she told herself, then she could break down.

The ground at the cemetery felt wet and spongy beneath her feet as she climbed from the carriage. The air smelled of damp earth and rotting wood. The graveyard sat high on the ridge above the city, but Bebe couldn't bring herself to look down at the flooding and destruction in the town below. The river had become her enemy, snatching Horatio from her arms and turning her world upside down. The future seemed hidden from her sight, as completely as Roseton's once-familiar streets lay hidden from view. God seemed very far away.

"Whatever will I do?" she asked herself again and again. "Whatever will I do?"

She didn't hear a word the minister said as they prepared to bury Horatio. She was aware of Mother Garner sitting stiffly by her side, but a vast ocean could have filled the space between them. Neither of them could offer comfort to the other. Horatio's mother never shed a tear throughout the ordeal, while Bebe's tears never stopped flowing.

At last the burial service came to an end and a line of mourners walked past, offering Bebe their condolences. Among the strangers was a familiar face: Neal MacLeod's. He removed his hat to bow slightly, and his golden hair—so like Horatio's—shone in the pale spring sunlight.

"Mrs. Garner . . . Beatrice . . ." he began. "I'm so sorry for your loss—"

"You!" They had been sitting in chairs beside the grave, but Mrs. Garner stood suddenly, toppling hers. "How dare you come here?" Her face shook with fury beneath her black net veil.

Bebe sprang to her feet, too. "Mr. MacLeod manages our tannery, Mother Garner—"

"I know exactly who he is!" she said in a harsh whisper. "And who his sister is!"

Neal ducked his head, his face bright with shame. "I'm very sorry for upsetting you. Please excuse me." He turned and hurried away, just as he had run from Bebe on her last day at the tannery. Her tears started again as she remembered how Horatio also had turned away from her on their last day. *"Let me go, Bebe. Let me do this."* He had received what he'd wanted most in life—a chance to redeem his past. But he was never coming home to her.

Home. Bebe returned to the huge, gaudy house that had never been a home to her, hating it more than ever before. The servants tiptoed from room to room, staring at their shoes. Lucy was inconsolable, crying for her father, unable to understand his death, and blaming Bebe for it, for some unfathomable reason. Mrs. Garner never left her room or her bed, numbing her grief with laudanum. And as badly as Bebe longed to lie down in a fog of sleep, as well, she knew it was up to her to keep the household moving forward. Each day felt longer and darker than the previous one.

"A Mr. William Harris is here to see you, ma'am," the maid told Bebe one afternoon. She had been dozing in a chair in the bedroom she had once shared with Horatio when the knock on her door awakened her. It took her a moment to recall that Mr. Harris was the family's attorney.

"Show him into the parlor, please. Tell him I'll be right down." Bebe stood to straighten the wrinkles from her black crepe mourning dress and tidy her hair. When she gazed at her reflection in the mirror she hardly recognized herself.

"I've come to talk about your husband's will," Mr. Harris began after offering his condolences once again. "I know that you and your family are still grieving, but I believe that your husband would want his estate to be settled quickly, and for you to know how things stand financially."

"Yes," she murmured. "Thank you." She heard the lawyer speaking, but she was still groggy with sleep and grief and had trouble comprehending him. The word *will* reminded her of a verse of Scripture—*"Not my will, but thine, be done."* Jesus' words echoed through her mind as Mr. Harris continued.

"Horatio made provisions in his will for his mother and daughter, of course, but you have inherited the bulk of your husband's estate: this home, the tannery, his real estate holdings, bank accounts, and shares of stocks and bonds. I will be happy to provide the details, if you wish—perhaps at a better time. But for now, I want to assure you that the business is doing very well, thanks to

Neal MacLeod, and to let you know that your life can continue as before. Nothing will need to change."

She looked up at him, certain he had missed something very important. "But everything will change, Mr. Harris. Horatio is gone."

"I know, I know. And again, I'm very sorry for your loss. But I want you to know that you have been very well provided for, Mrs. Garner—and for many of my clients that isn't always the case. Too often, I'm afraid, widows are forced to change their entire way of life after such a loss. Their lives are never the same."

After Mr. Harris left, Bebe sat in the parlor, unmoving. The attorney had done his best to reassure her that her life wouldn't change, but she knew that it wasn't true. Once again, she would have to start all over again. How many times had she been in this place? Three weeks ago she had been ready for a new start as she'd packed Horatio's bags to go to the fishing cabin. Would it have worked this time? Would he have remained sober? And if so, for how long?

*"Nothing will need to change,"* Mr. Harris had said, but the truth was, nothing would ever be the same. *"Remember how life changed when the war started and the boys left home?"* Mama had once told her. *"And how it changed again when Franklin had to leave? Life is like that, Beatrice—always changing, always flowing forward like a stream. Things never stay the same. And we have to move on and change, too."*

*"What if I don't want things to change?"* Bebe had asked her mother.

*"You can't fight against the current. You need to trust God and be prepared for wherever the river of life will take you next."*

Trust God. Was she angry with God? How could Bebe be angry when He had answered her prayers? She had prayed that Horatio would return to the cabin and sober up, and he had. God had answered Horatio's prayers, too, finally granting him the courage and redemption he had long sought. *"Not my will, but thine, be done."* Bebe repeated the verse over and over, praying that she could mean it.

For the next few weeks, Bebe watched from her bedroom window as the floodwaters receded and the townspeople prepared to rebuild Roseton. In most ways her life hadn't changed, just as Mr. Harris had promised. She had lived without Horatio's companionship for a very long time, even though they'd shared the same house, the same bedroom. But as she thought about the provisions of Horatio's will—and about God's will—she became increasingly aware that a great injustice had been done. When she finally made up her mind what should be done about it, Bebe made an appointment with Mr. Harris, then sent Neal MacLeod a note, asking him to meet her at the lawyer's office.

Bebe hadn't been to the downtown area in weeks, and as her carriage drove through the streets she saw the last remnants of the floodwaters and piles of debris still waiting to be burned. A muddy watermark stained many of the surviving buildings, showing how high the water level had reached. Mr. Harris's office on Central Avenue stood high enough above the river to be spared, for the most part.

Neal was already waiting in the outer office when Bebe arrived. He looked unchanged to her, as sturdy and strong and capable as ever. He stood up the moment she entered. "Listen, Beatrice, I want to apologize again for upsetting Mrs. Garner at the funeral. I didn't know that she would recognize me. I wasn't aware that she knew about . . . about Mary and me."

"It's not your fault, Neal. I didn't know, either. She never said a word to me about you and Mary in all the years I've lived with her." She was about to ask Neal how he was doing when Mr. Harris emerged from his office.

"Please come in, Mrs. Garner, and have a seat." He waited until

Bebe and Neal were seated in front of his desk and then said, "Once again, I want to say how sorry I am for your loss. Your husband will be remembered as a very great man in this town."

"Thank you, Mr. Harris. You know our foreman, Neal MacLeod, don't you?"

"Yes, of course." The two men shook hands. "What can I do for you, Mrs. Garner?"

Bebe lifted her chin. "You told me that according to Horatio's will, I have inherited all of his property, including the tannery. But now that I've had time to think about it, I don't believe this arrangement is entirely fair. Mr. Garner had two sons—Horatio and Neal. I believe that, by rights, half of the tannery belongs to Neal."

Neal shifted in his chair, suddenly uncomfortable. "What? Wait a minute. . . . You can't be serious."

"Yes, I'm quite serious."

"But . . . I mean . . . that's obviously not what my father wanted or he would have—"

"I disagree. Your father thought very highly of you and wanted *you* to run the tannery, not Horatio. The reason he didn't acknowledge you publicly was to spare his wife's feelings. But since Mrs. Garner is aware of the truth, I believe that his two sons should each inherit half of his business." She turned to face the lawyer. "I would like you to transfer half ownership to Neal, Mr. Harris."

"Wait!" Neal interrupted again. "I don't think you should do this, Beatrice. I . . . I *can't* let you do this."

"Why not? You've been operating the tannery all these years, so it's not as though I'm giving it to you for free—you've earned it. You're the one who has made it profitable. Besides, if part ownership is in your hands, then my daughter and I will be even better off than we are now. I'm sure you'll be motivated to work even harder if half of the tannery belongs to you."

Neal slumped back in his seat, shaking his head in disbelief, but Bebe remained determined. "Can you arrange for the transfer, Mr. Harris?"

The lawyer had been watching and listening without commenting, but he finally spoke up. "Are you certain you wish to do this, Mrs. Garner?"

"Yes. I'm absolutely certain."

"Very well. I'll respect your wishes. I'll prepare all of the necessary documents and deeds."

Neal followed Bebe outside afterward, stopping her as they reached the curb. "I still can't believe you would do this, Beatrice. It's a very kind, generous thing to do. I don't know how I can ever thank you."

"It was the right thing to do, Neal. You're Mr. Garner's son— I'm only his daughter-in-law. Besides, I watched you work at the tannery for more than a year, remember? I saw how much you love that place, how it has become part of you."

"Yes . . . well . . . in any case, thank you. I'll make certain you won't regret it."

Bebe's carriage was parked nearby and the driver had opened the door for her. She had accomplished her task and had no reason to linger, yet neither she nor Neal seemed in a hurry to leave.

He cleared his throat. "Maybe . . . maybe this isn't the best time to discuss this, for I know that you loved your husband and that you're still in mourning. But I think you also know that I . . . I have feelings for you."

"Yes. I know," she said softly.

"During the time we worked together, it would have been wrong to tell you how I felt because you were a married woman. But now it's no longer a sin. . . . I fell in love with you, Beatrice. Whenever I've thought about you for the past year and a half, I've wished that I had told you."

"I knew. And you must have known that I fell in love with you, too. I realized too late that it was wrong. I should have guarded my heart better."

Neal had been staring at his feet as they talked, but he finally looked up at her. "Someday . . . in a year or two . . . do you think there could ever be a future for us?" She saw love and hope and fear in his unguarded expression.

"Oh, Neal . . ." She closed her eyes, longing to share his hope, longing to fall into his arms. "I would love to believe that we might have a future together after enough time has passed, after I finish grieving for Horatio. But Mrs. Garner knows who you are. And if I left her to be with you . . ." Bebe shook her head. "I could never hurt her that way."

Neal exhaled. "Yes, of course. I understand." The muscles in his face worked as he battled his emotions. "I'm a reminder of her husband's infidelity."

"She has lost so much more than we have. Her husband betrayed her, her only son is dead, and the only thing she has left, besides Lucy and me, is her social position. I can't take that away from her. Believe me, I don't want to stay in that horrible house and live an empty life. I would much rather be with you. But I have to stay, for her sake."

*Do the right thing*, Bebe's mother would have told her, *and trust God to bring good out of it.* But she wondered as she watched Neal wipe away a tear that had escaped, if she ever would find the contentment and peace that Hannah had found.

"I might have chosen differently before I started working for the Temperance Union," Bebe continued. "I used to think only of myself and what I wanted. But if there's one thing I've learned from that amazing group of women, it's that God puts other people in our life so that we won't have to suffer through it alone. I can't leave Mrs. Garner all alone. God loves her, even if I find it hard to. And I'm responsible before God for how I treat her."

"You're a good woman, Beatrice," he said, swallowing. "I never dreamed you would give me a share in the tannery. In fact, whenever I've thought about you and the possibility of a future together, I was afraid that it would seem as though I was pursuing you so that I could inherit it. It never would have been my intention to marry you for the business."

"I know, Neal. I know you would never do that."

"Well . . . maybe we should leave things the way they are—strictly business." He looked up at her again, and she saw both love and pain in his eyes. She still could change her mind; she had only to speak the word and they could be together.

"Strictly business," she whispered. She could barely see him through her tears. Bebe loved Horatio. He had just died, and she still couldn't accept his loss. But she loved Neal MacLeod, too. Was such a thing possible?

"Are you going to be all right?" he asked. She nodded. "You could always come back to work with me at the tannery, you know."

"The tannery is your life's work, not mine. I have to move forward, not backward. And change is a part of life. I learned that growing up on the farm—sowing, growing, harvesting—life always goes on."

"What will you do, then?"

It was becoming clear to Bebe that she would continue her work with the Temperance Union even though her family was no longer affected. As the wife of Roseton's new hero, her voice would carry a great deal of clout. "With so much reconstruction taking place around here," she said, "I need to make sure that all the saloons aren't rebuilt, as well."

"I know how smart and capable you are. I have no doubt at all that you'll succeed in whatever you try to accomplish."

"Thank you."

The street had been free of traffic as they'd talked, but when a wagon and team of horses approached, Neal took Bebe's arm and gently guided her away from the curb so the approaching vehicle wouldn't splash them. "Why does life have to be so hard?" she asked after it passed.

"I don't know. I guess that's just the way it is." He released her arm and began backing away from her, as he always did. She wanted to embrace him one last time but knew that she didn't dare.

"Thank you again, for what you did with the tannery," he said. "I'll run it well, for both our sakes. I'll make sure that you're always well provided for."

"I know I'm in good hands. Good-bye, Neal."

"Good-bye."

Bebe took one long, last look at him as he continued to back away from her. Then he finally turned and hurried off. "God go with you," she whispered.

Bebe went upstairs to her mother-in-law's room and knocked on her door as soon as she returned home. Trading a future with Neal MacLeod for a future with Mrs. Garner had been one of the hardest things she had ever done, but she knew she had made the right decision. Again, she thought of the words *Not my will, but thine, be done.*

"Mother Garner?" she said after knocking a second time. "It's me, Beatrice." When she still didn't hear a reply, she went inside. The shades were drawn in the unkempt room, and Mrs. Garner lay buried beneath a mound of blankets and pillows. Bebe scooped up the tin of laudanum pills from her nightstand and slipped it into her pocket, then opened all the curtains and window shades.

"What do you think you're doing?" Mrs. Garner asked. The pillows muffled her voice.

"You have to get up, Mother Garner. You need to answer all of these condolence cards."

"You do it."

"I already answered the ones that were addressed to me. But good manners require you to respond to the ones addressed to you."

"Who are you to lecture me about good manners?"

Bebe drew a deep breath and slowly let it out. "I share your grief, Mother Garner. I loved Horatio, too. But he wouldn't want us to stop living. He would want us to carry on with our lives and learn to be happy again."

The covers rustled as Mrs. Garner sat up, leaning on her elbows. "What reason do I have to be happy? I have no one left."

"That's not true. You have Lucy . . . and me."

Mrs. Garner stared at Bebe as if questioning her sincerity. "I suppose you'll sell my home out from under me now, and everything will change. You never wanted anything to do with this house or our way of life."

"I'm not selling the house, and nothing is going to change. You're Horatio's mother, and he loved you. I'll always take care of you, for his sake. And for Lucy's sake. She loves you, too."

Mrs. Garner's eyes were cold as she stared at Bebe. "If you hadn't made him go up to that cabin with you, he would have been here at home where it was safe when the dam burst."

Her mother-in-law's words couldn't hurt Bebe. She had punished herself with them a hundred times since Horatio died. "Maybe so," she said quietly. "But thousands of innocent people would be dead." She walked toward the door, then turned back. "I'm going to send Herta up with a tray of food. You need to eat something, Mother Garner, and regain your strength. I'm planning to invite a small group of your friends to come for tea next week. They are concerned about you. Besides, according to all the etiquette books, holding a small reception is the proper thing to do."

Bebe felt a double measure of sorrow as she descended the

stairs to speak with the cook—sorrow over Horatio and over Neal. Yet God seemed very close to her at that moment, as close as He had been the first time she'd prayed in front of a saloon. Loving her mother-in-law was the task that He had given to Bebe for now. And though nearly everything else in her life had been taken away, God was still with her.

And she was going to be fine.

e⁓

By the time Grandma Bebe finished telling her story, I was crying. Tears flowed down her cheeks, too. I felt terrible for putting them there. I never should have made her relive that terrible day—much less relive it during Alice's wedding reception. The musicians played a stately waltz, people laughed and danced—while we cried our eyes out.

"I'm sorry," I said, hugging her. "I heard about the Great Flood of 1876 in school but no one ever told me what my grandfather did. Why didn't you tell me this story before?"

"Don't be silly. You've heard the story."

I shook my head. "No, I haven't. . . . I don't even know where he's buried."

"I'll take you there some time. . . . Well, I'm ready to leave, are you? There is entirely too much drinking at this shindig for me to want to stay."

I told Daddy we were going home, and I climbed into Grandma's car with her. I expected her to go straight home, but instead she drove to Garner Park and stopped at a spot overlooking the river.

"I know you've been to this park before, Harriet. You must have seen the monument stone."

"I guess I have," I said with a shrug. "I know your name is

Garner and that this is Garner Park, but my name is Sherwood . . . and I guess I never gave it much thought."

"Well, come on, then."

Dew dampened my shoes as we walked across the grass. A half-moon lit the way for us, and stars shone above our heads. Grandma halted beside a granite marker that was taller than she was. It looked like a giant tombstone. I had never bothered to read the engraving before, but this time I did: *In memory of Horatio T. Garner, whose courage and heroism saved thousands of lives in the Great Flood, March 25, 1876.* The names of the fifty-six other people who had perished along with him were inscribed beneath his name in smaller letters.

"The city proclaimed your grandfather a hero," Grandma told me. "They named this park after him. They said he saved thousands of lives, but my poor Horatio was washed away with the floodwaters. They found his body nearly a mile downstream." She sighed and gestured to the trees and pathways and flower beds all around us. "This park is where The Flats used to be. After the disaster, the city decided to move the workers' neighborhood to higher ground. They built those levies along the riverbanks for protection."

"No one ever told me," I said softly.

"Well." She sighed again. "I can't imagine why not. My Horatio was quite famous, dear." She gazed off at the distant river. "It was always very hard for me to talk about losing Horatio. I imagine it must have been even harder for your mother. How do you explain heroism to a child, especially when she misses her daddy?" Grandma Bebe pulled a handkerchief out of her sleeve and wiped her eyes.

"I'm sorry, Grandma. I didn't mean to spoil this happy day."

"You didn't spoil it, dear," she said with a smile. "Joy and sorrow are two sides of the same coin. They both come in seasons, just like floods and droughts. I loved my Horatio. I think about him nearly every day."

She reached to take my hand and we walked side by side, back to her car.

"He was a good man underneath it all," she said as she slid behind the steering wheel. "But in a way, he really died years earlier on a battlefield in Virginia. I guess it just takes some men longer than others to fall down dead. My brother Joseph was one of the lucky ones who died quickly."

I was afraid to ask any more questions, but as we drove away, I wondered when Grandma had moved out of Horatio's big mansion on the ridge. She had lived in her modest house overlooking the river for as long as I'd known her. The view from her bedroom window was of the river. I wondered if it reminded her of Horatio.

She halted the car in front of her garage, but we didn't get out right away. The gaslights up and down the street gave off a warm glow as we sat in the dark, talking.

"I loved him, Harriet. There was goodness and joy in him in spite of all the sorrow he brought into our lives. If only he could have believed in himself and overcome his drinking. But alcohol had a grip on him, and he couldn't shake free. That's why it should be outlawed. It ruined the life of a good man.

"Some people call our temperance crusade the Women's Whiskey War," Grandma continued. "And it is a war, make no mistake about that. We've had to fight hard to make this community aware of all the hardship that comes from alcohol, aware of the children who live in appalling conditions and die from poor health because their fathers drink away all of their earnings. We'll do whatever it takes to win this war, whether it means praying in front of saloons or smashing whiskey barrels at the train depot."

"But after Horatio died, you had no reason to keep fighting, did you? Why not just live peacefully?"

"I couldn't do that. I knew about the evil of alcohol firsthand. What better work could I ever do than to help others fight it? The other women and I do what we need to do—and lives are saved. I would like to think that in his short, tragic life, Horatio saved this town from more than the flood."

"But you did all the work, Grandma, not Horatio."

She shook her head. "Marriage is always a partnership, dear. I loved Horatio."

"How could you still love him after everything he put you through?"

"Love isn't always a feeling. Sometimes it's a decision. I can only pray that you and Alice will find love and meaning in your marriages, too."

"I'm never getting married," I mumbled, crossing my arms. I meant it now more than ever before. Why suffer all that pain and sorrow?

Grandma smiled at me through her tears. "We shall see, Harriet, my dear. We shall see."

CHAPTER

21

Who knew that life in jail could be so boring? Grandma Bebe had been arrested several times, so you'd think she would have at least mentioned it. If only someone would bring me a book to read—I would have even settled for some needlework to help while away the hours, and heaven knows I never have been one to sit and stitch. I seemed to be the only person in jail that day, which meant I had no one to talk to. Time passed as slowly and as annoyingly as a dripping faucet.

I finally sat up and ate my lunch. The glistening tapioca pudding wore down my resistance. I never could turn down a good bowl of tapioca. When that was gone and I had licked every slick, lumpy morsel off the bowl and spoon, I decided I might as well eat the vegetable soup and the bread, too. There is no point in attempting a hunger strike if you're going to make an exception and gobble down your dessert.

"The soup was watery and the bread was dry," I told the man who came to retrieve my lunch tray.

"Ain't that a pity now?" I could tell by his smirk that he didn't care. He slammed the cell door closed as if to remind me that I was incarcerated.

The afternoon dragged even more slowly than the morning had. Worrying about my fate didn't help my mood, either. Prohibition had become the law of the land only a few months ago, and I was one of the very first people in Roseton to get caught breaking it. I had no idea how long my jail term might last. Spending one day in this place was bad enough; I couldn't imagine spending several years this way. If prison was meant to be a deterrent to a life of crime, then I was ready to repent of my misdeeds and forswear all criminal behavior forever.

I slumped against the cold brick wall and sighed. I had been asking myself the same questions over and over ever since Tommy had locked me in here last night. How in the world had I ended up here, so far from where I imagined life would take me? And how would I ever find my way back to where I should be? I had hoped to stumble upon the answers by reminiscing about my grandmother's life. So far, it hadn't worked.

When my supper tray arrived hours later, I was very surprised to see that once again, Tommy O'Reilly delivered it. "Is our town so short of policemen that you not only have to arrest all the criminals but feed them, as well?" I asked.

"I was worried about you, Harriet. I wanted to see how you were doing."

I tried to think of a witty retort but couldn't. Boredom had dulled my mind. "I'm fine," I said, "considering my circumstances."

What really confused me was the fact that I was happy to see him. Both times that Tommy had made an appearance I had felt a jolt of adrenaline go through me, just as it had when we were kids. Back then, the spurt would come as I readied myself for a fight. But he was behaving so nicely today. Why was my heart speeding up? Could it be a learned reaction that I'd developed over the years? I didn't want to believe that it was because Tommy had grown into a good-looking man with a grin like ivory piano keys.

"Here you go," Tommy said as the cell door creaked open. "Dinner is served."

This time he came all the way inside and set the tray on my lap. The aroma of roast beef drifted up to my nostrils. A mound of mashed potatoes with gravy and a pile of green beans lay alongside the slab of meat. There was a hefty slice of chocolate cake for dessert. My traitorous mouth began to water.

"Thanks," I told him.

Tommy started to leave but made it only as far as the cell door before turning back. "Are you sure I can't do anything else for you, Harriet?"

I studied him with suspicion. Why was he being so nice? Why couldn't he have been this nice during our school years instead of tormenting me day after day? He had been nice last night, too, when he'd stopped my car and seemed to genuinely regret the need to arrest me.

"As a matter of fact, there is something you can do," I told him as I speared a forkful of mashed potatoes. "You can notify the Sunday school superintendent at my church that I won't be available to teach my class tomorrow—unless the girls want to come down here for their lesson."

"Harriet . . ." he said with a sigh.

"Tommy . . ." I said, imitating him.

"I don't understand you," he said, leaning against the bars. "I never did. You were never like any of the other girls in school."

"Oh? How was I different? Aside from the fact that I stood up to you and the other girls all ran away in fear?" I continued to eat my dinner. Mother would call it unladylike to talk with my mouth full or to eat in front of someone who wasn't eating, but I was hungry.

Tommy smiled. "You were always just like this—sassy and bold. And you were also a lot brighter than the other kids, even the boys." He hesitated, and he appeared to be considering something. "I've been thinking about your arrest all day, Harriet. I want you to tell me your story again. How did you end up with all that bootleg liquor in your car?"

"I knew you weren't listening to me last night."

"You weren't exactly reasonable last night."

After a moment's reflection I knew it was true.

"The thing I don't understand," he continued, "is that your grandmother is notorious here in Roseton for busting up saloons and smashing whiskey barrels. We have quite a collection of hatchets that once belonged to her."

"I used to buy her a new one for Christmas every year."

"So why are you carting liquor around for a bunch of bootleggers?"

I didn't reply. My reasons no longer made sense to me in the light of day. I sawed into my roast beef with the dull knife.

"I was thinking that maybe I could get you out of jail myself," Tommy continued. "I'm off duty until Monday. I could keep you under house arrest until your hearing before a judge—and in the meantime, maybe you can explain everything to me in a calm, reasonable fashion."

"You coming to Sunday school with me, too?" I asked with my mouth full.

He shrugged. "I suppose I'll have to."

I studied him with narrowed eyes. "Is this some sort of policeman's trick?"

"What would I gain from it?"

"I don't know—fame, a big promotion for capturing such a notorious criminal. Maybe you dream of becoming police superintendent like your father."

"You have quite an imagination, Harriet."

"I've studied police procedure, you know," I said with a half grin. "I'm a big fan of 'The Keystone Cops' and Fatty Arbuckle."

"Hey, me too! There's a new episode playing at the movie theatre this week—have you seen it yet?"

I gestured to my surroundings and shook my head before gulping the last bite of my chocolate cake.

"So what do you say, Harriet—have you had your fill of this place? Are you ready to be set free?"

I knew I should keep my mouth shut and let Tommy spring me from jail rather than spend another night here, but I couldn't let my suspicions rest. "I need to know why you would do this," I told him.

"Look, I live in this town, too, so I'd like it to be a safe, law-abiding place. My job is to keep the peace and arrest people who break the law. Our hands have been full of lawbreakers ever since Prohibition started. The moment the government made liquor against the law—which I think is a good thing, by the way—there was suddenly a lot of money to be made by breaking that law. It's supposed to be up to the federal agents to enforce Prohibition, but there aren't enough of them to go around."

"I think it's ironic that we're both on the same side for once, Tommy."

"Yeah, me too." He smiled his magnificent smile, erasing all traces of the bully I once knew. "Listen, why are we still talking in here? Let me see about getting you out of jail, all right?"

I remembered how the farmer and his sons had pulled Grandma and me out of the mud. Maybe this was one of those times when it was better to be rescued than to be stubbornly self-sufficient. *"There is no shame in changing direction,"* Grandma had said.

"All right. If you insist, Tommy. But I really have no place to go."

"Where are your parents? And your famous grandmother? . . . Although, under the circumstances, I think I understand why you may not want to call her. Don't you have a married sister who lives here in town?"

"You seem to know quite a lot about me."

"Roseton isn't that big. Listen, do you really want to spend another night in this place?"

"Not if I can help it."

"Sit tight, then," he said as he took my supper tray. "I'll be back."

"I'm not going anywhere," I assured him. I lay down on the cot and folded my hands behind my head as he hurried out, locking the door behind him.

Funny he should ask about my parents. My mother's life was another complicated story. I decided to consider the part that she played in this drama while I waited for Tommy to return.

&

My mother's childhood was worlds apart from the simple farm life that Grandma Bebe had known. Lucretia "Lucy" Garner was born with the proverbial silver spoon in her mouth, and she knew it. She quickly acquired a taste for the finer things in life, and by the time she learned to walk, any lesser type of spoon left a very bad flavor on her palate.

Her earliest memory, so she has told me, was of the day she peeked over the upstairs railing when she was supposed to be napping and saw Grandmother Garner's elegant friends arriving for afternoon tea. Lucy looked down at their flower-strewn hats and swirling satin gowns and thought they looked like the brilliantly colored birds in one of her picture books. When the ladies all disappeared into the parlor, Lucy tiptoed down the stairs to follow them, their voices and laughter drawing her like the sound of gurgling water.

Inside the echoing room, Grandmother's finest china teacups clinked and tinkled along with the laughter. Silver serving pieces that usually rested on the dining room sideboard shone in all their glory on marble-topped side tables. Parlor maids in black uniforms and starched white aprons flitted around like chickadees, serving the guests. Lucy stared in openmouthed awe at the beautiful spectacle.

Then the nanny, who should have been watching Lucy, caught up with her and snatched her away from the doorway. "You're supposed to be taking a nap," she whispered as she carried her toward the stairs. Lucy howled in protest.

Grandmother Garner set down her teacup and strode into the foyer to see what all the fuss was about. "Whatever is the matter, Lucy darling?"

"I don't want to take a nap, Grandmama. I want to come to your party."

Mrs. Garner smiled regally, careful not to disturb her calm composure. She reminded Lucy of a queen in a fairy tale, royally elegant with her swishing dresses and straight-backed posture, commanding obeisance from all the household servants and respect from all the society matrons. "You certainly shall attend one day, my dear. But first, we must make certain you are properly attired and instructed. These social gatherings require a great deal of training, you know. Now, toddle along upstairs and I will talk to your father about it tonight—there's no sense trying to discuss anything important with your mother."

Lucy wasn't happy about being left out of the festivities, but she did what she was told. And Grandmother Garner kept her promise. The very next day she gave Lucy a miniature porcelain tea set decorated with red roses and gold trim so she could begin to learn the rituals. The porcelain felt cool and smooth beneath Lucy's fingers.

"You must be very careful when you play with it, Lucy. You wouldn't want to break any of the pieces."

"I would never break it, Grandmama!" She carried the tea set up to her playroom so she could recreate her grandmother's party, planning to invite her stuffed bear and all of her dolls. She invited Mama the next morning at breakfast. "I'm having a tea party today like Grandmama's. Will you come?"

"I'm sorry, darling, but I have to go down to the tannery to work." Mama was always going to the tannery and was seldom home during the day. Every morning after breakfast she would pin on her hat and kiss Lucy good-bye, and she wouldn't return until suppertime.

Lucy decided to invite Daddy, instead. He slept very late every day, and she wasn't allowed to see him until he woke up. But when the maid brought him his tray of coffee and toast, Lucy tiptoed into his bedroom along with her as she did nearly every morning.

"I'm having a tea party today, Daddy. Would you like to come?" He squinted at her as if the room were very bright, even though all the curtains were still drawn. Then he smiled.

"Are men allowed to come? Your grandmother never invites men to her tea parties, you know." He pulled himself upright in bed so the servant could set the tray on his lap, then patted a place beside him, inviting Lucy to sit. She climbed up next to him and held out her hand for a lump of sugar. He gave her two. They both laughed at their familiar ritual as she savored the sugar's crunchy sweetness.

"It's *my* party, Daddy, and I can invite whoever I want, and I want you." He tousled her hair, then leaned over to kiss her forehead. Lucy loved her daddy's scent, like the rum cakes their cook made at Christmastime. The smell of bay rum aftershave always reminded Lucy of him.

Later that afternoon, when Lucy had everything ready, her father came to her tea party, sitting cross-legged on the playroom floor beside her, wearing his blue silk bathrobe. He held a tiny teacup in his hand and made slurping noises as he pretended to drink. Cook had baked tea cakes with pink frosting for Lucy to serve along with the pretend tea. They laughed and laughed. Lucy loved her carefree, golden-haired daddy—the most handsome daddy in the whole world. When she looked at herself in the mirror on her dressing table, she could see that she had fair hair and blue eyes just like his. She didn't look at all like Mama, who had dark hair and dark eyes and a dark frown.

Once Lucy began to learn proper social skills, Grandmother Garner planned a glorious party for her fifth birthday in May of 1874. Grandmother's friends filled the parlor, wearing their colorful afternoon gowns and bringing their little daughters and granddaughters along with them. It was a real grown-up tea party—Lucy's first. Her dress was the prettiest one, hand-sewn by Grandmother's seamstress and decorated with imported lace and embroidered smocking. Lucy stood in the front foyer to properly greet her guests, saying "Welcome" and "So glad you could come" just as Grandmama had taught her. She loved the envious looks the other girls gave her when they saw her dress and the satin bows that Nanny had tied in her shining golden ringlets.

Everyone brought Lucy a beautifully wrapped present, and she gave each child a little present to take home. The dining room table overflowed with food and candy and other treats, and Lucy ate and ate until her stomach ached. Then Cook brought in a towering cake with birthday candles. "Make a wish and blow them out, dear," Grandmama said.

Lucy closed her eyes and silently wished that Mother and Daddy could be there for her party. She must have closed her eyes too tightly, because when she opened them again, the candles seemed to waver behind a curtain of tears. It took her two tries to blow out all five candles.

A few minutes later, part of Lucy's wish came true when her mother rushed home from the tannery in time to eat a piece of birthday cake. She wasn't dressed as elegantly as the other women were, and she looked small and plain and out of place among the guests with their glittering necklaces and earrings. Lucy was sorry she had wasted her birthday wish.

"Where's Daddy? Why didn't he come?" she asked.

"I wish he could be here, Lucy. He loves you so much." Mother quickly finished her cake and swallowed her tea, then took Lucy aside. "I need to go back to work now," she whispered. "I love you, sweetheart."

Daddy didn't return home until very late that night after Lucy was already asleep. He tiptoed into her room carrying a candle and sat down on the edge of her bed, softly calling her name and stroking her fair hair until she woke up. She recognized his sweet scent. "Hi, Daddy."

"Hey, my darling girl. I'm so sorry I had to miss your birthday party. Something important came up, and I couldn't get away." Even in the middle of the night Daddy seemed happy, his face glowing with pleasure—unlike Mama, who always looked vexed and worried.

"That's okay, Daddy," she said sleepily. "Grandma didn't invite any men. You would have been the only one there."

"But I didn't forget your birthday, sweetheart. Here. I brought you a present." He held out a small box, and Lucy scrambled to sit up so she could unwrap it. Inside was a fine golden chain with a dark green gemstone dangling from it, shaped like a teardrop. "It's an emerald, sweetheart. Your birthstone. Here, let me put it on you." He fumbled to fasten the clasp around her neck. When he finished, Lucy hugged him tightly.

"I'll never, ever take it off! I love you, Daddy, more than anyone in the whole world."

"And I love you, too. Now, make a wish and blow out the candle, sweetheart. I'll see you in the morning."

Lucy didn't know what to wish for. She had everything she could ever want, except . . . maybe . . . a pony of her very own. She closed her eyes and wished for one, then blew out her father's candle.

Most of Lucy's days were spent with her nanny, but sometimes Grandmama would invite Lucy into her bedroom suite to read to her from etiquette books or look at fashion magazines. "I'm going to teach you how to be a proper young woman so you can attend society events someday," she told her. "You should be very proud of your high standing in this town. Our family owns one of the largest businesses. You can marry anyone you choose." At age five, Lucy imagined that getting married would be like kissing the handsome prince in the fairy tales Mother used to read to her—the end of the story, not the beginning.

Lucy admired her austere grandmother but was a little in awe of her. She especially loved the stately way her grandmother walked and the swishing sound her skirts made. "You can learn how to walk the same way, Lucy, by balancing a book on top of your head for practice." Grandmama showed her how, and Lucy practiced and practiced with Nanny, but no matter how hard she tried, Lucy couldn't get her dresses to make the swishing sound.

"I want more petticoats so my dresses sound like Grandmama's," she told her mother one morning at breakfast.

Mother laid down her newspaper and frowned. "You have enough petticoats. You're a little girl, Lucy. How can you run around and play in such stiff clothing?"

313

"I don't want to run, I want petticoats! Buy me some right now!" She stamped her foot for emphasis. Mother's frown deepened.

"Lucy, you may not talk to me that way."

Lucy had learned how to throw a temper tantrum to make Nanny do her bidding, and she decided to throw one now for her mother, kicking her feet and making as much racket as she could. Nanny ran into the dining room in alarm, but Mother calmly returned to her newspaper. "Carry Lucy to her room until she can control herself," she ordered. But as soon as Mother left for the tannery, Grandmother Garner came to Lucy's rescue.

"There, there, don't cry, darling. If you want more petticoats, we'll go shopping today and buy you some."

Lucy loved to shop. The carriage driver took them down to Central Avenue and Lucy held Grandmother's hand as they went from store to store, buying three of the prettiest, noisiest petticoats they could find. When Mother came home at suppertime, Lucy twirled in happy circles to show them to her—and to let her know that she had won the contest. Mama sighed and frowned and looked unhappy. Mother always gazed at Lucy as if she were aboard a ship that was slowly sailing away. She wondered why Mother didn't jump on board with her.

Then one day her mother didn't leave to go to the tannery after breakfast. Lucy found her sitting at the little writing desk in the morning room, instead. "What are you doing, Mama?"

"I'm writing letters to some very important people, dear." She didn't look up.

"Why?"

"Because I need to convince them to make some changes in our community, and—" She paused, finally looking up from her work. "It's hard to explain, Lucy."

"Are you going to the tannery after you finish writing the letters?"

When Mother's eyes filled with tears, Lucy feared she had said something wrong. "I won't be working there anymore," she said softly.

Lucy thought it was going to be wonderful to have her mother home again, but nothing changed very much in the months that followed. Mother's new work always occupied her: writing letters, reading pamphlets, organizing meetings. She never attended Grandmama's tea parties even though she was at home, nor she did she go calling in the afternoon like all of the other women did. But nearly every evening after dinner, Mother gathered up her picket signs and banners and left the house, staying out until long after Lucy fell asleep. Daddy seemed very angry with her and Lucy overheard him shouting at her one morning after the maid brought him his coffee. Lucy stood outside his bedroom door, listening.

"Where are my friends and I supposed to go now that you've closed down the place?"

"That's the point," Mother said. "You're not supposed to go anywhere. You're supposed to stop drinking every night and stay home with us." Her voice sounded very calm even though Daddy was angry. "I'm doing this for Lucy's sake. She loves you so much, you know. But how will she feel in a few years when she learns the truth about where you spend all your time?"

"You wouldn't tell her!"

"No, of course not. But other people here in town know the truth, and someday she'll find out, too, and it will destroy her love for you. Please, Horatio. I'm begging you to stop."

"Go away and leave me alone."

Lucy had no idea what they were fighting about, but everyone she loved seemed angry and sad all the time, even Grandmama. The tension made Lucy feel sad, too. And frightened. Her nanny tried to keep her occupied during the day and always closed the door to Lucy's playroom or bedroom or took her for a walk when her parents began to argue. But one morning on Nanny's day off, Lucy overheard her mother and grandmother fighting as she tiptoed downstairs for breakfast.

"I insist that you stop these crazy campaigns of yours," Grandmama said. "They are an embarrassment to me, to our family, and to yourself. You should be ashamed of such behavior." Lucy could tell by the sound of Grandmama's voice that her face was turning very red.

Mother's voice sounded as hard and tight as a fist when she replied. "Your son is the one who should be ashamed and embarrassed, not me. Why don't you ask him how he spends his evenings?"

"Because it's none of my business. Besides, his actions aren't described in vivid detail on the front pages of the newspaper every morning the way yours are."

"I spend my evenings praying and singing hymns—how is that disgraceful?"

"Because you do it on street corners in the most disreputable parts of town and in the company of the most disreputable sort of people. Don't you care at all about Lucy's future?"

Lucy's cheeks started growing warm when she heard her name. She worried that she had caused the argument somehow, but she didn't know what she had done. She wanted to run into the dining room and tell them to stop fighting, but every time in the past that she had come between the two women, she always felt like the rope in a game of tug-of-war, pulled in opposite directions.

"I care very much about my daughter's future," Mother continued. "And in that future she deserves to have a father she can respect."

"What about a mother she can respect? You're earning a terrible reputation in this town with your shenanigans."

"I'm trying to improve this town by closing down the multitude of saloons that have sprouted like weeds, and if some people don't like that, it's just too bad. Are you aware of the social problems caused by alcohol? You can read all about them in the Temperance Union's newsletter. Or you can open your eyes and see what's happening in your very own home."

"I can't talk to you anymore. You not only have no common sense, you've become some sort of religious fanatic."

"You're calling me a fanatic because I trust God and ask for His help? Or is it because I've chosen not to attend your church anymore?"

"That so-called church you attend is filled with religious fanatics just like yourself. There isn't a respectable citizen among them."

"Thank God for that! Thank God they're not too respectable to offer help during a cholera epidemic or to give aid to families with drunken husbands and fathers. I won't spend one more Sabbath in a church that ignores Christ's command to help the poor. Maybe you're comfortable in such a place, but I'm not."

As soon as the topic switched to churches, Lucy began backing away from the door to run upstairs. When Mother had decided to join a different church than the one Grandmama always went to, Lucy had felt like a piece of taffy, stretched and pulled in two directions at once. The tug-of-war continued until the two women finally asked Lucy to choose which church she liked the best. She hadn't known what to say. Of course, she wanted to please her mother, but she didn't know any of the other girls at Mother's church, and besides, they dressed so differently than she did. In the end, Lucy chose her grandmother's elegant church because that was the one that Daddy used to go to when he was a little boy. The distance between Lucy and her mother seemed to grow wider each day.

In the spring of 1876, Grandmother began planning a lavish

party for Lucy's seventh birthday. Lucy decided to ask for a pony that year, along with her very own pony cart to ride around in. But when she followed the maid into her father's bedroom one morning with his coffee and toast, she sensed right away that something had changed. For one thing, Mother was in his bedroom, too, and she was stuffing Daddy's clothes and toiletries into a suitcase. Daddy sat on the edge of the bed with his shoulders slumped. He looked very sad. His blue eyes weren't sparkling anymore, and he had dark circles beneath them.

"Are you going away on a trip, Daddy?" she asked.

Mother answered before he did. "We're going to stay at Grandfather Garner's fishing cabin for a few days."

Lucy skirted around her mother and ran to him. "I want to come on the trip, too, Daddy."

He tucked a strand of her hair behind her ear. "You wouldn't like it up at the cabin, sweetheart."

"Yes I would. I want to go. Why can't I go?" She stomped her foot and started to cry, certain that Daddy would give in, but her mother gripped her firmly by the shoulders and turned her around.

"Stop it, Lucy, and listen to me. Remember when Nanny took you upstairs to the attic and showed you where the servants sleep? Well, the cabin that we're going to is even more rustic than the attic is. It has spiders living there. And mice."

"You're just saying that. It's not true. I want to go!" Her tantrum didn't do any good. Her mother finished packing and prepared to leave.

"I'm sorry, Lucy," Daddy said as he kissed her good-bye. "I promise to buy you a very special present for your birthday when I get home."

"A pony. I want my own pony."

Daddy smiled faintly, but he didn't promise. Lucy tried one last time to throw a tantrum to get her own way, but Nanny held her back until her parents' runabout disappeared from sight.

She was playing with her dolls in the playroom a week later when Mother burst into the house shouting, "Lucy! Lucy, where are you?"

Lucy stood and went to the playroom door. "I'm up here, Mama." Her mother bounded up the stairs in a very unladylike way, then hugged Lucy so tightly it made her ribs hurt.

"Thank God! Thank God!" Mother murmured. She wasn't wearing a hat and the rain had soaked her clothing and hair. Her body shivered so badly it might have been snowing outside instead of raining. Daddy came inside, too, shouting something about the dam on Iroquois Lake. He rang the service bell to summon all the servants. Grandmama came out of her room and tried to get Daddy to close the front door and change out of his wet clothes, but he wouldn't listen.

Lucy had no idea what was going on, but everyone was shouting, and the household had never been in such an uproar. It made her feel very frightened. She started down the stairs toward her father, calling, "Daddy, Daddy!" but her mother caught her instead, and wouldn't let go of her until after her father left with the carriage driver. "Daddy! I want my daddy!" she wept, but it was too late. He was gone. Lucy fled into her grandmother's arms, instead.

"There, there," she soothed. "Come, my dearest. I'll tell Cook to fix us some tea and cookies."

Before Lucy had time to finish her cookies, Mother and Grandmama began to quarrel. The servants started moving all of Grandmama's pretty things out of the parlor and upstairs to her bedroom. Then Daddy came back with a carriage load of strangers—horrible, dirty people who crowded into Lucy's house, dripping water on the carpets and hardwood floors. Most of them were children, foul-smelling and dressed in rags, and elderly people with wrinkled faces, who spoke in languages she couldn't understand.

"Lift me up, Daddy. Carry me." She reached up to him but he only patted her head.

"Not now, sweetheart. I'm all wet. Your nice dress will get all wet."

"I don't care." She wanted his arms around her and everything changed back to the way it used to be, so she could go into his bedroom and talk to him every day.

She blamed her mother for all of this chaos. Mother was giving everyone directions and inviting them into the house, saying, "Please, come inside and get warm. We have food and hot coffee prepared." But when Mother suddenly said, "Come, Lucy. Let's take these children upstairs and show them where your playroom is," Lucy was too horrified to reply. She was desperate to stop the horrible children from going into her special room and was about to shout "No!" and throw a tantrum, but Grandmother Garner spoke up first.

"You can't be serious, Beatrice. These people can't be trusted. They'll break all of Lucy's nice things."

Mother waved her away. "I don't want Lucy to grow up to be selfish," she said. Lucy couldn't think what to do! Mother plunged ahead, saying, "Come, children. This way. Lucy, you go first and show them where your playroom is." The raggedy children started moving up the stairs.

"Aren't you going to stop her?" Grandmother asked Daddy. He shook his head. Lucy scrambled up the stairs as fast as she could go, racing toward the playroom to protect her toys. She would get the servants to help her move everything into Grandmama's room the way they had moved all of the valuables out of the parlor and dining room.

Lucy reached the playroom first, ready to scream or cry or

throw a tantrum, if need be, in order to keep the dirty children out. But a strange thing happened when the first few children reached the playroom behind her: Instead of running and grabbing and breaking her things, they stood huddled near the door, as unmoving as store mannequins, gazing around the huge room. The pause gave Lucy a few moments to calm down.

Then one little boy, the bravest one, took two halting steps inside. He had hair the color of wet sand and ragged clothing that hung from his slender body like a scarecrow's. She couldn't tell if all of the spots on his dirt-smudged his face were freckles or filth. He made a sweeping gesture with his scrawny arm, pointing to her shelves and toy boxes and to the pile of dolls in the middle of the floor that she had been playing with a few hours ago. "What are all these things?" he asked.

"They're called toys. Haven't you ever seen toys before?"

He lifted one bony shoulder in what might have been a shrug. "What do you do with them?"

Lucy had never met such a stupid boy. "What do you think you do? You play with them!" She watched as his gaze roamed the room, taking it all in. Then he spotted her wooden rocking horse and he took a few more steps inside, halting alongside it.

"What's this for?" He reached out his hand to stroke the horse-hair mane.

"You ride on it. Like this." She pulled the horse out of his reach and climbed on, gripping the handles to rock back and forth. The horse was a baby's toy, and Lucy had been bored with it for the past year, but when she saw the boy and all of the other children watching in amazement and admiration she decided that she liked the rocking horse again.

"Can I try it?" the boy asked.

"You mean, '*may* I?' " He looked at her as if she had spoken a foreign language. "You're supposed to say '*may*' I try it, not '*can*' I."

"I want to ride it," he said matter-of-factly, and Lucy recognized something in his gray eyes, a deep sadness that seemed very much like her own.

"Well . . . I suppose you may," she told him. "But you'd better be careful and not break it."

A huge smile spread across his face as he climbed on. She guessed that he was a little older than she was because his two front teeth were growing in and her baby teeth were just falling out. He had holes in his shirt and one button missing. The other three buttons didn't match each other. His pants were too short, his shoes too large. He wasn't wearing socks. But he laughed out loud as he rocked back and forth, and it was such a joyous sound that Lucy couldn't help smiling.

The other children watched him from the doorway, and since the stampede she'd feared hadn't happened, Lucy began walking around the room taking toys off the shelves, showing everyone how to play with them. She didn't show them her newest doll or her very special things like the porcelain tea set, but she decided that the strangers could play with her older toys and the things she had outgrown. Slowly, tentatively, the children inched forward to watch. Their mothers stayed close beside them and seemed as awestruck as they were.

"This is my rubber ball," Lucy said, showing two children how to roll it across the floor to each other. "And this is called a top." Three other children took turns spinning it. One little girl seemed content to rock Lucy's empty wooden doll cradle. Another hugged her old, worn-out rag doll in her arms. "Watch this," Lucy said as she taught two youngsters how to build a tower with her wooden blocks. They took turns building and toppling the blocks. She gave two small girls her chalkboard and some chalk to use. When everyone was occupied, she walked back to the first boy, who was still rocking on her horse, grinning as if it was the most fun he'd ever had.

"What's your name?" she asked him.

"Danny Carver. What's yours?"

"Lucretia Frances Garner. You may call me Lucy."

"I like your horse."

"It's all right, I suppose. Daddy is going to buy me a real pony for my birthday."

"I like this one."

"Well, when is your birthday? Why don't you ask your daddy to buy one for you?"

His smile faded. He lifted his shoulder in another shrug. "We got no room for one. Our house is too small. . . . Hey, can my brother have a turn?"

"I suppose so. If he's careful."

Danny helped a smaller boy climb on, and while he rocked, Lucy decided to show Danny her wooden train. He seemed more fascinated with the train than she had ever been, coupling and uncoupling each of the cars and imitating a train whistle as he pushed it across the floor.

A little while later, more children arrived. As the afternoon grew late, some of the youngest children fell asleep on their mothers' laps. Everyone was behaving nicely until the servants came into the playroom with a tray of sandwiches and set it on Lucy's table. Danny and the other children dropped their playthings and raced toward the food. They had no manners at all, snatching up the sandwiches in their filthy fingers and gobbling them down as if they hadn't eaten in a very long time. They created such an uproar that Grandmother came into the playroom to see what the racket was all about.

"What's going on in here, Lucy? Are you all right?" Her queenly face was no longer serene, and she looked angry and fearful. Lucy could tell that she didn't like all the upheaval in their household. "Come, Lucy. Let's take your nice things to another room." She helped Lucy gather up her favorite dolls and her tea set and carry them into Grandmama's bedroom suite. Lucy stayed there, eating from the tray of food the servants brought them, and later fell asleep in her grandmother's arms.

Lucy lost track of how many days the ragged, dirty strangers lived in her house, but it seemed like a very long time. They occupied every room downstairs, sleeping on the floor and eating her food and playing with her toys. She made friends with Danny, but the other children were too shy to talk to her or even tell her their names. Danny took turns playing with each of her toys, but what fascinated him the most were her picture books. She sat on the floor beside him one afternoon and told him the stories from memory. He studied each page with such concentration that she often grew impatient and pulled the book from his hands to turn to the next page. She had never met anyone quite like him before.

Years later, Lucy saw photographs of the disaster and learned what the Great Flood of 1876 had done to her town while Danny and the other children had stayed at her house. The photos showed mountains of mud as high as the door lintels; piles of debris and downed trees; vast lakes of water that surrounded all of the buildings and flooded the city's main street where she used to go shopping. The neighborhood where Danny and the other children had lived resembled a garbage heap.

Lucy waited and waited for her Daddy to return home, but he never did. When all of the dirty people were gone and the house was quiet once again, she asked, "When is Daddy coming home?"

Mother pulled her into her arms and held her tightly. "He isn't coming home, Lucy." Mother shivered, even though the room felt warm. Lucy didn't understand what her mother meant.

"Well, where is Daddy going to live from now on if he isn't coming home? I want to go live with him."

"I'm sorry, but you can't, Lucy. He died in the flood and now he's in heaven. He'll be laid to rest in the cemetery beside Grandfather Garner."

Everyone called Lucy's daddy a hero and said how courageous and brave he was, but Lucy didn't care what he had done for everyone else in town. She wanted her daddy back, dressed in his blue satin bathrobe, smiling and giving her lumps of sugar while he drank his morning coffee. Her last glimpse of him had been when he had walked out of the front door and into the rain.

The memorial service was like a bad dream, with everyone dressed in black and walking as if they were asleep. Mother couldn't stop crying, but Grandmama held her head high and tried not to show her feelings in public, just as she had taught Lucy to do. Hundreds of people filled the church along with huge bouquets of flowers, but Lucy's father wasn't there. When she'd had enough of all the sorrow and the meaningless words, Lucy sank down in the aisle of the church and threw a tantrum.

"I want my Daddy!"

For the first time in her life, she didn't get what she wanted.

CHAPTER

22

I will always remember Alice's wedding because of what I learned about Grandfather Horatio that night. And just as the Great Flood of 1876 proved to be a turning point in Grandma Bebe's life, the wedding opened a floodgate of changes in my mother's life. That's when she woke up one morning and discovered that she had nothing to do. She turned to me, sizing me up as her next project like a bear circling a bee tree, wondering how she could get at all that honey.

"Nothing doing, Mama!" I held up my hands, backing away like Neal MacLeod used to do. I had to stop when I backed into a wall. "I don't want you to turn me into another Alice. And there won't be another wedding, because I'm never getting married!"

She poked at my short hair, wrinkling her nose. "You're like a wild thing, Harriet, and it's all my fault. I should have kept a closer eye on you. As it is, I fear I've let you go for much too long."

I grabbed the telephone and called Grandma Bebe, pleading with her to come over and rescue me. "Please hurry!" I begged. "You should see the way Mother looks at me—like she wants to cinch my waist in a corset and pin a gigantic hat on my head. I won't let her do it, I tell you! I'll run away from home, first!"

"Calm down, Harriet. I'll be over as soon as I can."

By the time Grandma arrived, Mother had all of my bureau drawers open and the doors to my wardrobe thrown wide. She was shaking her head and clicking her tongue as she examined my clothing. "This won't do . . . and this *certainly* won't do. . . ."

"See?" I whispered to Grandma. "I told you she's lost her mind."

Grandma nodded and approached Mother as if soothing a spooked stallion. "Lucy, listen to me. You need to leave Harriet alone. She is already her own person. Alice was very much like you, but Harriet isn't like you at all."

Mother turned to us, smoothing back her golden hair, wild from her rummaging. Her eyes had a wild look to them, too. "But whatever will Harriet do in life? She has no aptitude for proper manners and absolutely no social contacts."

"I don't have any manners or social contacts, either," Grandma said, "and I'm perfectly happy. You know very well that when you were growing up, I wanted nothing to do with Grandmother Garner's women's clubs and teas. But I let you get involved with her social set, even though I thought you were wasting your time, because that was what you wanted. Alice wanted that type of life, too, but Harriet doesn't. Besides, times are changing. Women are moving beyond the home and developing interests other than marriage and motherhood."

Mother's expression showed her horror. "But what else is there? I will not have Harriet getting caught up in all your protests and things. I don't want her singing hymns outside those disreputable saloons and marching in parades."

"Neither do I, dear. And I don't think she wants to be involved in my work, either. But think about it, Lucy—would you have wanted me to force you to take up all of my causes? You can't expect Harriet to become like you any more than you would have wanted to become like me."

"But she's turning into a wild thing," Mother insisted. "Just last week I received another note from school about her unladylike behavior."

Grandma gave me a glance that was more conspiratorial than condemnatory. "What did she do this time?"

"She kicked the police superintendent's son in the shins!"

"He deserved it, Grandma. Tommy O'Reilly is a big, mean bully!"

Grandma paused before responding, biting her lip as if laughter might bubble out any moment. "All I'm saying is, we have to let our children lead their own lives. Let Harriet be herself, Lucy. Let her find her own way in life. She's a smart young woman. She'll do all right."

Mother sighed and pushed the wardrobe doors closed. I sank down on my bed with relief. But Grandma Bebe turned to me, her forefinger raised as she gently scolded me. "I want you to promise your mother that you'll behave in school from now on. No more shin-kicking, do you hear?"

"I'll try." It would be a small price to pay for my freedom. I thought the episode was over, but when I glanced at my mother I could see that she was still upset.

"I was always a disappointment to you, wasn't I?" Mother murmured. She was talking to Grandma Bebe.

"I was wrong to feel that way, dear," Grandma replied. "I had to learn what you're learning now—that our daughters aren't the same people we are, nor are they extensions of ourselves. They are unique individuals in God's eyes, responsible to Him for the choices they make, not to their mothers."

"I know you've always thought my life was shallow because I didn't share your values or your passion for all of your causes—"

"It isn't up to me to judge anyone's life."

"But I always knew you felt that way. That's probably why we were never close."

Grandma Bebe's expression turned sad. "I'm afraid it goes back a few more generations before us," she said. "My mother was dismayed by the choices I made, too—marrying Horatio, not being a woman of prayer like she was. The letters she wrote to me were very carefully worded, but I avoided visiting her because I could see that we valued different things and that she was disappointed in my choices. By the time I became involved with the Temperance Union and learned what it meant to really lean on God, my mother was already in heaven."

Mother closed the drawers to my bureau, then leaned against it. "Grandmother Garner understood me, even if you didn't. I knew exactly how to win her approval. But I always felt as though pleasing her meant displeasing you."

I listened to their conversation, aware that I was repeating their pattern. My mother was disappointed in me, too. We would probably never be close because I refused to join her social world. But the things that were important to Mother just didn't matter to me. I wanted to please her and make her proud of me, but it seemed impossible unless I turned myself into another Alice. I also wanted to make Grandma Bebe proud of me, but pleasing her meant disappointing my mother. I felt hopelessly confused.

"I was not the wife that Mrs. Garner would have chosen for her son," Grandma Bebe continued. "I was an embarrassment to her and to you. Admit it, Lucy. I still embarrass you, sometimes."

"Yes, I admit it. And I still don't want a life like yours. But lately, when I look at my life, it seems like such a waste. . . ."

I sat up in concern when I saw that Mother was close to tears.

I was afraid that I had caused them. It wouldn't hurt to *try* to be more ladylike in the future. But my behavior wasn't what had upset her.

"I keep thinking of all that time I wasted making sure that Alice's wedding was perfect . . . all the money I spent . . . I just wanted her to be happy, and now . . . now . . ."

"When one era in our life comes to an end," Grandma said, "and we have to start all over again, it can be a good thing. It gives us a chance to decide what's really important. Nobody likes change, Lucy. But even if everything else is taken away, God is still with us."

Mother didn't seem to hear her. "I just want you to be happy, too, Harriet," she said, turning to me. "Why won't you let me do that?"

*I'll be happy if you leave me alone,* I wanted to say, but Grandma said it for me.

"Harriet has to find her own happiness in life, and living to please another person is never going to accomplish that. Living to please God is what matters. Meanwhile, we have to trust that He'll arrange the events in Harriet's life in order to lead her to the purpose He has for her."

I looked to see what my mother's response would be, but it seemed as though she had suddenly popped open an umbrella to fend off Grandma's words and keep them from soaking in. Her spine stiffened and she assumed the faint smile and detached pose she always adopted for her society friends.

"Would you like some coffee, Mother? I'll go and ask Bess if there is any left." She floated from the room as if we had just arrived to pay a social call and she'd been neglecting her duties. Grandma looked at me and shrugged.

Grandma Bebe may have won me a reprieve from a life of foolish fashion, but my mother still drifted aimlessly without a project.

I watched her wander around like a child who had lost her way, turning in circles on an unfamiliar street, searching for the way home. I felt torn. I hated seeing her so sad, but I wasn't willing to sacrifice my liberty for her happiness.

Then at breakfast one Saturday morning, Father slid his newspaper across the table to her before leaving for work. "There's an article on the front page you might like to read. It's about your father."

Mother read the social pages every day but seldom looked at the rest of the news, insisting that it only distressed her. *"I would rather not know what's going on in the world,"* I'd once heard her tell Alice. *"I have enough to concern me in my own household. I'll leave it up to the politicians to fix the messes they create. That's their job."*

The United States had managed to fight a war with Spain right under Mother's dainty nose without her ever knowing about it. I don't think she was aware that the *Titanic* had sunk two months before Alice's wedding, either, killing thousands of people. After all, Mother had flowers to choose and invitations to address.

But as I spread a thick layer of orange marmalade on my toast, I saw her reach for the paper and pull it toward her as if it were a sack of snakes. She opened it to the front page. When I looked up again, her face had turned so white I thought I might have to run and get the smelling salts. She had tears in her eyes as she laid the paper on the table again.

"Mother? Are you all right?"

She nodded, but I could see that she wasn't. When she stood and tried to walk, her legs didn't seem to work right, as if she were wearing someone else's shoes. Somehow, she managed to wobble from the room and climb the stairs.

I grabbed the newspaper, of course, and quickly scanned the front page. The feature story wasn't even about Horatio, but about a local man who had leaped into the Iroquois River to rescue some children after their homemade raft had capsized. He managed to drag three of the boys to safety, but he and a fourth boy drowned after the current swept them away. The mayor called him a hero. A brief sidebar article reminded readers of Horatio Garner's heroism thirty-six years ago during the Great Flood of 1876.

Mother never returned to finish her breakfast. I reread the two paragraphs about her father, failing to see how the matter-of-fact prose could have evoked such a dramatic response. After the strange way she had reacted the other day in my bedroom, I feared that my mother would need a sanatorium soon. Father had left for work, and since our hired girl wanted to clear the breakfast table, I tiptoed upstairs and knocked on Mother's bedroom door. I heard weeping.

"Mother? Are you all right?"

"Go away, Harriet."

I decided to walk to Grandma Bebe's house and see if the story had affected her the same way. I found Grandma seated at her cluttered table, counting names on a batch of petitions. She held up a finger to keep me from interrupting.

"Did you see the story in the newspaper about Horatio?" I asked when she finished.

"I saw it."

"Are you all right?"

"Why wouldn't I be, dear? The flood happened nearly forty years ago."

"Mother read the story and she got so upset she started crying. For a minute there, I thought she was going to faint."

Grandma removed her spectacles and laid them on the table. "Oh, dear. Lucy never reads the paper. I was hoping she wouldn't see the front page."

"Daddy gave it to her. I read the article, too, and there were only two paragraphs about Grandpa Horatio. I don't know why her face turned so white. I nearly ran for the smelling salts."

Grandma slowly shook her head. "I don't think it was the story about Horatio that upset her. Lucy was——" She halted, covering her mouth with her fingers as if she had already said too much. That made me curious to hear more, of course. I stepped into the kitchen and got out Grandma's teapot and two cups. While the kettle heated on the stove, I flopped down on a dining room chair with my legs outstretched to let Grandma know I wasn't going anywhere until she explained herself. Mother would have told me to sit up straight and cross my ankles, but I could be myself at Grandma's house.

"Well?" I prompted.

Grandma had been staring out of the window while I'd put the kettle on to boil, and she turned to me as if she'd forgotten I was there. "Hmm?"

"Mother has been acting very strange and melancholy ever since Alice's wedding," I said to get her started. "But today, when she read the newspaper, it was like the Iroquois Dam had burst all over again."

"Your mother has been working too hard. She's overwrought." Grandma played with a corner of the paper in front of her. She was looking through the window, not at me. I knew she was hiding something.

"You should have seen her reaction, Grandma. She went upstairs to her room, and I could hear her crying, even though the door was closed. Is she going to be all right?"

"It depends on whether or not she turns to God for help. It can be a very difficult time for a woman when her children don't need her anymore. You'll see, one day."

"No I won't because I'm never getting married, remember?" I

waited, but Grandma still said nothing. I huffed in frustration. "Are you going to tell me why the newspaper made her cry or not?"

She closed her eyes. "Your mother knew the man who drowned."

"What?" I grabbed Grandma's copy of the newspaper, lying open on the table, and sucked in my breath when I reread his name: Daniel Carver. "Was he the same Danny who played on her rocking horse during the flood?"

Grandma's brows lifted in surprise. "Why, yes . . . how did you know about that?"

"Mother told me the story, once." I could tell there was a lot more to this mystery, so I waited, jiggling my foot impatiently. "Was that the only time Mother met this Danny fellow?"

She glanced at me, then quickly looked away. "I think your mother should decide whether or not to tell you about Daniel Carver."

Now I was thoroughly intrigued. And frustrated. "But she won't tell me! Mother never talks about anything interesting or important—just the news on the social page."

The kettle whistled, and Grandma got up to turn it off. She didn't pour the water into a teapot, though. "I think you should go home and talk to her, Harriet. If she's as upset as you say she is, maybe talking about it will help."

"You come, too, Grandma. We'll both talk to her."

She shook her head. "Your mother misses Alice very much. You don't have to take Alice's place, but you should try to spend a little more time with your mother. Get to know each other."

I winced at the idea of spending time with my mother, especially if she was going to weep, but it seemed to be the only way I would ever hear the whole story. I hemmed and hawed until I realized that Grandma wasn't going to change her mind, then I trudged home again.

I found Mother in her little sitting room upstairs. A pile of correspondence sat in front of her but the pen was still in the inkwell, the stationery untouched. She sat with her hands folded in her lap as she stared out of the window above her desk. The wadded handkerchief on her desktop looked very damp.

"I'm so sorry about your friend Danny Carver, Mother."

Her eyes looked red and swollen as she turned to me. "I haven't thought about Danny in years, and now I see his name on the front page . . . and such a tragedy."

Her tears started again. A childhood friendship of two or three days didn't explain so much grief. I made myself comfortable on the floor at her feet and waited to hear the story.

⁓

A brass band played a dirge in the distance as Lucy stood on a grassy rise, gazing at the river that had swept her father away when she was a child. The shimmering water appeared deceptively placid, and she had trouble imagining that it could have done so much damage eleven years ago or caused so much sorrow.

She hadn't wanted to come to this commemorative event today, but her mother had insisted. "It wouldn't be right if you didn't come, Lucy. After all, they are honoring your father. Besides, Grandmother Garner might need you."

Lucy had watched in detached silence as city officials dedicated Garner Park to her father's memory and unveiled the newly erected monument stone. The town's brass band played mournful music and a group of soldiers who had served in the army with Horatio saluted in tribute. Grandmother Garner, the honored guest for the ceremony, had presented a wreath in her son's memory. Now Lucy had drifted away from all the fuss while the city's elite soothed Grandmother Garner and Mother talked with Uncle Franklin, who had arrived by train for the event.

For the moment Lucy stood alone, trying to find the daddy she remembered in all the glowing tributes she had just heard. No one had mentioned how his eyes had sparkled when he looked at her, or how he would laugh as they sipped pretend tea together. She worried that she would forget what he looked like. She had a photograph of him in his army uniform and another of him with his arm around her mother's shoulder, taken shortly after they were married, but neither photograph had captured the father Lucy remembered.

The brass band finished their dirge and began playing a lively march. Lucy didn't hear the man approach until he spoke to her. "You're Horatio Garner's daughter, aren't you?"

She turned to see a tall young man who was about her age. She backed up a step when she saw that he was a common laborer. "How do you know me? Who are you?"

"My name is Danny Carver. I met you once before, but you probably don't remember."

Lucy couldn't imagine ever meeting him. His overalls and work shirt were stained with red clay from the brick factory. He ran his hand through his hair, which was the color of wet sand, and she saw red stains beneath his fingernails and in the creases of his knuckles.

"I came to your mansion during the flood. You let me play in your playroom and ride on your rocking horse."

He smiled—a wry grin that laughed at the world—and Lucy did remember him suddenly. But she was too proud to admit it. "Dozens of children stayed with us during the flood," she said primly.

"I know. And I always respected your family for that."

Lucy didn't respond. She had been taught to act very coolly toward young men who were attracted to her beauty, especially unsuitable strangers.

"I just wanted to tell you how sorry I was about your father—even though it happened eleven years ago. He saved my life, you know."

"He saved many lives."

"Yeah, but he saved me in person. He came up to my family's apartment and warned all of us to get out. Said the dam was about to break. My grandmother was old and couldn't walk too good, so your father carried her out to his carriage in his arms."

Lucy watched Danny's face as he spoke and saw that his emotion was genuine, his sneer a shield of defense. "Then your father came back for me and my brother. He put Jake on his shoulders because the water was so deep, but he said I looked like a big brave fellow, and he was sure I could get through it on my own. My mother had to carry the baby. I remember how cold the water was as I waded into it, and how your father whistled 'Yankee Doodle' as if we had nothing at all to worry about. He let me hang on to the back of his coat, and he lifted me up into his fancy carriage when I finally made it there. I had never ridden in a carriage before. "

Tears came to Lucy's eyes as Danny brought her father to life again. She had forgotten how he had loved to whistle.

"We lost everything in the flood," Danny continued. "Not even a blanket or a tin pot was left. Our tenement and everything in it simply vanished. All that remained of our neighborhood were piles of junk and tons of mud. But at least we got out alive. Your father was a brave man."

"Thank you. It was very kind of you to tell me your story. I miss my father. You might have been one of the last persons to see him alive."

"I was on my way over there," he said, pointing to the levy. "I wanted to see where our apartment used to stand. Want to walk there with me?" He had a kind face, a respectful voice, and Lucy thought that he might be nice looking if he were properly dressed. She glanced back at the crowd and saw that her mother and grandmother were still occupied.

"I would like that," she replied. They started walking together, with Lucy carefully picking her way in her dainty shoes. He slowed his stride to match hers.

"Do you remember what The Flats used to look like before the flood?" he asked.

"No. I'm sorry, but I was only six years old at the time."

"Yeah, and you probably weren't allowed down in this part of town, were you? . . . No, don't apologize," he said as she started to. "I don't blame your family for keeping you away from that place. You probably shouldn't go near the new workers' neighborhood they built to replace it, either."

He halted a few minutes later in the middle of a bare, grassy area and pointed to the place where they stood. "Here. This is where I used to live."

Lucy glanced around and saw nothing that made this spot of land distinguishable from the rest of the park. "How do you know that this is the place?"

"See that church steeple on the hill across the river?" he asked, pointing to it. "I used to see it from my apartment window. It was straight across the river." He paused, closing his eyes for a moment. "My tenement was three stories tall with four apartments on each floor—packed with people of all ages, shapes, and colors. You could hear three or four languages at a time, and people yelling, laughing, cursing . . . babies crying . . . It seemed like there was always laundry hanging out, day and night, and I remember that our drinking water tasted terrible. But all the families watched out for each other, you know?" He smiled his crooked grin again. Lucy nodded, but she had no idea what he meant.

"Most of the fathers worked at the brickyard or in your tannery. None of us had very much, but it was home. We lived on the top floor, and I loved to watch the boats go by on the river. We'd go for a swim in the summer when our apartment got too hot, and my father used to take me fishing sometimes on Sunday afternoons. That was his only day off. . . . He died in the flood, too."

Lucy stared at him in surprise. "Why didn't he get out when you did?"

"He was at work when the alarm sounded. They shut down the brick factory and told everyone to get to higher ground, but he decided to help with the evacuation. They said he was trying to convince two elderly sisters to leave their house. It was further downstream and right on the riverbank. When the logjam at the railroad trestle broke, the river swept the house and all three of them away."

"I'm so sorry!" Lucy rested her hand on his arm. "It seems we have something in common then, don't we?" She had never met anyone who truly understood her loss, and she felt a kinship with him.

He raked his fingers through his sandy hair and nodded. "The word *hero* never meant much to me when I was a kid. It didn't change the fact that my father was never coming back. I couldn't understand why he left us. I was furious."

"I've always felt the same way. I would much rather have my father back than have him applauded as a hero. To tell you the truth, I didn't care about all the people he saved. I didn't know any of them. I felt like they stole my daddy from me. My eighteenth birthday is coming soon, and he won't be here to celebrate it with me. The other girls will all get roses from their fathers when we graduate from the female academy in a few months, but my father won't be there." She stopped, surprised by the strength of the emotions Danny had stirred. Then she realized what she had just said. "I'm sorry. You were one of those people he saved. I didn't mean—"

"That's okay. I know exactly how you feel. For a long time I used to hate those two stubborn old sisters who wouldn't leave their house. I figured they'd killed my father just as surely as if they'd stabbed a knife through his heart. It probably wasn't right to hate them, but he was dead and their stubbornness was to blame."

"I blamed the entire town. I hated the mayor and the police and the firemen—it was their job to save and protect people, not my father's." Lucy didn't say it aloud, but she also blamed her mother. It had been her fault that Daddy went up to the cabin in the first place. If he had stayed home, he never would have known about the dam. He would have been drinking his coffee in bed when the dam burst. But Lucy didn't tell Danny that part, because if her father had lived, he and his family would have died.

The band played a lively tune in the background as they stood side by side remembering the disaster, and it seemed inappropriate. She suddenly thought of something else. "Your father's name must be on the new memorial, too."

"It is. That's why I came today. I wanted to see it."

"Well, I would like to see it, too. Will you show it to me?"

"Sure." They walked back across the grass together, but when Lucy looked closely at the granite marker, she regretted her request. Her father's name stood above all the others, chiseled in huge letters. She found Henry Carver's name listed below it in much smaller letters.

"That's not fair," she murmured. "They died doing the very same thing."

"Life is seldom fair, Miss Garner. And you know what else? They put the names of the two spinster sisters my father was trying to save on there, too. See?"

Lucy looked where he pointed and read their names: *Elizabeth Dawes, Esther Dawes.* It seemed so unfair. As Lucy's memories returned, she recalled how angry and cheated she had felt in the weeks following the flood.

"Our home was a terribly sad place after my father died," she said. "I was planning a huge party for my seventh birthday, but I never had it. I was going to ask Daddy for a pony—a real one this time, not a wooden one like the one you rode. That probably sounds selfish and petty considering all that you lost, but I was very young and I couldn't understand all the changes in my life."

There must have been changes in Danny's life, too, she realized. How had his family survived? Lucy's family had income from the tannery, and she hadn't lost her home. She had never given much thought to all of the people whose homes had been destroyed while hers had been spared. The differences seemed unfair to her now—like the big and little letters on the monument.

"How did you get by after your father died?" she asked. "Where did you live?"

"We managed." He lifted one shoulder in a casual shrug, and she recalled the gesture from eleven years ago. "They set up a tent city for a while, and it developed into a sort of shantytown."

"Who supported your family?"

When Danny didn't answer right away, Lucy was sorry she had asked. He looked away but not before she saw his cheeks flush. "My mother found work. And I did odd jobs and things—delivering ice and newspapers, running errands. I took a job at the brickyard when I was fourteen. They thought I was much older."

"Lucy!" She whirled at the sound of her grandmother's voice. "It's time to leave."

"Good-bye, Daniel. Thank you—" But before Lucy could finish, Grandmother Garner gripped her arm and yanked her away.

"Why in the world were you talking to that person?" Her voice sounded as cold and hard as the monument stone. "Don't you know it's unseemly to talk to such people?"

"He was telling me about Daddy. He said that Daddy rescued him from the flood and saved his life."

"You can't believe a word those people say. They'll tell you anything to win your trust."

"But it's true, Grandmama. Danny's father died in the flood, too. He was helping Daddy save people. I saw his name on the marker."

Grandmother didn't seem to be listening. "It's bad enough that your mother fraternizes with those people, which is why she isn't invited to all of the places that you and I are. But you mustn't ruin it for yourself the way she did. Come along now."

Lucy glanced over her shoulder as her grandmother led her away, but Daniel Carver had disappeared in the milling crowd. As Lucy rode home in the carriage, her heart felt lighter in spite of the somber occasion and the memories it had evoked. For the first time in her life, she had met someone who understood the loss she had lived with for so many years—someone who understood that a father couldn't be remembered in a granite marker and flowered wreaths.

**23**

Lucy was reading a book in her room a few evenings later when one of the servants interrupted her. "I'm sorry to disturb you, Miss Lucy, but there is someone at the back door asking to speak with you. He is not a respectable gentleman and I refused to let him in the house, but he insisted that I—"

"Did he tell you his name?"

"Yes, Miss Lucy. Daniel Carver." Lucy's skin prickled and warmed as if she had stepped into a tub of steaming water. "Shall I send him away, Miss Lucy?"

"No! I'll speak with him." Lucy found it hard not to run. She used the servants' stairs to get to the back door, aware that her grandmother would never allow Danny into her house, nor would she want Lucy speaking with him. She couldn't say exactly what drew her, but her heart raced as if she had run up all those steps instead of down them.

Danny Carver smiled when he saw her, his admiration as clear as his gaze, then he snatched off his hat and lowered his head. "Excuse me for bothering you again, Miss Garner, but after we talked the other

day I remembered something that's been eating at me all these years."
He dug in his pocket and pulled out a small lump of wood, handing
it to her. It took Lucy a moment to recognize it as a toy boxcar just
like the one that had belonged to her little wooden train.

"It's yours," he said. "I stole it from your playroom eleven years
ago. I've felt sorry about it ever since and more than a little guilty,
but I was too ashamed to walk all the way up here and return it
to you. Besides, my life was . . . Well, things were pretty hard after
the flood. But anyway, I wanted to give it back to you. I knew it was
wrong to steal."

"Then why did you take it?"

He lifted his shoulder in a shrug. She followed him as he turned
and walked a few paces into the garden, then hoisted himself onto
the low stone wall. She remained standing.

"I don't really know why I took it. But this house, all your toys
and things, all the food . . . it felt like a dream. I guess I wanted
something that would help me remember that it was real. Then
when I found out we'd lost everything in the flood . . . I don't know,
but for a long time that little boxcar was the only thing I owned.
My father was dead, and it reminded me of him for some reason.
And I didn't want to forget him."

"To tell you the truth, I never even noticed it was missing. I had
so much more." She spun one of the little wooden wheels with her
finger, aware that she took for granted her way of life and all her
possessions. It occurred to her that she was the one who should
feel guilty, not Daniel.

Lucy was silent for so long that Daniel finally slid off the wall, brushing dirt from the seat of his pants, and said, "I guess I should go."

"No, wait! I-I enjoyed talking with you the other day."

He smiled his crooked grin. "Yeah, me too."

"Tell me more about yourself. Where do you live now? What's
your life like?"

"There isn't much to tell. I've worked in the brickyard for the past six years—"

"Six years? How old are you? And what about school?"

His only reply was a shake of his head as he hoisted his lanky body onto the wall again. "I live in a boardinghouse in New Town— that's the workingman's part of town that they built to replace The Flats. And I'm twenty."

"Do you live all alone? What about your family?"

"I don't have one, really. My baby sister died the first winter after the flood, and my brother, Jake, has been on his own almost as long as I have. We don't see our mother much."

The tragedy he had faced made Lucy feel ashamed of her pampered life. She was glad that the darkness hid her flushed cheeks. "Why did you let me go on and on about not having a seventh birthday party or a new pony?"

"Because I don't think grief and loss are something you can measure, Miss Garner. We both have a hole in our childhood where our fathers used to be, and that makes us alike, no matter how different we are."

"Please, call me Lucy."

"If you want." Except for his first glance, Danny had averted his eyes the entire time he'd talked to her, as if he'd been taught that laborers didn't look wealthy young ladies in the eye. But he looked at her now in a way that made her heart pound.

"Do you have a girlfriend?" she asked. He shook his head, his gaze still fastened on her. Lucy knew how to make polite conversation, but she struggled for something to say. "Do you enjoy your work?"

"Not really. It's boring and backbreaking. But I consider myself lucky to have a job at all. Especially with all the new immigrants coming to town who would gladly do my job for less money."

"Is there some other job you'd rather have in the future?"

He scratched his head. "I guess I just don't think that way, Lucy. I

345

know what you're really trying to ask—what am I looking forward to in the future, what do I hope for and all that. You mentioned yesterday that you were graduating from school soon, so I assume you're looking forward to starting something new. But things don't work that way for people like me. If we have a decent job, we hang on to it. Maybe we'll wind up as foreman someday and make a little extra money, maybe not. But from where I stand, the future looks pretty much like the present, so why waste time trying to see into it?"

His words appalled Lucy. "How can you live without hope?"

He gave his now-familiar shrug. "I guess you don't miss what you never had."

"You've lived your entire life without hope?"

"Pretty much. I used to hope that my father would come back, but that didn't get me anywhere. And for a while I hoped that my mother would change, but . . ." He looked away.

"Let me help you, Danny. I can talk to our foreman at the tannery and see if he can get you a better job, and—"

He held up his hands to stop her. "Don't start down that road, Lucy. It isn't going to take me anywhere. Believe me, I know."

"I . . . I don't know what to say. I've never met anyone like you before."

"Listen, why don't you tell me more about your life?"

"Because it seems shallow and selfish beside yours."

"I would still like to hear about it. If you want to be friends, that is."

"Yes, I really would like to be friends. You're the only person I've ever met who understands how I've felt all these years about losing my father."

"Good. Then tell me what it's like to be Miss Lucy Garner."

"Well . . . I live here with my mother and grandmother. I don't have any sisters or brothers." She could hear the apologetic tone of her voice and was certain that Danny could hear it, too. "I attend a small, private female academy here in town—I'll graduate in a few months."

"What do they teach you in school?"

She was ashamed to tell him she was taking classes in French and watercolor painting and piano. "I like geography," she said, instead. "It's interesting to learn about other countries. Grandmama said that I might—" Lucy stopped, embarrassed to say that they had talked about traveling to Europe someday. "My grandmother has been to Paris," she amended, "and she says it is very beautiful."

"Do you have any boyfriends?"

"No." She was glad he couldn't see her blushing. "We see boys at social events, but it's all very stiff and artificial. I've never talked with any of them the way I'm talking with you. And not even my best friend understands how I feel about losing my father. But then how could she, since her father is still alive? It's so nice to know that you understand."

"Miss Lucy?" She recognized the butler's voice and turned to see him standing near the back door. "It's chilly out here. I think you'd better come inside."

"I'll be right there, Robert."

Danny slid off the wall again. "I'll come back another time if you want, and we can talk some more. Which room is yours?" He tilted his head toward the rear of her mansion. "I'll throw some pebbles at your window to get your attention, next time. I don't think your servants like me very much."

"It's that window," she said, pointing. "The second one from the left."

"Well, I'd better get going. My day starts pretty early."

"Please keep this," Lucy said, pushing the little boxcar back into his hands. His skin felt as rough as an emery board. "I think it means much more to you than to me."

He looked surprised. "Thanks. Have a good evening, Miss Garner—I mean, Lucy. Until next time . . . ?"

"Yes. Good night, Daniel."

e

Four months later, Lucy sat near her bedroom window on a warm July night, waiting for Daniel's now-familiar signal. As soon as she heard the tap of a pebble against the glass, she hurried down the back staircase, then carefully closed the outside door behind her, hoping that none of the servants had heard her leaving the house. She stood on the back step for a moment as her eyes adjusted to the darkness, then saw Daniel standing in the shadows near the carriage house. She ran to him and let him pull her into his arms. Lucy felt at home there, comfortable with his embrace, his touch.

"I've told myself a dozen times to stop coming to see you," he murmured, "but I can't make myself stop."

"I don't want you to stop."

"Come on, let's find a better place to talk," he said, taking her hand. "There's a full moon tonight, and I don't want your servants to see us." He led her further into the garden, stopping when he found a bench beneath the rose trellis, where they could hide from view. The summer night was warm, the moon very bright, and she could see his beloved face clearly by the light of the moon. Something was bothering him.

"Why would you want to stop coming?" she asked. "We always have so much to talk about, don't we?"

"Yes. But I've been wondering where this can possibly lead."

"I-I don't know what you mean." She traced her fingers along his jaw, feeling the rough stubble of his whiskers. She had grown to love the roughness of his skin, the coarseness of his work clothes, the hardness of his muscles. Everything in her world was soft and refined, and she loved the novelty of him.

"Come on, Lucy. I think you know that we've become much more than friends. I think you know that I'm falling in love with you."

They had never talked about love before, and it made Lucy's heart speed up. She had wondered during the past few weeks if this was what love felt like: wanting to be with Daniel all the time; counting the minutes and seconds until night fell and she would hear the pebble strike her window; wishing the time they spent together could last twice as long as the time they spent apart. She had read about love in romance novels, of course, but books couldn't begin to describe the happy, breathless way she felt whenever she was with him.

*I'm falling in love with you.* No one had ever said those words to Lucy before, and she felt like whirling in giddy circles the way she had as a child with her brand-new petticoats. Danny Carver loved her! And she loved him, too, she was certain of it. So why had he turned so serious? Why was he talking about not coming anymore? She couldn't bear the thought of never seeing him again.

"Is that such a bad thing?" she asked. "That we've become more than friends?"

Danny released her hand and stood up. "No, of course it isn't a bad thing. But . . . but that river down there isn't a bad thing, either, when it's flowing along nicely. But when it goes beyond its banks, when it goes into places it shouldn't . . . that's when trouble happens."

"I don't understand." She watched him pace in front of her, a frown on his face, and she was afraid that he was angry with her.

"I don't belong up here on the ridge, in your world. And I know for sure that you don't belong down in mine. I've overstepped my bounds, Lucy, and it can't end well. For either of us."

"But I don't want it to end."

"I know." His frown melted into a look of sadness. "Me, either. But I don't see how . . ." He paused, clearing his throat as if to rid it of the emotion that thickened his voice. "The first time I came here, I told you that I didn't dare to gaze into my future and start hoping for things to change, because my future was always going to look like my present. That's the way things are in my world. And I was fine with that—until I met you. Now when I look into the future, I want you there beside me. But I don't see any way that we can possibly be together—and I'm not fine with that."

"But there has to be a way, Daniel. What if I asked my family to give you a job at the tannery? I know how hard you work, how honest and good-hearted you are."

"They will never allow it," he said, continuing to pace in front of her. "They would say I'm only after your money."

"But that isn't true. I know it isn't."

"They would point out that I never finished school. That I can barely read and write."

"But you're not stupid, Daniel. You could easily get an education if someone gave you a chance. You could be anything you wanted to be."

He stopped and looked at her. "But that's just it. I wouldn't even know what to wish for." He sank down beside her on the bench again. "Everything I own fits into a room in a boardinghouse that I share with three other men. You're used to . . . to all of this." He made a sweeping gesture with his arm.

"That doesn't matter. My mother came from a very poor family, too, but my father loved her and married her anyway, and she came here to live. I would gladly share everything I have with you."

"I don't know if I could ever get used to a place like this. Besides, I saw the way your grandmother looked at me the first day we talked in Garner Park. You saw it, too, I know you did. She would never accept me."

"She looks only at the outside of people." Lucy swallowed the bitter taste of guilt, knowing she had done the same thing before she met Daniel. "If people only knew you the way I do—"

"Don't give me hope, Lucy. You'll only break both of our hearts in the end."

"But it can't end! Please don't stop coming to see me. Give me a chance to figure out how to make this work. There has to be a way that we can be together."

He took her face in his hands and kissed her. Afterward, they clung to each other.

"I'll keep coming as long as you want me to, Lucy. When the night comes that you don't answer my signal"—he nodded toward her bedroom window—"then I'll know that it's over."

Lucy stayed awake for most of the night, trying to figure out a way that she and Daniel could be together. She considered eloping, coming home a married woman and forcing her family to accept him, but she was too afraid to leave home on her own. She had never ventured anywhere without a chaperone or with friends or family.

Her thoughts kept returning to her mother and how she had come from humble beginnings to live in this house, eventually adjusting to this life. Bebe still wasn't afraid to "fraternize with the riffraff," as Grandmother Garner called it. Lucy realized that the only solution was to get her mother on her side. She had to talk Bebe into helping her and Danny so they could be together. After a short, restless night of sleep, Lucy began a conversation with her mother at the breakfast table the following morning.

"I wish there weren't barriers between rich people and poor people," she said as she pushed scrambled eggs around on her plate.

"Education is the key," Bebe said. "If we can help poor children get an education, we'll give them a better chance in life. That's one of our Temperance Union's goals."

Lucy resisted rolling her eyes. For her mother, the Union was always foremost in her mind. She tried a different approach. "Did you marry Daddy for his money?"

Bebe finished stirring milk into her tea and laid down her spoon. "Maybe I did, in a way. I worked so hard during the war, doing my brothers' chores on the farm, that I think I liked the idea of having servants. It overwhelmed me to think that such a wealthy, sophisticated man as your father wanted to marry me. But I truly loved him, Lucy. Most of all, I married for love."

Lucy twisted her napkin nervously. "And what advice would you give someone who wanted to do the same thing—marry for love, I mean—in spite of other differences?"

"I would say . . . that they should think twice. It took me years and years to adjust to our differences, and in many ways I still haven't adjusted, as you well know. I embarrass you at times. I'm not like all of your friends' mothers, am I?"

Lucy didn't know what to say. She remembered how small and plain and out of place her mother looked at the graduation reception a few months ago. As Lucy fumbled for what to say next, her mother suddenly reached for her hand and took it in both of hers. "I know about him, Lucy. I know all about Daniel Carver. That's who you're really talking about, isn't it?"

"How . . . how do you know?" she asked in a whisper.

"The servants told me. They've known for some time that you've been sneaking out at night to see him."

Lucy pulled her hand free. "How dare they spy on us!"

"They did it because they love you, Lucy. Robert and Herta and Peter have known you since the day you were born. They would never let you come to harm or allow a stranger to take advantage of you."

Lucy imagined them peeking at her and Daniel through the curtains, seeing all their private moments together, and her anger threatened to boil over. "If you knew all about Danny, I'm surprised you didn't lock me in my room and forbid me to see him!"

"I considered it," Bebe said calmly. "But then I recalled the night that Horatio asked my father for permission to marry me.

And I remembered that it wouldn't have mattered if my father had refused—I would have defied him. I didn't want you to make a mistake out of anger or defiance, Lucy. Marriage is one of the biggest decisions you'll ever make. . . . And you're so young."

"I'm older than you were."

"Not by much. And that's why I'm glad you're asking me for advice."

"But I'm not asking for advice—I'm asking you to help us. You can give Danny a decent-paying job in the tannery. You can let him move in here, like you did."

"What about your friends? What advice do they have for you?"

"They're so shallow and superficial. I can't talk to any of them the way I talk to Danny. And never about important things."

"So you haven't told your friends about Danny?"

"They wouldn't understand. But Danny lost his father, too. He shares the grief I've felt all these years."

"I share it, too, Lucy. I lost your father, too. And I found comfort in God, not in another person. He knows what it's like to lose someone dear to Him."

"Why do you keep changing the subject? Are you going to help me or not?"

"I am trying to help you. You need to think everything through so you can make a mature, informed decision."

Lucy exhaled, forcing herself to be calm so her mother would take her side. "I'm sorry. Go on."

"Can you picture Danny at all your social events? Or are you going to give up your social life?"

"He could learn to fit in. He's very smart, Mother. And the rules of etiquette aren't that hard to learn."

"Danny Carver could hire the finest tailor," Bebe said quietly, "and get every detail of your social world letter-perfect, and he still wouldn't be accepted. Believe me, I know. Besides, have you asked him if he wants to be part of all that? I know I never did. I hated it. What if Danny hates it, too?"

Lucy saw him in her mind, seated at her grandmother's elegant dinner table, hiding behind his careless half shrug and his laugh-at-the world grin, and knew that he would hate every minute of it—especially Grandmother Garner's cold, undisguised disdain. Lucy let her mother's question go unanswered.

"So the real question is," Bebe continued, "are you willing to change for him? That's what you must decide. Don't expect him to change. You're the one who must change. Do you love him that much? Could you give up your way of life and live in his world for his sake? Or are you expecting him to fit into yours?"

"It doesn't matter where we live. I love him, Mother. I know you're going to say that I'm too young and that I don't know what love really is, but it's true—I love Daniel Carver!"

"I believe you. But even when people love each other, it doesn't always mean that they should get married."

"Are you talking about Daddy? Are you sorry that you married him?"

"No. I'm talking about someone else." Her mother looked away, sighing softly. "After your father died, someone else asked me to marry him."

Lucy's jaw dropped in shock. "Who?"

"It doesn't matter, dear. I loved him but I didn't marry him because . . . because I knew it would hurt you and Grandmother Garner. You would have felt that I was betraying your father. I can tell that I've shocked you now, even though your father has been gone for more than a decade."

Lucy struggled to digest this news as her mother continued. "Grandmother Garner will feel even more shocked and angry and betrayed than you do right now if you marry Danny. It will break her heart. You're all she has. That's why you need to carefully consider if you really want to do this to her."

Lucy recalled how her grandmother had yanked her away from Danny on the day the memorial stone was dedicated. But she also knew that her grandmother had never denied her anything she'd wanted. "Grandmother always lets me have what I want. She won't stand in the way of my happiness."

"You might be surprised, Lucy. She would have gladly had my marriage annulled even though she knew I made Horatio happy. . . . Listen, there is one more question you need to consider, and it's an important one. What about Danny's faith? My mother tried to advise me to make sure your father and I had a common faith in God. No marriage can get along without Him at the center."

Lucy had no idea what Danny believed. They had never talked about God or religion. "What difference does it make what church he goes to?" she asked.

"I didn't ask about his church—I asked about his faith. There is a huge difference."

Bebe's questions frustrated Lucy. She wanted answers, not questions. "So, will you help Danny and me or not?"

Bebe wrapped her hands around her teacup, staring down at it as if deep in thought. "I want you to make a well-informed decision, not one you'll long regret," she finally replied. "If you promise to agree to my conditions first, then I'll agree to help you."

Hope and suspicion battled inside Lucy. "What do you want me to do?"

"Tell Danny you can't see him for two weeks."

"Mother, no!"

"True love can certainly endure a separation of two weeks. You both could use some time apart to get some perspective on your relationship. That's my first condition—and the servants will be sure to let me know if you try to cheat. During that time, I want you to come with me to get a firsthand look at the world that Daniel comes from. It's important that you understand him and why he thinks the way he does. You've never been to New Town, have you?"

"Danny and I aren't going to be living there, so I don't see the point. But I'll go, if you insist. Is that all?"

"No. I know that you've been invited to the Midsummer Ball at the Opera House later this month. Grandmother Garner is looking forward to showing you off to the town's royalty. I want you to go with her and enter into the festivities with the same enthusiasm you would have shown if Daniel Carver wasn't in the picture. Those three things are all I'm asking you to do."

Lucy knew that her mother was trying to shock her by taking her to New Town, but she made up her mind not to be shocked. As for Grandmother Garner and the ball, Lucy didn't see how it would hurt to go. She could get on her grandmother's good side by being cooperative, and maybe then she could talk to Grandmama about Daniel. The hardest condition would be spending two weeks away from him, but that was a small price to pay for a lifetime together.

"I'll agree to all three conditions," she told her mother, "so start counting off the two weeks. I'll tell Danny tonight."

Two days later, Lucy accompanied her mother to New Town. "A woman who attends my church just had a baby," Bebe told her. "Our ladies' group always brings a meal to new mothers, along with some clothes and things. I told the other ladies that we would deliver everything."

The working-class neighborhood was just as Lucy had expected it to be: overcrowded, smelly, and disgusting, but she worked hard to hide her shock from her mother. She thought of her beloved Daniel growing up in such a sad environment, and she was all the more determined to lift him out of this way of life.

So many ragged children played in the street that Lucy feared the horses would trample one of them as the carriage waded through the melee. The driver halted in front of a dilapidated two-story building with several of its windows boarded up. It looked as though it already was falling apart, even though the neighborhood had been built only eleven years ago, after the flood. Lucy hooked the basket of food over her arm, steeling herself to go inside and get this "lesson" over with. But before she could take a single step, dozens of children mobbed her, thrusting their filthy hands in her face and shouting, "Please, miss! Please! You have a penny for me?"

She wanted to turn and flee to the safety of the carriage, but her mother simply smiled and shouted to them above the noise. "All right, children. Let us through, please. We have to bring these things to Anna Walsh and her new baby. We'll have something for all of you when we come out."

The clamoring mob parted, and Lucy and Bebe made their way up the steps and into the building. The smell of urine assaulted Lucy in the vestibule. "Oh! That's revolting!" she said before she could stop herself. Bebe said nothing as she led the way upstairs to the second floor. The apartment door was open, and she knocked on the doorframe and peered inside.

"Anna? It's me, Bebe Garner."

"Come in, Mrs. Garner, come in."

The room was tiny and smelled of kerosene and perspiration. It was so hot that Lucy couldn't breathe. Not even a hint of a breeze blew though the windows, which stood dangerously open to the two-story drop below. Two toddlers sat bare-naked on the wooden floor. A line of laundry was strung across one end of the room, dripping into a sink and onto the floor. Anna Walsh sat on a sagging bed on the other end of the room, nursing her baby. She couldn't have been much older than Lucy was, but she looked as timeworn as Grandmother Garner. She thanked Bebe over and over for the food and clothing and other supplies.

"Is there something more we can do for you while we're here?" Bebe asked. "Do you have some work that my daughter, Lucy, and I can help you with?"

Mrs. Walsh wouldn't hear of letting them work for her, and after Bebe rocked the new baby for a few minutes and the two women chatted, she and Lucy left again.

"An apartment like this is all that Daniel can afford on his salary," Bebe told her on the way down the stairs. "This is how you would have to live, unless he relies on you to support him." Lucy nodded, refusing to reply. "My experience tells me that most men take a great deal of pride in being the breadwinner. How do you think Daniel will feel, knowing he has to rely on his wealthy wife for charity for the rest of his life?"

"He's willing to work if you give him a chance. He could work for us at the tannery."

"That decision isn't entirely up to me. I would have to talk it over with Mr. MacLeod."

Before they emerged from the building, Bebe pulled a bag of penny candy from her basket and held it out to Lucy. "Here. You can pass these out to the children."

Lucy shrank back. "I don't want to. You do it." She would need to take a bath after touching all those filthy fingers. But her mother pushed the bag into her hands.

"I have a pocketful of pennies to pass out."

Lucy did as she was told, gritting her teeth and bearing her penance. She would be home soon. And once the two weeks were over, she could be with Daniel.

"How much do you know about Daniel's parents?" Bebe asked on the ride home.

"His father died while helping people escape from the flood, just like Daddy did."

"And his mother?"

"He doesn't talk much about her."

"I think I know why," Bebe said quietly. "I met Mrs. Carver a few years ago in one of the saloons we were trying to close down. Do you understand what it means if I tell you that Daniel's mother survived after her husband died by selling her body?"

"You're lying! You're just trying to shock me!"

"No, it's the truth, Lucy. I'm trying to help you understand the man you love. Women aren't paid the same wages as men, even if they do the same job in the same factory. They can never earn enough to pay the rent and feed their children. Besides, who would watch her children while she worked a twelve-hour shift? After Mrs. Carver's husband died, she must have faced all those dilemmas. The only way she could make a living and keep a roof over her head was to solicit business in a saloon every night."

Lucy didn't reply. She couldn't stop the tears that rolled down her face. It explained why Danny had quit school and gone to work at such a young age. And why he wouldn't talk about his mother.

"Mrs. Carver's situation is one of the things that our Temperance League is working so hard to change. If we could get equal wages for women and affordable housing and childcare for widows like her, they wouldn't be forced into such a tragic position. I'm certain that Daniel feels shame because of what his mother does, and I'm sorry that you were forced to see his shame. But you know your grandmother and her friends very well, Lucy. Will they ever accept Daniel, knowing what his mother does for a living?"

"That's not fair! It's none of their business!"

"Life isn't fair. That's what I'm trying to show you. And you need to remember that it will be just as difficult for Daniel to change and enter your world as it would be for you to enter his."

Lucy longed to talk to Daniel about what she'd seen today. She wanted to tell him that she loved him and that the differences between them didn't matter. And she wanted to hear him say the same thing.

But she also knew that she could never shame him by admitting that she knew the truth about his mother. Unless he chose to tell her, it would be one secret that would always stand between them.

At dinner that evening Grandmother Garner began making plans for the Midsummer Ball. "Lucy, darling, we need to go shopping as soon as possible. If we don't order our new gowns soon, all of the finest seamstresses will be spoken for."

"Why don't we go first thing tomorrow morning, Grandmama?"

Lucy loved to shop. She and her grandmother drove downtown as soon as the stores opened the next day. But as they made their rounds, it distressed Lucy to realize that her grandmother had a hard time keeping up. When had Grandmother Garner become so frail and out of breath, her steps so slow and halting?

"Sit down, Grandmama," Lucy said over and over. "You should rest a bit. We don't have to keep going."

"Nonsense. I'll be fine." But Lucy listened to her painful wheezing and worried, just the same.

As they paged through pattern books and selected fabric and lace and ribbon, Lucy couldn't help remembering all of the happy hours she had spent shopping with her grandmother as a child. She tried to imagine the two of them sitting side by side this way, choosing the wedding gown she would wear when she married Daniel, and found that she couldn't do it. Her mother had been right about that much. If Lucy married Daniel Carver, she would break her beloved grandmother's heart.

Lucy forced all these disturbing thoughts from her mind over the next few days as she prepared for the ball. She made luncheon dates with some of her school friends to compare notes about their dresses and giggle about all the young gentlemen they would meet at the upcoming event. She had forgotten how much she enjoyed their girl talk, even though she found herself avoiding their questions about what she'd been doing all summer. As the day of the ball neared, Lucy grew more and more excited. She no longer thought about Daniel a dozen times a day as she had when the separation first began. She was much too busy deciding how to arrange her hair and which shoes would be more comfortable for dancing. When the night finally arrived, Lucy felt like a princess in a fairy tale.

"You look beautiful, my darling girl," Grandmother said as Lucy descended the stairs. "The young men will be fighting to fill your dance program." And they did. The moment Lucy entered the ballroom, dozens of young men in tuxedos clamored for a chance to dance with her, the way the street urchins had clamored for pennies. She was swept away into the glory of it all, surrounded by colorful ball gowns and flowers, glittering candles and elegant music. And she loved every elegant minute of it. Lucy never wanted the evening to end.

Halfway though the ball, Grandmother Garner parted the sea of Lucy's admirers and linked arms with her. "Come, my dear. There is someone I'd very much like you to meet. I hope you saved a dance or two for him."

Lucy could tell that she dazzled John Sherwood the moment they met, and she savored the power she held over him. She was discovering how much fun it was to flirt and tease and make a man laugh at all her charms. And John instantly held her interest, as well. His hands were soft and clean, his scent spicy and intoxicating. His tuxedo was the finest one she'd seen all evening, exquisitely tailored to fit his tall, sturdy body.

"I had it custom made," he explained. "Our family owns several men's haberdasheries, here and in various neighboring towns. But now that I've graduated college and have entered the family business, I have plans to expand our stores and turn them into fine department stores like the one I've visited in Chicago recently.

LYNN AUSTIN

Imagine, floor after floor with everything a woman could ever want to shop for, all under one roof."

"I would be your most devoted customer, Mr. Sherwood," she said with a smile. She tossed her dance card aside to waltz with him for the remainder of the evening, listening in awe as he described his recent trip to Paris.

"I would like to ask your family for permission to court you," he said as the night drew to a close. "May I?"

For the first time all evening, Lucy thought of Daniel. She tried to picture him there at the ball, but he wasn't wearing a tuxedo or whirling with her around the ballroom floor. Instead, she could only imagine him standing near the door, looking ashamed and uncomfortable in his coarse, work-stained clothes. Once again, Lucy knew that her mother had been right—Daniel would hate all of this. And he would never fit in.

"In fact, Miss Garner," John Sherwood continued, "our family is planning a dinner party for next Thursday evening. If you are free, would you be kind enough to join us?"

"I would love to," she replied. She began planning what she would wear, forgetting that her two-week separation from Daniel ended that night.

On Thursday evening, when Danny Carver tossed a pebble against her bedroom window, Lucy wasn't home to hear it.

e‑

"I was so shallow, Harriet!" Mother said when she finished telling me her story. "I liked my pampered life too much, and in the end that's what I chose. I wanted to wear beautiful gowns and attend lovely parties and travel to Paris. I loved wealth and ease more than I loved Danny."

"Didn't you love Father at all?" I asked in horror.

"Of course I did," she said, blowing her nose. "But I thought I loved Danny, too, and I decided not to marry him for very selfish reasons. I didn't want to be poor and live in New Town and have a mother-in-law like his mother. And I knew he would never fit into the life I wanted, either."

I exhaled, alarmed to learn how close my mother had come to throwing everything away for Daniel Carver. I admired Grandma Bebe even more for her wisdom and ingenuity.

"Don't get me wrong," Mother said, "I care very deeply for your father. We've had a good life and two beautiful children together. It's just that . . . I confess to feeling guilty at times for the pain I must have caused Danny. I've often wondered what became of him and what our life together might have been like. Who would I be today if I had chosen differently? And now he's dead." She blew her nose again and dropped the handkerchief onto her desk.

"Lately, I can barely look at myself in the mirror," she said tearfully. "I look around at my elegant home and my wardrobe filled with clothes . . . I think about how much money I just spent on Alice's wedding, and I'm horrified with myself. My father was a hero who died saving people! My mother has dedicated her life to helping others and improving our community. And me? All I ever think about is myself, Harriet . . . only myself. . . ."

I didn't know what to say to my mother. I reached for her hand and patted it uselessly, saying nothing.

**24**

The day after Mother told me about Daniel Carver, we went to church as usual. She seemed to be holding herself together during the service, but that afternoon, while my father dozed on our sun porch, my mother dressed in black from head to toe and pinned a huge black hat on her head. "Where are you going?" I asked her.

"I've decided to attend Danny's funeral." She lowered the black mesh veil over her face, which still looked red and puffy to me. I was worried about her. She certainly hadn't been herself lately. I would have called Grandma Bebe again for help, but I remembered the advice she had given me about spending more time with my mother.

"I'll go with you, if you want," I said. I thought she would refuse, but she didn't. I quickly changed back into my church clothes while she called a taxi—Mother didn't drive. And she would have fainted dead away on the floor if she ever found out that I did.

We arrived at the cemetery near New Town at the same time as the funeral procession. We remained at a discreet distance, standing in the shade of a huge oak tree that had obviously survived the Great Flood. "It said in the newspaper that Danny had a wife and four daughters," Mother whispered to me. "I wonder what will become of them."

We saw them a few minutes later, dressed in black and seated in chairs beside the open grave. But I counted six women, not five. Maybe the blowsy gray-haired one was his disreputable mother.

"Danny once told me how difficult it is for widows and orphans to survive without a father," my mother said. "His mother was a widow, and she—" A sob caught in her throat. She slid her handkerchief beneath her veil to wipe her tears.

A dozen raggedy young boys suddenly surged forward to gather around Danny's grave. I wondered if the three boys he had rescued were among them. They parted as the pallbearers moved Danny's casket into place, then a man in a ministerial collar stepped forward to speak. I nudged my mother closer to the gravesite so I could hear what he was saying.

"Danny Carver died the same way he lived—helping others. He was a true hero. Some of you may remember Danny from his earlier years, and if so, you know how the Lord transformed his life when he came to know Jesus. By his own confession, Danny found hope, for the first time in his life, in Christ. Afterward, he spread that hope to everyone he met, not caring that his own circumstances hadn't changed, but working to provide a better future for others. That was how his ministry to these young boys began. Danny fed them from his own table, bought shoes for those who needed them, took youngsters fishing on Sunday afternoons, and encouraged them to stay in school and get a good education. Above all, he shared his faith with these boys." The minister's voice choked with emotion, and he paused to clear his throat. "I'm sure the Lord must have a good reason why He needed Danny Carver in heaven, but frankly, I don't know how we'll get along without him here on earth."

Mother sobbed beneath her veil as the six pallbearers lowered the simple wooden coffin into the ground. We could hear the hollow thumps as his family dropped clods of earth on top of it. As the other mourners filed past to pay their respects, Mother moved forward, as well. I stayed close beside her as she halted in front of the minister.

"I would like to do something for his family," she told him. "If . . . if they need money . . ."

Up close, I could see that the minister's face had been ravaged by his grief. His voice was hoarse with it, too. "Money is important, of course. But it's really a matter of vision. Danny Carver could look into a young person's future and see hope when everyone else in New Town saw it as hopeless. I don't know where we'll ever find another man like him."

"Please, tell me what I can to do for his family. Shall I bring them a meal? That seems so paltry. I want to help, but I'm not sure what to do."

He shook his head like a man trying to awaken from a bad dream. "Come and see me next week," he said. "I-I can't think straight at the moment. I still have the funeral for the young boy who drowned. I'm sorry . . ." Another woman got his attention, and he turned to speak with her.

While my mother had been talking to the minister, I noticed that the gray-haired woman, whom I had assumed to be Danny's mother, had been listening to their conversation. She rose abruptly from her chair and strode toward us, and I could tell by her stiff posture and glaring eyes that she wasn't coming over to thank us for attending. I wanted to grab my mother and run, but I was too slow.

"You rich women from up on the ridge are all alike!" Her voice was low and filled with rage. I could smell alcohol on her breath as she leaned close to us. "You leave your pretty little world, do a few acts of charity, and go home again. You think you're better than everybody else, and you look down on women like me from on high. But we're the ones your husbands turn to for love and excitement. There would be no need for us if rich men like your husband weren't willing to pay for our services." She turned and strode away again before I could draw a shocked breath.

Mother was quiet all the way home. I was sure she would collapse in another fit of weeping as soon as she reached her bedroom, and I figured I should call Grandma Bebe right away. But as we stepped from the cab, Mother turned to me and said, "I'm going to do something meaningful with my life from now on, Harriet. Just wait and see if I don't!" She marched upstairs and changed out of her mourning garb without shedding another tear.

The way the women in Mother's club tell the story, she barreled into their next meeting like Annie Oakley riding into the Wild West Show with guns blazing. "Ladies, I have a project for our club to undertake. If you would like to join me, I would be happy for your help. If not, I plan to tackle it with or without your help."

The president inched toward Mother as if she may not have fired all of her ammunition yet and might still pose a danger. "Are you feeling all right, Lucy?"

"I have never felt better. But I've been thinking about how shallow we have become in our elegant little women's club. All we ever focus on in our meetings is ourselves—improving ourselves and entertaining ourselves and pampering ourselves. What about service to our community? Isn't it time that we, who have been so richly blessed, did something to help the women and children in Roseton who aren't as fortunate as we are? I, for one, have vowed to commit myself to bettering the lives of the downtrodden here in our town."

The president patted Mother's shoulder as if soothing a

barking dog. "There, there . . . Why don't you sit down, Lucy. You don't need to shout. You're among friends."

"No, thank you. I can think much better standing up."

"Tell us your plan, Lucy," a matron in the front row said. "We're listening."

"I would like to start by doing something for the family of our New Town hero, Daniel Carver. As you know, my father, Horatio Garner, died as a hero in the Great Flood of 1876. My family was well provided for by his estate, but unfortunately that isn't true for Mr. Carver's family. He labored in the brickyard all of his life. His wife and daughters have no way to support themselves now."

"What do you suggest?"

"I suggest that we provide some sort of short-term relief for them, certainly. We can at least help his wife and daughters find employment—perhaps as domestics in our homes. But the Carvers aren't the first family to lose their sole breadwinner, and they certainly won't be the last one. Why not invest the money that we usually spend entertaining ourselves every month to start a charitable foundation to help the women and children of New Town who have nowhere else to turn?"

"Good idea," someone called out. "Write up a motion, and we'll vote on it at our next meeting."

Mother smiled. "I'll do that—but there's more." The club's president had been about to lift her gavel, but she settled back in her seat.

"I spoke with the pastor of Daniel Carver's church," Mother continued, "and I learned that before he died, Mr. Carver dedicated all of his spare time to helping the young boys who lived in New Town. You see, unlike our sons, those poor boys have little hope for a better life. If their fathers worked in the brickyard, that's where they're destined to work, too. Daniel's vision was to start a boy's club for them—a place where they could be encouraged to dream of a better life. I would like to help him make that vision a reality."

It is a credit to my mother's charming personality and newly awakened leadership skills that the women in her club embraced her proposals. Not every woman shared her enthusiasm, certainly, but enough of the important ones did to quickly endow Roseton's new charitable fund. They also sent a delegation to other towns to research how they had sponsored boys' clubs. Mother stopped her weepy-eyed moping and launched into her new tasks with the same energy that she'd poured into planning Alice's wedding. The change in Mother seemed instantaneous and complete. I didn't understand it. And I certainly didn't like it. Neither did my father.

He threw down his napkin at the dinner table one night, interrupting Mother's rant about the town council's resistance to change, and shouted, "What has gotten into you? I thought you wanted nothing to do with your eccentric mother and her crazy causes."

"Perhaps I finally see the point of them," she said quietly.

"Why now, Lucy? Why all of a sudden?"

"Why not now?"

Father exhaled. He sounded like one of our overheated radiators when the repairman vented the steam. "I think you should go up to Saratoga Springs for a few weeks and take a cure. I'm worried that you're heading for a nervous breakdown. You overtaxed yourself with Alice's wedding."

The calm, placid expression never left Mother's face. She had worn it ever since we returned from Daniel Carver's funeral, and it worried me. It was so unlike her usual worried, hand-wringing appearance. "Going to Saratoga won't change a thing, John. I'm tired of all my vain, empty pursuits. I'm starting a new life."

Father and I exchanged looks. "You're still a wife and mother, Lucy. Aren't they the most important roles there are for a woman?"

"Of course they are. And the work I'm doing in our community is a natural extension of those roles. Why not share my motherly skills with families in real need?"

"What about Harriet? She needs a mother, too, you know."

"Harriet doesn't need me," Mother said with a wave of her hand. "She never did need me. No, my life is going to change now that Alice has left home, and it may as well be for the better."

"For the *better*? What more could you possibly want, Lucy?" Father slapped the table in exasperation. "I provide for all your needs, you don't have to lift a finger here at home, you have your women's club and dozens of friends—why isn't that enough, all of a sudden?"

"I don't know, John . . . but it just isn't."

I started going to Grandma Bebe's house after school every day since Mother was never at home anymore. I was helping Grandma design a newspaper advertisement for the Temperance Union one afternoon when Mother burst into our cozy little world, uninvited.

"I can't even begin to tell you how frustrated I am," she said as she unwound the fur boa from around her neck. "I was certain that our mayor and city council would welcome our plans. After all, we're simply trying to improve Roseton and the lives of its women and children. Imagine my surprise when they turned down our request to convert the old Columbia Building into a boys' club! They wouldn't even let us explain our proposal at the town council meeting. It seems there's a long-standing bylaw that doesn't allow women to attend the meetings unless they're invited, and they refused to invite us! Can you imagine? I would love to see every last one of those hardhearted scoundrels voted out of office at the next election, but—"

"But women aren't allowed to vote," Grandma finished. "It's a vicious circle, Lucy. That's why the Women's Christian Temperance Union joined forces with the suffrage movement. The male politicians have continued to ignore our demands, which means we can't accomplish anything worthwhile until we have a voice."

"I know! Our women's club was so frustrated today that we passed a unanimous resolution to enroll our club in the National American Woman Suffrage Association."

"Well, glory be!" Grandma Bebe leaped up and threw her arms around Mother. "I never thought I'd see the day when you would finally live up to your namesake! I named you after Lucretia Mott, you know. Grandmother Garner must be rolling over in her grave."

I sat slumped in the chair with my arms folded and my legs outstretched, pouting. My mother didn't even try to correct my posture. I was angry about the change in my mother and didn't know why.

The changes continued, building in momentum and menace like a great storm. The only things I had ever seen my mother reading were the society pages and party invitations, but now that she was receiving information about the women's movement, she read religiously. Her reading also included the daily newspaper. My father was not at all happy about sharing it with her every morning.

"Must you drip orange marmalade on the stock market report?" he grumbled. "My fingers are sticking to the page."

"But, John, how will I be able to vote intelligently once I do win the right to vote, if I don't know what's going on in the world?"

"Can't you read my newspaper while I'm at work?"

Of course not. She would be busy with meetings all day. Father left for work muttering darkly beneath his breath.

Instead of lecturing me about poise and manners, my mother

now delivered sermons on woman suffrage at every meal as if she expected me to memorize the details of the movement the way I'd once memorized which fork to use for my shrimp.

"Are you aware, Harriet, that Elizabeth Cady Stanton, Lucretia Mott, and the other women signed the Declaration of Sentiments and Resolutions in Seneca Falls, New York, on the same day that Grandma Bebe was born?"

"Yes, Mother," I said dully. "Grandma told me all about it."

"July 19, 1848, was a very important day for all women. But I must say, we don't seem to have made much progress in the past sixty-four years. . . ."

I deliberately slurped my orange juice and said, "That's because the suffrage movement didn't have you helping them." My sarcasm was wasted on her.

"I was a mere child, Harriet, when Susan B. Anthony delivered ten thousand signatures to the U.S. Senate, asking for a suffrage amendment. That was in 1877, the year after the Great Flood, and those men laughed right in her face. The following year she persuaded a senator to propose the amendment again, and it has been introduced every year since—and defeated every year since, I'm sorry to say."

"Am I supposed to be memorizing all of this for a quiz or something?" I asked, licking jam from my fingers.

"I wish I had done more to help, all those years," she said with a sigh, "instead of shopping and sipping tea all day."

I rolled my eyes and reached across the table for more toast, instead of politely asking her to pass it to me. She never even noticed.

"Of course, I shouldn't say that we've made no progress at all, Harriet. There are five states that have already granted women the right to vote. Wyoming was the first one, then Colorado, Utah,

Idaho . . . and what was the other one again . . . ?" She stared at the ceiling above the china cabinet, scratching her chin.

"Washington," I told her.

"What did you say, Harriet?"

"I said, Washington State granted voting rights to women, too. Grandma Bebe told me all about it."

"Yes, I believe you're right about Washington. Very good, Harriet."

I was afraid she might pat me on the head. I grabbed my toast, scraped back my chair, and fled without waiting to be excused. My mother was taking all of the fun out of swimming against the stream.

I wondered where in the world all of these changes were taking my mother, and I soon found out—to Pennsylvania Avenue in Washington, D.C. Nearly one year after Alice's wedding and Daniel Carver's funeral had begun the transformation process, Mother decided to travel to Washington on the eve of President Woodrow Wilson's inauguration to take part in a huge suffrage parade. I had heard her and Grandma Bebe discussing it and wondered when she would muster up the nerve to ask my father for permission to attend. I wanted to be there to watch the fireworks.

I knew she was up to something one morning when she came to the breakfast table dressed in blue—Father's favorite color—and wearing his favorite perfume. I also noticed that the orange marmalade was missing, replaced by cherry jam, another of his favorites. As he began unfolding the morning newspaper, she began her appeal. "I would very much like to go to Washington, John, and take part in the suffrage parade next week."

"Don't be ridiculous."

"Let me explain why I want to go. Women need to be able to vote in order to be good mothers and protect children's interests. We deserve the right to participate in decisions that will affect our homes and families—issues like better education, free public libraries, and playgrounds for poor children. We're not only caretakers in our own homes; we're caretakers of our communities. But we have no voice, John."

"Do I really have to listen to all of this? Can't I eat my breakfast in peace?" He made the mistake of looking up at Mother. She smiled at him. My mother was still a very beautiful woman, able to blindside my father with her charms.

"If you give me your blessing, dear," she said, "I'll spare you the speech and the sermon. Otherwise, if I have to convince you of the rightness of our cause and the reason for our methods, it might take some time, and you won't get to work until well after lunchtime."

"It isn't necessary to preach to me." He finally managed to tear his eyes away from her. He started scanning the headlines.

"I can show you the materials that the organization sent us describing the march, if you're interested."

"I'm not."

"It's a very well-organized event. Prominent women from all across the country will be there, including Miss Helen Keller."

"I'm not married to Helen Keller, nor is she responsible for running my home and raising my daughter."

"So, may I go, dear?"

He looked up again. "What happens if I say no?"

I wondered if she would turn on the tears. Perhaps Father was wondering the same thing. But Mother didn't even reach for her handkerchief.

"Why, I suppose . . . I suppose I will go to Washington just the same."

For a moment he looked stunned. "Then why bother asking me?" He raised his newspaper like a shield and disappeared behind it.

"Well, I . . . I would like to know that I have your blessing, John."

He was silent for a long moment before lowering the paper again. "Promise me that you won't turn into your mother."

"Good heavens, John!" She had no trouble at all looking appalled. "This is going to be a nice, peaceful march down a very respectable street, not a prayer meeting in front of a saloon. We simply want to get our point across to the new president, and all the other politicians who are ignoring us, that we deserve to be heard. I would never take up any cause that requires me to raise an axe or lower my dignity. Mother and I are two entirely different people."

When it looked as though my father was about to give in, I decided to speak up. "May I go, too?"

They answered simultaneously. "No!"

"Don't be ridiculous," my father added.

"You're only thirteen," my mother said. "You can't miss school, Harriet."

I begged and pleaded to be allowed to come, but to no avail. I even threatened to leave home and travel down to Washington on my own, but Mother knew it was an empty threat. I didn't have money for a train ticket, and it was a very long walk from central Pennsylvania to Pennsylvania Avenue. I burned with envy when my mother and Grandma Bebe left without me.

The train they took to Washington was very crowded, with barely an empty seat. Lucy hated being crushed together with a carful of rude, smelly strangers, even if it was for a worthy cause. It turned out that the overflowing train was just the beginning of Lucy's ordeal. Once she and Bebe reached Washington, they could barely move through the train station, much less find a cab to drive them to where the parade started. Grandma Bebe linked arms with her to prevent them from becoming separated and said, "Let's walk, Lucy. I'm sure it isn't that far."

They started toward Pennsylvania Avenue, following groups of excited, sign-toting women. The closer they got to the starting place, the more crowded the streets became.

"Isn't this intoxicating?" Bebe asked. "There's something about being part of a group, united for one cause, that's so energizing! It's like we're tiny drops of water in a powerful stream, all flowing in the same direction toward the same goal. I feel like shouting!"

Lucy had never shouted in her life and couldn't have shouted now even if she had wanted to. She couldn't seem to draw a breath as strangers pressed in on her from all sides. The march seemed like a disorganized mess to her, with chattering women milling around, drums rattling, and uniformed musicians warming up on their instruments. The parade floats sat mired in the muddy grass, looking as though they weren't going anywhere.

"Who's in charge?" Lucy asked. "When are we going to get started? Where are we supposed to go?" She had been too excited to sleep well the last few nights and had risen early to catch the train. Now she felt close to tears. She could no longer see how being part of this swarming, chaotic throng was going to help her win the right to vote.

"According to the instructions I received," Bebe told her, "we're supposed to march with our state delegation. Let's walk this way and look for their banner, shall we? I see New York State's sign . . . and there's Virginia's over there . . ."

"Oh, look, Mother . . ." Lucy pulled Bebe to a halt to watch a cluster of professional women lining up, grouped by their occupations. She saw nurses in white uniforms and stiff caps, women doctors with white coats, and college women in their academic gowns. "I feel so inadequate compared to them," she murmured.

"I'm only a housewife." She felt close to tears again, but Bebe pulled her forward.

"You mustn't think that way, dear. You know what an important job motherhood is. Come on, I think I see our Pennsylvania banner over there."

They found a place to stand among their state delegation, and someone handed Lucy a picket sign to carry. Her legs were already weary from so much walking and standing, and she hadn't even begun marching yet. The streets were so crowded! Lucy was about to lay down her picket sign and pull a folding fan from her bag to cool her flushed face when she saw that the first few groups were starting to line up in an orderly fashion. She caught a glimpse of a woman wearing a white cape and riding on a white horse, preparing to lead the march down Pennsylvania Avenue. The parade finally began to move. The colorful floats eased off the grass and onto the pavement. The marching bands fell into their ranks and began to play. The music cheered her.

"I would have loved to meet some of the pioneers of the women's movement," Bebe said. "According to the printed program, they are among the first ones marching today. It seems fitting, doesn't it? They led the way for women, and now they are leading the way in the parade."

"There are so many people here!" Lucy said, feeling faint again. "How many do you suppose are marching?"

"I think they expected around five thousand women from all across the country. The politicians will have to take notice of us from now on. They can no longer justify excluding us."

The crowd moved and swarmed around Lucy like a living thing as more and more groups started marching down the parade route. She couldn't breathe. She needed to sit down somewhere. She was searching around frantically for a place to sit when the signal came that her state delegation was next. Lucy and her mother lined up like soldiers and marched out onto Pennsylvania Avenue.

"Isn't this marvelous?" Bebe asked.

To Lucy, it was anything but marvelous. The gawking spectators who lined the parade route were mostly men, in town for the next day's presidential inauguration. They stared at her as she marched past, making her feel naked and exposed. It was one thing to dress up for a ball or to be on display for her husband's important clients. It was quite another thing to parade down a public street with a picket sign, deliberately drawing attention to herself. It went against everything that Grandmother Garner had taught her. Proper young ladies did not allow themselves to be publicly conspicuous.

In spite of Lucy's self-consciousness, everything went well for the first few blocks. Then she sensed a change in the mood when one of the spectators shouted, "Go back to your kitchens, where you belong!" The other men rewarded him with cheers and laughter, and soon more men began to jeer and shout. The farther the women walked, the worse the taunting became. Lucy was shocked to hear cursing and foul language and filthy jokes. She forced herself not to cry.

"Ignore them, Lucy," Bebe told her. "It's to their shame, not ours."

Lucy knew that her mother had sometimes endured public humiliation while holding vigils in front of saloons, but Lucy had never been treated this way in her life. Women were supposed to be revered and respected, not made to be the butt of jokes.

Soon the men were no longer content to stand alongside the curb and shout rude comments. Hundreds of them surged into the street to try to halt the parade. When the men had managed to squeeze the procession down to a single file, Lucy dropped her sign on the ground and gripped her mother's arm, terrified that they would become separated.

"Keep moving forward, ladies," Bebe shouted to encourage everyone. "We can't let these brutes stop us." Lucy held on tightly. She saw several policemen up ahead and breathed a sigh of relief, certain they would restore order. Instead, the policemen joined in the mockery, laughing at the crudest, most ribald jokes Lucy had ever heard. Bebe shouted above the noise, "Pay no attention to them, ladies. Keep marching."

The women's perseverance seemed to anger the men. Lucy saw rough hands reaching out toward her, grabbing and shoving and groping. Someone stuck his foot in her path and she stumbled forward, nearly tripping. She lost her grip on her mother's arm, and when she turned to find her, Lucy saw another woman trip and fall flat on the pavement. A second woman tripped over the first one, then others tumbled down on top of them. She heard Bebe shouting, "Stop! Help them up! They're being trampled!"

In spite of her tiny stature, Bebe managed to steer the parade around the fallen women, then she quickly took charge, helping the uninjured ones to their feet. But the women on the very bottom of the pile hadn't fared so well. Several of them sat on the pavement moaning, bruised and bleeding. One woman cradled a broken arm, another a rapidly swelling ankle. The first woman to fall wasn't moving at all.

"Somebody call an ambulance," Bebe shouted. "People are injured over here." Lucy stood above her mother, wringing her hands. "Go on without me, dear," Bebe told her. "I'm going to stay here until the ambulance comes."

"No. I don't want to get separated." Lucy backed away a few steps and watched as Bebe and a few other women tried to administer first aid. She felt faint and wished she had brought her smelling salts. The parade that continued to stream past them seemed absurd to her now. What good were decorated floats and marching bands when women sat huddled on the street, mocked and weeping and bleeding?

"Where is the ambulance?" Bebe asked again and again. When it finally arrived, the driver was as enraged as the women were.

"I would have been here sooner, but they wouldn't let me through! I had to fight my way through all the spectators just to get here. I'm sorry, but I had to park about a block away."

"Come on," Bebe said, "I'll help you get these people to the ambulance." Lucy followed her mother and the others, feeling nauseous. The taunting continued, even though it was obvious that the women were injured. Lucy battled tears. Women were supposed to be placed on a pedestal, admired as gentle creatures, the weaker sex. She wanted nothing more to do with this march. All she wanted to do was to go home and crawl into her bed and weep.

Lucy never did reach the end of the parade route at the Treasury Building. She read about the inspiring pageant that she had missed in the newspaper the next day. One hundred women and children had presented an allegorical tableau on the steps of the building, dressed in flowing robes and colorful scarves to portray Justice, Charity, Liberty, Peace, and Hope. Trumpets had sounded and a dove of peace had been released. The *New York Times* called it "One of the most impressively beautiful spectacles ever staged in this country." Meanwhile, Woodrow Wilson, the newly elected president, had arrived at the railway station expecting to see a huge crowd and had found only a handful of people. Everyone else was watching the suffrage parade.

Lucy also learned that more than one hundred women had to be shuttled to the hospital by ambulance before the day ended. The chief of police had finally called the secretary of war, requesting that the cavalry be sent from Fort Myer to help control the crowd. They arrived too late to do Lucy's dignity any good. After the last patient had been helped to a hospital, Bebe finally noticed Lucy sitting forlornly on the curb.

"My poor dear," she said, stroking her windblown hair from her face. "Where would you like to go? Shall we find the other marchers and see the end of the parade?"

"I want to go home."

They walked the eight blocks to the train station. Lucy paid for two extra fares so they could have a compartment all to themselves. The tears she had bravely held back all day could finally flow.

"I feel dirty and tattered and heckled and scorned. I've worked so hard for the suffrage movement, but it hasn't done one bit of good. Those men will never accept us as equals."

"Why are you doing all of this, Lucy? Why did you want to go to the march today?"

"Because I vowed to change and to become a better person. Alice is married now, and Harriet doesn't need me, and . . . and I just felt so empty and worthless. I could barely get out of bed in the morning."

"Oh, Lucy, only God can fill the emptiness you feel. Why didn't you turn to Him?"

"Because I couldn't! I needed to make it up to Him first, for the way I've lived all these years and for all of the shallow choices I've made. I felt so guilty for the way I treated Daniel. He died a hero, just like Daddy and his own father had, while I've done nothing worthwhile all of these years."

"Listen," Bebe said as she pushed her own handkerchief into Lucy's hand. "Harriet told me what Daniel's pastor said at the funeral, and it sounds to me that Daniel's faith was what motivated him. He didn't just pull up his socks one morning and resolve to be a better person. God changed him from the inside out."

"I tried to change and do something meaningful for God, but

I'm just so tired of it all. I didn't feel like I was part of the parade today—I hated it!"

"I think you may have gotten everything turned around, dear. You're supposed to work *with* God, not *for* Him. Let Him change you first, and then He'll give you the strength and motivation you need for each task."

"Well, what am I supposed to do now?"

"You need to stop all this work and go away by yourself for a while. Start talking to God. Let Him fill the emptiness in your life. Then, once you get to know Him, He'll tell you what He wants you to accomplish next."

Lucy couldn't seem to stop crying. "I'm so sorry for disappointing you. I'm sorry I can't do all of the things you do."

"Oh, Lucy," Bebe said, pulling her into her arms. "I don't expect you to fight the same battles that I do. We're two different people, just as my mother and I were two different people. God arranged the events in my life to give me a different task than the one He gave to Hannah, and He has a different plan for you, too. Once you put God in the center of your life, I know He's going to use you. And He's going to use you just the way you are right now."

"But how can He? I'm so shallow and empty-headed and . . . and all I've ever cared about is socializing."

"Do you honestly believe that women should have the right to vote?"

"Yes, but I hated marching and picketing and being heckled today. I would rather die than make a public spectacle of myself again. If God tells me that I have to do that all over again—"

"God has never told anyone to grab a picket sign and march for woman suffrage. What He does tell us to do is to feed the hungry and help the oppressed and share His love with others. Women of faith could change the world if we were given half a chance.

But what we've discovered is that we won't get that chance until we're treated as equals. The fight for suffrage is simply a means to a greater end."

Lucy blew her nose, then leaned her head against Bebe's shoulder. She wondered how her mother had grown so wise.

"God never asks you to be someone you're not, Lucy. He asks you to use the talents you already have. You are in a perfect position to use your club friendships and the social connections you have to butter up our legislators and convince them to support suffrage. Have tea with politicians' wives, get them to support our cause, too, so they'll pressure their husbands. Hold dinners and other events to raise funds for candidates who do endorse suffrage. Your natural charm and social skills will get you through doors that are closed to me. And these are things that you love to do and are skilled at doing."

They were almost home. Lucy finally dried her tears and pulled herself together. "Will you promise me something, Mother?"

"What's that, dear?"

"Promise me you won't tell John what happened today. Or how useless I was."

Bebe hugged her tightly. "Your secret is safe with me, Lucy."

Much to my surprise, Tommy O'Reilly returned to my cell with the necessary paper work to spring me from jail. I had been rescued. I stood outside on the front steps of the police station a few minutes later and inhaled deeply. Fresh air and freedom had never smelled so good.

Tommy took my elbow and guided me forward. "Now that I've sprung you from jail, where would you like me to take you?"

"I know the secret password to a little speakeasy down the block."

"Very funny, Harriet. How about if I take you home?"

"Well, I suppose I should go home and prepare my Sunday school lesson for tomorrow. . . ."

"Seriously? You mean you weren't making that up about teaching Sunday school?"

"I knew you didn't believe a word I said."

"That's not what I meant, Harriet."

"No? What exactly did you mean?" I stopped walking and stood with my arms crossed, feeling belligerent for some reason. Tommy halted, as well.

"I meant that you're so smart and modern. . . . Sunday school seems so . . . old-fashioned. Aren't Sunday school teachers usually elderly women with snowy hair and whalebone corsets and high-button shoes?"

I had to laugh, in spite of myself. "You're describing the teachers I had when I was a girl. Look, I may be modern in some ways, but I'm old-fashioned in others. If you're really going to keep me on a leash all weekend, then you'll have to come to Sunday school with me tomorrow."

"Fine. So, should I take you home now? So you can prepare your lesson?"

I remembered that I would have to face my father if I went home, and I shook my head. "No. I don't want to go home. Take me to that café over there and buy me a cup of coffee."

I thought he would argue with me, but he didn't. We walked across the street, and since Tommy was wearing his police uniform he was greeted with smiles and nods of respect as we entered the café. We took a seat in a booth. Tommy's coffee was free. Our waitress batted her eyes at him and offered him a piece of blueberry pie to go with it. "It's free, too, Officer O'Reilly. Just for you." I don't know why, but I had the urge to kick her in the shins.

He gave her his finest smile. "No thanks, Sue. Just coffee tonight."

Once we had our coffee in front of us, Tommy picked up where he had left off. "Listen, Harriet, I'm sure your family must be very worried about you. It's been nearly twenty-four hours since I arrested you. Why don't you at least call them and let them know you're all right?"

"Has anyone telephoned the police station looking for me?"

"Not that I'm aware of."

"Well, there you are." He continued to stare at me, waiting, and I knew I owed him an explanation. "Look, I can't call my grandmother. She joined the Women's Christian Temperance Union and took the pledge not to drink alcohol before I was even born. After all the hard work she has done to get Prohibition passed . . . well, she'll murder me. And then you'll have to arrest her, too."

"I understand that. But what about your parents?"

"My mother isn't worried about me because she isn't even home."

"Where is she?" He poured about a tablespoonful of sugar into his coffee and stirred it patiently.

"Don't you ever read the newspaper, Tommy? The U.S. House of Representatives passed a suffrage bill in January of 1918, and—"

"I was over in France in 1918. I think I missed that piece of news."

"You fought in the war?" I asked in awe. He nodded. "Was it as bad as everyone said it was, with mustard gas and trenches and everything?" He nodded again. Who knew that Tommy O'Reilly's life could be so interesting? I wanted to pursue this topic of conversation further, but Tommy was a relentless interrogator.

"Let's get back to your mother."

"I haven't seen much of her since the bill passed and the momentum started building toward a suffrage amendment. And by the way, did you hear about the women who protested outside the White House all during the war? Wasn't it ironic that President Wilson had you fighting for freedom and democracy halfway around the world while denying those same democratic freedoms to half of the population of America—its women? Did you hear how the suffragettes were eventually thrown into jail and force-fed with tubes shoved down their throats when they went on a hunger strike?"

He held up his hand to stop me. "So is that where your mother is? In jail?"

"Are you kidding? She wouldn't be caught dead in jail. She prefers to work behind the scenes, throwing parties for political candidates—she's great at throwing parties. Anyway, last year the suffrage bill passed in the Senate, too, but then it had to be ratified by two-thirds of the states. She has been hard at work, and now all we need is one more vote. My mother is in Tennessee right now, probably on her knees, praying for their legislature to ratify the amendment. If they vote to pass it, we'll win. Women will finally have the right to vote."

"That's a fascinating story, Harriet. So tell me, is your father in Tennessee, too?"

His question caught me by surprise. "Huh? . . . No. No, he's here in town. But I don't want to involve him."

"You're his daughter. I'm sure if you had called him last night, he would have come down and bailed you out of jail, wouldn't he?"

"Not unless I cried a gallon of tears. That's what Alice and my mother used to do whenever Grandma Bebe got arrested, but I'm not the type to weep and beg. Why do you think women want the right to vote, Tommy? It's so we can stand on our own two feet and be taken seriously. We're tired of depending on a man to run to our rescue and bail us out whenever we're in trouble."

Tommy bit his lip, staring at his coffee and frowning fiercely in what I guessed was a desperate struggle not to laugh. "What's so funny?" I asked.

"Nothing."

I suddenly figured out the joke, and it was on me. My indignation vanished. "Oh. You're a man. And you just bailed me out of jail, didn't you?"

"It seemed like the gentlemanly thing to do." His smile broke free, and I almost smiled in return. "But I didn't think of it as rescuing you," he quickly assured me. "If I've learned anything about you over the years, Harriet Sherwood, it's that you can take care of yourself. I'm sure you would have managed just fine if you had to spend another night or two locked up. Even the trustee was a little frightened by you. But I know there has to be more to your story than what I can see on the surface."

"And so you're going to follow me around like this until you crack the case? Our city is going to need a pretty big police force if they have to assign one cop for every person out on bail."

He looked down at his coffee. He was still stirring it relentlessly, causing a tiny typhoon in the cup. "I have a confession to make, Harriet. I don't have to follow you all around. I trust you not to flee. I'm following you because I want to."

"Because you want to—what? Torment me? That's what you always did best, you know. All through school, you were always pulling my pigtails or taunting me or bullying me."

"You know why I did all those things?" he asked. He looked up at me with a shy grin on his face. "Because I liked you."

"You're joking. If you liked me, then tormenting me was a pretty stupid way to show it."

"I know. But I was a kid," he said with a shrug. "What did I know about women? I liked you because you weren't like all the other girls. You had guts. You were just a little bit of a thing—you still are. Yet you stood up to me like someone three times your size. I admired you for that. I still do. I just wish that you hadn't . . . you know . . ."

"Broken the law?"

"That's what we need to talk about. Tell me what's going on. Convince me that you're innocent."

"I'm not innocent. You caught me red-handed. . . . But there are innocent people involved. And as I told you last night, they're the ones I'm trying to help. The really bad criminals are the ones who belong in jail. But if the people I'm protecting are arrested, then innocent children are going to go hungry."

"Then help me catch the real criminals."

"If I do that, if we catch the bigger crooks, will you let me and the others go free?"

"I'll do my best, Harriet."

"How do I know I can trust you to keep your word?"

He looked hurt. "People can change, you know. I'm not the same bully I was when we were in school. Besides, I think you can trust me more than some federal agent you've never met before, can't you?"

"I guess so . . . I'm in a whole pile of trouble, aren't I?"

"I'm afraid so."

He had become so solemn that I began wringing my hands like the heroine in a melodrama. "Oh no! Please save me, Tommy! I'll go insane if I have to remain behind bars! The meat was so rubbery that I bent the knife, and the tapioca pudding came out of the bowl in one huge, gummy lump and—"

"I wish you would be serious."

"I'm sorry." And I was. "I'm sorry I became involved in this mess in the first place. If I could do it all over again, I would do everything differently."

"Why did you do it?"

"I'm still not exactly sure. . . ."

But after thinking about it for the past twenty-four hours, I was beginning to figure it out. The waitress brought us more coffee, and Tommy sat back and listened patiently while I told him.

⁓

In April of 1917, two months before I graduated from high school, America went to war. I thought I had drawn a nice, neat map for my life, but the war turned out to be one of those unexpected changes Grandma Bebe had warned me about. I had every intention of steering a course straight toward college in the fall, but the rudder slipped from my grasp and I drifted, instead, into a job at my father's department store.

My change of course started where so many other events in my life have started—at the breakfast table. It was a beautiful morning in May and my father had just read an article in the newspaper about the new Selective Service Act that required all men between the ages of twenty-one and thirty-one to register for the draft. His newspaper rustled like a forest fire as he refolded it angrily and voiced his frustration.

"I don't know how I'm expected to run a business without employees. According to this article, nearly all of my department managers, buyers, and bookkeepers are about to be drafted. I've had several good men enlist already, and it's impossible to find anyone to replace them."

"I could do it," I said. "I could work for you." The prospect of a long, boring summer loomed ahead of me now that both my mother and grandmother were occupied with their causes. Neither one of them would allow me to come with them and get involved—licking stamps didn't count, in my opinion. "Why don't you hire me to work in your store, Father?"

"Don't be ridiculous." He waved me away without even considering the idea.

"I'm serious!" I banged my fist on the table to get his attention, rattling his coffee cup. He looked up, startled. "I'm graduating from school in two weeks and I have nothing else to do. I'm very smart, according to all my teachers. Twice as smart as any boy. Why won't you hire me?"

"Because these aren't jobs for women."

"Why not? What difference does my gender make? Your male employees just sit behind desks all day anyway, don't they?"

"The only women I hire are all salesclerks. My department managers, buyers, and bookkeepers are men."

"Why?"

"Because that's the way it's done."

"Well, you might have to change the way it's done now that we're at war. Grandma Bebe had to take over for her brothers when they went to war, and she ended up doing all their farm chores—plowing and baling hay and everything. And then she helped run her husband's factory when he was . . . unwell."

"Your grandmother's example is hardly one that I want my daughters to follow," he said, shaking his head. "Women have no business running a factory or a department store. And besides, aren't you supposed to be going to college soon?"

"Not until the fall. I have all summer free. And if you give me a job, it might help me decide what I want to study in college. Won't you at least think about it?"

"Women work fine as salesclerks, but I don't need any more clerks at the moment. I need managers—men."

I huffed in frustration. "The United States government is hiring women in Washington to fill men's positions because of the shortage. I just read about it in the paper the other day. If the government thinks women are capable of doing men's work, why not hire them for your store? All I'm asking for is a tiny little department to manage."

"My department managers are all men. You're a woman." My father was repeating himself. Either he had run out of arguments or he wasn't listening to me.

"Your managers *were* all men," I told him. "You just said yourself that they were all leaving to enlist or were about to be drafted—and that there aren't any men to replace them. I would say you're out of options." When Father didn't reply, I added, "I could dress up in a man's suit and tie, if you think it would help."

"Don't be ridiculous."

"Look, you need employees, right? What's so hard about a manager's job that a woman couldn't do it?"

"It's a question of respect. The salesclerks are mostly young women your age. Managers need to be mature. They need to be men."

"But I'm the store owner's daughter. That should win me some respect. And believe me, I can be very bossy—the boys at school tell me I'm bossy all the time. "

The more I thought about it, the more I liked the idea of working in the department store, but my father looked as though he wasn't even going to consider it. I was wondering how I could convince him when, much to my surprise, my mother rose to my defense—and she did so without resorting to tears.

"Why don't you let her try it, John? What could it hurt? If you need help as badly as you say you do, it seems you should give Harriet a chance. She is very quick to learn things, you know."

"Yes, Father. Why not let me try it? Let's say . . . for two weeks? If you're not completely happy with the work I'm doing by then, I'll agree to come home again."

I don't think anyone was as surprised as I was when my father finally agreed. It showed how truly desperate he was for help. I would have gone to the store with him that very morning, but he made me wait until after graduation. "I need to shuffle people around and find a suitable department for you to manage," he explained.

He didn't want me to run Ladies' Fashions or the Millinery Department, because I wasn't the least bit fashionable. I couldn't tell a Gainesboro hat from a Shepherdess style. Likewise, I was the wrong person to run the Jewelry, Perfume, and Shoe departments.

All of the men's departments were off the list because the middle-aged male clerks—not to mention the customers—would never take me seriously. "The Children's Department is much too important," Father said, "to be managed by a woman with a strong aversion to marriage and children"—and I had been outspoken about both. In the end, Father ranked all of the departments in order of importance and gave me the most unimportant one he could find: China, Glassware, and Silver Goods.

"What an excellent choice for me, Father," I said, pretending to be overjoyed. "As you know, I'll bring a great deal of experience to my work. Mother has trained me quite well in understanding the differences between a salad plate and a dessert plate, between a tablespoon and a dessert spoon, between a—"

"That's quite enough, Harriet."

"But I was just explaining about the differences—"

"The most important difference you need to know is that male managers don't aggravate me with their excessive talking."

"Yes, sir."

I had never even seen the China, Glassware, and Silver Goods Department in my father's store until my first day of work. It was in such an out-of-the-way location in the basement of his vast emporium that I was going to need a map to find it again tomorrow. Mine was a small department with only three salesclerks, Bertha, Claudia, and Maude. They weren't much older than I was. Their shifts were staggered so that no more than two of them were on duty at one time, and only Bertha and Claudia were there to greet me on my first day. They stood at attention in my father's presence, gracing me with a small curtsy after he introduced me as Miss Sherwood, their new department manager. Next, Father showed me my desk—piled high with sample catalogs, invoices, and order forms—behind a curtain in the back room. I shared the space with three other department managers and shelves full of inventory.

"You can ask Mr. Foster from Linens, Pillows, and Bedding to show you how we do things," Father said. He nodded toward an elderly gentleman at the neighboring desk, who looked as though he had been selling pillows and bedding since the War Between the States.

The first thing I did after my father returned to his office was to peruse my new domain on the showroom floor. It consisted of a tall shelf of glassware on the back wall and four long display counters—one for ridiculously elaborate silver serving pieces, another for silver tableware in silk-lined boxes, and two for porcelain dishware. My two salesclerks were busy trying to look industrious. Bertha twirled a feather duster over the glassware while Claudia rubbed tarnish off a silver pickle castor as if she expected a genie to pop out and grant her three wishes.

"Tell me how my predecessor used to run this department," I said after gathering them into a huddle. They looked at each other, then at me.

"Mr. Osgood had his rules," Claudia said, "and as long as we remembered them, he left us alone."

"What kind of rules? Can you give me some examples?"

Claudia gazed at the ceiling as if she had pinned a crib sheet up there. "Um . . . we had to say, 'May I help you, ma'am?' right away whenever a customer came. And when there weren't any customers we had to keep busy. No sitting allowed."

"And we can't chew gum," Bertha added—although I thought I spotted a wad of it tucked in her cheek. "Our clothes have to be pressed and neat, our hair clean and tidy, and our shoes shined. And if we get married, we lose our jobs."

The last rule seemed arbitrary and unfair to me, but I kept my thoughts to myself. "Do you like working here?" I asked.

Not surprisingly, they both replied, "Yes, ma'am."

I spent the entire day familiarizing myself with all of the paper work I would be required to do and listening as Mr. Linens, Pillows, and Bedding droned on and on about ledger books and accounting practices. My eyes started to glaze over, and if I hadn't pleaded so fervently for this job in the first place, I might have decided to enlist in the army myself. When I emerged from my underground kingdom at the end of the day, I was glad to see sunlight again.

"How was your first day?" Mother asked.

"Wonderful! I learned so much! I never knew they made sterling silver mustard pots." I didn't mention that we hadn't had a single customer. At least reordering new stock would be simple.

By the end of my first week as manager of China, Glassware, and Silver Goods, I knew I had to do something differently in my department or die of boredom. I decided to go on a spying mission to our competitors' stores, comparing their selection and services to ours. I returned to give Bertha, Claudia, and Maude my report.

"The clerks in the other stores acted so haughty and superior, they made me feel like I was trespassing. I was afraid to peruse the shelves or ask them any questions. I don't want you to be that stuffy. Smile and be friendly to our customers. Ask about the occasion for the gift and whom they are buying it for. Show some interest in our customers."

I got the standard reply of "Yes, ma'am." But as I turned to leave, I thought I heard Bertha whisper, "What customers?"

Yes, something would have to be done about the customer problem.

During my second week of work, I marched into Father's office on the top floor and asked, "What's my budget for newspaper advertisements?" He stared at me as if he'd forgotten my name. "I'm great at writing ads," I told him. "I used to help Grandma Bebe write them all the time."

"Budget?" he finally replied. "You don't have a budget. Our

advertising department handles everything. That's their job. Your job is to sell china, glassware, and silver goods."

"How am I supposed to do that if nobody can even find my department?"

"Well, it's your job as manager to figure that out. Now go away and stop bothering me, Harriet. I'm busy."

I spent a week pacing the floor of my department, desperately searching for an idea. "How would you describe our typical customer?" I asked my salesclerks one day. Claudia began to giggle as if the notion of having actual customers was hilarious.

Bertha pushed her gum aside with her tongue and said, "They're mostly girls who are about to get married. They come in to pick out their wedding presents."

I sat at my desk in the back room beside Mr. Linens—whom I suspected was asleep most of the time—and thought about it some more.

I came up with a brilliant idea.

I ran up the stairs from the basement two at a time—the elevator was much too slow—and hurried outside to the nearest newsstand, where I bought all three of our town's daily papers. When I got back to my department, breathless, I gave one to Bertha, one to Maude, and kept the third. "Open it to the social pages," I told them, "and find the engagement announcements for me." They did as they were told, but they were eyeing me warily. "Now, add up the engagements. How many are there?" Bertha counted four, Maude had three, and I struck gold with seven.

"Here's my idea: Sherwood's Department Store is going to offer the happy bride-to-be a free sterling silver serving spoon in her choice of four different patterns as our way of congratulating her."

"Free?" Bertha echoed, nearly swallowing her gum.

"Yes, free. Once she has that first spoon, you see, it will be your job to convince her that she needs the rest of the set, as well. That means service for at least twelve with all of the accessories to go with it—gravy ladles, carving knives, pickle forks, jelly knives, salad sets. And why not add a beautiful set of berry spoons and shrimp forks?"

My staff appeared dubious, but they set to work cutting out the engagement announcements for me while I got out order forms for Rogers Brothers Silver and boldly ordered six sets of serving spoons in four of our most popular patterns. Then I went upstairs—taking the elevator this time—and borrowed several sheets of Sherwood's Department Store stationery from my father's office. That evening I typed up letters of congratulations on Grandma Bebe's typewriter to all fourteen prospective brides. I mailed them on my way to work the next day.

"Now, this is the most important part," I told my clerks. "The free spoons are going to be in a box on my desk, but don't run into the back room and bring it out to the customer right away. Make her wait a few minutes so she has time to wander past our display counters and examine the dishes and the sterling silver tea sets while she's waiting. Suggest that she sign up for our wedding registry. The free spoon will draw new customers in, and before you know it, every bride in town will have registered their silverware selections at our store."

My gamble worked. All fourteen brides-to-be hurried into the store for their free spoon. I sent out more letters. Business boomed. Then my father heard about my scheme.

"What's this I hear about you giving away my stock for free?" he asked at the dinner table one evening.

I quickly explained my idea to him and finished by saying, "It's just a serving spoon. And dozens of new customers have come in already to get theirs."

"Can't you give away teaspoons? They're cheaper."

"I know, but a teaspoon is too small. The bride will toss it into her hope chest and forget about it. But a serving spoon carries a lot more weight. It's big and shiny and elegant, and she'll put it on her bureau top and dream about serving mashed potatoes to her new husband every evening."

"Don't be ridiculous."

"You won't think I'm ridiculous when you see our sales figures in a couple of months. I've sent out thirty-five letters so far. And do you know how many brides came in for their free spoon? Every single one of them. We counted them. And every single one of them signed up for our gift registry. You can bet they'll be back for the rest of their silverware in the pattern of their choice."

"Well . . . I suppose you can continue."

"You won't be sorry. But listen, Father. I'm going to need some help typing letters. I can't keep doing them all myself. Grandma's typewriter ribbon is about worn out and my salesclerks need me on the floor."

"I suppose my secretary can do them."

By the time summer ended, China, Glassware, and Silver Goods was thriving down in the basement of Sherwood's Department Store.

And I loved my job.

I was supposed to start college in the fall of 1917, but I no longer wanted to go. "You need me at the store," I told my father. "The war is far from over, and besides, the college campus is like a ghost town with all the young men overseas." From my desk in the back room I could hear Bertha, Claudia, and Maude bemoaning the shortage of men, too, as they kept our stock shiny in between customers. But they complained about the shortage for an entirely different reason than my father did. All three of my clerks desperately wanted to get married and live happily ever after, but only Bertha had a steady boyfriend. His name was Lyle, and she worried about him constantly.

"He's going to get called up, I just know it!"

He did.

"He's going away for training, and I'm going to miss him so much!"

She did.

"I'm going to worry myself sick if he gets sent overseas."

She did after he did.

One weekend in November, Claudia and Maude asked if they could work extra hours to cover Bertha's shift and give her the weekend off. "Lyle is home on leave," Claudia explained. "This will be the last time Bertha will get to see him before he sails for France." I gave her the time off. She cried for days after he left. Once Lyle landed in France, Bertha kept track of his steps and all the battles he fought more diligently than General Pershing did. Her daily news reports brought the war right into China, Glassware, and Silver Goods. It didn't look like the war would be over anytime soon, which was bad news for Bertha and Lyle, but it was great news for me. I loved my job.

I did miss spending time with Grandma Bebe, however, now that I worked such long hours. In December, she called one day to ask if I would drive her to the train station and water her violets while she was away. "Where are you going, Grandma?" I asked.

"To Washington, dear. I don't know if you've been following the news, but the prohibition amendment is coming up for a vote before both houses of Congress this month. I can't sit quietly at home and wonder about the results. I've waited much too long to see this day and worked much too hard for it."

I was happy for her, but a little sad that I had become so wrapped up in my job that I had lost track of her progress. America had been fighting in Europe for only nine months, but Grandma Bebe had been waging war against alcohol since she was my age. I eagerly awaited news from her in Washington. On December 17, the House of Representatives voted to pass the amendment. The next day the Senate did the same. I thought Grandma Bebe would be triumphant when I picked her up at the train station again, but she seemed surprisingly subdued. Considering how hard she had worked to get the amendment passed, it seemed to me that she should be jubilant—even if she couldn't toast her success with champagne.

"What's wrong, Grandma?"

"We can't sit back and rest just yet. The amendment still needs to be ratified—which means getting thirty-six out of the forty-eight states to approve it. Many state legislatures won't even get around to voting until after the Christmas recess."

"How many years have you been fighting this battle, Grandma?"

"Oh, I don't know . . . let me think. We started our local chapter of the WCTU before the Great Flood of 1876 . . . so it has to be more than forty years by now."

"So it shouldn't be too hard to wait a few more weeks until after Christmas, should it?"

"We'll still have our work cut out for us, though," she said with a sigh. "The temperance chapters in each state will have to work to get the amendment before the state governments, which means talking to legislators, signing petitions, gathering support . . . Yes, we still have a lot of work to do. But I keep thinking of all the families and the children whose lives are ruined by this evil every day. They are the reason I'm doing this, Harriet."

I carried her suitcase into her house for her and saw the mountains of paper on her dining room table, and I wondered what Grandma would do with herself once the amendment passed. I knew what she would do if it didn't pass—continue working, of course.

Christmas approached, and as I was strolling past Woolworth's on my lunch hour one day and saw rolls of brightly colored wrapping paper in their store window, I came up with a great idea for the holidays: free gift-wrapping. I went inside and bought a dozen rolls of paper and fifty yards of ribbon with my own money. When I told my staff my idea, Bertha claimed to be an expert at wrapping packages. She offered to teach my other salesclerks how to do it.

"First you fold the ends in like this . . . then you crease it real good. . . ." I watched Bertha work, admiring her graceful hands—and suddenly noticed a plain gold band on the ring finger of her left hand. "And then you tie it like this. See, Miss Sherwood? Doesn't it look pretty?"

She looked up, expecting praise, and must have seen my puzzled frown. She looked down again, following my gaze, and gasped. She snatched the ring off her hand and stuffed it into her pocket, but of course it was too late.

"You're married." It came out as a statement, not a question.

"Please don't fire me, Miss Sherwood! Please! I need this job and—"

"You and Lyle got married."

Tears filled her eyes at the mention of Lyle's name. "We eloped the weekend before he was shipped overseas. I wanted to be with him and be his wife so badly . . . just in case he . . . you know . . ."

I was too surprised to reply, even though I shouldn't have been surprised at all. Bertha had talked about Lyle constantly since I began working at the store seven months ago. She was in love and love led to marriage. I had seen the same starry-eyed look in my customers' eyes when they came in for their free spoon, a symbol of their brand-new life. And even though I had forsworn love and marriage and all the rest, there were times when I looked at all those brides-to-be and I felt something very close to jealousy. I felt it now after learning the truth about Bertha and her beloved Lyle.

"I know there's a rule that says I can't work in this department store and be married," Bertha said between sobs, "but Lyle and I need the money, Miss Sherwood, and I don't want a factory job. And I can't just sit at home all day, either, because I'll go crazy worrying about Lyle and—"

"I'm not going to fire you, Bertha."

"Y-you're not?"

"I always thought it was unfair to fire a perfectly good salesclerk just because she got married. When men get married, the store gives them a raise."

"But . . . but your father is the one who made that rule in the first place, and you might get into trouble if—"

"My father's rule is unfair, and I'm not afraid to tell him so—if he asks."

Justice was on my side. I thought of my great-grandmother Hannah, who had defied the unfair Fugitive Slave Law. Nevertheless, I didn't plan to confront my father unless I got caught. "I'll look the other way, Bertha. But make sure you don't wear the ring to work again." She hugged me in gratitude.

Free gift-wrapping turned out to be another successful idea, and other departments throughout the store soon copied it. My father, however, never breathed a word of praise or acknowledgment to me.

January of 1918 turned out to be brutally cold, and business slumped when a deadly flu epidemic swept across the nation. I begged Grandma Bebe to cancel all her meetings and stay home so she wouldn't risk getting sick. For once, she listened to my advice. My mother traveled to Washington with a group of her friends after President Wilson spoke up publicly in support of the suffrage amendment. She was in the audience chamber in the House of Representatives on January 20 when they narrowly passed the amendment. But she arrived home discouraged after the Senate decided to postpone the debate on the amendment until the fall.

Meanwhile, state legislatures across the country began to ratify Grandma Bebe's prohibition amendment, bringing the total to eleven states by the time spring arrived and the wedding season was about to begin. Of course, the war meant fewer weddings, since a sizable percentage of prospective grooms were overseas, but that didn't stop me from coming up with more new ideas for China,

Glassware, and Silver Goods. In fact, when Mr. Linens, Pillows, and Bedding announced that he was retiring, I begged Father to combine the two departments and allow me to run both of them. The Linens Department couldn't be that hard to manage, since I suspected that Mr. Linens had actually been asleep at his desk for the past few years.

"We could call it the Home Goods Department," I told Father. "Our slogan could be 'Everything a woman needs for a comfortable home.' " I hatched plans to pair damask tablecloths and napkins with my dishes and glassware to create beautiful table settings for our customers to covet. "There may not be too many weddings this year," I told Father, "but once the soldiers return . . ."

My father eventually agreed. He had no choice. He couldn't find a replacement for Mr. Linens, Pillows, and Bedding no matter how hard he tried. My kingdom expanded to twice its size, and I was on my way to becoming the queen of the basement of Sherwood's Department Store. In April I decided to have a Hope Chest Sale in my combined departments. Young ladies could prepare for the day when their sweethearts returned from France to pop the question by making sure their hope chests were well stocked with china and bed linens.

One morning as we were setting up for the sale, I took a good look at Bertha and realized that she was pregnant. "Please don't fire me, please!" she begged when I pulled her into the back room for a talk. "I'll go crazy at home all day, and we really, really need the money, Miss Sherwood, especially with a baby on the way. Please!"

I had grown very fond of all my clerks by now, but I would especially hate to lose Bertha. She was my best salesgirl and could probably talk the Rogers Brothers silversmiths into buying one of their own pickle castors from us. I was counting on her to teach my new clerks from Linens, Pillows, and Bedding how to sweet-talk our customers into buying more than they intended during the Hope Chest Sale.

I gave the matter a great deal of thought and decided that I could disguise Bertha's condition for a while longer if I gave blue cotton smocks to all of my salesclerks to wear over their clothing. I told my father that not only would the baggy smocks protect the girls' blouses from tarnish stains, but our customers would be able to distinguish our staff members much more easily in their smocks.

The Hope Chest Sale was such a success that I decided it should become an annual event. Bertha continued to work for a few more months. When she began to waddle, the girls and I gave her a baby shower in the back room after the store closed on her last day. I sent her a sterling silver teething ring and a twenty-five dollar war bond after she gave birth to Lyle Jr. in August.

Life couldn't have been better for me. I was enjoying my work and accomplishing great things for our store—maybe not of the caliber of Mother's and Grandmother's accomplishments, but I couldn't help noticing that we were all working hard for our community, each in our own way. And in the past, women in our nation hadn't been allowed to accomplish very much at all.

By fall, almost half of the required states had ratified Grandma's Prohibition Amendment. I held a sale in my new Home Goods Department on warm bedding and china teapots in preparation for winter. And my mother and her suffragette friends were waiting anxiously for the promised debate in the Senate on the woman suffrage amendment. When the amendment lost by only three votes, Mother was heartbroken. And furious. But she refused to give up.

"We'll show those hardheaded old men," she told me. "There's an election coming in November, and we're going to target all of the senators who voted against the bill to make sure they lose their Senate seats. The amendment is going to pass the next time, you'll see."

On November 11, everyone rejoiced when the armistice was signed. The war in Europe was over. I visited Bertha and her baby and learned that her husband, Lyle, had managed to survive the war unharmed. He was coming home. I hired three more sales-clerks and ordered a case of silver serving spoons in anticipation of the flood of engagements that would soon follow.

During the first two weeks of January 1919, there was a flurry of voting all across the country as more and more states ratified Grandma Bebe's prohibition amendment. Then, on January 16, Wyoming became the thirty-sixth state to ratify it. She now had the necessary votes to officially amend the United States Constitution to prohibit alcohol. The saloons she had fought so hard to close would have to shutter their doors for good. Grandma Bebe invited me to the celebration at her house, along with Millie White and all of the other longtime members of the Women's Christian Temperance Union. No one at the party needed champagne in order to cel-ebrate. It was a good thing the amendment passed when it did, too, because Grandma was seventy years old, and I couldn't help noticing that she was starting to slow down. Her days of smashing whiskey barrels at the train depot were all behind her.

She was jubilant, though, her cheeks glowing like a school-girl's. "The last time I felt this ecstatic," she told me, "was the day I learned that the slaves had been set free. . . . Or maybe it was when I learned how to soar on my brothers' swing with the sky above me and the wind in my hair. . . . Or it might have been when I first saw Niagara Falls with my dear, sweet Horatio by my side. . . ."

Meanwhile, Mother's goals were also within sight. She had worked hard to help pro-suffrage candidates get elected to the Senate, and on June 4, 1919, when a vote was taken once again, the woman suffrage amendment passed. Once thirty-six states ratified the amendment, women would achieve equality at last. I couldn't help feeling proud of the women in my family. Great-Grandma Hannah had helped bring about the abolition of slavery. Grandma Bebe had saved America from Demon Rum. And now Mother was close to victory, as well. All three women had worked hard and had accomplished their goals—and my mind spun with all the plans I had for our family's flourishing department store.

Two days after my mother's latest victory for woman suffrage, my father called me upstairs to his office at work. I assumed it was to congratulate me on three straight months of record sales figures in the Home Goods Department. With the surge of engagements and June weddings, I was mailing out letters and handing out free spoons at a record rate. I strode confidently into Father's office and found him conversing with a tall young man with an army haircut.

"Harriet, I would like you to meet Robert Morton. He was discharged recently from the army, and I've just hired him to manage my Home Goods Department."

I think I stopped breathing for a moment. I tried not to panic. I managed to swallow my fear and say, "How nice for you. And which department will I be managing from now on?"

Father looked confused. "You're going off to college."

"What? No I'm not! I like working here."

Father had the good sense to ask Mr. Morton to kindly wait outside. Then he cleared his throat and said, "Now, Harriet, I admit that you've done a good job here. But you always knew that your position was only temporary."

"No I didn't—"

"This is men's work."

"What!"

"And now that the war is over and the men have returned home, it's time to give them their jobs back."

"But it's *my* job, not theirs! I'm the one who created the Home Goods Department in the first place. I'm the one who boosted sales to record numbers by giving away spoons. I don't want to go to college anymore. I want to keep managing my department, just like I've been doing for the past two years."

"Mr. Morton has a family to support."

"I don't care! There must be another job in the store you can give him. Or at least give me a different job to do. You hire lots of people, don't you?"

"The women who work for me are all salesclerks and typists. I'm sure you don't want one of those jobs."

"Why do you keep insisting that there's such a thing as men's work and women's work? Don't you know that women have done all sorts of 'men's jobs' during the war? There were women car mechanics and telegraph operators and streetcar drivers. Women worked on factory assembly lines and plowed fields and served as traffic cops."

"But they aren't doing those things anymore, Harriet. The soldiers have come home and they need their jobs back."

"But those aren't *their* jobs anymore!"

"You can go to college in the fall like you planned. Isn't that what you wanted to do?"

"I don't want to go to college anymore, I want my job back! I want to work in this store—our family's store. Your father let you join the business years ago, didn't he? Suppose I was your son instead of your daughter."

"That would be different."

My pulse rate soared along with my anger. "Why? Why would it be any different?"

"Men have to work to support their families. Women get married and have children."

"Not me! I'm never getting married!"

"It doesn't matter if you get married or not, Harriet. My mind is made up."

I hated myself for it, but I began to cry. I couldn't help it. "Please, Father. Please let me stay here and work for you. I want to come into the business with you."

My tears made him uncomfortable, but they didn't change his mind. He started leading me toward the door. "I'm sorry, but it just isn't done. Now, if you were to settle down with a husband someday and he wanted to work for me, I would consider bringing him into the business."

There aren't enough words to describe my outrage.

I don't know how long I stood outside his office door and wept. His secretary came over with a handkerchief to console me but wisely refrained from asking me what was wrong. When I finally dried my tears, I went downstairs to say good-bye to the girls in my department. I didn't see any reason to delay my departure, nor would I stick around and help Mr. Morton learn how to manage the department he had just stolen from me. I gave free spoons to Maude and Claudia, who had both become engaged to returning servicemen. Then I left Sherwood's Department Store for good.

It was pouring rain outside, but I was so furious that I didn't care how wet I got. I walked all the way to Grandma Bebe's house, remembering how she had walked through a downpour, too, after leaving her job at the tannery—and leaving Neal MacLeod. I knew that she would understand the terrible loss I felt at that moment, if not my rage.

"Why, you poor thing," she said when I appeared at her door, shivering. "Where's your umbrella? Why aren't you at work?"

The second question brought more tears. "Father fired me!"

"Fired you? Why? What happened?"

"He said that since the servicemen have all returned, he doesn't need me anymore. It's so unfair!"

Grandma Bebe pulled me into her arms and let me cry. Even in my anger and grief I was aware of how frail she had become—and how dear she was to me. When I finished crying, she took me into her kitchen and made tea.

"You're right, Harriet. That was completely unfair of him. But I don't suppose anyone is going to convince him to change his mind, are they?"

I shook my head, rainwater dripping from my hair. "Even Mother's and Alice's tears wouldn't do me any good this time."

Grandma fetched a towel and gave it to me to dry off. "I know that right now you want sympathy more than advice, Harriet, but I'm going to give you some advice anyway. Just two words: Trust God."

I looked away. She was right—I didn't want to hear it.

"You have to trust that He is arranging the events in your life in order to lead you to the purpose He has for you," she continued. "Sometimes those events are tragic and painful. But He uses them to shape us into the people He wants us to become."

"But I loved my job. And I was good at it!"

"Did you ever stop to think that maybe God has an even better job for you? You're so young, Harriet, and working at the store was the first challenge you ever faced on your own. But what if God has planned something even better for your future? Would you want to end up stuck at the store all your life and missing something great? Remember poor Horatio and how much he disliked working in his father's business? I always thought he was destined for better, greater things, but he was stuck there. He had no choice. He was expected to continue his father's work. And poor Neal MacLeod, who was so well suited for the job, was written right out of his father's will."

I tossed the wet towel down on the floor. "Life is so unfair."

"Yes, it is. But in spite of that fact, we can trust God to always do

what is best for us—best for *His* purposes. If working at the store is
His choice for you, then He'll arrange circumstances to lead you
back there. Maybe your father's attitude will change. But in the
meantime, go to college. Find out more about yourself and your
gifts. Women will be able to vote soon, and then watch out. There
will be no limit to what we can accomplish."

"My life was going along so nicely," I said. "And now I have
nothing."

"Remember what my mother once told me, Harriet? She said,
'Life is always changing, always flowing forward like a stream.
Things never stay the same. And we have to move on and change,
too.' She was right, you know."

I heard what Grandma was saying, but disappointment and
rage kept her words from sinking in. "I want to move in with you,"
I told her. "I hate my father and I'm never going home again!"

She stood to pour water from the boiling kettle, then said,
"You may stay for a day or two. . . . After all, I would hate to see you
commit patricide. But eventually you will have to forgive him."

"Never! What he did was unforgivable!"

Grandma smiled sadly. "Your father grew up in an era when a
man's role was that of provider and protector. Whether men went
to war or to work, they did it so that the women they loved could
stay home where they were safe and cherished. That's the way
your father was raised, and in his mind he is doing what's best for
you—saving you from being forced to earn a living. He thinks he's
your knight in shining armor, doing battle in the business world
so that he can give you and your mother everything you need,
without you having to lift a finger. That's the only way he knows to
show his love for you. He can't change his role overnight. Imagine
how threatened men like your father must feel now that women
are coming into their own, working in professional fields, voting
to change things. Look how much your mother has changed in

the past few years. In many ways, your father's entire way of life is coming apart."

"Don't ask me to feel sorry for him, Grandma. I can't do it."

"I know, dear. But you are going to have to forgive him."

I closed my eyes, picturing my beloved Home Goods Department, knowing I would never work there again. I shook my head. "Forgiving him is impossible."

## 27

I decided to start college in the fall of 1919 and faced a new injustice. When I reapplied to the school that had accepted me two years ago, I discovered that the admissions office was now giving preference to the men who had served their country during the war. And because so many men enrolled that fall, there was no room for me. Grandma Bebe would have told me that it was another instance of God ordering the circumstances in my life for His purposes, but if that was the case, I was starting to feel pretty angry with God, too.

I ended up attending a small female college in Roseton and living at home. My classes weren't nearly as challenging as my job had been. I signed up for a liberal arts degree with no clear goals in mind.

On January 29, 1920, Grandma Bebe's prohibition amendment went into effect. It was now officially against the law to manufacture, transport, or sell alcoholic beverages in the United States. "You have a right to be proud," I told Grandma. "You've accomplished all your goals."

She must have detected a note of jealousy or maybe bitterness in my voice, because she caressed my cheek and said, "Your day will come, Harriet. Just be patient."

That August I was on summer break and sitting around feeling sorry for myself when Maude called to tell me that Bertha and Lyle had just had a second child. I decided to pay Bertha a visit and surprise her with a gift. I found her in tears.

"Bertha, what's wrong?" It was probably a stupid question. She had a runny-nosed two-year-old hanging on to her apron and a fussy newborn in her arms. The apartment looked much too cramped for a family of four, and the temperature inside felt ten degrees hotter than outside. I would weep, too, if I were Bertha.

"Oh, Miss Sherwood. Lyle and I are in a terrible pickle. He . . . oh, maybe I shouldn't tell you. He said not to tell anybody, but I . . . I just don't know what we're going to do!"

I guided her to a chair so she could finish feeding the baby, then gave her two-year-old the stuffed bear I had brought him. Both children were content momentarily, so I encouraged Bertha to confide in me. "You know that I would never share your secrets with anyone—and maybe there's something I can do to help."

Bertha wiped her eyes on the burping cloth that was slung over her shoulder. "You see this crummy apartment? It was all we could afford, and now we can't even afford to live here. If we don't pay the rent by next week, they're going to throw us out."

"I thought Lyle had a good job."

"He did! But they went on strike a month ago and now we're all out of money."

"Maybe I could loan—"

"I'm not even to the worse part, Miss Sherwood."

I could see that this might take a while, so I sat down on one of Bertha's splintery kitchen chairs to listen.

"Please don't get me wrong. My Lyle is a very good man, and

he knows that he never should have done such a stupid thing, but with two children to take care of and no money for the rent, he was desperate. So when a friend told him how he could make a little extra money . . . well . . ." Bertha's voice dropped to a whisper. "He got mixed up with the wrong kind of people, and . . . and he agreed to smuggle liquor across the border from Canada."

"Oh my."

"Transporting liquor is against the law, Miss Sherwood, and if Lyle gets thrown into jail, we'll starve. I didn't know he was planning to do it until it was too late. He had already gone up to Canada and he never said a word about it until I saw him bringing all the crates of liquor and beer into the apartment, and I—"

"Wait a minute, slow down. He brought the liquor in here?"

"Yes, here! Lyle hid it here in our apartment."

I took a quick glance around the two rooms and knew it wouldn't be too hard for me or anyone else to find it. The baby had fallen asleep in Bertha's arms, so she laid him in a laundry basket that she was using for his cradle. Now that her hands were empty, she began wringing them. "I don't know what to do!"

"Why didn't Lyle just deliver his cargo right away?" I asked. "Why bring it here?"

"They told him to wait a couple of days and to use a different car in case the police were watching him and were planning to follow him to the delivery place. When he told me all this . . . honestly, Miss Sherwood, I had a fit! We have two children to think about. Lyle told the people that they would have to come here and get the liquor themselves, but they explained that transporting it is the part that's against the law. They said that Lyle has to deliver it, but now he's afraid to. And I'm afraid to let him. Oh, I just don't know what to do!"

"If I were you, I think I would dump it all down the sink."

"We can't. The people loaned him the money to drive up to

Canada and buy it. Beer costs five dollars a case up there and sells for twenty-five dollars a case down here, and after Lyle pays the people back, plus a little bit for interest, we were supposed to keep the rest. Now we're in even more debt."

It sounded like a very well-planned operation where the bad guys made desperate people like Lyle and Bertha take all of the risks. "Have you considered going to the police?" I asked.

"We can't. Lyle broke the law. We'll starve while he's in jail, and once he has a prison record, he'll never be able to get another job. I know you're very smart, Miss Sherwood, and you're always thinking up new ideas and things—please tell me what we should do."

"Wow." I couldn't think of anything else to say. I ran my hands through my short hair as I pondered Bertha's dilemma.

She was an excellent salesclerk, but she would never be able to find a job now that she was married. Besides, who would take care of her children? The women like Millie White who had come to Grandma Bebe for help had faced the same dead end, and Grandma had begun her temperance crusade to help them. My mother's involvement with the suffrage movement had started after Daniel Carver's wife and children were also left destitute. Mother had enlisted the help of her women's club the very next day. Now it was my turn to come up with a solution to rescue someone in need. I rose from the chair and started to pace.

I could borrow Grandma Bebe's car and deliver the liquor myself, but I would be taking a huge risk. Then again, Great-Grandma Hannah had taken a risk when she hid escaped slaves in the back of her wagon. And Grandma Bebe had not only risked contracting cholera in order to help out, but she had been willing to go to jail to close down saloons. My mother had risked losing her reputation and all of her society friends when she stood up in front of her club members and declared her intention to help families in need. And I wanted to help this family.

"I'll deliver the liquor," I told Bertha. "And collect your money."

"Y-you will?"

"Yes. But I need you to swear to me that you and Lyle will never do anything this stupid again."

"I do swear! On my very life! And I'll make sure that Lyle swears, too."

I borrowed Grandma's car that evening. As I drove back to Bertha's apartment I felt like Joan of Arc or Queen Esther, or some other noble heroine racing to the rescue. I admit that the thought of breaking the law—for a worthy cause—was very exciting. And heaven knows I hadn't had much excitement in my life lately.

My apprehension began as I watched Lyle loading all the liquor into the car. "I never imagined that there would be so much of it," I told him.

"Yeah," he said, wiping sweat from his forehead. "And I don't think it's all going to fit in your trunk."

"How did you get all of this across the border?"

"They gave me a special car to drive, with compartments to hide it all in."

"Well, I'm not making two trips," I said. "You'll have to pile the rest of it in the back seat and cover it with a blanket. I want to get this over with."

Lyle gave me the address where I was supposed to deliver the liquor, along with his profuse thanks. "Good luck, Miss Sherwood."

I started the car and took a moment to wipe my sweating palms on my thighs before shifting into gear. The excitement I had felt on the way over began to drain away once I started driving through town. Fear replaced it. What in the world was I doing? I pushed down on the accelerator, driving a little faster, eager to get my good deed over with. That's when I heard the siren behind me.

My first impulse was to press the accelerator all the way to the floor and make a run for it, but then I recalled how Hannah had stopped and waited for her pursuers. I pulled the car over to the side of the road, hoping the police car would drive past, hoping the blaring siren wasn't meant for me, after all. But the police car came to a stop behind me. I thought I knew how Grandma Bebe felt when the bounty hunters had halted their horses beside her wagon and the dogs started sniffing around. I tried to act calm, but my entire body was trembling. Imagine my surprise when I looked in the mirror and recognized the officer who was walking up to my car window.

"Would you step out of the car, please?" Tommy asked.

I could barely stand and found I had to lean against the fender for support. Too late, I noticed that the blanket had slipped off, exposing my cargo in the back seat. I watched in a daze as Tommy uncorked one of the bottles and sniffed. How could this be happening to me?

"I'm going to have to arrest you, Harriet," Tommy said. He seemed truly surprised. I was even more surprised. Unlike my great-grandmother Hannah, I had been caught with the goods!

$\backsim$

"So you see?" I told Tommy, "I did it to help a friend in need. Bertha and Lyle have two small children, and I don't have anyone to worry about but myself. I don't intend to make a career of rum running, and neither do they. I just wanted to do a good deed."

I didn't tell Tommy, but after thinking about it for the past twenty-four hours, I also think that I did it because I was angry with all of the maddeningly heroic people in my family: Great-Grandma Hannah, who helped free millions of slaves; Grandpa Horatio, who saved an entire town; and Grandma Bebe, who not only conquered Demon Rum in our family and our town but also helped the entire nation go dry. And even my lovely, shallow, socialite mother was about to succeed in a way that would change the life of every woman in America. And what had I ever done?

"I come from a long line of heroes and heroines, Tommy, and I wanted my chance to be brave. But there aren't any more causes to fight for. I've been left out and left behind. I'm plain-faced and ordinary. And now, apparently, I'm also a criminal."

"I don't know where you got that idea," Tommy said, looking up at me. "You're not plain-faced. And you're certainly not ordinary."

"Thanks." I wasn't sure if I believed him. I wondered if he believed me.

"The funny thing is," Tommy said, leaning back in the booth, "I believe your story."

"You do?"

"No one could make up something as wild as that," he said with a grin.

I felt only a small measure of relief. "So I guess Lyle was right. I guess the police were watching his house, after all."

Tommy's brow furrowed. "I wasn't watching his house. I stopped you because you were driving too fast."

"You're joking!"

"No. When I saw that it was you, I was going to let you go with a warning—but then I spotted all those bottles in the back seat and I had no choice."

"The blanket must have slipped off."

"Apparently. The liquor was in plain sight."

"Poor Lyle," I said with a sigh. "I don't know how he'll ever pay back all the money he owes. Some very big people are going to be awfully mad at him."

The furrow in Tommy's brow deepened, but I didn't think

he was worried about Lyle and Bertha. "So that means . . . Lyle's customers must still be waiting for their delivery," he murmured.

"I suppose they are. . . . Why? What are you thinking?"

"I was thinking that if I called in some federal agents to help me, we could go raid the place. You had an awful lot of alcohol in your car, Harriet, so I'm guessing it must be a very large operation. Do you still have the address?"

"I do."

Tommy leaned forward, his gaze intense. "Listen, if you give it to me and we're able to catch the big guys, maybe the judge will be more lenient toward you and your friends for cooperating."

I did some quick thinking, and I didn't like Tommy's idea. "Your plan would get my friends into trouble, and right now you don't have any evidence against them. The liquor was in my car. But if you go crashing in to catch the bad guys, they will think Lyle tipped you off. And if Lyle doesn't pay back the money he borrowed, he and Bertha will be even worse off than when they started."

"Maybe so, but—"

"I have a better idea. Let me make the delivery and collect Lyle's money first. Then you can move in and make your arrests."

"I can't involve you in this. It's much too dangerous."

"Well, I'm not giving you the address unless we do it my way." I crossed my arms and lifted my chin. Tommy would recognize the pose.

"Now, Harriet—"

"Look, I was going to drive there last night and make the delivery, so how is this any more dangerous? Please, let me try to undo some of the harm I've already done."

We argued about it until we had each drunk enough coffee to keep us awake for a week. In the end, Tommy reluctantly agreed with my plan, since it was the only way he would ever make the arrest and close down a secret gin joint. We walked back across the street to the police station. Night had fallen by now, and it was dark outside.

I sat in a wooden chair in the back room and listened while Tommy made some phone calls and enlisted two federal agents to help him. "Okay, it's all set up," he finally told me. "Your car is still behind the police station, where my partner parked it last night. The alcohol is in the evidence room, but we'll put it all back in the car. . . . Listen, are you sure you won't change your mind and just give me the address?"

"Quite sure."

I watched the police load all of the liquor into my car. I felt exhausted. I hadn't slept very well last night on that squeaky iron bunk, and I just wanted to get this over with and go home.

"I still have reservations about this," Tommy said as I slid behind the steering wheel. "I don't like putting you in danger."

"You didn't put me in danger. I did it to myself with my misguided notion of becoming a heroine. Besides, you'll be watching out for me tonight, right?"

"Every step of the way."

"And listen, Tommy. Please wait until I drive away so the bad guys won't think Lyle tipped you off. And please let him and Bertha keep the money. They really need it."

"I'll do my best."

"Thanks. Okay, then," I said with a sigh, "let's get going. I have a Sunday school lesson to prepare, remember?"

I put the car in gear and drove away, careful not to speed this time. My nerves felt jitterier than they had last night—but that might have been from all the coffee. The address Lyle had given me was on the other side of town and belonged to a run-down warehouse next to the brickyard. I could see the dark void of the river behind it and Garner Park in the distance. Tommy and his agent friends would be disappointed if this turned out to be just a storage facility and not a gin joint, after all. Presumably he had followed me, even though I hadn't seen his car's headlights.

I pulled around to the back of the building as Lyle had instructed me to do. The windows were all boarded up, but I did see a door. I parked as close to it as I could and got out of the car. I knew that I should have been nervous or excited or something, but I wasn't. I felt wide awake from all the coffee, but otherwise numb. I took a deep breath and knocked on the door. A middle-aged woman wearing a lot of lipstick and rouge opened it a moment later. I was relieved to hear lively music and laughter coming from inside. It was a gin joint. Tommy would be pleased.

"I have a delivery from Lyle," I told her.

"Just a moment."

She closed the door, and as I stood waiting in the shadowy alley, I suddenly realized why Tommy had been worried about my safety. These people could tie me up and toss me into the river and keep both the liquor and the money. Who would ever know? I hoped he was watching out for me.

The door opened again, and three burly men came out. I backed up a few steps, but they were interested in my cargo, not me. The woman held the door open for them, counting the bottles as they carried the crates inside. When they finished, she pulled a fat wad of bills from her pocket and paid me.

That was it. The end of my adventure. The police didn't swoop in with guns blazing, as I half expected them to do. The alley was quiet except for a train whistle in the distance. Tommy and I hadn't discussed what I should do afterward, so I got back into Grandma's car and drove to her house. She was in her nightgown and robe.

"Where in the world have you been?" she asked when she saw me. "You look like someone dragged you through a mud puddle."

"You would never believe it."

"You joined the circus and they shot you out of a cannon?"

"No . . . I spent last night and all day today in jail."

"Oh, dear. Well, you'd better sit down and tell me all about it."
I followed her into her dining room, then halted in shock when
I saw her table. It was bare! I was looking at a shiny wooden table-
top for the first time in my life. There wasn't a paper or leaflet in
sight—only my grandmother's Bible lying open on top of it.

"Grandma! What happened?"

"I cleaned my table off," she said with a flip of her hand. "And
it was about time, too, don't you think? But sit down, dear, and tell
me why you were in jail."

I drew a breath as if I were about to leap off Grandma's swing
into the river. My words all came out at once. "I'm only out on bail
and I'm still in a whole lot of trouble, but Tommy said he would
testify in court that my story was true and he thinks the judge
might be lenient with me because I cooperated with the police
and helped them arrest the really bad guys."

I had just thrown a great deal of information at her, but when
I paused to take another breath, she had only one question for
me. She smiled when she asked it. "Who's Tommy?"

"Huh? . . . Oh, you wouldn't believe that, either."

"Try me."

"He's Tommy O'Reilly, the police superintendent's son.
Remember the bully whose shins I used to kick all the time? Well,
he grew up to be a policeman, and he's the one who arrested me
last night."

"For kicking him in the shins?"

I shook my head. I felt close to tears because I was afraid to tell
her the truth. "I was only trying to help a friend, Grandma. I wanted
to do something brave and noble and heroic like you and Mother
and Great-Grandma Hannah did. I even prayed for help the way

nah did, and asked God to blind Tommy's eyes, but it didn't ⸮ any good. He saw what I had in my car, and he arrested me."

"I'm guessing you weren't hiding slaves."

"No," I mumbled. "Alcohol."

"I see."

"I don't understand why God didn't answer my prayer like He did for Hannah. She broke the law, too, by helping slaves escape."

"Prayer isn't a magic trick, Harriet. When my mother prayed, it was to a Savior she knew and loved and talked to all the time."

I propped my elbows on the table and rested my head in my hands. "I'm so sorry, Grandma. I know you must be so disappointed in me. I know how hard you fought for this law and how much you hate alcohol, and the only reason I did it was because a friend was in trouble and she has two small children who were going to suffer, and besides, I wasn't going to drink any of it or make any money for myself, but even so, I wouldn't blame you if you were furious with me and—"

"Harriet, Harriet . . . I'm not angry with you." She stood next to my chair and wrapped her arms around me, resting her cheek on my hair. I hugged her tightly in return and sobbed. When I finally stopped crying, she sat down on a chair beside me.

"You're right, I have worked hard to make certain that alcohol was banned. I've devoted my entire life to temperance because I saw how much pain and suffering alcohol caused. But you know what? Every day now I read in the paper about the crime spree that Prohibition has caused, and I wonder if I've been fighting the wrong battle all these years."

"What do you mean?"

"Jesus' harshest words were for the moral guardians of His day—the Pharisees. They wanted to dictate morality, too, but Jesus called them hypocrites and whitewashed tombs. It isn't our calling as Christians to write laws that force people to live moral lives. As much as our communities might need it, and as bad as things are, imposing our morality on others isn't the answer. It doesn't work. People may be forced to give up alcohol, but they are still going to hell. That's our calling—to bring people to Christ—not to force them to behave the way we want them to or to solve all their external problems."

She reached for my hand and held it in her own. Her skin felt as soft and fragile as tissue paper. "We can make stricter laws, Harriet, but people will just figure out a way around them if their hearts are hardened. The Emancipation Proclamation freed the slaves, but it couldn't make people accept the Negroes. They're still hated and treated unfairly and given only the poorest paying jobs. When the suffrage amendment passes and women are allowed to vote, there will still be many more battles to win. Men who are biased against women aren't going to treat us equally overnight. No, there aren't enough laws in the world to change human nature. We've had the Ten Commandments since Moses' time, and people still murder and steal every day. Only God can change people."

"But your work wasn't in vain, Grandma, just because people are breaking the Prohibition laws."

"That's true. But I've come to realize that our short time here on earth isn't about what we accomplish, but about what sort of people we become. I'm at the end of my life now, but when I look back on the work I've done, I see that God was using it to teach me to care about someone besides myself. He's been working compassion in your mother, too. And also in you, judging by the risk you just took for your friends. And God also uses our circumstances to teach us to rely on Him. That was the first lesson I ever learned when I helped deliver those slaves in our wagon. That's why my mother brought me with her in the first place. She told me that we

stronger every time our faith is tested. That's how we learn
trust God."

"Am I ever going to get a real task to do?" I asked. I gestured to
her barren dining room table. "Look—your work is all done. Even
the table is finally cleared off. And Mother's suffrage amendment
only needs one more state to approve it and it will become a law,
too. What's left for me to accomplish?"

"Harriet, God has already given you a task to do for Him."

"He has? What is it?"

"Jesus told us to go into all the world and preach the gospel
to every creature."

I sighed. "Where in the world do I begin doing that job?"

Grandma smiled. "Why, you start by teaching your Sunday
school class tomorrow."

It seemed like a very paltry beginning.

I thanked Grandma for forgiving me and went home so she
could go to bed. I tried to sneak into the house and go upstairs to
work on my lesson, but my father must have heard me because he
came out to the hallway.

"Where have you been?" he asked.

I was about to give a sarcastic reply, asking the reason for his
sudden concern for my welfare, but he broke into a smile.

"I've been waiting all evening to tell you the good news. Look,
your mother sent us a telegram." He waved a yellow paper in
the air. "It says, 'Tennessee voted to ratify. Suffrage amendment
passed!' "

I could see that Father was proud of my mother, happy for her.
He loved her. And maybe the fact that he could celebrate Mother's
victory meant that his attitude toward women was slowly beginning
to change. Grandma was right; he was a good man at heart.

"That is good news," I said.

"Yes . . . and perhaps Lucy will stay home from now on." He

didn't add *where she belongs*, but I could tell that he was thinking it. I thought about all the changes he had endured since my mother became a suffragette, and I felt sorry for him. Sympathy was a tiny step toward forgiving him.

"Thanks for waiting up to tell me the news," I said.

I went upstairs to my room and opened my Sunday school book to tomorrow's lesson—and I laughed out loud at God's timing. The lesson was on one of Jesus' most famous parables. Two men decided to build houses, one on a rock, the other on sand. The storms came and the floodwaters rose—just like the great flood that had taken Grandpa Horatio's life. The foolish man's house, which must have been built in a place like The Flats, was demolished by the floodwaters. But the wise man's house, built high on a ridge like the Garners' home, was able to withstand the deluge.

This was the lesson that Grandma Bebe had been trying to teach me all along. It wasn't enough to build my life on doing good deeds and heroic things such as helping Bertha and Lyle. I needed to get to know Jesus first, and obey His commands.

And I knew very well that one of those commands was to forgive my father the way God had forgiven me. I closed my eyes and prayed—a real prayer this time.

∼

I had just finished dressing for Sunday school the next morning when I heard a knock on our front door. I sprinted down the stairs and opened it to find Tommy O'Reilly on my doorstep. I was surprisingly happy to see him. And judging by the grin on his face, he was happy to see me, too.

"What are you doing here?" I asked. "Don't tell me you've come with leg irons to haul me back to jail?"

"Not at all. I'm supposed to be watching you so you don't flee to Canada, remember?"

427

Well, you're just in time to help me repair my still. I'm turning in alcohol into gin down in the basement."

"Very funny."

"How did it go last night?" I asked, leaning against the door-frame.

"The federal agents were quite impressed. The warehouse you led us to was a speakeasy, and we found a lot of valuable evidence inside. We uncovered a large rum-running operation, involving people in several communities. Yes, I would say it went very well."

"Congratulations."

"Thanks." Tommy had an incredible smile.

"Now, if you're really intent on watching my every move," I told him, "I'm on my way to church to teach my Sunday school class."

Tommy hesitated, ducking his head as a shy grin spread across his face. "Listen, Harriet. May I come with you as a friend and not as your jailer? I would really like to be . . . um . . . friends."

Now it was my turn to hesitate. I knew I had foresworn love and marriage and all the rest, but Tommy O'Reilly had changed a lot in the past few years. And my attitude toward him had changed, as well.

"I would like to be friends, too," I finally said.

I could almost hear the roar of a waterfall in the distance and Grandma Bebe laughing as she said, *We shall see, Harriet, my dear. We shall see.*

## DISCUSSION QUESTIONS

1. Throughout the novel, Harriet is trying to answer the question, "How did I end up here in jail?" What insights does she gain from recalling Great-Grandma Hannah's story? Grandma Bebe's story? Her mother Lucy's story? How does she ultimately answer the question?

2. What strengths did each of the four women—Hannah, Bebe, Lucy, and Harriet—possess? What were each woman's weaknesses?

3. Which woman did you identify with the most? Why?

4. Hannah tells Bebe, " 'Smooth seas don't produce skillful sailors.' . . . God uses the turbulent times in our lives to prepare us for His purposes—if we'll let Him." What were some of the rough waters in each woman's life that led them closer to God?

5. After the episode with the bounty hunters, Hannah tells Bebe, "Someday . . . God is going to give you a task to do in your own time and place. Then you'll have to put your faith in Him as you follow your conscience." What tasks did each woman feel God was giving her to do? How did the circumstances in her life lead her to this task?

6. Near the end of the book, Grandma Bebe tells Harriet, "Our short time here on earth isn't about what we accomplish, but

about what sort of people we become." What are your thoughts regarding her comments? What other insights did Bebe share with Harriet regarding each Christian's task?

7. Grandma Bebe is born on the same day, month, and year that the first Women's Rights Convention was held. The story ends with the news that the suffrage amendment has passed. How did each woman's "cause" contribute to its passage: Hannah and the Anti-Slavery Society? Bebe and the Women's Christian Temperance Union? Lucy and her women's club? Harriet's job and the need for workers during World War I?

8. What was your reaction when Harriet's father "fired" her from her job in the department store? How would you have reacted in that situation? As a young woman living in 1919, what recourse did she have to fight his decision? What other instances of discrimination against women did you see in the story?

9. What was the prevailing attitude toward women and their roles in each generation throughout the book? Did you see a change in any of these attitudes? If so, what caused it?

10. What qualities did each woman see in the man she married: Hannah and Henry? Bebe and Horatio? Lucy and John? What qualities do you think Harriet and Tommy are beginning to see in each other? Do you think Bebe should have married Neal MacLeod? Should Lucy have married Daniel Carver? Why or why not?

11. What do you think the next chapter in Harriet's life will be?

DON'T MISS ANY OF THESE NOVELS FROM

# Lynn Austin!

As three sisters flee unexpected sorrow and a tainted past, they find they have nothing to rely on except each other—and hope for a second chance.

*Until We Reach Home*

Venturing to Chicago during the 1893 World's Fair, Violet Hayes has one goal: to find her mother. When her investigation uncovers missing pieces of her family's past, what she finally finds is priceless.

*A Proper Pursuit*

As four women watch their loved ones fight in World War II, they in turn answer the nation's call for help. Together they struggle toward a new understanding of what love and sacrifice truly mean.

*A Woman's Place*

Like her mother and grandmother before her, Kathleen fled her past to start a new life. Thirty-five years later, can she find healing for the wounds that cut so deep?

*All She Ever Wanted*

Recently widowed, Eliza is wary of the new hired help. But Gabe's gentle ways around the farm draw her to him. Yet she fears he hides motives that could jeopardize all she has struggled to attain.

*Hidden Places*

For five decades a devastating secret has haunted Emma Bauer—and the lives of her descendants. Can she finally manage the courage to set right her wrongs and shatter the cycle that rules their lives?

*Eve's Daughters*